The Unexpected Guest

A Novel Out of Africa

Samantha Ford

Published on Amazon Via KDP
All Rights Reserved.
Copyright © 2021 Samantha Ford
(ISBN 9798492292287)

No part of this book may be reproduced or transmitted in any form or by any means, graphic, electronic, or mechanical, including photocopying, recording, taping or by any information storage or retrieval system, without the permission in writing from the copyright holder.

The right of Samantha Ford to be identified as the author of this work has been asserted in accordance with the Copyright, Designs and Patents Act 1988 sections 77 and 78.

This is a work of fiction. The characters and their actions are entirely fictitious. Any resemblance to persons living or dead is entirely coincidental.

******

Also by Samantha Ford

The Zanzibar Affair

The House Called Mbabati

A Gathering of Dust

The Ambassador's Daughter

In this story I have re-introduced Jack Taylor, Detective Piet Joubert, Kia and Jabu. All characters I became fond of in my previous book called The Ambassador's Daughter. There you will find their original story.

Amazon Reviews

"This is simply the best book I've read in a very long time. This talented lady brings Africa alive. Wilbur Smith you have some competition…"

"A cracking good story with a totally unexpected twist at the end!"
John Gordon Davis – author of Hold My Hand I'm Dying

"Having read all Wilbur Smith's books, this author ranks up with the best of them. Best read I've had for years!" Peter C. Morgan

Dedication: For my little brother Robert. Only a whisper away…

Acknowledgements

I would like to thank the following for their unswerving support on this long lonely road called writing.

My sister, Jackie, who held my hand every step of the way even though I knew she was dreading having to read the manuscript over and over again…

My close friend Mark Baldwin who has, once again, designed a stunning cover for my story, it even took my breath away!

mark@creativemix.co.za

Michel Girardin, who is somewhat of a legend in the South African safari business. He guided me through life in the Sabi Sands, what happens where, the rules and regulations, and the wild life. I have bent a few of the facts to suit the story. Sorry if I moved the trees and a few other things, around a bit…

michel@djuma.co.za

My brilliant editor Gail Williams who has the ability to make me laugh and cry at the same time and doesn't miss a trick… or a mistake.

www.gailbwilliams.co.uk

Brian Stephens for taking away the pain of formatting and preparing the book for publication. Another great job, thank you.

brian@moulinwebsitedesign.com

My thanks to Nicky Fitzgerald, another legend in the safari business, for allowing me to use the shot of her glorious camp, Angama Mara, in Kenya, taken by www.dookphoto.com

angama.com

Finally, to my friend Brian in Canada. Thank you for your complete and utter faith in me as a writer and your unswerving support in so many ways.

All the characters are fictitious but I have taken the liberty of adjusting geographical locations to fit the story. Poaching is a huge and troubling problem, especially here in South Africa. There are strict rules as to whom may traverse through private reserves. Again, here I have bent some of the rules to fit the story.

I have never been a political person but I am an avid follower of world news. Some of the events referred to in this story are true and factual, but others are my own reflections and not meant to refer to any political point of view.

Finally, to you the readers, thank you for all the fantastic reviews on Amazon. Without reviews an author will struggle to sell their books. To be compared to John Gordon Davis, one of Southern Africa's most loved authors, and to Wilbur Smith, is indeed a huge compliment.

Thank you for purchasing this book, I hope it brings back wonderful memories to all of you who have ever had the privilege of living in Africa.

Through the long nights she walks beside you in your dreams. Your eyelids flutter with indelible memories. Your hands reach out wanting to hold them close again.

You awake with a sense of being somewhere else, but this somewhere else has dissipated. Your heart tightens with a longing to return to the place of your dreams. A place you knew and loved – Africa.

The barking of dogs, the noise of endless traffic, the screaming sirens, and the urgency of another day seeps through your windows, and into your awakening mind.

The sky is dark with rain, the bare branches tap rhythmically against the window. You close your eyes and sink back into that other familiar world.

In the distance of this other place, you hear your childlike voice, echoing through the bush as you run wild, free and barefoot chasing the sun, the sky so wide and blue. The wavering grasses the colour of a lion's mane, whispering their secrets through the veld, as they brush against your legs. The majestic jacaranda trees laying a bruised carpet of purple and blue beneath your small dusty feet.

You hear the sound of Africans singing, in perfect harmony. Their voices as clear as your dreams and memories. Your tears return.

High above a bird of prey dips then holds still, hovering on the thermals, watching you as you dance through your childhood days, with no fear of the future, only the joy of being where you are.

Then at the end of the day, an almost biblical sky, the glorious colours of molten gold and pink as the fiery red sun sinks below the horizon, the bleached white wings of birds etched against the sky, the darkening silhouettes of trees and the lingering shadows over the cooling bush. From far away comes the rasping throaty sound of a lion as he calls to his pride.

Though you may have travelled to another place, far from Africa, she did not leave you.

She is waiting for you.

Chapter One
South Africa

The little girl lifted her head in terror as she listened to the hideous cackling giggle from a hyena, somewhere close by. Clinging to the high branch of the tree she stayed still, her heart thumping. Tears trickled down her mosquito bitten cheeks as she tried to stifle her sobs and remain silent.

She had no idea how long she had been making her way through the wilderness. She'd been brought up in the bush and knew its ways; knew what could be eaten and what was poisonous. She understood the habits of the animals and did not fear them.

But now she was frightened.

Her sister had been badly hurt when they had been pulled from the vehicle. She had torn off her shirt to try and staunch the blood flow from the deep cut on her left leg. A few hours after they had set off to find help, Susie stumbled and slowed, then sank to her knees, her face contorted with pain.

"Up, up!"

"It's no-good Abby," she whispered. "I can't walk any further. Leave me here, you'll be faster on your own, I'll slow you down. We need somewhere shady for me to shelter from the sun. Here help me over there," she pointed to a stubby tree. "I'll be alright, but hurry. Make sure you bend some branches as you go along so you can find your way back to me – okay?" Susie winced as she reached for her rucksack.

"Here's some rusks, and a bottle of water, take sips, make it last until you find someone. Take my jumper in case you get cold."

Abby helped her sister to the shade of the tree, unable to conceal her fear. She looked wildly around until she found a stout branch lying on the ground, picking it up she looked at Susie and made chopping motions on the ground, and on the bush next to her.

Susie nodded, her eyes already closing with the fierce pain in her leg, her face ashen. "I'll keep the stick close by and use it to keep any animals away. Go, Abby, go. Promise you'll come back. Promise?"

Abby nodded. "Back, back..." she whispered brokenly.

She bent and put her arms around her big sister, holding her tight as she tried to contain her sobs and terror at what had happened to them, and what might lay ahead.

"Try and find a river Abby, then follow it alright. But don't go near the edge. It will lead somewhere and you'll find help. I know it's hard for you to talk, but you must try. Don't sleep or rest on the ground. Find a tree and sleep in the branches, it will keep you safe - I'll sleep in the branches of this one." Her eyes closed and her head lolled back against the tree.

Abby stood on shaking legs, taking one last look at her sister, she started to run, the little rucksack bouncing wildly on her back.

Chapter Two

The sun, as it sank, changed the stark outlines of the trees, rendering them black, the water hole turning from molten gold to pink then red. The sounds shifted from the soft grunts of the hot animals as they grazed, to the shrill sounds of the coming night. Birds flew back to roost, settling as they awaited the familiar calls of the predators as they lifted their torpid bodies and ventured out into the dusk, anxious to fill their hungry stomachs.

Jabu manoeuvred his dark green safari vehicle, with its tiered seats, through the thick bush, his keen eyes scanning the land for anything unusual. As he changed gear, he smiled to himself. Life went on in the African bush, unchanged for hundreds, maybe thousands of years, the animals getting on with what they had to do. Mate, produce and protect their young, hunt, and eventually die. No thoughts of what was going on in the other world of 'animals.' Politics, power, money – it had no meaning in the world he inhabited.

Lives began and ended, wars were fought, money was made and squandered, people toppled in and out of love, then consumed with hope, searched once more for it, and throughout it all the bush endured.

He looked up and watched the whiteness of the birds' wings as they were silhouetted against a blood red sky, a lone cry of a fish eagle gave its last haunting call before night fall.

His eyes searched the bush looking for the familiar hiding places of the nocturnal predators, he leaned over the side of his door and scanned the parched dirt road for the spoor of the animals who had passed through during the day, along with the hovering dragonflies, the dung beetles, the butterflies and other small creatures, which made up the whole of this unique reserve.

Night fell quickly, as it does in Africa. The twin cones of the headlights made little impression on the darkness in front of him. He turned on the spotlight at the front of the vehicle, and watched the bush and the dirt track ahead.

It was his favourite time of the day, getting away from the game lodge for an hour, away from his guests who were out on their own game drives through the vast rolling bush of South Africa's world-renowned private reserve, the Sabi Sands, where the game lodge called Infinity was situated.

His vehicle bucked and rocked as he went off road, parting the thick bush, making his way to the river. The water was low and muddy as it made its sluggish way through the dry terrain. He could smell rain in the distance, hear the low rumble of thunder, later tonight there would be a storm and the rains would come to cool and cleanse the sweltering bush, replenishing the river where the animals came to drink.

The warning of a cyclone approaching the Mozambique coastline may well have a ripple effect, which could bring unseasonal heavy rains and the possibility of flooding. But he had come to learn television weather reporters liked to be dramatic, like newsreaders; warning of treacherous conditions to come, but invariably the warnings were downgraded to a different category and hardly affected them at all.

Jabu stopped the vehicle and turned off the engine. He lifted his head, his finely honed senses on high alert. Something had disturbed the normal rhythm of the bush this evening. He looked around trying to fathom what it might be. He knew it wasn't the outline of the vehicle or the sound of its engine, the animals were well used to the shape and sound, and had no fear of the intrusion into their territory.

He checked his watch and reluctantly turned on the ignition. Time to get back and make ready for the return of his twelve guests.

They seemed a nice mix; two American couples, two German women, two English couples and two singles, one an English doctor, of what he was not certain, and a retired Italian gentleman in his sixties.

The lodge had ten tented suites, the owner had wanted her camp to be small and intimate, where guests and staff alike could get to know each other. Not for her a twenty bedroomed lodge, she didn't want to cater for what she referred to as a never-ending stream of one-night stands who were here today and gone tomorrow. This, she had declared, she would leave to the big boys and the package tour operators.

The beckoning light of the lanterns at the lodge were a beacon in the darkening bush, never failing to lift his heart with deep satisfaction.

In his career he had worked at three lodges, becoming head ranger in all of them, his goal had always been to manage one. But where he had been working before here, he had known it would never happen. The owner's son had that position, it would never be his.

Then Caroline Gordon had blown into his life. Finally, he was now the manager of her exquisite lodge called Infinity.

He had realised his dream and turned it into reality.

*****

Running a lodge, such as this, was challenging work, the guests were not always easy, their expectations high; hoping to see the big five on their first game drive. But the bush and the animals cared little for their expectations. They appeared when they felt like it, or not at all.

Jabu had been brought up in the bush, he knew this was where he belonged. His skills as a tracker and ranger made it easy to find the smallest dung beetle to the mighty herds of elephant who roamed through the endless terrain, following their ancient ancestral paths.

Using these skills, he could find any animal. The job of an experienced ranger was to present theatre, expectations and excitement. This was all part of the great safari experience.

He pulled up and parked his land cruiser next to the generator. As he walked up the path to the lodge, he automatically checked the paths were swept, the lanterns placed strategically in the trees and on the high wooden walkways, so the guests could find their way to and from their suites in the dark.

He checked the bar and nodded at the barman as he polished the various glasses and prepared for the return of their guests who would be thirsty after their long game drive, despite having enjoyed their sundowners watching the sun go down, casting a pink blush over the distant hills and bush. They would want to shower and change before dinner.

The outside dining area was alight with lanterns. Tables and chairs were set under the darkening trees, candles, already lit, quivered in their glass domes on the tables. Tall wine glasses winked and glowed from their light; heavy silver cutlery polished to perfection added a final elegant touch.

Satisfied, he made his way to his quarters to take a quick outside shower before changing his khaki bush shirt for a fresh one, and his shorts for long trousers. The mosquitoes would rise like small dark clouds, hungry for blood, with the heavy humid air.

He closed his eyes as the warm water cascaded over his body and thought about his brief drive in the bush.

Something was bothering him and he couldn't put his finger on exactly what it was.

Jabu towelled himself off then changed into his fresh clothes. As he did up the buttons he looked out into the blackness of the night, hearing the grumbling of far-off thunder as it rolled over the cooling bush. The tail end of the cyclone would hit them tomorrow evening. He made a mental note to move the safari vehicles to higher ground.

Something had been off out there tonight his inherited ancestral senses told him. What had upset the rhythm and the timelessness of the bush? There had been a slight shift in the behaviour of some of the animals, and it wasn't the fear of approaching predators, or the possibility of a violent storm.

Chapter Three

Jabu checked each table and paused to chat to his guests, he gestured to one of the waiters to fill an empty wine glass, then adjusted one of the lanterns, before making his way to the seating deck with a view across the water hole.

Discreetly placed spot lights, hidden in the trees and grasses, casting a soft glow across the wide expanse of water. He threw more wood on the fire and sat in one of the canvas chairs waiting for his guests to finish their dinner and join him. The sense of unease he had felt earlier, lingered with him.

His guests made their way to the fire, leaning back in their chairs and sofas as they drank in the glorious velvet skies and stunning starscape above them. Waiters took their orders for a final drink before they would retire to their suites after a day filled with sun, heat, good food, and the added bonus, on the evening game drive, of seeing a pride of lions enjoying their kill.

From out of the dark night a lone elephant approached the water hole. In the distance the thunder rumbled again, the clouds were gathering smothering the star filled skies. Getting closer, Jabu thought, as he watched the big bull drink thirstily.

Suddenly Jabu saw a flash of white and red and leaned forward. Something else was approaching the water hole. He narrowed his eyes and tried to focus on the movement.

The guests were also peering into the darkness, their conversation tapering off as they tried to pinpoint what Jabu was looking so intently at.

A bolt of lightning streaked across the sky, lighting up the ground beneath and around the water hole.

"My God," gasped one of his American guests. "Is that a child?"

Jabu's body stiffened as he held up his hand, then put a finger to his lips. The mighty elephant seemed unaware of any other presence.

"Keep still, no sudden moves; voices will carry across water," he whispered.

What seemed to be a small child, wearing something red, sank to the ground and lay still. A massive clap of thunder made everyone jump, before it clattered and grumbled off into the distance, followed by the faint patter of the first raindrops on the deck.

"Do something, Jabu," the Italian guest whispered urgently. "The elephant might hurt it!"

Jabu again held up his hand. "Please stay as quiet and still as you can. No-one will be able to go near the elephant, it's too dangerous. Let's give him a moment and hope he wanders off. Then I'll go and see what's happening over there."

The old bull elephant lifted his trunk as if trying to pick up the scent of the inert body lying near the water hole. He made his ponderous way towards it.

The guests gave a collective gasp of pure horror.

Lowering his trunk, he ran it over the crumpled body, then stood unmoving for a few moments, before ambling back into the bush, the only sound carried across the water, was the breaking and snapping of branches as he made his way through the dark undergrowth.

Jabu stood slowly. "Everyone please remain seated," he said quietly. "There may be more elephants out there." He looked around at his guests, finding the face he was looking for. "Olivia?"

Her eyes filled with disbelief, Olivia turned to Jabu, speaking softly as he had requested. "Yes?"

"You're a doctor. Medical doctor?"

"Yes I am. How can I help. Do you want me to come with you? I need to get my bag..." she whispered.

"No, no thank you. One of the rangers will go back with you to your suite, to make sure you get there safely. There are a lot of animals around tonight and they can get quite close to the camp.

"Donovan," he nodded to one of his rangers, "will show you to the owner's cottage after you've collected your bag. We'll use that, the lighting is better. I'll bring the child, if it is a child, to you. I'm not sure what we might be dealing with here. What kind of condition it might be in?"

"Of course, I'll go and make preparations. Be careful how you carry the child, support the head. As you said, heaven alone knows what we might be dealing with here."

Jabu beckoned to another of his rangers. "Come with me Lovemore, bring your rifle, fire warning shots only if absolutely necessary. Let's go and see what's happening."

Jabu made his way cautiously around the wide water hole, Lovemore following closely behind, watching for any movement, rifle at the ready.

The hidden spotlights in the trees gave them enough light to guide them towards the shape lying on the ground. Making their way to the opposite side of the water hole, Jabu knelt. It was starting to rain hard. He wiped the wetness from his face and eyes with his sleeve.

He turned on his torch. His breath caught in his throat. A girl child, as far as he could tell. Her face and body were badly scratched and bruised, one eye swollen. The dark hair matted and dull. Her red shorts and shirt torn and ragged.

Jabu felt for her pulse. It fluttered beneath his fingers. He turned her over checking for any serious injuries. Then he carefully lifted her in his arms, holding her close to his chest to try and shield her from the rain, as they made their way slowly back to the lodge.

Lovemore again following closely behind, his rifle shiny with rain, steady in his hands, as he scanned the bush for any potential danger.

"How can this be, Jabu." Lovemore whispered. "Where did this child come from? There are no other camps for many miles, there have been no reports of any accidents, this we would have heard about on our radios."

Jabu shook his head, anxious to get the child to the safe care of Doctor Olivia.

The guests stood as Jabu mounted the short steps to the deck of the lodge. The shock showing on their faces as they looked at the broken child he carried. The little face bloated, burnt and bruised, the arms hanging limply, the clothes torn and now sodden.

Helplessly they asked if there was anything they could do.

"I'll let you know. The most important thing now is to get her to Olivia. Please don't be alarmed. I'll let you know the situation once the doctor has assessed the child."

The waiters moved in quickly, their faces creased with concern, as they attended to their agitated guests.

Chapter Four

Doctor Olivia Hamilton was waiting at the entrance to the owner's cottage, her brow puckered with anxiety.

"I've prepared as much as I can. I've cleared the office desk. We need to lie the patient on something solid."

She looked closely at the child. "It's a girl, probably about six, maybe older but she's quite small."

Jabu laid her gently on the desk and stepped back.

Olivia checked the child's vital signs and frowned, then examined her eyes with a small torch, and frowned again. Reaching for a pair of scissors, Olivia began to cut the ragged clothes from the girl's body. Checking her for any other injuries, she reached for the warm bowl of water she had prepared and carefully washed the child's dirty wasted body.

"She's dangerously dehydrated, Jabu, her pulse is weak and her eyes are not reacting to light. She's covered with bites, mosquitoes I would imagine. Her skin is badly burned from the sun, so many blisters. I need to get some liquid into her quickly, she's hanging on by a thread at the moment. She has a high fever, much too high, her body is pulsating with heat."

Jabu looked at the doctor, then at the girl. "What else do you need? We have everything to cover almost all eventualities, being so far from any town or clinic."

"Do you have oxygen Jabu. Any IV fluids?"

Jabu shook his head, his forehead creased with concern. "No. Lodges don't carry anything like that. If administered incorrectly there's a huge liability risk. Give me a minute, let me see what I can find."

Olivia sucked in her breath. "Dear God, is this a snake bite?"

Jabu leaned forward seeing the tiny puncture marks. "Yes, but I'm not sure what kind of snake, venomous though. Judging by the amount of mosquito bites on her, it's likely she may have malaria as well. It would give her the fever and high temperature."

Olivia took a deep breath. "This is probably why her system seems to be shutting down." She turned back to the child, whose lips were now tinged with blue. "Come on little girl, come on…Jabu bring me whatever you have, but hurry."

Olivia had dealt with many emergencies in her career, but then she had had all the sophisticated equipment a London hospital could offer. But this? Out in the middle of the bush? The child didn't stand much of a chance without first class medical facilities.

Snake bites, she knew, could be fatal and this was not an area of her expertise, and malaria was a killer. It claimed thousands of lives each year in Africa.

*****

Jabu raced back to the main office. He made an urgent call to the private air ambulance company in Nelspruit, giving them the co-ordinates of the lodge.

Pulling out the first aid box, he rummaged through it. All the rangers had first aid knowledge, but not anything like enough for this kind of emergency.

His mind flicked back to the girl, her lips beginning to turn blue. He thought about the snake bite on her leg.

His father, Eza, was a descendant of the San people. His ancestors had roamed the desert plains of the Kalahari for centuries. They had had no need of modern medicines or science. Their knowledge was passed down through the generations. Their potions, natural herbs and poultices, had enabled them to treat any malady, any emergency whatever the situation, however remote the area was.

Eza had passed this knowledge to his son.

Jabu picked up the first aid box then loped back to his own quarters. At the back of the drawer, he pulled out the pouch made of soft goat skin.

Working quickly, he mixed the two potions as he had been taught by his father.

Chapter Five

Doctor Olivia saw the tall shadow of Jabu silhouetted against the outside of the owner's cottage and breathed a sigh of relief.

Jabu dropped the first aid box on the table next to the child. He bent over her; her breathing was shallow. The snake bite was now hot, red and swollen. He checked her darkening feet. The snake was a bad one.

He placed his two bowls of herbal paste on the table, giving them a final mix.

Olivia frowned. "I need medicine for this child, Jabu. I need it urgently…" her voice trailed off. "What on earth are you doing?"

"You have to trust me, Olivia. I know what I'm doing. If we want to save this child, then let me do what's necessary."

"I need anti-snake venom, Jabu, not some grey looking paste?" she said, her voice edged with anger and frustration.

He glanced at her briefly, the muscles on his face rigid, before looking at the child and peeling back the sheet from her body. "We have nothing to lose Olivia. This child is dying, let me try to help her."

Olivia watched as he carefully spread the grey paste over the puncture wounds on the child's leg, speaking softly in a language she had never heard before, with its clicks, murmurs, and soft musical sounds.

Jabu sat back and waited. It would take some time for the potion to draw out the poison. Time something the girl had precious little of.

Olivia checked the child's blood pressure and other vital signs.

Tears of frustration filled her eyes. "I don't think we can save her Jabu. I don't know what I'm dealing with here. I think we may be too late."

"Stay with her Olivia, she'll sense your presence, she'll know she's safe, and we're trying to help her. But in the end, it will be up to her. I have no idea what she's been through, how long she's been wandering around the bush, what she's eaten – I don't know. We can only do the best we can."

He looked at Olivia's stricken face. "I've made contact with the air ambulance company in Nelspruit, about two hours away from here. They can't send the chopper tonight, it's a no-fly zone here in the bush after dark, too dangerous, and the weather's closing in.

"They'll be here first thing in the morning and take," he paused and looked at the broken body of the child in front of him, "this little one, where she'll get first class medical attention. We have some of the finest doctors in the world here. But what I would ask is for you to go with her.

"It's possible she might have heard your voice. I know this is not what you expected when you booked your safari, but it is what it is. Will you go with her? The lodge owner will cover all your expenses."

Olivia didn't hesitate. "Of course, I'll go with her. Now I need to check for head injuries, but her hair is so matted it's almost impossible. God knows what's crawling around in her hair. But I have to check."

She looked at Jabu's shaven head. "Bring me whatever you use to shave your own head Jabu. But hurry."

Olivia cut what she could of the girl's dark curly hair, then reached for the shaving instrument Jabu had returned with, and carefully shaved the child's head before bathing her scalp.

*****

Jabu checked the poultice he had applied to the snake bite and nodded, satisfied. He reached for the other bowl he had brought back with him, carefully he stirred the liquid with a short root and bent over the desk. The wind growled outside of the cottage and rattled the canvas roof covering.

"What's the liquid for Jabu? I'm not feeling comfortable with all this mumbo jumbo stuff. You could be causing more harm than good."

Jabu's jaw tightened, as he touched the girl's lips with the root. "My ancestors have been using these cures for hundreds of years. They work, Olivia, but you also have to combine their healing powers with trust and faith. Tiny drops of this liquid will help not only with her dehydration but also with the effects of the venom. It will help with the cuts, the open sores, the blisters and the bites she has all over her body."

He dabbed her lips again. "See if you can get some of this into her, it will bring down the fever. You and I have nothing to lose by using these potions – but the child will die if we do nothing. Tomorrow the medics will take over and treat her with the kind of modern medicine you think she needs. Meanwhile you and I, well, we're all she has right now."

Olivia reached out and stroked the girl's arm. "I'm sorry Jabu, it was insensitive of me. I know you're trying to help. Give me the bowl. How often must she have some of this?"

"Every twenty minutes, use the root to keep her lips moist, it will give her a little liquid. Don't touch the poultice on her leg, it's drawing the poison out of the snake bite. Some of the swelling and redness has already receded. It's a good sign."

"Jabu, the language you were whispering to her, what is it?"

He looked at her, a ghost of a smile hovering on his lips. "You mean the mumbo jumbo? It's my mother tongue, the language of my people, the San people, the Grique people, it's one of the oldest languages in the world. Softer than others, more soothing. Even if she doesn't understand me, the words will bring her comfort, they always do."

Lightning slashed through the dark night following by a boom of thunder which rolled around the skies. The rain came down hard and fast, like a drum roll, as it beat against the sturdy tented canopy.

Olivia looked up briefly, pausing in her ministrations of her little patient.

"Is it a sign from your Gods Jabu? A good one maybe?"

Jabu stood. "It's possible. They move in mysterious ways, a bit like your God, if I recall from your bible," he said with a half-smile. "I must go and check on the other guests. I'll be back as soon as they have retired. Keep administering my mumbo jumbo medicine, won't you?"

Despite the dire situation Olivia now found herself in with her patient she couldn't help the shadow of a smile flickering across her lips.

Jabu had a droll sense of humour, given the circumstances.

She crossed herself, sending a prayer to the only God she knew, then bent to her patient, the bowl trembling in her hands.

"Who are you. Where on earth did you come from? My name is Olivia and I'm a doctor, can you hear me? Tomorrow I'll come with you to the hospital. I'll stay with you until you're better and until we locate your parents and find out who you are. You're safe now."

The girl didn't move, her thin chest caving in, as she fought to breath. Fleetingly it crossed Olivia's mind, that perhaps the child didn't even speak English. She started to drip the potion onto her lips, using the root Jabu had stirred the mixture with.

How could a child survive out there in the bush with all the wild animals – and judging by the state of her it must have been for some time. She was practically a skeleton, her small cheeks sunken, her eyes swollen.

Olivia put the bowl down and gently lifted her, taking her through to the bedroom. Covering her with a blanket she slumped into the chair next to the bed and held the child's limp hand.

There was nothing more she could do, only wait and pray.

Chapter Six

Jabu returned to his guests, who were now sheltering from the rain under the covered section of the deck. Only the two American couples remained, the others had retired for the night. The fire now hissing with damp dying embers.

"How is the child Jabu, will it be alright?" Helen raised her voice against the drumming of the rain.

"It's a girl, Helen, probably about six. She's in a bad way, she has a high fever, lots of mosquito bites, open sores and sun burn. She was also bitten by a snake, but Olivia is looking after her until the air ambulance arrives at first light. Once she gets to the hospital she'll be in excellent hands. Olivia is going with her."

"Oh my," the other woman, Melody breathed, her face white with shock, her hand covering her mouth. "How can a child appear out of the bush in the middle of no-where? She must have been through a terrifying experience, poor little thing. Do you think there was some kind of accident, a plane crash or something? I mean she must have come from somewhere. She must belong to someone?"

"Yeah," her husband Chuck replied. "Could have been a plane crash, those little aircraft don't look too solid to me. I nearly had a heart attack when we landed on your air strip, well, a dirt road is what I thought it was."

The wind was picking up, the rain sweeping across the bush, the women reaching for the warm mohair blankets hanging on the back of their chairs.

Jabu stared at the water hole as the fierce wind sent white topped ripples across the surface. "I don't have any answers I'm afraid. I was hoping to go out with Lovemore, once the little girl and Olivia were safely on their way to hospital," he looked at the now torrential rain and mist, "but any tracks she may have made, will be washed away with all this weather. But we'll go out tomorrow, at first light, and see what we can find.

"One thing is for sure," Jabu continued, "there have been no accidents reported, small planes or otherwise. We would have heard about it on the bush telegraph."

"Bush telegraph?" Helen's husband Larry asked.

"We call it bush telegraph where news travels fast, but it's the two-way radio system all the lodges have. We keep in constant touch. If there had been a plane crash all of us would know about it."

"Maybe she'd been staying at another game lodge and wandered off?" said Melody.

Jabu shook his head. "No, that would have been impossible. Most game lodges in this reserve don't allow children under the age of twelve. The main concern of all lodge managers and rangers is the safety of their guests. They keep a close eye on all of them, know where they are at any given time. It would have been impossible for anyone to wander off without someone noticing. Lovemore has checked with the other lodges, no-one has reported a child missing."

Helen wrapped her blanket around her and shivered. "So, what will happen to her then Jabu?"

"The first priority is to get her to the hospital and stabilise her. I will contact the police, they need to get involved to try and trace her family, and, more to the point, find out how exactly did a child end up in the bush, wandering around on her own."

Melody took a shaky sip of her coffee. "I guess the media will get involved, it should produce some results surely? Someone must have noticed their child was missing. Maybe they've already reported it. With no newspapers out here in the bush, you wouldn't know anything about it would you Jabu?"

"If anyone had gone missing all the lodges in the vicinity would have been in touch with each other, with us. If there had been an accident somewhere on the reserve, we would all know about it. But we've heard nothing, as I said, Lovemore has checked."

He stood up at the star-stricken night. "Looks like the weather is closing in. Time for bed, I think. There's nothing more we can do at the moment."

His guests stood up, abandoning their blankets on their chairs. "I'm sorry you had to witness such a distressing incident. I hope it hasn't spoiled your safari experience."

"Oh, not at all," Melody exclaimed. "It's the child we're all so worried about, honey. I wish there was more we could do. You will let us know if we can help in any way? If things need to be paid for, we're all so willing to contribute for what is needed, medical expenses, anything to help her."

Jabu felt his throat tighten. He had had some difficult American guests over the years, but on the whole, he found them kind, generous, courteous and caring. These four had not been found wanting and he was touched by their concern.

"It's kind of you, I appreciate your offer. The owner of the lodge has insurance to cover any emergency. The child will be well cared for, as will Doctor Hamilton. She's going to stay with her until she recovers.

"I'll wish you all goodnight. The air ambulance will be here at dawn, it's a chopper so I hope it won't disturb you too much. I'll see you back to your suites."

Once they were safely inside, Jabu returned to the fire to make sure it was extinguished. He looked across the water hole before turning off the spot lights. He narrowed his eyes, there standing in the place he had found the girl, stood the big bull elephant again. He could tell by the shape of his tusks and ears, it was the same one.

Shaking his head, he turned off the lights, the bush and water hole now plunged into an impenetrable blackness. He made his way back to Olivia.

His unique instincts had not let him down. The animals had no fear of the low rumble of a safari vehicle, but they must have sensed the presence of the terrified child as she had made her way towards the lights of the lodge, desperately looking for help.

*****

Olivia was sitting next to the bed holding the girl's hand, sleeping in the chair. She looked exhausted. He bent over the child and checked the poultice on her leg. The swelling was going down, her breathing a little easier. The bowl next to the bed was almost empty. Olivia was doing a wonderful job considering the circumstances.

Olivia's eyes fluttered open and he held a finger to his lips.

"You need to get a few hours' sleep; tomorrow is going to be a stressful day for you. The air ambulance will be here at daybreak. I'll bring the medics to you as soon as they arrive."

Olivia nodded and reached tiredly for the bowl. "I had to give her CPR, Jabu, we nearly lost her. But thankfully I have her back. The shock of all this is going to be difficult for her to handle if she survives. But I won't leave her. I'll sleep in the chair."

He patted her hand. "She'll survive Olivia, she will."

Chapter Seven

The thwap, thwap, thwap, of the helicopter's rotor blades startled and scattered the animals and birds from the bush surrounding the lodge. This they were not used to.

The bright red logo of the air ambulance emblazoned on the helicopter's side panels added a dash of colour and hope to the grey misty morning. It hovered for a few moments then dropped down on the sodden lawns in front of the lodge.

Jabu stood waiting, the rain pattering on his dark green waterproof cape, covering his head and body. His guests watched from inside the lodge wrapped in blankets against the cold. The morning game drive had been cancelled due to the bad weather conditions. It would have been impossible to see anything through the thick grey curtains of rain.

The rotor blades slowed then stopped. Three medics tumbled out carrying a stretcher and all the other equipment required in an emergency. Jabu introduced himself, then ran ahead of them, leading the way to the cottage.

Olivia stood as they entered, her luggage at the entrance, already packed by a member of staff.

The medics listened to as she briefed them on her patient and where she had been found, then moving swiftly to the side of the inert girl's body, they unpacked their equipment.

Hooking her up to the much-needed intravenous drip, they checked her vital signs. One of the medics looked up when she saw the grey paste spread over the patient's leg and raised her eyebrow.

"Snake bite," murmured Olivia, "we did the best we could using local medicines." She glanced at Jabu.

The medic turned back to the patient. "Any other sort of local medicines used here?"

Jabu who was standing near the door shook his head at Olivia.

Olivia frowned. "No, nothing. I did the best I could under the circumstances."

"You did a great job Doctor Hamilton. Now let's get her wrapped up and on to some oxygen. Her vital signs are erratic, her blood pressure is low and she has a worrying high fever, as you know."

The medic signalled to her crew, her brow furrowed with anxiety. "Doctor Hamilton, how did this child suddenly appear from the bush. How long was she out there?"

Jabu moved forward. "We have no idea, but be assured we'll investigate with the co-operation of the police, once the weather clears."

*****

The team lifted the child up with skilled experienced hands, and put her on the stretcher. They made their way back to the helicopter, sheltering their patient from the heavy rain, the intravenous bag hooked up to the stand. Once inside the child was given the much-needed oxygen.

Olivia hurried after them, carrying her medical bag.

"Olivia! Olivia!"

She turned, holding her hair back as the rotor blades of the helicopter began to turn, blowing her wet hair across her face and eyes. Melody was running towards her, a blanket thrown over her shoulders and head.

"Please take this Olivia, it's been in our family for generations. I want the little girl to have it. We still have our family, past and present. This child may have lost hers. Will you give it to her?"

Olivia looked at a small, well-worn bible, Melody had placed in her hand and felt exhausted tears threatening. "Yes, of course, thank you. So, very kind of you."

"I've put our contact details inside. If there's anything, anything at all, we can do to help, please get in touch. You will let us know what happens, won't you?"

Not given to demonstrations of affection, Olivia put her arms around Melody. "Thank you, Melody, thank you for giving such a precious family gift to a child you don't know, someone none of us knows. I promise I'll keep in touch."

Holding the old bible, Olivia ducked her head and joined her patient in the helicopter.

"I'm here, my child, I'm here," she said softly, as she clambered in. "I'll stay with you." She slipped the bible into the side of her bag, then strapped herself in.

Turning back to the child she picked up the small hand, hot and limp in her own, careful not to get in the way of the medics working intently on her.

*****

Jabu watched as the helicopter lifted off, he raised his arm in farewell, then turned and walked back to his guests who were waiting for him.

"Time for breakfast, I think, and some much-needed hot coffee. The child is in safe hands now, Olivia is with her, and will stay with her."

Showing some relief, the guests made their way to the dining area.

Jabu checked his watch. He had to make a difficult call to New York. The owner, Caroline, needed to know before the press latched on to the story.

His priority the night before had been the child, his guests and the approaching storm. Caroline would have expected him to get his priorities right before he called her.

He had made the difficult decision to turn off the wi-fi connection at the lodge as soon as Olivia had taken charge of the child, knowing it would stave off any unwanted publicity before the facts were known. But he knew it wouldn't be for long. He could hardly blame any of his guests, or the managers of the other lodges, for wanting to share the night of drama with their family and friends.

All his guests were scheduled to leave today, the new arrivals were expected to arrive at lunch time.

Once he had made his report to the police, the media would be on to it. Social media would whip it around the world in seconds. This was the sort of unusual story which made headlines around the world.

Chapter Eight

Jabu was exhausted, but there was still much to be done. The first thing was to search the bush for any clues as to which direction the child may have come from. In this weather, it would be nearly impossible. But they would have to try.

He still had another priority call to make … to the police, and this he did.

*****

The last of the guests had departed unaware they were in for a bumpy water-logged bush road drive back to the airport, before taking their commercial flight to Johannesburg.

Jabu made a calculated decision. He would call his neighbouring lodges and see if they could take his incoming guests, if they had availability. The police would be arriving and would want to begin their investigation. He didn't want his new guests to be confronted by police vehicles when they arrived. That would be a disaster. Not what they would expect on the first day of their safari.

The rangers moved all but one of the safari vehicles to higher ground, should the river rise whilst they were away, then clambered into the remaining one with Jabu at the wheel, the engine already running.

The rain was unyielding as it pattered rhythmically on their waterproof capes. The wind howled, whipping the trees into a frenzy of movement, the bushes bending back and forth, the long grasses bent double by the force of it.

The vehicle made its way slowly through the gloomy sodden bush, the tyres squelching, throwing up mud and spattering it on the doors and windscreen, stones pinged against the chassis of the vehicle.

Herds of impala, kudu and buffalo, sheltered under the trees and bushes, their coats darkened by the deluge. Monkeys clung to the swaying branches, their fur clumping with the wetness, their worried eyes blinking away the rain drops as they clutched each other.

Jabu looked at the now purple and bruised clouds gathered above. The tail end of the cyclone was upon them. A searing flash of crackling lightning lit up the vehicle and the rangers. The thunder boomed and roared in retaliation.

The wind responded with a short burst of rage, rocking and ripping through the branches and leaves of the trees, then stilled, as if holding its breath, before launching into another tirade of rage and fury, tearing the branches from their hosts and hurling them to the ground where they rolled and bucked as they were blown away.

Jabu looked at what was normally a dusty dry track, the water was rippling down it, spreading to the bush at the sides. He could hear the roar of the river as it broke its banks. He felt a tap on his shoulder. Lovemore, his head ranger, was shaking his head.

Jabu gave him the thumbs up sign. It was hopeless. There would be no evidence of the girl's progress in the bush now, no tracks to follow, the water would have eliminated any signs. The situation could become dangerous with the rising water and the lightning.

Reluctantly, he turned the vehicle around and gingerly made his way back, thankful his lodge was on higher ground and built on sturdy stilts. Other lodges, he knew, would not be so lucky.

He had booked their incoming guests into two different lodges, far enough away from the swollen river to ensure their safety.

The lodges built close to the river would bear the brunt of the dangerous weather and the flooding making its way to them. Their guests would have to be evacuated for their own safety. This had happened some years before when the river had burst its banks. Crocodiles, with no sense of direction, had floated through some of the lodges, who had not been quick enough to evacuate their guests, causing panic and hysteria. Dead bodies of animals, who could not outrun the speeding water, had been carried down the river as they bumped against the guest rooms at the stricken lodges.

Jabu would go back and secure their lodge, then wait out the storm. He thanked the Gods, for the second time, for sparing the child's life. She would never have survived a storm of this magnitude on her own. She would have been swept away by the raging torrent of water, and drowned.

The police would arrive soon, unless they decided to wait out the storm until the weather settled.

Jabu knew they would find no trace of his little unexpected guest. There would be nothing left to give them any clues as to which direction she might have come from or where she might have been.

But they would come.

*****

Later that day the police vehicle pulled up at the now empty lodge.

Jabu met them at the entrance, introduced himself, and led them into the covered sitting area of the lodge. The sky was clearing and a watery sun had made its appearance. The staff had moved the dining room chairs and tables from the outside deck and stacked them inside. Raindrops hung from the branches of the trees, the deck now soaked and deserted.

The two police officers looked around them and Jabu could see the resentment in their eyes. He knew members of the police force were not well paid. To see all the luxury around them and knowing it was owned by a European woman, who lived in America, was not going to make for a good start.

Jabu ordered coffee, and once they were all settled, he gave them his statement. The younger of the two made notes, his expression sullen.

"Mr Klassens," the senior officer said, "we have already done as much as we can to find the family of this child, but no-one has come forward with any information, or reported a child missing. The Nelspruit police are handling the case but instructed us to come from Hazyview, our station being closer to where the girl was found here."

Jabu inclined his head. "But you will be mounting a search? My rangers and I have attempted to find evidence of where she might have come from, what route she may have taken, before she arrived here," he raised his shoulder in a half shrug, "well, I'm sure you are well aware there was a bad storm. Any tracks would have been washed away when the river burst its banks. We found nothing." He sat forward. "Perhaps a chopper could be used to fly low over the bush, maybe the pilot would be able to spot something?"

The senior policeman carefully returned his empty cup to the silver tray. "I'm afraid it won't be possible," he said with a weary sigh. "We have few resources at our disposal and a limited budget. As you say, any evidence out there would have been destroyed by the storm. It would be a waste of valuable police time and we are only a small station.

The child is now safe in hospital, there's nothing more we can do out here until the weather settles.

"I suggest, if you think a chopper will reveal any further evidence, you might ask the owner of this lodge," he glanced at his notebook, "Ms Gordon, I think you said, to finance it?"

Jabu held back his frustration. "There will be no need for me to contact the owner and ask for permission to finance a private search. I'm the general manager of this lodge and also her partner, she trusts me." He let this information sink in.

"However, I will need permission from the police to do this, as you know. The Parks Board authorities don't allow just anyone to fly over the area. It's tightly controlled, guests of safari lodges are allowed, parks board officials, of course, the choppers used to track down poachers, and for emergencies such as we had here. The authorities, to give permission for a private search, will need instructions from the police to allow me to go ahead."

Jabu looked at the senior policeman. "I will need this co-operation from you as a matter of urgency. I want to search the area thoroughly and see if we can find any trace of an accident, any debris at all. When can I expect the necessary permissions Inspector?"

The inspector shifted in his chair and looked around the room.

Jabu continued when there was no response from him. "The press pack will be anxious to learn more about this little girl. It would be good public relations for the police if they were seen to be doing as much as they possibly could to assist, not so? Especially as all expenses would be met by Ms Gordon, and myself, personally."

The inspector rammed his hat on his head, and stood up. "I will see what can be arranged, Mr Klassens."

Jabu showed them out and watched the tail lights of the vehicle as it made its slippery way through the thick congealing mud to the entry gate of the lodge.

Shaking his head Jabu walked back inside. It still surprised him, having fought so hard and for so long, and having their own government now, twenty-two years later, there was still such racial emotion in his country. He knew under the surface, and especially with the many luxury game lodges in the area, mostly owned by Europeans, there was resentment.

To his mind the lodges offered thousands of jobs to previously unemployed rural Africans. There were hundreds of South Africans all over the country who worked tirelessly to help those who couldn't help themselves. Many Afrikaner farmers, the backbone of the country's farming and agricultural industry, had trained their fellow countrymen to farm and feed themselves and their families, and had given them land to set them up.

Farmers, who owned vast wine estates in the Western Cape, had given land freely to their workers, letting them have full use of all the vineyard's farming equipment so they could grow their own grapes and produce their own wine, and helped with the marketing of it, alongside their own brand.

Jabu walked out on to the deck of the empty lodge. Some things would never change, he knew. All over the world it was the same, the divide between the haves and the have nots.

The police had performed their duty by coming to the lodge but he knew they could do little to follow up the story, or help in any other way. They were under staffed and working within tight budgets.

The police had had some bad press over the years, not all of them, of course, but there were whispers of bribes, corruption, papers being mislaid, hijackings masterminded. The list was endless.

He smiled to himself. The permission for him to launch his own private search over the bush would not be long in coming, he was quite sure, the police would welcome some good publicity.

The weather was clearing. It was time to open up the lodge again. Tomorrow he would retrieve his guests from the other lodges, then organise for a private chopper and pilot to be on stand-by.

Chapter Nine
New York

The elevator pinged as it arrived at the fifth floor in the store on 56th Street in New York City. Caroline heard the light footsteps as a potential customer made their way towards the book section.

Oak floors were partially covered by expensive Persian rugs, leather wing back chairs were dotted around ready to take the weight off the feet of weary shoppers in need of rest. The shop was a little chunk of England set amongst the towering skyscrapers.

The other floors sold shooting clothing, and accessories, and handmade shoes, both for men and women. The sixth floor was dedicated to its core business – bespoke guns.

There were three sections to the impressive floor, where Caroline worked; the art gallery filled with pictures of African wildlife and birds and beasts of America and England. The African wildlife was easily recognisable to Caroline, but the various birds of America and England still remained a complete mystery to her.

The book department held books on every kind of dog imaginable, mostly English sporting dog and how to train them in the field. One corner, which she avoided, had coffee table books filled with hideous shots of wild, and endangered, animals mounted in vast private rooms of wealthy American hunters.

The other corner she loved was the books on Africa. Some first editions, lots of photography books by renowned wild life photographers, and shelves and shelves of historical books the store bought from private collections.

Hunters from years gone by had penned their tales of life in unchartered terrains, when shooting big game was something to be admired. Thankfully, not any more.

There were no more recent books about hunting. Like poachers they aroused fury and protests all around the world. Their blatant postings on the internet as they cradled a dead lion, elephant or giraffe in their arms, caused outrage, forcing the hunters to run and hide for their own safety, when they returned home.

Initially when she was being shown around by a member of staff, she had noticed there were three other people there on the fifth floor.

The book expert, the art expert and the salesman who processed all the purchases through the till. All she had to do was sit at her rather impressive desk and set up her safari business.

She had made it clear to the British company who had offered her the position in New York, that she would not, under any circumstances, handle any big game hunting safaris, even though the company had been arranging such safaris to Africa for over eighty years. The shop specialised in all things English and African related. The Americans loved it.

Now wanting to move away from hunting and all the bad publicity it brought with it, they had decided to offer photographic safaris instead. They had hired Caroline to set up the new side of their business.

On her first day there, over two years ago, Caroline had glanced at the antique clock on the wall and wondered if she had arrived too early. Where were the other members of staff?

Two hours later she realised there were not going to be any other members of staff. Her heart had plummeted. Although highly skilled in her own field, she had never been involved in the world of retail and knew precious little about art and books. As for the cash register which hunched like a bad-tempered hippo in the corner, well it made her feel rather faint to say the least.

Elegant shoppers walked through the three adjoining rooms, browsing through the books on Africa, wandered round the art gallery, always stopping at the safari desk to ask questions about Africa, and what it was like there. Her racks of expensive glossy brochures and the stunning shots of game lodges all beautifully framed, graced the walls and spoke of another world which they could only wonder about.

Caroline's enthusiasm for Africa, her impressive knowledge of the lodges in East and Southern Africa, the landscapes, the people and the culture, soon had the business rolling in. Plus, she owned a lodge there herself.

The one Jabu ran.

*****

Caroline looked up from the complicated itinerary she was putting together.

A woman she judged to be in her early fifties, gave her a quick smile as she made her way through to the art gallery.

Discreetly Caroline studied her. She was of medium height, her straw-coloured hair swept back from her forehead and tethered back in a thick plait which snaked down her straight back. Her long legs were encased in khaki trousers, sporting button down pockets, a startingly white shirt, beautifully tailored, was tucked into her narrow waist. Her feet encased in soft beige safari boots.

The woman turned and smiled, almost as though she had felt she was being studied. Around her neck she was wearing a cream bone choker, held together at the front with a round medallion sporting two small feathers. On both wrists she wore an assortment of bracelets which Caroline immediately recognised as the beadwork made by the Ndebele people of South Africa.

Caroline smiled back at her. "I love your jewellery – so African. May I help you with anything?"

"No, my dear, thank you," she replied, her very English vowels clipped.

Not American then. Caroline watched as she studied one of the pieces of art, with its vast landscape, the endless deep blue skies, the flat-topped trees, and a herd of elephant leaving a trail of dust in their wake. The woman stood there for some time, not moving, then turned and walked to Caroline's desk.

Her smile widened as she looked at the photograph decorating the wall at the side of Caroline's desk. "What a perfectly wonderful photograph, what I wouldn't give to be sitting in one of those chairs watching the game come down to the water hole to drink."

Caroline turned her head and looked at the photograph she never tired of, which happened to be her own lodge. Two director's chairs, a table set for two beneath a large shady tree, the crisp white cloth billowing in the breeze. The sky a mixture of pink and red, a hurricane lamp glowing on the table refracting prisms of light from the crystal glassware. She turned back to the woman now standing in front of her.

"Yes, I agree. I often wish I was sitting there with someone interesting. New York is exciting, but, oh my, it certainly is noisy."

The woman lowered herself into the comfortable leather chair opposite Caroline's desk. "My dear, you sound quite English but I hear another accent somewhere?"

Caroline smiled. "South African. I was brought up there but have travelled all over the world most of my life. But my heart and soul will always be in Africa – it has a tremendous pull for anyone who has lived there."

"Indeed, it does. A hard place to leave."

"I noticed you liked a particular painting," Caroline gestured towards the elephants. "The David Shepherd."

"Yes," the woman said, "I grew up in Kenya. I've lived there all my life. He captures everything just so, don't you think?"

Caroline smiled in agreement. "I know Kenya, I've been there many times. The first time when I was only nine years old. My father was posted to a place called Gil Gil. He was with the British military."

The woman's bracelets rattled softly on her slim wrists. "Ah, yes, I know it well. Marvellous boarding school there where young children went before being bundled off to another boarding school in England. Must have been difficult for them having to wear thick woolly knee length socks, after running around barefoot in the sunshine and having such freedom growing up."

Caroline held out her hand. "I'm Caroline Gordon by the way."

"Hello, Caroline. Grace Chambers."

"So, are you living here in New York now Grace?"

"No, I'm only passing through. My son used to live here. I have a little unfinished business to attend to. I'm trying to make my mind up about something. It's a long story."

Caroline looked around the empty floor, feeling an instant rapport with this woman from Kenya. "Well, why not tell me your story? No-one seems to require my attention at the moment, as you can see," she said wistfully.

Grace gazed at the magnificent photograph next to Caroline's desk and sighed deeply. "My daughter was born in Kenya, as was my son, then, like so many other children, we had to send them to England, to a boarding school, to complete their education.

"They came back to Kenya for holidays but Megan changed. She saw her future in the UK. She went to university there, met a fellow student, fell in love, and that was it. Then she married him. Tim chose to go back to Kenya, well, for a while anyway."

Caroline nodded encouraging Grace to continue with her story.

"When Megan's babies arrived, I went back to the UK to see them. She'd settled into her new life, adapted to all things British, including the weather, and she was perfectly happy. I stayed a month but found it difficult to fit into such a different way of life."

Caroline grinned at her. "Yes, I tried living there for a few months, but I couldn't hack it either. It was, well, so different."

Grace looked down at the bracelets on her wrists and adjusted them slightly. "Megan begged me to think about leaving Kenya and make a new life with them." She looked up at Caroline.

"Are you sure you want to hear all this? I don't want to take up your time?"

Caroline nodded her head enthusiastically. "Of course, speaking to someone from Africa is a refreshing change from listening to New Yorkers. They speak so fast, don't they?"

Grace smiled and continued. "I discussed it with my friends back home and heard all the stories, the pressure put on them by their children to leave the country they had been born and brought up in, to be with their children, and grandchildren."

She looked back at the photograph on the wall. "Many of them caved in under the pressure and sold up everything before taking off for Australia, Canada, the UK or wherever their children lived. Suddenly they were in a strange country, they knew no-one, they lived in tiny little flats or houses, paying high rents, with a quality of life which paled into insignificance after the carefree, friendly, social life they had always known in Kenya."

She touched the choker around her neck. "The huge supermarkets with their hundreds of choices of produce were rather daunting after being used to the local *duka,* back home, where they knew the owner, found whatever they wanted and sometimes only needed to sign a chit, then pay at the end of the month."

She paused as the scream of a siren passed by outside. "Initially they saw their children and grandchildren on a fairly regular basis, mostly when they were needed to baby-sit," Grace said wryly.

Caroline tapped her nail on the pile of glossy brochures on her desk. "Yes, I've heard the stories as well. People sort of shrink when they're unhappy, fold into themselves. But I heard the more courageous grandparents did turn their back on what they considered an alien and lonely life, and returned to Africa. That takes a lot of courage."

Grace nodded. "Yes, it does. Those who returned to the country they loved, had to start all over again. But they were home, the sun was shining they were happy, and that's what counts Caroline, being happy. Even if some of them found they were now living in reduced circumstances."

Caroline changed the subject sensing it was upsetting the woman sitting opposite her. "Was your husband a Kenyan?"

"Yes, he was. He worked with the government on various dairy projects all around the country. We lived out in the bush, it was basic, but I don't think I'd ever been happier. We were miles away from anywhere so I home schooled both of my children."

She fiddled with her bracelets again. "Before I was married, I was a nursing sister at the Aga Khan hospital in Nairobi. It's where I met my husband, Craig. He'd been admitted to hospital with a particularly bad bout of malaria, I nursed him through it."

Caroline glanced at her computer. No new emails required her attention, the complicated itinerary could wait a few hours. She wanted to hear more of the story.

"So, is Craig here in the city with you, helping you with the unfinished business you mentioned?"

Grace leaned back in the chair, her smooth brow now creased. "No. We moved back to Nairobi from our bush home when it was obvious the children needed to go to a proper school."

She lifted her shoulders. "He met someone else. You know what Kenya is like, a social whirlwind, lots of good-looking girls and guys with too much time on their hands.

"The new woman in his life worked in a bush camp somewhere, doing some research on ticks and mosquitoes. Craig decided he wanted to go back to the life we had had, but not with me."

Caroline saw a shadow of sadness cross the attractive face in front of her. "It must have been tough for you."

Grace smiled. "It was tough to start with, but when someone finds someone else more attractive, all they want is to be with them. They don't look too far down the line to see what the fall-out might be. You can't hang onto someone who doesn't want you anymore, Caroline, no matter how hard you try.

"Once the children were settled into their boarding school I went to Mombasa and lived there, and worked at a small rural hospital. The years whizzed past, the children grew up and spread their wings. I missed my children. The job wasn't enough for me anymore. So, under a great deal of pressure, I gave in and tried to adapt to life in the UK, close to Megan."

She clasped her hands together. "I knew the UK wouldn't work for me, but I did try to adapt, anyway, I came back to Kenya."

"And your son. Where does he live now?"

Grace looked down at her hands. "I'm not sure where he is now. He was a game ranger at a rather expensive lodge in the Sabi Sands. He was offered a job there and left Kenya for South Africa.

"He fell in love with one of the guests, and moved here to New York."

Grace's large blue eyes filled with regret. "It didn't last of course, the glamour of it all." Her voice faltered. "It was all over for Tim. He should have stayed in Africa, where he belonged."

Caroline looked up. A young couple were looking through the brochures for African safaris, displayed opposite the lift doors.

Grace had noticed them too, and stood. "I must be going. Lovely to meet you Caroline, I've taken up far too much of your time, but it was good to talk to someone who understands how it is in Africa."

Caroline watched her walk away. She sensed Grace was trying to make the best of things but clearly she was in limbo, torn between where she wanted to be, and where her family thought she should be.

Caroline herself had fallen into the same honey trap. She had been working at a game lodge in South Africa, as the manager, and fell in love with a charismatic American who seemed to have such empathy for the way she lived, he'd also come from New York. Like a lot of South Africans at the time, when her own country was in turmoil, she imagined a place anywhere else. He promised her the world, a different world, she fell for it, and him, then married him.

After leaving the lodge and moving to New York, she was happy, happier than she had ever been. Then Andrew blew her away with a gift on their second wedding anniversary. He had bought the lodge they had met in.

*****

Five years later Andrew dropped a bomb on her life. Caroline had spent more time than he anticipated at their lodge, travelling back to South Africa on a regular basis.

Andrew had been a social animal, invited, as a top cosmetic surgeon, to all the glamour and glitz of the New York social life, after all it had been his hunting ground for new clients.

Predictably he had met someone who he thought he could make more beautiful than she already was.

The divorce was acrimonious. Caroline was shattered, but she hung onto her dream – her game lodge in Africa.

Andrew, flying high with his new love, agreed she could have it. But during the divorce proceedings, the lodge had lost its place in the international market. Rumours spread about the divorce, would someone else buy it? Tour operators looked nervously at it. How would this look after they had promoted it internationally to their travellers? They couldn't be sure and gradually moved away from promoting it, finding safer options.

Caroline had found herself with no bookings and no manager. She had let the staff go and closed down the lodge. The old Caretaker had kept his eyes on things, but the isolation of the place and lack of any other human contact had taken its toll on him and, after a few months, he had found another job.

But the divorce settlement had made her eyes water – to say it was generous was an understatement.

When the divorce was finalised, she had immediately flown back to South Africa and from Johannesburg taken the short flight to the small bush airport, then a private charter to her empty lodge.

That was eighteen months ago, long before the child arrived at the water hole, and before she met Jabu.

Chapter Ten
South Africa

An empty lodge is irresistible to creatures of the bush. Caroline had seen the thatch was beginning to sag and fray from the main lodge area. The twenty modest guest rooms had generously made their empty space available to birds, bats, monkeys, snakes, insects and small animals. The private pools were green and slimy with leaves, branches and other detritus.

For hours she had walked around checking the rooms, seeing the yellowing bed linen, the spider's webs, the scurrying insects and the overgrown grounds around the lodge.

Caroline had started to imagine something quite different. She didn't want the ten-star luxury everyone else was emulating. She wanted more of an old-fashioned safari experience. After all, she reasoned, how much time did guests spend in their opulent rooms?

Caroline knew it was only wealthy international guests who could afford the super expensive lodges, and probably had the same thing in their own homes. Outdoor showers and decks, fabulous views across the hills and valleys, okay they didn't have the wild animals of Africa, but they had their own wild life, both two and four legged.

No, she wanted something different. Guests would expect some luxury, proper plumbing, snow white sheets on their beds, but was it necessary to have all the rose petals on the pillows, the packaged range of toiletries in the bathrooms? The fruit basket wrapped in cellophane, tied with a ribbon. To her mind that smacked of ubiquitous chain hotels, and luxury resorts with too many rooms.

In order to immerse guests in Africa, she reasoned, you had to give them the expected standard of luxury, but make them feel the real essence of the land, feel its heartbeat.

The food would have to be sublime, the service impeccable, but the greatest experience of being on safari had to be the animals. To embrace and feel the African safari her guests needed to peel the layers away from their extraordinary wealthy lives and, literally, come down to earth. Feel and immerse themselves in the bush around them.

She envisioned a tented camp, with a difference. No English style armchairs, no leather studded high winged chairs. No. The touches of luxury would come from safaris taken a time long gone, when they used a lot of campaign furniture, comfortable, and very collectable now, but with an authentic feel of Africa.

Caroline needed someone with exceptional abilities to oversee the refurbishments she had in mind, to get things up and running. He, or she, would need the bush experience only a qualified professional ranger had. They would need to be good with people from all over the world, difficult or otherwise, with their different cultures and languages, and have leadership qualities because when the lodge re-opened Caroline needed that someone to run her camp, and become her manager.

Through her contacts and friends in the industry, one name came up time and time again.

Jabu.

She had wiped the leaves and dust from one of the outside chairs and sat, pulling out his file from her briefcase.

Jabu had been born in a rural village in the Eastern Cape, with a direct bloodline to the ancient people of the desert. The San people.

An English couple had taken him under their wing and given him the education he needed to become a ranger. He left school with adequate exam passes but with no desire to go to university, however his knowledge of the bush, the animals, birds, plants, trees and insects, was apparently encyclopaedic. All these things he had learned from his father. He could have easily gained a first-class degree in botany, zoology or entomology. She liked what she had read about him.

She looked at his photograph: he was tall for a Griqua man, his eyes were the colour of wild honey, his shaved head gave him a noble look. Around his neck he wore a slim necklace of turquoise beads, around his wrists were beads and elephant hair bracelets. A good-looking man.

Caroline read on: his parents had lived a simple life, in their village in the bush, his mother a quilt maker, his father a shepherd. He had a sister who had gone into the world of publishing, producing life style books and magazines which were a huge success, according to all the information she had garnered on him. Jabu was unmarried and had no children.

She had tucked the file back in her briefcase and stood up, stretching her slight body working out the kinks in her back from all the flights she had taken recently.

The old lodge had been built on a small hill, surrounded by ancient jackalberry trees, with irresistible berries which attracted birds and small antelope, and tall leadwood trees with their generous shawl of leaves. The view across the bush was breath-taking. In the distance she could see the familiar dead tree, bereft of any leaves. Its long-blackened branches reaching almost accusingly for the sky. It gave the place a mystical - spiritual feel.

The Sabi Sands private reserve, where the lodge was situated, stretched for sixty-five hectares, sharing fifty kilometres of the western boundary bordering the Kruger Park. In the early nineties the fences had been taken down allowing the prolific game to traverse vast stretches of grazing land between other reserves and the Kruger Park itself.

There were plenty of super luxury lodges in this area, but none would compare to her refurbished one, surrounded by the gentle rolling hills of Africa, and the majestic Drakensberg mountains watching over from a distance. She would outshine them all.

*****

Caroline had booked into the lodge where she knew Jabu to be working. She had spent some time walking around, noticing all the clay pots sprouting porcupine quills, the excessive African art hanging from the walls, the carved wooden animals dotting all the tables, the solid English furniture, the leather winged back chairs studded with brass buttons. She had shaken her head.

Why bring so much international style into an African game lodge, she thought. Surely this is what guests were trying to get away from?

Her suite was lovely enough but, once again, full of excessive *objets d'art*, the bathroom crowded with miniature bottles of shampoos, body lotions, and other beauty products. In each corner there was a carving of some sort, and, again an excess of African art hanging on the walls.

On the carved table surrounded by bronze lizards, wooden bowls and woven baskets, stood a stiff arrangement of fruit wrapped in cellophane tied with a ribbon…

The feel, the sense of Africa, she concluded, was not to be found in the interior of her suite, that was outside, in all its savage beauty. The smell of the bush, the sound of the birds and the animals, the colours of the trees and bushes. Nature in all its glory.

*****

As the evening approached and darkness fell, she had watched the game ranger Jabu entertaining his guests. He moved between the tables with grace and confidence; she was impressed.

Finally, he had made his way to her table. "Hello. Caroline, I think? I'm Jabu."

The moment she had been waiting for had finally arrived.

He smiled down at her. "No-one should ever be on their own in the bush, the animals never are, but sometimes being alone is alright, don't you think?"

Caroline returned his smile; he was astute as well. "Yes, I think being alone is quite alright. Would you like to join me?"

Jabu sat. "So, where are you from, Caroline?"

"At the moment I live in New York, but I was born here in South Africa, excuse the slight American drawl. I'll drop it one day and revert to my native twang."

Jabu picked up a leaf from the table and twirled it around his fingers. "You look a little pre-occupied, you haven't mixed with our other guests, and I understand you passed on going on a game drive."

He flicked the leaf away. "Your thoughts seem to be miles away. I've noticed you scribbling away in your notepad – are you writing a book?"

She grinned at him. "No. I'm making a few sketches for a new project I want to do."

"Here in South Africa or the States?"

"Here in South Africa, in fact, right here in the bush. I'm looking for someone like you Jabu."

He raised his eyebrows. "I'm not quite sure what you've found, or what you're looking for, but why someone like me?"

Caroline took a sip from her wine glass. "I have a game lodge, completely deserted, no guests. But it's a beautiful place, Jabu, a place with true potential. It's not super luxury, but it has a magic all of its own, the game and bird life is fantastic."

She draped her scarf around her shoulders against the cooling night air. "I'm looking for someone to manage it, someone who will have a stake in it, a passion for it."

"I think I know which lodge this is, been empty a while, yes? Would it be Porcupine Peak by any chance?"

"Yes, and the first thing I'm going to do is change the name, change the style, make it more a sort of Hemingway experience but with all the modern facilities a guest would expect."

Jabu glanced round at his other guests, checking they were all being looked after, but she could see he was listening.

"Jabu, I don't only want a manager, I want an exceptional person to run the place. I'll offer a good salary with all the perks, and a stake in the business. I believe a lodge manager, to feel the passion and commitment, should be a stakeholder. I'm prepared to offer that as well."

Jabu ran his hand over his head. "What's the time frame for the refurbishment of this run-down empty lodge?"

"I want to start as soon as possible. I have all the ideas of how I would like to see it, and I have a generous budget to get things going. I even have rather a clever idea for marketing it under its new name."

Jabu sat back in his chair and frowned. "There are so many lodges in this area, all over the country, in fact. The competition is fierce, you'll be up against a lot."

Caroline shrugged. "It doesn't faze me one little bit. I've been in the safari business for years. I've visited most of the game lodges both here, and in Kenya, Zimbabwe, and Botswana. The Kenyans have things right, the way they do it with a mix of both old and new is spot on. Botswana camps have a different feel altogether, perhaps more rustic but with all the facilities, it works there with the Okavango Delta and all the waterways.

"Zimbabwe, of course, struggles to get tourists, what with all the problems they have. There are some lovely lodges there but no international guests. Hopefully, sometime in the future the situation will change." She swirled her wine glass around contemplatively.

"The lodges here in South Africa, are a mix of rustic, simple and, quite frankly, so sumptuous some of them, in my opinion, detract from the wild life experience – and as for the rates they charge!"

She looked over his shoulder at the sun setting over the bush. "I've stayed in a few of these luxury game lodges and, yes, they were stunning, but honestly some were a bit over the top. One lodge used to change the furniture around, every few days, in the main areas so the guests wouldn't get bored.

"Another place I stayed in had a lot of glass walls and windows in the room, and whilst I was at dinner, they changed things around. I didn't notice when I came back from dinner, it was only when I woke in the night to use the bathroom and walked into a sheet of glass, which I swear wasn't there before, and nearly broke my nose."

Jabu's body shook with laughter.

"Don't laugh it was true. The next day, with a throbbing nose, I asked the manager how many guests had walked into the glass windows thinking they were doors. He looked straight at me and said '*You mean this month or this year?*'

She shook her head. "As for all the rose petals on the bed? No," she said firmly. "That is not what a safari is all about. I'm going to be different with my lodge."

Jabu stood. "Most entertaining Caroline, but I like your vision, and I agree, there is always room for something different in the game lodge industry. Let me give it some thought."

Caroline watched him turn towards his other guests and smiled. He was perfect for the job, and, if she was not mistaken, he was interested.

She called him back and played her trump card. "Oh Jabu, wait a minute. You do know this lodge is up for sale, don't you? No guarantees the new owners might keep you on – you're safer with me. You'll have a future."

Chapter Eleven

The next day Caroline gathered all her sketches, architect's drawings, and a heavy file of papers with all her plans, then made her way to the main seating area of the lodge. She left a message with the receptionist. She would like to meet with Jabu as soon as it was convenient.

Caroline ordered coffee then settled in one of the chairs and spread her sketches over the table in front of her, glancing up occasionally to watch the small black faced vervet monkeys trying to snatch bread rolls and fruit from the long trestle breakfast table. Waiters flicked at them with their serving cloths, much to the amusement of the guests, scattering them back to the trees where they chattered to each other, waiting for another opportunity.

Half an hour later Jabu found her there. "Morning Caroline, sleep well?"

"Morning Jabu. No, far too much on my mind. Spent most of the night scribbling away as you call it. Take a look at these?"

Jabu sat and studied the sketches Caroline had been working on.

"No walls. Only glass. Like the lodge you nearly broke your nose in?"

"Yes. No walls, no thatch, only canvas and glass, and I won't be changing the furniture around every night. Each suite will have a sort of Bedouin look, surrounded by glass and built on stilts."

She ran a finger over one of the sketches. "The suites will be sheltered by cream canvas, like an East African safari style tent. When the guests arrive the glass walls will be covered by soft white muslin curtains, wall to wall. Each suite will have its own personal butler, and when he has deposited their luggage, he'll sweep open the curtains and their jaws will drop – it will be like being suspended in the air in the middle of the bush. What do you think?"

Jabu looked at the logistics of it all, as he flipped through her sketches. "Well, it will certainly be different," he murmured, not looking up.

Caroline lifted another sketch. "The glass doors, leading to their private deck will slide back letting in any breeze, it will be like sleeping in the trees. The guests will be protected from mozzies and other insects by their mosquito nets. The only solid door will be at the entrance to their suite. I want to ship them in from Lamu. You know, those beautiful hand carved doors with brass studs?"

Jabu shook his head. "No, but I have a feeling I'm about to find out."

Caroline looked up innocently. "Does this mean you're at least thinking about my proposal then?"

He held up his hand. "There's a lot to think about first. I spoke to the management here this morning Caroline. You're right the owners are going to sell and the new owners have the right to select who they wish to have working for them. They've assured me I would still have a job, but, quite frankly, I don't like the way this is being handled."

"How did you know it was going to be sold before any of us did?"

Caroline raised an eyebrow. "I hear these things, I know a lot of people in the business, not much moves without me knowing or hearing about it, how do you think I found you?

"I agree, Jabu, the current owners should have been a little more upfront about it, especially to you. But I'm looking on the positive side. If you should decide to join me, I want you to handpick the best of your staff and rangers, from here, or other lodges, to come and work with us. They'll be well paid and have more perks than most lodges offer these days. They'll have their own quarters, a distance from the lodge, of course, and again, should you decide to join me Jabu, you can design your own living quarters, but closer to the lodge than the other members of staff."

She pushed her hair behind her ears. "I'll need my own place with an office attached. Also, I'll need other accommodation to house pilots who might need to stay overnight, and friends."

She grinned at him. "I won't insist you surround yourself with glass and muslin curtains, I promise.

"So, what's it going to be Jabu. Are you going to join me on my big project?"

He smiled at her. "You don't let the bush grow under your feet do you Caroline? I only met you yesterday. But I like your energy and your passion for the project. I like the look of your potential new lodge. I think it will be magnificent. Very different.

"Let's discuss the terms and condition. I'll need a written contract of course," he said with a wide smile.

*****

For the next two hours Jabu and Caroline hammered out the conditions of the contract, and when they would tear down the old lodge and start building the new one.

"Here's the business plan, including the staff we'll need, Jabu. Housekeeping, food and beverages manager, rangers, chef, groundsmen, etc. Pick the best for us and I'll leave you to train them up. All the furniture from the old lodge will be used to furnish the new staff quarters. Throw away anything past its sell-by date. I'll need your advice on the safari vehicles. We need new ones."

She opened her bulging file of papers. "I already have the building company we'll use, they're based in Nelspruit. Ditto the architect. Ready to go when we are. The accountant is in place, he's also based in Nelspruit. I want to use as many of the local people as possible, but the final decision as to who we take on, will be yours to make. I want the lodge finished in nine months Jabu. The building contractor has promised me as many people as we need, and assures me it can be done."

Jabu raised his eyebrow. "Nine months?"

"Yeah. The grand opening will be at the end of November. I have big plans for that."

She flicked through her file. "All the furniture and furnishings have been chosen and paid for. I've sourced a lot of colonial style pieces for decoration, from a shop in London. Again, only waiting to be shipped out. The interior designer may well want to add to this, depending on their vision."

Caroline hefted the heavy file over to Jabu. I have all the original paperwork in New York. This is for you to work with. Any suggestions would be most welcome, anything you think I may have missed, let me know."

Both well satisfied they ordered more coffee and sat back, smiling at each other.

Caroline blew her fringe back. "Phew! Going to be a hot one today, I think."

She leaned forward and reached for her notebook. "I'm going to put you on the payroll with immediate effect, as a consultant until you've worked out when you can officially start. I have complete faith you'll find the right people to staff our lodge. Let me have your bank details when you have a moment."

Caroline took a sip of her now cold coffee. "Right, all I need to find is an interior decorator…"

Jabu signalled to a waiter to bring them fresh coffee. "I thought this would have been your job, Caroline."

"Unfortunately, not. Although I will give a thorough briefing to whoever I find to do the interiors. You see Jabu, I won't be here."

He looked at her, startled. "Where will you be? New York?"

She smiled at him. "I told you I had a big plan for the marketing, and I have. I also plan on bringing out the top journalists from the glossy lifestyle magazines in New York City, London and Paris for our opening. It would be useful, to lure the journalists even more, if I could bag a minor British Royal to officially open the lodge. I'm still working on that.

"There's a prestigious store in New York City. They were looking for someone to set up a safari desk, that was a couple of years ago when I was going through my divorce. They wanted me. I needed something to do, so I took the job.

"I used to push the lodges I knew in East and Southern Africa. Mine, was already running down, I couldn't send those sorts of clients there. But I listened to what they wanted."

She laughed. "Now I'll be pushing our lodge as hard as I can. Clients will be impressed. I'll know so much about our particular, as yet, nameless game lodge. I won't be telling them it's ours, of course.

"When I can describe it in great detail, and answer any questions they throw at me, they'll have the confidence to book. Americans, especially, need the reassurance, they ask a thousand questions, and I'll have the answers to every one of them." She said triumphantly.

"You see, Jabu. Lodge owners, or their representatives, from all over Africa, go to the international travel shows all over the world. Not only is it hugely expensive to attend, what with the airfares and hotel expenses, entertaining the tour operators etc thrown in. But the competition is fierce."

She lifted her face to the October sun and closed her eyes for a moment. "In my opinion there are too many lodges to choose from. Somehow you have to have an edge. If the owners of the lodges are wealthy, well, they can afford to throw thousands of dollars of advertising at it. But most lodge owners are not in that kind of position."

Jabu reached for his coffee. "So, what's the edge we'll have over all the other lodges? Especially as ours isn't even built yet?"

"The edge?" She rubbed her hands together gleefully. "The clients will come through the door of the fancy store in Manhattan and right into my arms at the safari desk. Clients nearly always book their safari a good year in advance, so we have plenty of time."

Jabu glanced briefly at his watch. "Well, you certainly seem to have worked hard with your plans Caroline, I'm impressed. I only hope I'll be able to keep up with you."

Caroline leaned over and shook his hand, already feeling quite comfortable with him, knowing she had made the right decision.

"I'll visit our building site at least every two months, even if it's only for a long week-end. But I'm at the end of an email and will work with you on any decisions to be made."

Caroline took a sip of her coffee and shuddered. "We need to up the game with the coffee in our lodge, this stuff tastes as though it came out of a tin." She pushed her cup to one side.

She gathered up her papers and files, straightening their edges into a neat pile. "Now I need to find an interior designer who has the same vision as me and won't mind spending weeks in the bush, battling the bugs, the heat and other crawly things, like snakes, without freaking out.

"The interior designer I'm looking for needs to have a certain temperament. There won't be any room for tantrums, they'll be working under a lot of pressure in pretty tough, hot, and noisy conditions. Camping out mostly."

Jabu leaned forward resting his chin on his hands. "I think I know of someone. Someone with vision and who doesn't freak out if a snake slithers past or the bugs and mozzies become too much to bear."

"You do. Who? Not everyone wants to spend weeks in the middle of nowhere on a building site you know, Jabu, camping out in a tent, and it needs to be someone you can work closely with."

"My sister. She works for a lifestyle magazine, freelance, in Cape Town. Top of her game. She's featured many game lodges where she was involved with the interiors. She knows her craft and she doesn't mind the bush at all, she was brought up in it."

Caroline perked up immediately. "Okay, tell me more. What's her name?"

"Kia. Kia Klassens."

Caroline's eyes lit up. "Yes, I've heard of her, seen some of her work, it's excellent. How do I get hold of her? Is she still in Cape Town?"

Jabu nodded. "She is now. She went to London for a while, but she's back and looking for work."

"Right. Give me her details. I'm going to Cape Town tomorrow. I already have interviews lined up with another three interior designers there, but I would like to meet Kia."

They both stood. "Better get packed then. I'll get my lawyer to draw up your contract, as we discussed, as soon as I get back to the States."

Caroline shook his hand again. "I have a meeting set up with the architect and the building company in Nelspruit on Thursday. I want to start with the reconstruction of the new lodge immediately. All the contractors and their contact details are in the file. They'll be in touch with you on Friday to introduce themselves."

She rubbed her hands together happily, then stopped and clicked her fingers. "That's it! The lodge will be called Infinity. The word means timelessness, limitless – it's perfect don't you think?"

"No Rhino Lodge? No Elephant's Way? No animals in the name, or birds, beetles or fish or anything?" But he was smiling.

"Nope – only Infinity – it's perfect. Not even Infinity Lodge."

"Infinity it is then – yes, I like it."

"One more thing Caroline," he called after her.

"Yes?"

"If you should decide to take Kia on as your interior designer, well, there's something you need to know about her."

Caroline came back and sat again. "What would that be then?"

*****

An hour later Caroline sat back in her chair utterly speechless, which was unusual for her. The story of Kia was the most fascinating thing she had ever heard in her life. Of course, she had read something about it in the media, and on line, but had forgotten about it.

"So," Jabu said, "you will understand why she won't want to talk about her personal life, which would be a natural thing to ask if you were to consider taking her on. She's intensely private. There were so many people involved and she wants to protect them all."

47

"Yes, of course, I understand. May I tell her you told me all of this. Will that be alright?"

He nodded. "Yes, I'll also let her know."

"This experience she went through. How is she now?"

"It took time for her to adjust, but she has. She's happy with her life now. You don't need to worry about her mental state, if that is a concern of yours."

"Thank you Jabu, of course this will stay between the three of us. I'm intrigued to meet her now. What a story – what an ending."

Jabu stood. "Better go and give in my notice I think, then I'll start working my way through your files."

Chapter Twelve

The flight into Cape Town was as spectacular as the city itself. Caroline looked down at the rows and rows of shanty town shacks, a sharp contrast to the glittering pools, landscaped lawns, and impressive houses, soon unrolling in front of her eyes.

There was Table Mountain, possibly the oldest mountain on the planet, brooding over the city, the deep blue sea endlessly lapped the pristine shores, with a collar of white. The heavy traffic wove in and out along the snaking motorways below her, the tall buildings almost touched the clouds which were already beginning to gather.

The plane touched gently down and came to a halt outside the arrival's terminal.

Caroline collected her luggage and hire car, then drove into the city, staggered at the development of properties and buildings, and the increased density of the traffic since she was last here ten years ago.

The city had changed beyond recognition, except for the flat-topped brooding mountain, which would never change, carelessly throwing its white tablecloth of clouds over it, giving the much-needed moisture to the plants and small animals which thrived in the rugged bush on its sides.

She checked into the Table Bay hotel at the Victoria and Alfred Waterfront, marvelling at how well developed it had become, designer names in the shopping mall, well-heeled shoppers, both local and international, swinging their glossy bags, and so many restaurants catering to all tastes, and budgets.

Lining the outside of the mall were umbrellas with their logos, wine bars, wine shops, tourists' boats, water lapping at their sides as they waited for their passengers to take the pilgrimage to Robben Island where Nelson Mandela had been incarcerated for so many years.

Seals, their black shiny bodies, long white whiskers, and round black eyes, bobbed up and down in the harbour. The place was vibrant with life.

Caroline's first interior designer was due in twenty minutes, he was meeting her at the hotel. She checked in and unpacked her small bag, collected her files and laptop, then made her way to the lounge and out to the deck of the hotel.

A south-easterly wind, the tail end of the famous Cape Doctor, well known for cleansing the city of dust, dirt and impurities, was gathering momentum. Hurriedly she moved back into the serenity of the hotel lounge, letting reception know this was where she would be conducting her interviews, giving the interviewee names, and where she would be sitting.

Two hours later she had interviewed three of the potential designers, and dismissed them all as lacking the qualities, the passion and the vision, she was seeking.

Over and above their impeccable credentials, she knew the most important thing of all would be the ability to work with the strong minded, and strong willed, Jabu.

She had considered one as a possibility, Brett. But when she told him of the conditions he would have to work in, the amount of time he would have to spend there especially when the lodge was near completion, and in the blazing heat, with all the insects, snakes, and clouds of mosquitoes, who would surely come. That he would have to sleep in a tent, with the wild animals milling around the place, he had thrown his hands up in horror, squealing he only worked on projects in the city. So, he was out.

Caroline checked her watch. Kia was due any minute.

She watched the tall slender girl approach, carrying a slim briefcase. She looked enchanting in a simple white linen dress, offset by an exquisite turquoise belt and matching shoes. Her long hair was braided with small turquoise beads.

Caroline stood and held out her hand. "Hello, Kia, I'm Caroline, let's sit. What can I order for you. Tea, coffee, glass of wine?"

Kia smiled, her eyes the colour of fresh mint. "Mineral water, thanks."

The waiter delivered two bottles of sparkling mineral water and two tall glasses filled with ice and a slice of lemon.

"Okay, Kia. Jabu has told me all about you, your extraordinary story. Let's leave it there, and I'll tell you all about the place we're going to call Infinity."

An hour later, having pored over all Caroline's sketches, Kia sat back, her braids clicking softly with the movement. The turquoise beaded necklace around her neck identical to her brother's.

"I'd love to be involved in this. Working with Jabu would be a dream come true. I haven't seen him for a long time, too long."

Having studied Kia's portfolio, Caroline's mind was already warming to this young woman. But there was one question that needed to be asked.

"You realise, Kia, if this all works out, you'll be spending weeks out in the bush working on the project, especially when it nears completion. I hope it won't interfere with your personal life in any way?"

A shadow crossed Kia's face but was quickly gone. "There was someone in my life but it didn't work out the way either of us anticipated it might. Both our expectations were too high, I think. I'll be happy to sit out in the bush with Jabu and no personal complications."

Caroline gave her a wide smile, absolutely delighted with her answer. "The job is yours Kia. You and Jabu will make a great team. Now what ideas do you have for this lodge of mine?"

They chatted for another two hours. Kia had quickly grasped the vision Caroline had for Infinity and made a few suggestions of her own.

She picked up the photographs of the existing lodge and shuffled through them until she found the one she was looking for.

Kia held it up. "Maybe an idea, Caroline. This tree." she pointed to an old tree, generously leaved, set slightly away from the lodge. "We could have a star bed here. It will face away from the lodge which will ensure absolute privacy."

Caroline raised her eyebrows. "I've heard of them, but not seen them here in South Africa. I saw one in Kenya, a bit rustic, a nice idea, but I'm not sure."

Kia turned back to the photograph. "I wasn't thinking rustic. I was thinking luxury. The shape of this tree is perfect. We could build a platform out for a sumptuous bed. Surround it with glass, in keeping with the other suites, but no roof, only layers of mosquito netting, suspended from the branch here." She pointed at the photograph.

"The glass doors would slide back, so the guests would literally be sleeping under the stars, almost floating in the universe.

"For privacy," Kia continued with a wide grin, "after all it would lend itself to nights of passion, the guests could pull the white muslin curtains across the glass, do what they want to do, then afterwards, pull back the curtains, slide open the glass doors and float into Paradise."

Caroline was warming to her idea. "Go on."

"No need for luggage etc. There would be an add on charge for a night under the stars. Their luggage would stay in their suite, they would dine with the other guests, then drift off with one of the night watch men, who would see them up the short ladder to heaven. He'll have a thatched dwelling for shelter, and be on call, by buzzer, if the couple should need him.

"The night watch, would be there the whole night, at a discreet distance, of course, so they would be safe. I think it would be fabulous."

Caroline took a sip of her water as she looked at the tree in the photograph. "What happens if it rains, with nothing but the stars to keep the guests dry?"

Kia pointed to the tree. "See here. The tree is perfectly formed for what we need. If it should rain there will be a canvas roof which can be rolled out to provide shelter. Even if the guests won't be able to see any stars, it will still be a wonderful experience to lie there listening to the rain pattering, or thundering down on the canvas. Wonderful for the senses, and that's what a safari should be all about, right?"

Kia took a delicate sip of her water. "The night watch would smell the rain long before it arrived, all he would have to do is crank the handle and the canvas roof will roll out."

Caroline hugged herself. "Excellent, I love this idea. Yes, I want to do this – over to you then Kia. You design and furnish it."

"By the way," Caroline continued enthusiastically. "I don't want any kind of reception desks, or computers on display. Guests will have the forms to fill in, at their leisure, once they get to their suites. The butlers will collect them when they've been completed. Of course, we will have computers, but they'll be concealed in the back office along with all the other admin paperwork.

"I want as little of the real world, the world our guests will be escaping from, as possible. This will be the key to everything I have envisaged. Also, no clay pots, porcupine quills, paintings on every wall – no, no art at all, once in their suites the guests will have the best art to look at in the world – the bush, the birds, the butterflies, the monkeys, the squirrels and any small antelope which may wander by."

Chapter Fourteen

Caroline was doing what she did best. The expensively dressed, obviously wealthy, couple sitting opposite her wanted her to plan their safari of a life time. No expense spared. Caroline positively purred, she loved designing a safari where there was no budget.

"We'll be taking our bodyguard with us, of course, his name's Alwyn. Any problems with that?"

Caroline shook her head. "No problems at all, Mr Lewis. Alwyn will have to check his gun in, of course, at arrivals and departures, with the correct paperwork and gun permits. The only slight problem will be Botswana. The government will not allow private individuals in with guns."

Her client frowned with annoyance. "Well can't you make a plan, speak to someone, pay someone? We never go anywhere without Alwyn, and he's always armed."

Caroline smiled sweetly at him. "I'm afraid it's out of the question Mr Lewis. But you are going to be way out in one of the most remote parts of Botswana, on an elephant back safari. You can't possibly come to any harm out there, I promise. But if you prefer, I can change the itinerary around and leave Botswana out."

Mrs Lewis reached across and squeezed his hand. "Aw, honey," she said petulantly, "we have to go to Botswana. I want to meet the American guy who rescued all the elephants from a circus here in the States, and released them into the wild, back in Africa where they came from. It was going to be the highlight of my trip."

Mr Lewis sighed. "Well, I guess if the government won't allow Alwyn in with his gun, well, we'll have to make another plan."

Caroline smiled at him with relish. "I'll tell you how we can overcome this problem. Maybe Alwyn, when he gets to the camp, could spend a couple of hours making some sort of spear, I'm quite sure one of the rangers will be delighted to help."

Mrs Lewis's face brightened. "You see, honey, I told you she was the best in New York to arrange a safari to Africa with. The spear sounds good."

Mr Lewis inclined his head. "Okay then let's go with that. Now the other thing is this. To get to this camp you say we have to fly in one of those small aircraft?"

"Yes, Mr Lewis, that is correct. Botswana have some of the best bush pilots in Africa."

"Um, the thing is…"

Caroline kept a straight face. She knew exactly what was coming next.

Mr Lewis squirmed in his chair, looking uncomfortable. "See the thing is," he repeated, "we have our own pilot here in the States, of course. I'd like to have a bit of background on the pilot who will be flying us around the bush."

"Like what sort of background Mr Lewis?" She asked innocently, a smile fixed on her face.

"Well, you know, where he trained and such like?"

Caroline opened her Botswana file and drew out several photographs. "These are the pilots the company use to get their guests to the camps. Choose which one you would like to fly you and I'll book him, or her."

Mr Lewis mopped his brow with a hand-crafted handkerchief, even though the fifth floor was freezing, and shuffled through the photographs of the European and African pilots.

He stabbed his finger at one of the photographs. "Let's take this guy Patrick McNeil. He looks mature, we'll feel comfortable with him."

Caroline kept her face neutral. She had flown many times with African pilots and they were superb. America still had a long way to go before they would ever accept this in anywhere but their own country. But it was a fabulous booking and it's what she did. Made dreams come true. Turned dreams into reality.

"Now, after Botswana you wanted to stay in a lodge in South Africa. I have the perfect spot for you – it's called Infinity – everyone's talking about it. I highly recommend it. Let me tell you about it and then you can ask as many questions as you like, I'll have all the answers I'm quite sure. It's booked up well in advance, but I know the owner.

"They don't have brochures. With this calibre of lodge, they only need word of mouth to fill the place, but they do have a web-site, here, take a look at this."

Mrs Lewis stood up and wandered through to look at the African paintings.

Mr Lewis studied the web-site, then beamed at her. "Caroline, book us, and Alwyn, in to this place called Infinity for a week, also we'd like to have a night under the stars in the place in the trees. It looks awesome. Probably the nearest thing I'll get to heaven until I get there."

He laughed at his own joke, but she could see, despite his immense wealth, he was fascinated with her lodge, and all it offered.

"Hey, honey," he called to his wife. "Come and take a look at this?"

Mrs Lewis slid back into her chair and stared at the web site. "My goodness, out there under the stars all by ourselves?"

Caroline looked at her. "Only for one night, if you would like to. It's a magnificent experience you won't get anywhere else."

Mrs Lewis looked at her nails. "Will there be a hairdryer there?"

Caroline straightened her face. "No, not under the stars. But there will, of course, be one in your suite, and, after all, no-one will see you there – only the stars. There's a night watchman who will be at a discreet distance, so no need for Alwyn. But if it will make you feel more comfortable, Alwyn can spend the night in the guard house, with his spear."

Mr Lewis leaned over towards his wife and winked. "And me, darlin' I'll be there, but I won't be looking at the stars or your hair – well not 'til later."

Mrs Lewis pulled slightly back from her husband. "Well, I suppose it will be quite nice…" she said hesitantly.

Mr Lewis grinned at Caroline. "She's so excited about this trip, she's going to have some work done on her face."

Caroline held her smile for as long as she could.

She had a sudden longing for Africa, where life seemed more real and women didn't go and have face lifts before they went on holiday.

Chapter Fifteen

The lift pinged a week later and Caroline looked up. "Well, hello Grace. Lovely to see you again."

Grace smiled. "I've come for a taste of Africa."

Caroline indicated the chair in front of her desk. "Come and sit."

Grace smiled, a girlish grin spreading across her make-up free face. A beautiful face, Caroline thought.

The phone purred again, on Caroline's desk. *Sorry* she mouthed at Grace.

An Executor of a deceased estate had called her some days ago when she was busy with the Lewis safari, asking if she would display a piece of work, from the estate, in the store. Slightly distracted and anxious to get a decision on their safari, she hadn't asked any questions as to the size, or even what it was, he wanted to display. She had agreed, expecting it to be a stuffed bird of some sort.

She picked up the phone. It was the store security. "Ma'am? There's a large crate on the sidewalk here, outside the store? They need to open it up because it's too big to get through the front door – it's, um, stuck ma'am."

"Okay. No problem, unpack it on the sidewalk and bring the contents up to me, would you?" Caroline turned back to Grace.

Once again, the phone purred. Caroline rolled her eyes. "Ma'am. I think you need to get down here, see, the thing is, it's stuck in the door now."

"What's stuck in the door?"

"Well, ma'am, it looks like a big lion, is all, an old scruffy one."

Caroline put the phone down and snorted with laughter. "Sorry Grace, there's something I have to attend to. We have a lion on the sidewalk with his face poking into the front of the shop."

Grace grabbed her bag. "I'm not going to miss this, let me tell you."

Caroline and Grace took the lift to the ground floor. Glaring at them, through the narrow front entrance to the shop, was a fully grown stuffed lion. His stiff mane unmoving, his mouth agape in a grimace of outrage, his coat dull, his teeth tinged with the colour of blood.

Caroline looked at it in horror. "Pull it out, guys," she shouted at the security guards. "Try the other end, it might work."

The lion was pulled out and its rear end pushed into the front door. This didn't work either. They pulled him out and stood him on the sidewalk.

Grace who was standing there, had tears of laughter running down her cheeks. She looked helplessly at Caroline, and lifted her hands, seemingly unable to offer any kind of solution.

Caroline looked around, the staff from the store, crowding at the door, were unable to contain their mirth, watching her trying to deal with a lion on the sidewalk of a busy Manhattan intersection. If anyone could sort the incident out it had to be the woman from Africa. Surely, she must know all about lions?

Determined to solve the situation, before it escalated into chaos, Caroline looked around then ran down to the basement, she returned dragging a large sheet of cloth behind her.

Valiantly she tried to cover the rigid lion with it, unfortunately there was a high wind blowing through the skyscrapers. Grace moved forward and lent her weight against the lion and his covering, trying to hold down the corner covering his outraged face, her shoulders shaking with laughter.

Pedestrians crowded around the wretched animal, horror and outrage on their faces. Out of the corner of her eye Caroline saw the television cameras. This will be bad publicity, she thought hysterically.

"Push the damn lion down the stairs into the basement. It will fit there," she shouted at the security guard.

Henry, the despatch clerk, born and brought up in the Bronx, looked at it briefly. He had seen all there was to be seen in New York city, but nothing quite like this. Gingerly he manoeuvred the lion upright, then wiping his hands down the front of his shirt, he returned to his packages and parcels, shaking his head in resignation.

The lion had found his temporary new home in the basement where the staff, no doubt, would come each day, give him a pat and hang their coats over his back. It would add another dimension to their lives – they had a lion in the basement. No way was Caroline going to have it displayed on her floor, it was hideous, and endorsed her loathing of the world of poaching and hunting.

She would contact the Executor who had sent it on consignment, and ask him to arrange for it to be removed immediately, even if she had to pay for the removal herself.

*****

Grace had insisted Caroline join her for a cocktail when she finished work.

Grace lifted her glass and clinked it against Caroline's. "Best fun day I've had since arriving here in New York. Let's toast the lion – he deserves it – a majestic beast delegated to the basement of a prestigious store. New York doesn't deserve him."

Caroline took a sip of her martini. "He won't be there for long I can assure you. But we must give the poor thing a name."

Grace smiled. "I remember a television programme, a long time ago, the lion was called Clarence. So, here's to Clarence, let's call him that for as long as he's in the basement on 56th street."

*****

Darkness was falling over the city. Grace looked at Caroline. She wasn't a beauty by any means, but not unattractive, somewhere in her late forties she guessed.

Her straight blond hair fell to her shoulders with a full fringe, she wore no make up to enhance her dark brown intelligent eyes, or cover the few freckles on her cheeks, her wide mouth housed even white teeth. But there was an energy about her, a passion for what she was doing. A woman who was comfortable with who she was, and like her, this woman didn't need to be anyone else other than who she was.

It seemed to her those children born in Africa had a certain confidence about who they were, but then, they had no other experience in life, other than how they had grown up, wild, bare foot, and running free. There was nothing to compare themselves with. They felt different.

"I know I found it difficult to adjust to a different life, a *completely* different life. But how did you manage?" Grace asked.

Caroline watched the rain sweeping over the sidewalk. "I didn't – I haven't. I mean look at the weather outside. It doesn't smell of anything, all I ever smell here are exhaust fumes. It doesn't evoke anything. It's just, well, rain. Something to be tolerated, as it washes the grime from the buildings. To us, in Africa, it's God's gift. Oh, the smell of it, the suddenness of it, the sound of it. It fires up the senses. The coolness as it splashes against your hot swollen summer feet, as you sit outside on the stoep watching as the ground hungrily soaks it up," she said wistfully.

Grace tried to lighten the mood a bit. "So, what's your most memorable experience here in New York?"

Caroline laughed. "So many. But the one which sticks in my mind was when I first started working in the store. Apart from the lion episode of today, which might top it…"

She took a handful of peanuts from the bowl on the bar. "As I told you, I was never into retail, I sold safaris. That's what I came here to do, not sell books and art, that wasn't part of the deal.

"All the bookings for safaris went through the London office for payment, so I didn't need to handle any money. Then one day, I hadn't been here more than a week, the accountant came to teach me how to process the sales of art and books through the ghastly beast who was lying in wait for me – the dreaded till.

'*Don't look so worried Caroline,*' she said to me, '*It's a piece of cake, and you really have to learn how to use it.*

'*What I want you to do is put in tutorial mode, and practice for a few hours. Pick out any customer's credit card in the system, and use the number, but remember, it must be in tutorial mode.*'

"So, I picked out a credit card number, and started to practice. I rang up a huge safari for about a hundred and twenty thousand dollars, then a dozen rare books, some pieces of artwork, worth thousands, chucked in a few bespoke fishing rods for good measure, and a couple of antique guns. Then hugely satisfied with my baptism of fire, I ran the whole thing through the till. I went back to what I do best, and forgot all about it.

"A few days later the accountant stomped down the stairs to my floor, her face worse than ashen."

'*Caroline!*' she said. '*We have one of our best customers on line, he wants to know why the store has run up nearly four hundred thousand dollars on his card!*'

She grinned at Grace. "I told her I had definitely put the damn beast on the mode thingy…

"What could I say? The customer was outraged. The next morning the cash register had been replaced by a large plant. Plants I can relate to. The beast in the corner was finally gone."

She laughed at the memory. "From then on any one who wanted to buy books or art had to pay for it downstairs."

Grace wiped tears of laughter from her eyes. "So, how long are you going to stay here in the city?"

"Well, I'm not exactly employed by the company, I'm more of a consultant on contract, so I can leave any time.

"In fact, maybe in a few months' time. I have another project I'm working on.

"I'll probably see the contract out and then go home. New York has been a fabulous adventure, as I'm sure your son Tim found out, but after a while it becomes like any other great city in the world, except it's damn expensive to live here. The thing I hate most is the massive rent I have to pay for a miniscule apartment. No wonder the streets are always busy here, people get cabin fever in their boxy apartments and have to get out. I'll never get used to it."

She helped herself to another handful of peanuts. "I haven't seen a sunset or any stars since I arrived here. I long for the open spaces, the endless skies and the star-studded velvet nights, the sounds of the bush as the sun sets, oh, and the delicious smell of a *braai*! Sometimes this city seems a bit overwhelming."

Grace glanced at her watch. "You sound a bit homesick. Tell you what, why don't we meet up for lunch tomorrow?"

Chapter Sixteen

Caroline sat back in the restaurants comfortable chair and patted her lips with an impossibly white napkin.

"God, the food in this city never disappoints. Lunch was fabulous, Grace, thank you. Nothing like a plate of pasta smothered with truffles. Divine."

Grace looked at her empty plate, impressed. "Nice to see someone with a good appetite. Most women here seem to live on a stick of celery and a lettuce leaf. I'm glad you enjoyed it."

Caroline sipped her water. "Well, to be honest, I can't afford to eat out in the city, all my money goes into my project, restaurants are way too expensive and not much fun on your own.

"But you've hardly touched your food, you don't seem to have much of an appetite yourself."

Grace pushed her plate to one side. "I normally have a good appetite but in the next day or two I have to make a difficult decision, it's sort of taken my desire to eat away."

Caroline waited for her to continue, but she didn't.

"Is there anything I can help you with?"

Grace shook her head. "Thank you, my dear, but this is something I must do alone."

The waiter came and removed their plates. Grace asked for the bill which was swiftly delivered. She signed with a flourish, retrieved her credit card from the soft leather case on the plate then stood, preparing to leave.

Caroline's phone vibrated on the table, she glanced at it.

Jabu.

"Sorry Grace, I have to take this call. Just give me a minute."

Grace sat down again.

"Jabu. What's up?"

Chapter Seventeen

"Caroline? Something happened here at the lodge and you need to hear it from me before anyone else."

As Jabu explained the situation, she could hear the tension in his voice.

"All the guests left yesterday as scheduled," he paused hearing the scream of sirens in the background, then he continued.

"I've moved our incoming guests to two other lodges, and closed ours for a day or two. I'm not saying this is a crime scene but I had to report the incident to the police. They'll want as little disturbance as possible in the area where we found the child. We'll assist in any way we can with our own trackers and rangers."

It was good to know that Jabu had moved swiftly and made the right decisions.

"Also, Caroline, the media will get hold of this story, it will be on all news stations in hours, then the internet will have it around the world in minutes, if it's not already out there.

"I had to mention it to the other lodge managers in the area, just to check if anyone had lost a child somewhere. Our last guests, who saw what happened, will no doubt talk about it, and who can blame them."

Caroline interrupted him. "I'm not concerned about the media. Infinity is on private property. No-one can get near us. But once the word gets out, they'll descend on the hospital. Please arrange for some private security company to guard the child's room, if you can, and if the hospital will allow it."

"Already done Caroline. The office in Nelspruit organised everything."

Caroline, cleared her throat. "Good. I agree with you about the next few days bookings. Inform the tour operators who booked their guests with us. Make up some feasible story to keep everyone happy, use the storm if necessary. We're covered by insurance if there are any problems."

She sighed. "Jabu, make sure the child gets the best medical attention in a private ward. Doctor Hamilton will, of course, be compensated for her time and we'll give her a full refund for her safari and her air fares. It's the least we can do. Whichever hotel she is staying in, we'll pay that bill as well."

There was a slight pause. "What are the chances the child will survive Jabu?"

"I can't answer that. A snake bite and malaria make for a toxic mix. It's a serious situation."

"If she survives Jabu, it may take some time to find her parents or other relatives. We have no idea which country she even comes from, unless she's able to tell us after such a ghastly experience. She'll be in a terrible state of shock.

"When you can, please speak to our guest the doctor, Olivia you said?"

She took a deep breath and continued. "If the authorities agree, and if the child does survive, perhaps she could come back to the lodge, away from the glare of the media which will be descending on the hospital as we speak. She'll be safe with us whilst the search goes on for her family. I need some time to sort things out here. I'll be with you as soon as I can. I'll let you know my flight details."

Caroline dropped her phone into her bag. There was so much to think about, so many things she needed to do as soon as possible.

"Sorry about that Grace, bit of a problem back at the lodge."

Grace smiled. "I gather an unexpected guest arrived at what I now presume is your own lodge. The photograph you have next to your desk?"

"Yes, no-one knows it's my lodge. Jabu is my manager, my partner. A little girl appeared out of the bush, she's in a bad way, as you no doubt gathered from my conversation. I have to get back as quickly as possible. See what I can do, and manage the media.

"I'll need some time to sort things out here. I'll have to hand over my forward bookings to the London office, then pack up my apartment. I won't be coming back. It looks as though Jabu will need all the help he can get with the current situation, and all the things he has to organise with the guests, the police and the search."

Grace nodded. "Yes, I think it's a wise decision, given the circumstances."

Caroline tapped away at her phone, then scrolled up and down.

"There's a South African Airways flight a week on Friday. It should give me enough time to get things done here. Jabu seems to be managing everything his end."

She smiled at Grace. "Maybe one day, when all this is over, you'll come and stay at my lodge, as my guest. I've enjoyed your company; it meant a lot to me. I hope you sort everything out with your son.

"Perhaps, sometime in the future, we can sit around the camp fire, and talk about our time here in New York. You will keep in touch, won't you?"

Grace hugged her. "Yes, of course I will. I would love to come to your lodge one day. Go well Caroline, I'll miss you."

*****

Grace watched Caroline race out of the restaurant. It must have been fate, she thought to herself. Caroline coming into her life.

Perhaps Caroline would be able to help her with what was left of hers.

Grace pulled out her phone. She would also be booking a flight out of the city. Her unfinished business was now finished. She just had one more thing to do.

That would be the hardest part of her plan, finding the right moment.

Chapter Eighteen

Caroline made her way through the crowded departure lounge at JFK. She wandered through the various shops, her large piece of hand luggage weighing heavily on her shoulder. All the cafés and bars were heaving with passengers. She found one outlet specialising in oysters and champagne, and not as crowded as the other fast-food venues. Spotting a vacant table for two, she made her way through the meandering crowds.

With a sigh of relief, she off-loaded her shoulder bag and sank into the chair. An expressionless waiter took her order. Half a dozen oysters and a glass of champagne.

Caroline watched the flights landing and departing, and the throng of passengers wandering around the duty-free shops and restaurants, wondering about the lives of all these people on the move. Where were they all going? Husbands, wives, brothers, sisters, friends, babies and children, teenagers, and, yes, lovers, married or otherwise. A seething mass of human emotions which would culminate in their country of destination.

"Hello Caroline!"

Startled, Caroline turned in her chair. "Grace, what on earth are you doing here?"

"Well, my dear, I'm flying off, like you. I spotted you as I made my way into this rather grand little oasis. Mmmm, those oysters look good, I think I might order some myself. You don't mind if I join you?"

Caroline smiled. "Of course not, it's lovely to see you. But where are you off to, you didn't mention you were leaving the city?"

Grace attracted the attention of the waiter and ordered her oysters and a glass of champagne. She waited until he returned with her order, before continuing.

"A change of plan, a last-minute thing. Well, here's to us Caroline. Tim is around somewhere," she gestured with her hand. "He was here all along in New York."

Caroline smiled, happy to see her new friend looking so pleased, although, she felt, a little tense. "That's marvellous. But how did you find him?"

"Well, it took some doing, but, you see, it's why I came here, to find out where he was. I knew he hadn't gone back to Africa. You'll meet him shortly."

"So, he's going home?"

"Yes, he's going home, back to the bush where he was happy."

Caroline checked her watch. "Look, Grace, now you're here, I need to go into duty free and buy a few things for some friends. Would you watch my bag? I won't be long."

"Go on then, go shop. I'll watch your bag for you and have another glass of champagne."

Caroline wandered through duty free, inhaling the glorious fragrances of hundreds of perfumes. Confident Grace was watching her luggage for her, she took her time.

Clutching her duty-free bags, Caroline wended her way back through the crowds to the Oyster Bar and the table where she had left her heavy bag.

Grace was gone.

Caroline looked around, slightly annoyed, her hand luggage stood forlornly by the empty seat. Maybe she'd gone off to the loo, knowing the waiter would watch over her bag.

The unsmiling waiter sidled up to her as she lowered herself into the chair. "Here's your bill, ma'am, your friend said you would settle it for her."

"Settle it for her? But where is she?"

The waited lifted both his hands, having seen more than he needed to in a busy airport lounge. "I have no idea ma'am."

Caroline took the folded leather case and opened it. There was the bill, a hand written note, and a photograph. She settled the bill much to the waiter's relief, then opened the folded note.

We were destined to meet, my dear Caroline. You won't understand this now, but trust me. My son, Tim, will shortly be on his way home, back to Africa, as I told you.

Me? Well, I am going somewhere else. I have no choice this time. Follow Tim for me please?

Caroline looked at the photograph – a good looking young man, his tawny, wheat coloured hair, lifting in the breeze, his wide blue eyes, the same colour as his mother's, laughing into the camera, his full lips embracing strong white teeth.

She flipped over the photograph and looked at the short message. *You'll find him, Caroline.*

Caroline looked around the crowded terminal. So, where was this Tim? She was flying to South Africa. Tim, his mother had said, was going back to Kenya. How was she supposed to follow him. Why would she. Why would Grace ask her to?

She heard her flight being called. Gathering her shopping bags and hand luggage she made her way to the departure gate, glancing around for a good-looking game ranger called Tim in case he had changed his destination and was on the flight to South Africa and not Kenya. Caroline handed her boarding card to the crew member, turned left into business class and made her way to her assigned seat.

A smiling member of the crew helped her stow her luggage in the overhead bin, it was wonderful to hear the old familiar accent of her homeland.

She settled in her seat and accepted the glass of champagne being offered. Her mind went back to the curious meeting in the departure lounge. One thing she was quite sure of, Grace Chambers hadn't pitched up by chance, she had planned to meet up with her. But why?

The whole incident was disturbing. She remembered at the end of their lunch together ten days or so ago, after Jabu's call, she had told Grace which day she planned to fly back to South Africa.

No, this was no coincidence. Where was Grace going that she had no choice about?

The giant aircraft roared down the runway, shuddering as it lifted off into the dark skies. Caroline looked down at the glittering lights of New York, and the millions of people who lived there in their tiny apartments, relentlessly pursuing their dreams of power and money, scurrying around like ants in search of something sweet and satisfying.

She levered her seat back and closed her eyes. Well, whoever Grace Chambers and her elusive son, Tim, were, she doubted whether she would see her again, unless she took her up on the invitation to come and stay at the lodge, which she now doubted. The whole thing was baffling.

She reached down into her briefcase and pulled out the thick file of paperwork she needed to go through.

Who was this little girl who had collapsed at the water hole at her lodge?

Chapter Nineteen
South Africa

Jabu heard the engines of the small plane before he spotted it as a dot in the now endless blue sky.

The dirt airstrip was still recovering from the heavy rains of the storm, but he knew bush pilots could land anywhere under most conditions. Caroline might have a bit of a bumpy landing.

He started the engine of the land cruiser as the aircraft touched down, then turned and made its way back to where he was parked. The pilot slid open the side window, opened the door, lowered the short steps and helped Caroline alight.

The pilot, Toby, retrieved her heavy luggage from the hold and backseats of the aircraft, along with some boxed provisions for the lodge, and helped Jabu carry them to the vehicle.

Then he climbed back into his seat and started up the plane. With a cheerful wave Toby taxied back down the slippery airstrip then turned ready to take off. The engines rumbled and he roared past them giving a final wave.

Caroline waited until the sound of the engines had receded then turned to Jabu, shaking his hand.

"How are things Jabu. How is the little girl now? Any news?"

Jabu pulled out from beneath the shade of the tree. "She's holding her own, at the moment, Olivia is with her, she doesn't leave her side. I don't think she expected to extend her stay by another two weeks, but she won't leave her and sits with her for hours every day, working with the other doctors. I think she's becoming anxious to hand over the responsibility of the girl and return to London. I'll get another update this afternoon."

Caroline looked over the lush landscape, drinking in the smell of damp earth, feeling herself relax after the seventeen-hour flight from New York to Johannesburg, then the domestic flight to the small airport in Hoedspruit, which serviced the passengers going on safari. Toby had met her there and flown her to the lodge.

Caroline put her sunglasses on. "Did the police find any tracks or trace of the child's journey through the bush?"

"No, they felt if there was anything to be found our rangers were more qualified than they were to find any debris or signs of an accident. I sent them a full report. We had one hell of a storm, as you know, which made it impossible for any of us to try and find out what happened. The police have, of course, opened a case file and will be following procedure. They're trying to work out if she is a local girl, or a tourist perhaps, who somehow became separated from her family. We did our own helicopter search, as you know, but found nothing."

He drove down a narrow track, manoeuvring his way around a fallen tree and keeping a watchful eye for any game which might suddenly bolt out of the bush and collide with the vehicle. "The police have been to the hospital in Nelspruit but the doctors wouldn't allow them in to see her, she's too weak and still in a precarious position, but she's stable."

Caroline nodded. "Shame, poor little soul. We must do everything we can to help her and find her parents, they must be frantic with worry."

Then she turned her head tiredly. "The bush looks magnificent Jabu, so green after the rains." She pointed to a herd of impala enjoying the fresh green shoots, their short white tails twitching as they grazed.

"Even though it's only a short time since the storm the animals look in excellent condition. We flew over herds of antelope, buffalo, and elephants, we saw a few rhinos as well. All looking good."

Jabu pulled up at the lodge and turned off the engine. Caroline gave a sigh of contentment. "It's looking fabulous, Jabu. Absolutely fabulous."

The East African style canopy canvas covering the glass suites were spotless as they nestled beneath and between the ancient trees, the sturdy wooden walkways swept clean of any drifting leaves.

Jabu lifted her luggage from the back seat and she followed him into the cool reception area. Tall leafy plants rustled in their tall elegant cream pots. The white tiled floor gave the immediate effect of coolness, a respite from the hot October sun. There was not a computer in sight.

Two, life size, bronze statues of leopards stood guard at the entrance, soft white ceiling to floor muslin curtains moved in the slight breeze on either side of them, like billowing ball gowns. Overhead three slender rattan fans paddled the hot dry air.

On one side of the entrance hall stood a cream, twelve drawer, vintage apothecary dresser, home to an eighty-year-old typewriter, alongside an elderly adding machine.

Out on another deck was the dining area. Ten tables, their simple cane chairs covered in heavy cream upholstery were covered with tablecloths sweeping the floor of the deck. Tall silver candelabra each holding eight white candles were sheltered from the elements by glass sheaths.

Come nightfall they would be lit, throwing shadows up into the trees, and prisms of lights over the silver cutlery, crystal glasses and the delicate cream, yellow centred frangipani flowers, nestling in silver bowls with their lingering sweet perfume.

Hurricane lamps were positioned amongst the branches all around the dining area, creating the romantic, old-world safari setting, Caroline had wanted.

Jabu left Caroline to unpack and made his way back to the kitchen to organise the wooden crates of produce to be collected from his vehicle.

*****

Caroline sat in her own private quarters, feeling the pressure of city life, the cacophony of noise, the never-ending sirens, pneumatic drills, droning traffic and honking horns gradually drift away into a different world.

There was a soft knock. "Come in."

Moses, one of the guest butlers, who was assigned to her when she was in residence, entered. "Welcome back Miss Caroline, it's good to see you again." He glanced around her room. *"Eish*, you have much luggage this time, more than before when you came to visit."

"Yes, Moses. I'm here to stay now. It's good to be back in the bush. I've missed it."

"Ah, then, this is good news. We are happy to have you back, here with us. Perhaps I can help you with your unpacking?"

Caroline glanced around at her two heavy suitcases and equally heavy hand luggage. "Yes, I would appreciate that, Moses. To say I'm tired would be an understatement." She stifled a yawn.

He gave her a wide smile. "I too would be very much tired if I had to fly in the long tube with small windows. If God was wishing for me to fly, he would surely have given me the wings of an eagle. I have no wish to go to other places where there is much noise and many many people." He shook his head. "I will bring you some tea."

"Thank you, Moses, tea would be lovely. Then I want to walk around the lodge and see how things are looking. Is the lodge full tonight? All guests out on a game drive? They should be by now."

"Only one suite empty, Miss Caroline, number four. The other guests are out on their game drive."

"Alright. I'll have a look at number four, after I've had my tea. I'll take it down on the viewing platform."

Moses padded away, humming happily.

*****

Her marketing strategy had worked. She was already booked up a year in advance. The journalists she had chosen had arrived the week after Infinity had officially opened a year ago. Twenty of them, all happy to share rooms, knowing Caroline had paid for their flights and provided the accommodation. She, of course, had been there for the opening.

It had been a triumph.

She hadn't been able to snag a Royal for the opening. Their official engagements had been booked years in advance. The one Royal who had been available had been featured in the news all over the world, with a sniff of scandal.

She had decided to let that one go. Besides, she had thought, a Royal would have been a nice lure, but the logistics of security and the normal entourage a Royal would bring, would have depleted the availability of the rooms. No, she had wanted the journalists. In lieu of a Royal and the entourage, she had invited life style journalists from Europe, the UK and the States.

All of them had accepted; anything to escape a long hard winter.

The journalists had produced glossy double page spreads in their ritzy magazines exalting the unique design and furnishing of Infinity and its abundant wild life, with glowing reports of the cuisine and service.

*****

Now Caroline wandered down to the viewing area, overlooking the waterhole. Moses brought her a tray of tea and some cucumber sandwiches.

She watched the animals coming to drink, lapping at the water as it rippled away over the surface. In the distance she could hear the cry of a fish-eagle, as it eagerly scanned the surface of the water for its supper. The dead tree still stretched its black arms to the sky. She felt the tension seep from her body.

Caroline looked over the wide expanse of the waterhole – where the child had been found, then gazed across the terrain of the wild dense bush, the high trees, the faraway rolling hills.

Where had this child come from. It was impossible to believe she had walked through the bush by herself?

The remnants of the storm, shortly after she was found, had destroyed any possible evidence of her journey. The storm had also kept the media away, although they would have found it impossible to enter the private reserve and her lodge, without being confronted at the security gates, and the guards who monitored all their expected arrivals. If they were not on the list, they were denied entry.

Once Caroline had checked out suite number four, she would call the hospital in Nelspruit, introduce herself, and ask to speak to Doctor Olivia Hamilton.

In her own way, Caroline felt a responsibility for the lost girl.

*****

Moses hung Caroline's clothes up in the wardrobe, carefully placing her shoes on the bar underneath. He shook his head. *Eish,* how could it be these ladies who flew in tubes with small windows, could wear these shoes with long points at the back, out here in the bush. Good for stabbing snakes, but not for anything else.

He turned to her heavy hand luggage, carefully placing her toiletries in the bathroom. The files he put on the table in the office, adjoining her suite.

At the bottom of the bag, he pulled out a small square box. Puzzled he turned it over in his hands. Where must this box be put? Perhaps in this box were more shoes.

He shook it. It was light. Too light for shoes. On the lid was a small cross of the Jesus people.

Not sure of where it belonged, he carefully placed it next to her shoes. If this, he thought, was a Jesus box, then it should be placed somewhere in the dark where this Jesus lived, because no-one had seen this Jesus person, for he did not wish to be seen.

He unzipped the pockets of the luggage and felt around inside. He pulled out an envelope addressed to Miss Caroline.

He opened a drawer and slipped the envelope inside, along with all the other paperwork which would be waiting for her attention.

Chapter Twenty

Caroline made her way to suite number four. Instead of thinking like an owner, she imagined herself as a guest. What would her first impressions be?

The hurricane lamps had already been lit and were strung amongst the trees either side of the wooden walkway.

The suite had already been prepared for her guests, though none were staying in this one tonight. The soft muslin curtains had been closed. Large cream coloured coir mats covered the floor. The impressive double bed already swathed in filmy mosquito netting.

Two wardrobes adapted from 1920's Gucci travelling luggage stood next to each other. Leather trunks and hat boxes were positioned around the room. An old wicker food hamper lay at the foot of the bed.

Through an alcove a copper bath with elaborately decorated feet gave way to a full glass window where guests could watch the scurrying squirrels, the vervet monkeys and the birds, as they washed the dust of a game drive away.

An old-fashioned butlers' tray held handmade soap, a frangipani flower embedded in the middle, made from the scent and oils of the frangipani flowers, produced by a boutique shop in Nelspruit.

Sliding back the curtains and glass door, Caroline stepped out onto the wooden deck. Two planter's chairs, from India, plump with white cushions, sat beside an old steamer trunk, now painted white, with its brass edgings. A set of binoculars and a telescope, Caroline's only nod to something modern, and the magazines the lodge had appeared in, were piled on top.

No rose petals scattered across the taut pristine crisp sheets, no fruit covered in cellophane to keep the bugs and flies away. No, if the guests required fresh fruit, they only had to use the buzzer and their butler would appear and bring it fresh from the kitchen.

If guest preferred to have breakfast in their suite amongst the trees, it would be delivered by the butler on a wheeled trolley, covered with silver domes. Tea, or coffee, would be served from the Victorian silverware. Dinner, if the guests preferred to be alone, would be served in the same manner.

A half-moon wall enclosed the outside shower, here guests could relish the great outdoors as they gazed at the bush beyond and, as darkness fell, the stars above.

Caroline lowered herself onto one of the planters' chairs and soaked it all up. A light movement caught her eye. A tiny dik-dik, the smallest of the antelope species, renowned for its shyness, stepped delicately out of the bush beneath her.

Its big brown eyes, locked on hers, its soft straight ears twitching as it tip-toed on elegant tiny hooves, out of the bush. High above a squirrel stopped, its tail briefly bushing up, before it went on its way foraging for food. She liked the squirrels, they used their tails, like a parasol, to brush up over their bodies and keep them cool from the intense sun and heat of the day.

Caroline leaned back and sighed. She had done it. Infinity was exquisite, a magical place in a spectacular setting.

Feeling the tiredness of her journey wash over her, she stood. The dik-dik, alarmed by her movement, skittered back into the safety of the bush, away from her prying eyes.

She closed the door behind her and made her way back to her own quarters.

Chapter Twenty-One

Caroline returned to her office and picked up the phone.
"I'd like to speak to Doctor Hamilton please, she's looking after the girl who was found at our lodge, Infinity?"

She waited, drumming her fingers on the side of the desk.

"Doctor Hamilton speaking."

"Hello, Doctor, this is Caroline Gordon. The little girl was found at our water hole. I want to thank you for all you did to help her, without you she would not have made it. Jabu told me all about it. How is she?"

"Ah, Caroline. Thank you for getting in touch, I've been waiting for your call.

"She's doing well. The fever is under control, there doesn't seem to be any ill effect from the snake bite – we have Jabu to thank for that. Of course, she's getting excellent medical attention here at the hospital. She's going to make it physically. But mentally I think the fall-out will be severe. She hasn't spoken yet. We have no idea what her native language might be.

"Whilst she was out in the bush, she must have survived by eating berries and leaves, and probably drank from the river. All her tests seem to point to this. Her vital signs are steady, but she is heavily sedated. She was lucky to have survived – I think we have a lot to thank Jabu for, even though I was highly suspicious of what I called his mumbo-jumbo potions he used on her. I owe him an apology. A big one."

Caroline smiled into the phone. "Well perhaps you may be able to do this in person Doctor Hamilton. The next problem will be what will happen to the child when she's released from hospital. Where will she go? Who will look after her?"

She heard Doctor Hamilton hesitate at the end of the telephone. "I'm not sure what happens here in South Africa. In England we have all sorts of infrastructures in place to deal with things like this. Lost children, missing children. But here I'm out of my depth. I don't know your country, or how it works. But it's vital this child doesn't end up in a foster home or some kind of state institution. She'll need a lot of care with people she can trust. This will be the key to unlocking her mind as to what happened to her."

"She'll be under psychiatric care then?"

"Yes, she will have to be assessed." Olivia continued. "The first thing is to try and find her family. It's been over two weeks since she was found. The international networks have, of course, picked up on this story, and it's all over the internet. The police are sifting through each bit of information but so far nothing has come to light. No-one has claimed her, although there are a lot of crazy people out there, who swear she belongs to them.

"There were pictures of her, in the media here, but I doubt she looks familiar to anyone. She was badly dehydrated, her skin and eyes sunken, her head shaved. Only her parents would recognise her, or any siblings she may have."

Caroline continued to drum her fingers on the desk, wondering how she could help with the situation.

"Would you be prepared to come back with her, if the authorities agree?"

Olivia sighed. "No, I'm sorry that won't be possible. I have to get back to London, I've already been here far longer than I anticipated. You need to think of a more long-term arrangement for the child, if indeed the authorities will allow it."

"Has the child responded to you in any way Doctor Hamilton?"

"I think she knows I'm here, but it's only what I'm assuming. She's drowsy when she looks at me, but she's not saying anything yet, which is understandable. She's traumatised, of course. Her eyes wander all over the place as if she is trying to work out where she is, and how she ended up here."

Caroline made up her mind. "I'll fly to Nelspruit as soon as I can. I'd like to meet her. I'm going to bring Jabu with me."

Chapter Twenty-Two

Jabu and Caroline made their way through the hospital corridors. The receptionist, after checking her list of who was allowed near the girl, and seeing Doctor Hamilton's name, gave them the directions they needed.

Jabu, acknowledged the security guard who was sitting outside the child's room. He pushed open the door of the private room and Caroline went ahead. Doctor Hamilton rose from her chair and smiled at Jabu.

She shook hands with Caroline and gestured to the bed. "Well, here she is."

Caroline looked at the slight figure on the bed. The child was asleep, her eyelashes casting a shadow over her cheeks.

Jabu leaned over and stroked her face. He spoke to her in the soft clicks, murmurs, and sounds of his people.

The child moved her head and opened her eyes. She held up her thin arms to him.

Instinctively Jabu put his arms around her, careful not to disturb the tubes surrounding her. He held her close to his chest, his eyes filling with tears.

Caroline and Olivia dabbed at their eyes. "Somehow," whispered Olivia, "the child knows him. An instinctive thing, I think. He spoke to her in his language when we found her. It seems to sooth her."

Jabu carefully laid the child back on the bed, but still kept hold of her hands in one of his.

The child's eyelashes fluttered as she went back into the world of escape, somewhere, presumably, where she felt safe. Her tight fists in Jabu's hand relaxed.

*****

Jabu, Caroline and Olivia, sat across the desk of the rooms of the child's doctor.

Olivia introduced him. "This is Doctor Delamere. He's the paediatrician looking after the child."

Caroline leaned forward and shook his hand, as did Jabu. "Doctor Delamere, we're concerned about what will happen to the girl once she's discharged from hospital. Is there any way we can help at all? We would like to take her back to the lodge until her family can be located. It's safe and secure there, away from the media's prying eyes."

Doctor Delamere steepled his fingers in front of him. "The child will probably be discharged from the hospital in the next few days. She's recovering well, all her vital signs are near normal.

"However, she will need to be assessed by a psychiatrist. She will be severely traumatised by whatever happened to her out there in the bush. We'll keep her here, of course, for the assessment. Depending on the outcome, it will then be up to the authorities to decide what will happen to her. She needs to be constantly monitored by a medical professional."

Olivia shifted in her chair. "Once she's been assessed and leaves hospital, what will happen to her, where will the authorities put her? In the UK we have social workers, a whole infrastructure for cases like this. But how will it work here in South Africa?"

Doctor Delamere ran his hands through his thinning hair. "She'll be put in a foster home with people who will have some experience of traumatised children, until her family can be found."

Caroline crossed her legs and leaned forward again. "Doctor Delamere," she said urgently, "it wouldn't be right to put her with complete strangers. Doctor Hamilton and I have watched the child react to Jabu, who found her at the water hole. She seemed to recognise him, held out her arms to him. Surely, she would be better off with us, on a temporary basis?"

Doctor Delamere scribbled on the pad in front of him, a frown creasing his forehead. "Well, it seems a positive sign, the way she reacted. Look, let's take this step by step. Let's see what the psychiatrists have to say and take it from there. I agree, the less this child has to deal with once she is released, the better she will be. Recognising Jabu is a positive sign. Clearly someone she feels she can trust. I'll have a word with my colleagues, see what we can come up with."

He stood. "I'm sorry, I must do my rounds now…"

Olivia, Jabu and Caroline made their way back to the girl's room.

Jabu leaned over her bed. Speaking to her in English. "Hey, little girl, we're going to make a plan for you. Would you like to come home with us?"

The child's eyes fluttered open, and once more she lifted her thin arms to Jabu. He gathered her to his chest and spoke to her in a language Olivia was now becoming familiar with, although she had no idea what he was talking about. But whatever he was saying seemed to work, the words seeming to calm and sooth her.

Olivia turned towards Caroline. "What language is he speaking? He told me once but I can't recall what it was."

"He's speaking the language of his people, the Griqua people, there's no other language like it. It's the language of the desert people, the San. One of the oldest languages in the world."

Olivia listened, fascinated. Whatever he was saying to the girl, she seemed to be listening. Her whole body leaning into his.

"Jabu never ceases to amaze me," she whispered. "When he brought me the child, that night, he saw the desperate state she was in. He used some kind of medicinal pastes and roots, to treat the snake bite and the malaria. I was, to put it mildly, a bit taken aback. I know nothing about traditional medicines. To be quite frank with you, if he hadn't used his medicines, the child would have died. I have the greatest respect for him now."

Caroline smiled. "You see Doctor Hamilton, in their culture, the culture of his people, once you have saved a life, this life is inextricably linked to your own. You have a duty to watch over it, care for it. This is what Jabu is doing now. He feels a responsibility for the girl's life. Nothing will take it away from him."

Olivia shook her head. "Scientists, technology, and medical experts have made huge strides over the past years, but, in my opinion now, it's more about the connection with the patient, and less about what they pump into their broken bodies."

Something she had now seen in a country far away from her own.

Chapter Twenty-Three

Caroline sat in her office, trying to concentrate on the pile of paperwork needing her attention, her forward bookings and all the other administrative work it took to keep a game lodge featured at the top of the international market.

But her thoughts kept straying back to the girl. Having never had a child of her own, she was surprised how she felt so responsible for this one, how protective.

She swatted a fly away from her face and reached for the white envelope with her name on it. Frowning she opened it, glancing to see who had sent it.

Grace?

My journey has been a long one, a hard one. But I feel I should tell you the truth now, something I didn't do when we met in New York.

I knew which flight you were on. I knew where I would find you if I was patient enough.

Nothing is ever as it appears, is it?

You see, my beloved son is dead. I know I gave you the impression he was alive. But this is not so.

The man he met at the lodge in the Sabi Sands, was hugely successful and wealthy.

I have tried over the years to come to terms with the fact Tim was not attracted to women. I wasn't surprised. No-one knows their child better than their mother.

It would appear there was an accident, at their home, in New York. Tim and his partner had a terrible row. Tim lost his footing on the staircase and plunged to his death. Pushed? I have no idea. It's a world I have no experience of. All I knew was my son was dead.

When Tim died, I wanted to know how and why. I needed answers to so many questions. But because he was married to this man, he was his next of kin, not me. No-one would tell me anything, not the police, not his doctor, no-one, not even the undertakers, the funeral directors.

It was impossible for me to deal with. The man he had married had more rights to him than I did. I was his mother, but I had no claim on my own child.

I was not going to give up. I wanted my son back.

So, I came to New York, I met with this person he called his husband. Jerome.

Jerome was nice enough, I suppose. It was an accident. This is what he told me.

Over his fire-place there was a small box. Inside was what was left of my son. I begged him to let me have the ashes so I could take him home. At first, he refused, but gradually I wore him down.

When I met you, this was what I was doing. Begging him to give me back my son, so I could take him home, where he belonged, where he would want to be.

The sadness for me, is this. I didn't have the money to take Tim back to Africa. I knew you were going back, back to the Sabi Sands where he was happy. Whilst you were shopping in the duty-free shops, I slipped his ashes into your luggage, with this letter you are holding, which I hope will explain things.

I can't go back to Kenya. I simply don't have the means to make my home there again.

So, it is with a heavy heart, I will have to go back to England and live with my daughter. Perhaps I will eventually get used to life there, but it's not what I want. I want to go home as well.

It is me who should scatter Tim's ashes in the place he loved. Now, dear Caroline, it is to you I turn and ask you carry out this final act of love for me.

Perhaps you would be kind enough to let me know if you are prepared to do this, and when? I will find a peaceful spot somewhere in the unfamiliar woods near my daughter's house in England and at least be with you and Tim in spirit, as you scatter his ashes in the place he belongs – Africa.

Grace

Caroline put down the letter, feeling the tears welling up in her eyes. Now she understood.

Grace had gone through something no mother should have to endure. Losing a child was beyond her imagination. The memories, the sadness, the disbelief and the struggle to come to terms with the loss of a child, and not being able to say her final goodbye to him.

She would carry out Grace's request to scatter Tim's ashes and she knew the perfect spot. Beneath the spiritual tree.

But where were Tim's ashes?

She called through to the kitchen and asked the chef to send Moses to her office when he saw him.

Ten minutes later there was a gentle knock on her door.

"Ah, Moses. I need to ask you something. When you unpacked my luggage did you find a small container of any kind?"

Moses frowned and shook his head. "No, Miss Caroline. No container. Only the small Jesus box. This I am putting at the back of the cupboard where the shoes are now living. The ones with the stabbing points for killing snakes. I am thinking the Jesus box should stay in the dark where this Jesus person is living, because he has not been seen by anyone."

Caroline shook her head trying to hide her smile. "Please get it for me Moses?"

Moses went through to her bedroom and returned, carrying the wooden box which he reverently placed on her desk.

"Here is the Jesus box, Miss Caroline."

Tim.

"Thank you, Moses." She shivered in spite of herself, realising Tim had been in her bedroom since she got back.

Moses left and made his way back to the kitchen, leaving Caroline staring at the wooden box. Thank God she hadn't been stopped at customs when she entered the country. She was quite sure carrying someone's ashes required legal documents of some sort.

Caroline would have been completely taken aback if the customs officers had found them. With no documents they would have confiscated the ashes, and Tim would be sitting on a shelf somewhere, in some soulless confiscated goods building.

Poor Grace would have been beside herself if she had lost Tim once again.

Chapter Twenty-Four

The following week Caroline received a call from the girl's doctor.

"How is she Doctor Delamere?"

"She's weak, but well on the road to recovery. Two physiatrists have seen her and both agree that to put her in any kind of foster home, with complete strangers would be detrimental to her mental health. She cries a great deal," he paused, "a great deal. She hasn't spoken a word. It's a difficult situation, heart breaking in fact."

Caroline caught her breath. "Does this mean she can come here, to us?"

"My colleagues and I agree this would be a good solution. From what you told me when we met, the child has some kind of affinity with your manager Jabu?"

She heard another phone chirping in the background. "However, we all agree she can't be discharged from hospital and go back to your lodge without medical supervision."

Caroline bit her lip, her mind searching for some kind of solution to the problem.

He cleared his throat. "I'm afraid the child will have to go to a foster home until we can find her family or relatives. I'm sorry."

Caroline put down the phone and went to look for Jabu.

She found him at the back of the lodge supervising some clearing of the bush. "Jabu. Can you spare a moment please?"

They sat out on the deck, in the shade, the leaves above them rustled in the breeze. Caroline brought him up to date on the current situation at the hospital.

Jabu looked thoughtfully into the distance before turning back to her. "Without some medical presence here, the doctors won't release her into our care. There's no point in fighting this Caroline, we're up against the authorities and the doctors.

"We'll have to hope she won't be in a foster home for too long, and someone will come looking for her."

He twisted the turquoise bracelet on his wrist. "I agree, the child should stay under some kind of medical supervision. We have no idea who she is, where she comes from, what language she speaks, or what happened to her. Her mind will have a lot to deal with, and neither you nor I have this kind of experience."

Caroline pushed her hair behind her ear. "I feel responsible for her Jabu. She seemed to recognise you and responded with trust. There must be something we can do?"

He stood, looking troubled. "I'm afraid not Caroline. We'll have to accept what the doctors have told you. There is nothing more we can do. Nothing more I can do."

Chapter Twenty-Five

Caroline tapped the pile of papers on her desk with her pen, feeling distracted after the call from Doctor Delamere and her conversation with Jabu. Her eyes wandered back to the wooden box on her desk.

Suddenly she straightened her back, sucking in her breath. Of course!

Haphazardly she rummaged through her pile of papers, scattering them all over her normally tidy desk, until she found the white envelope with Grace's letter.

Straightening it out she saw Grace's address at the top of the page and her telephone number in England.

Without a second thought, she punched it into her phone and held her breath.

She tapped her foot as she waited for someone to pick up.

"Hello. This is Megan."

"Hello Megan. My name is Caroline Gordon. I met your mother in New York. I wonder if I may speak to her. Is she there?"

Caroline sensed the slight hesitation. "Yes, she is here, but I'm afraid she's unwell at the moment."

"Oh, I'm sorry to hear that, but I need to speak to her, it's quite urgent."

"Look Miss Gordon," the girl said sounding weary, "my mother hasn't left her bedroom since she arrived back from New York. She's in a bad state of depression, so much so I can't get her to talk to me. She seems so terribly sad, which I understand given my brother's death."

"Yes, Megan, she told me. But I think if you ask her, she may speak to me."

"I'm sorry. I don't think she wants to talk to anyone. I'm so worried about her, she seems to have given up on life. She doesn't want to go anywhere, or do anything. I'm at my wits end, and she refuses to go to a doctor. So you can imagine the state of her mind."

Determined not to give up Caroline tried again. "Look Megan, I know all about Tim, how he died, how your mother fought so hard to reclaim his ashes. I met her again at the airport on my way home to South Africa.

"She was obviously on her way back to you in the UK, but whilst I was in the duty-free shop, she put Tim's ashes in my hand luggage, with a letter saying she couldn't afford the airfare back to South Africa to scatter his ashes as she so desperately wanted to do."

Caroline looked up at the box on her desk. "I have them here, at my lodge in the Sabi Sands. She's asked me to do this, scatter his ashes in the bush."

She could hear the tears in Megan's voice. "That's why she's so sad then. But I don't see how this changes anything. I'm losing my mother and I'm scared, because I can't reach her."

Caroline stood and paced around her office. "Well, I think I can. Let me speak to her please?"

Again, Caroline tapped her foot as she waited.

"Hello Caroline." Grace's normally strong voice sounded subdued. No, not subdued, defeated. As though she had been through enough and didn't have much fight left in her.

Caroline sat at her desk again. Not wasting any words, she got straight to the point. "Listen to me Grace. I have Tim's ashes right here at my lodge, as you wanted, they're here on my desk in front of me. You did the right thing under the circumstances, wanting the best for him, but I'm not willing to scatter his ashes, I'm sorry."

She heard a whimper on the line.

"However, there's something else I want to talk to you about. Remember the girl who appeared at the water hole, more dead than alive?"

"Yes, my dear," Grace said quietly. I do remember. How is she?"

"She's doing as well as expected. We don't know her name, she hasn't spoken yet. She's been assessed by two psychiatrists, and unless I do something damn quickly, she'll be fostered out, until her parents, or relatives can be located.

"We want to take care of her at the lodge, here where she was found. Jabu, my manager, is the only one the girl seems to trust. She has bonded with him somehow. He saved her life."

Caroline took a deep breath. "Grace. I want you to do something for *me* now.

"You were a senior nursing sister at one of the best hospitals in Nairobi, it's what you told me, right?"

"Yes, I was."

"You specialised in looking after children – yes?"

"Yes. But it was a long time ago Caroline."

"It's in your blood Grace. Now, are you going to help me out here or not. You do owe me, you know? I could have been in serious trouble if the customs officers had found Tim's ashes in my luggage. I had no legal documents to prove who he was."

"What do you need from me. How on earth can I possibly help you. I'm so far away."

Caroline stood up again and paced around her office. "I want you to come here. I want you to take this child under your wing and care for her at Infinity. We want her here but we can't have her unless she is under medical supervision. The doctors, and the authorities, will release her to us if someone with a medical background will look after her. You know how Africa works, after all you lived here for so many years.

"My only problem will be to get you a residence permit of some kind, and a legal right to work here."

"Oh, don't worry about that Caroline. I was born in South Africa; I can live and work there with no problems."

She could hear the hope in her friend's voice and smiled into the phone with relief.

"Okay then. This is what's going to happen. You're going to come back to Africa. You're going to help us make this child get better, whilst we search for her family. I'm going to book your flight now. I'll let you know the details; it'll be in the next day or so.

"You'll fly into Johannesburg and take a connecting flight to Nelspruit. I'll be waiting, with Jabu, at the airport. Then your work will begin. We'll take you to the hospital in Nelspruit where you'll meet your patient and the doctors who have attended her. You'll sign off all the paperwork, and bring our girl home to Infinity."

Grace's voice was low, but stronger now. "Thank you, Caroline, you have no idea…"

"No Grace, *you* have no idea. You're an answer to a prayer. We need you. The child needs you.

"You'll need to bring your paperwork, qualifications etc, proving your years as a senior nursing sister. It might help if you could wear your uniform. We must impress the doctors. You're the only hope we have."

Caroline took a deep breath. "And another thing. You and I will scatter Tim's ashes under my spiritual tree, it's a special place. Or, if you prefer you may want to do it alone, he is your son. He's safe here with me. He's waiting for you. We're all waiting for you."

Grace's voice, though slightly shaking with emotion, was now more as she remembered.

"I'll be there Caroline. I'll take over the responsibility of the child. I want to be with my son again. I want to come home."

Chapter Twenty-Six

Caroline checked the private accommodation which had been built to her specifications, set back a considerable way from the main lodge and the guest suites.

One of the four modest thatched cottages was perfect for Grace, it had two bedrooms, a sitting room with a dining alcove, and a tiny kitchen.

She was satisfied the child would not disturb her guests at this distance. The space was adequate for Grace and her soon-to-be, hopefully, new patient. She had no idea what a child's requirements might be, but Grace would.

*****

Jabu and Caroline watched as the domestic flight from Johannesburg touched down in Nelspruit and disgorged its passengers.

Caroline saw the familiar figure of Grace, in her nursing uniform, as she strode along with the other passengers making their way through the arrival's hall, her long thick plait bouncing on her back.

Caroline hugged Grace and introduced her to Jabu. "Welcome home Grace, and thank you for trusting us with what, if we are successful, some hope for the child's future."

Grace turned back to Jabu. "I've heard a lot about you and how you saved the child. I was brought up in Kenya so I'm sure we'll have some interesting discussions about conventional and traditional medicines. It's good to meet you."

Jabu smiled at her as he took her luggage.

Grace paused for a moment as they made their way to the hired car. "Do we know the child's name yet?"

Jabu and Caroline both shook their heads.

Grace straightened the epaulettes on her uniform. "Come on then, let's get to the hospital. You have no idea how good it felt when I disembarked, to feel the warm sun on my skin. Oh, the glorious smell of heat and dust, I've missed it!"

*****

Jabu and Caroline waited outside Doctor Delamere's office. Jabu sat and watched as Caroline paced up and down, twisting her cotton scarf through her hands.

Grace had been with the doctor for over an hour now. Was this a good sign? Would Grace's medical credentials be enough for the doctor to release the child into her experienced and capable hands?

The door opened and they both turned expectantly. Grace shook the doctor's hand, a large file tucked under her arm. She was smiling broadly.

"Right. Please show me my patient, Caroline."

They entered the silent room. The girl was sitting up in bed; all the tubes and wires had been removed, making her look even more fragile than before, she looked completely bewildered.

"You go first Jabu." Caroline said quietly, overwhelmed by the success of her plan.

Jabu sat on the side of the girl's bed. "Hello, little one. Remember me. It's Jabu."

Immediately the child lifted up her arms to him. Wrapping her arms around him she put her head against his neck.

Grace stood there mesmerised. The child had a definite connection with Jabu. She sat on the other side of the bed and indicated Jabu should unhook himself from the tight embrace. Reluctantly he did so.

Grace lifted the girl's hand and took control of the situation.

"Hello, my name is Grace. I'm going to be looking after you. "Caroline," she nodded towards her, "and Jabu are going to be with you. We're taking you home until we can find your family. You'll be safe with us."

The girl turned to look at Grace with her big blue troubled eyes.

"Ace," she whispered, "Cawo. Abu."

Jabu, Caroline and Grace looked at each other. The child had finally spoken.

"Yes. Now, you'll be needing some new clothes, right?" The child looked down at her hospital gown.

"Yes, of course you will. Now I'm going to go to the shops, with Caroline to find some new things for you. I think you might need some shoes as well, because you'll be walking around and you can't do that in your bare feet, can you?"

Grace smoothed back the stubble of the child's hair. "The nights and the mornings can be a little cold at the moment, so we'll get some pyjamas and slippers, so you'll feel warm and safe."

A shadow crossed the little face. "Now," continued Grace briskly, "we'll need some books for me to read to you, all children love stories. I'm going to buy you some colouring crayons so we can draw together, and maybe find some games to play."

The child seemed fascinated with Grace, although she kept a tight hold on Jabu's hand.

Grace continued. "When I was a little girl, like you, I had a favourite book, it was called The Velveteen Rabbit. Do you know the story?"

The child shook her head. "Well, it will be the first one I read to you. Would you like that?"

The child's eyelids fluttered. "Appy." The next minute she was asleep.

Grace tucked the blanket around her, then checked her pulse. "Well, it's a good start. The child understands English. Apparently, she hasn't spoken at all, to anyone, but I think Jabu being here gave her the courage she needed to start communicating. I know it was only a whisper but I think she said she was happy."

*****

Caroline and Grace left the room, leaving Jabu to watch over the girl. Caroline drove her friend into town. "Okay, where's our first port of call?"

"A shopping mall. We have to get clothes. Shorts, tops, underwear, jumpers, pyjamas, dressing gown, shoes, slippers, a sun hat and a toothbrush.

"We need to buy story books, including my favourite, lots of pads for drawing and writing, crayons, puzzles and a few educational toys to play with."

Caroline smiled happily at the busy traffic shimmering in the hot sun. "I suggest we get a cuddly toy of some sort, which I would like you to give to her, Caroline, you need to forge a connection to her as well. She needs something other than humans to comfort her. Something of her own."

Caroline parked outside the shopping mall, and turned to her. "You don't disappoint, Grace, I'm proud of you. Not only are you going to try and put her mind back together, you plan to home school her as well?"

Grace's forehead creased. "No, not really, but I do need to get into her mind, the only way to do this is to see what she's capable of, what she already knows. I need to get her to talk. Now, come on let's go shopping. I'm anxious to get back to her."

Two hours later the two women arrived back at the hospital, the car loaded with enough things, according to Grace, a young child would need.

Jabu was sitting with the girl, who was still asleep.

Grace sat in a chair next to him. "Jabu, before I do anything else I need you to give me every detail of how you found the child, the condition she was in, the medication you gave to her, and anything else which will help me understand the situation a little better. I need as much information as possible if I'm to get the child back on her feet again."

Caroline stood by the window watching the traffic as Jabu recounted the story of the night he found the girl.

Grace then dressed the sleepy child.

Caroline turned from the window, her face flushed and anxious. "The media are out there with all their damn cameras. Word seems to have spread around that our girl is being released. I don't want her to be blinded by flashing lights and questions being shouted at us. It will terrify her."

Jabu smiled at them. "Don't worry about the media. There's a back entrance to the hospital, although I'm sure the cameras are there as well.

"I'll carry her out, the media will assume I'm only another African carrying my own child. They will have no idea who I'm carrying."

Caroline and Grace looked at each other.

Jabu cocked his head. "Our concern is getting her to a safe place with as little disturbance as possible. I'll need the scarf you're wearing Caroline."

Caroline unwrapped it and handed it to Jabu. She rattled her car keys. "Right, let's do it then. We'll meet you at the end of Hospital Road," she glanced at her watch, "in ten minutes."

Jabu gathered the sleepy girl in his arms, covering her head with the cotton scarf he made his way out of the room.

At the back entrance he was surprised to see Doctor Delamere and six nurses waiting for him. They clapped as he walked past them with the child.

Jabu paused briefly. "Thank you, all of you. You saved her life."

Doctor Delamere stepped forward and put his hand on Jabu's shoulder. "No, Jabu, you saved her life. We have much to learn about traditional medicines. But we are locked into what we're allowed to prescribe," he sighed. "Go well, my friend, take care of our patient. Sister Grace is more than qualified to look after her. Let me know how she progresses won't you? At least once a week or I'll be in trouble with the authorities."

Jabu inclined his head and carried the child out.

In his pocket he carried the small bible which had lain next to the girl's bed throughout the days of her recovery. The family bible, Melody, their American guest had insisted Doctor Olivia give to her.

There were many Gods, he thought, which one was the more benevolent?

*****

Caroline and Grace, with Jabu carrying the child, made their way to the private aircraft waiting for them at Nelspruit airport,

Their pilot, Toby, stashed their luggage into the hold of the Cessna, then loaded his passengers. Caroline sat up front with Toby. Jabu and Grace sat in the seat behind, the child wedged in between them.

After the aircraft had taken off the child climbed onto Jabu's lap, her hands pressed flat against the window. Grace studied her. The child was watching the African bush speed away beneath them, as though she might be searching for something. Then her head dropped and she began to cry.

Jabu wrapped his arms around her. Grace tried to work out what had upset her. But one thing she had guessed. The child had been in a small aircraft before.

Chapter Twenty-Seven

The 4x4 land cruiser from the lodge collected them at the air strip. The child refused to get out of the aircraft.

Jabu reached up for her and she came into his arms willingly, her arms wrapping tightly around his neck. When they arrived at the back entrance to the lodge, the child once again, refused to get out of the vehicle by herself, holding her arms out to Jabu.

He carried her into the cottage and placed her on the sofa.

"Here we are, little one, this is your new home. Grace will be looking after you, she will be with you all the time, okay. I'll come and see you later when you've settled in."

The child looked utterly bewildered.

"Appy, abu, appy." Then she put her thumb in her mouth, and lay back on the cushions, watching him anxiously as he left.

Grace busied herself with unpacking all the clothes they had bought. Holding them up for her to see before she went through to the bedroom and folded them away in the drawers.

The child's eyes followed her, as she sucked on her thumb.

"Now, where shall we put all our new books, games and crayons?"

The child said nothing, her eyes watchful.

Grace took the things she'd bought from the stationery and book shop and piled them on the dining room table. "Would you like to come and help me?"

Still the child said nothing, as the tears coursed down her now wet cheeks.

Grace sat next to her and took her hand. "I know all of this seems confusing after being in the hospital. But you'll get used to it. The thing is, we need to have a name for you. Can you tell me your name?"

"Appy," the child whispered, taking her wet thumb out of her mouth for a moment.

"Well, I'm glad you're happy, even though you're crying. But we have to call you something."

The child shook her head.

"All right. Here's what we'll do. I'm going to call you, let me think…Meggy. I have a daughter and her name is Megan, when she was little, like you, we called her Meggy. Shall we call you this until you can tell us your real name?"

The child stared at her, her chest heaving with silent sobs.

Grace held her arms out. The child turned away from her and pressed her face into the cushion.

There was a light tap on the door and Caroline came in carrying a small brown teddy bear.

"I've brought our new guest a present…" her voice trailed off as she looked at the child curled up on the sofa. She looked at Grace, her eyebrow raised in question.

Grace pointed her head towards the bedroom. Caroline followed her. "She's a bit overwhelmed," she whispered to Caroline. "We have to give her time. She won't tell me her name so I said we would call her Meggy, until she tells us her own name. She hasn't moved from the sofa since we arrived, nor has she stopped crying. She's going to need a lot of love and care, after what she's been through. I can only imagine how terrifying that experience must have been for her.

"Why not give her the teddy bear and then we'll leave her to adjust to her new surroundings. I'll give her something to calm her down. Doctor Delamere gave me a few things he thought might help, plus the other medications she's on."

Caroline knelt next to the girl they would call Meggy.

"Hello Meggy. I like your name. I've brought you something; something of your own. Maybe you can find a name for him too."

Meggy didn't move. Caroline placed the teddy bear next to her. "We'll find your family, I promise."

*****

Caroline and Grace sat outside on the deck, watching the sun slide behind the trees. "Don't look so worried Caroline. We have to give her time to adjust. In a situation like this it's best to give the child time, let her come to me, to us. She'll only do this when she doesn't feel threatened.

"I've seen this sort of thing before. Now, I'm going to finish my unpacking, and give her a bath. If you'd arrange for the kitchen to send her something light to eat. Poached eggs I think, with some toast. Let's see what sort of food she likes. Then if you would ask Jabu to drop by to say good-night to her, I think she'll sleep better."

Caroline lit the hurricane lamp on the table. "Will you eat with her Grace, or should I send something up later for you?"

"Later I think, although I'm feeling a bit bushed, after the flight from London, and the grilling from the doctors," she paused. "I'd like to have Tim here with me tonight, if it's alright. I'd like to have him close, where I can see him."

"Of course. Let me organise the kitchen. Moses, who looks after me, will now look after you and Meggy as well. Anything you need, ask him. He's a dear old man, gentle and quiet. He has children and grandchildren of his own, he'll help you with Meggy. You'll need to take a break now and again. Moses will bring Tim to you…"

She reached over and squeezed Grace's hand. She pointed in the distance. "See that blackened dead tree over there?"

Grace peered out into the distance, as dusk began to draw in. "Yes, it seems to stand out all on its own."

Caroline wrapped her arms around herself as the air around them started to cool. "It's my spiritual tree Grace. I've always loved it. It might have been dead for a hundred years or so, but to me it seems eternal, ethereal, a symbol of something more enduring than life. I thought maybe Tim would like it, and you'll be able to see him from here."

Grace rubbed her tired eyes. "Yes, I think it would be perfect, he'd like that."

Chapter Twenty-Eight

Grace looked around the cottage and turned on the lights. It was beginning to feel a bit more like home and less like the accommodation for pilots or other non-guests at the lodge. As yet she hadn't walked around Infinity, but was looking forward to the time when she'd be able to.

She ran the bath and laid out Meggy's pyjamas; anxious to examine the child for herself, and read through the medical files Doctor Delamare had given to her, and the reports from the two psychiatrists.

She changed into her khaki trousers and a loose white shirt; the child had seen enough uniforms in the hospital.

Grace sat next to the child, who had not moved for over an hour now. "Your bath is ready. Then we'll get you into your pyjamas, before you have something to eat, then I'll read you a story."

She held out her hand. "Come along, I've put some bubbles in the water for you."

Still Meggy didn't move. Her eyes distrusting and frightened, as she sucked on her thumb.

"Oh well, I think you'll have to sleep out here then, and you'll be hungry if you don't eat. It would be a pity because Jabu said he would only come and say goodnight if you have your bath and eat something. Shall I tell him not to come then?"

She sat up. "Abu?" she whispered.

"Yes, he wants to see you. So, let's have your bath, shall we."

She looked at the floor then up at Grace, panic dancing in her eyes. She lifted up her arms. "Up, up!"

Grace narrowed her eyes, remembering how she wouldn't get out of the aircraft or into the vehicle unless Jabu was carrying her. "You want me to carry you?"

Meggy stared at the floor, drawing her knees to her thin chest.

Grace bent forward and lifted the fragile child into her arms. "Come on then, bath time."

*****

Meggy finished her poached eggs and toast. Now dressed in her pyjamas and dressing gown, she was watching the door.

Grace, as she washed the girl, had been shocked at how wasted her body was, seeing for the first time the scars, evidence of her hazardous time spent in the bush before she was found.

There was a gentle knock at the door and Jabu entered. "Up, up, abu," the child whispered to him.

"Well now, little one, I hear we have given you a name. Do you like it?"

The girl's eyes were anxious. "Appy, appy."

Jabu smiled at her. "Well, if you're happy, then so am I."

She held out her arms and Jabu scooped her up. "Tell you what Meggy, before Grace reads you a story, I'll take you outside. Let's see what we can hear and see, shall we?"

Grace smiled at their retreating backs. There was something about Jabu, Meggy connected with. She could hear him talking to her in that strange language, full of clicks and soft musical sounds.

Ten minutes later they were back. Jabu settled her into her bed. "Now, Grace will read you a story, and I'll come and see you tomorrow, to make sure you've eaten your breakfast."

Meggy snuggled into her bed. Grace walked out onto the deck with Jabu.

"You must be tired, Grace, it's been quite a day for you. Once you have Meggy settled, Moses will bring your dinner, then you can catch up on some sleep."

Grace tried to stifle a yawn. "Yes, I'm tired, but so far I think things are progressing well. What bothers me though is that Meggy doesn't seem to want to touch the floor with her feet, I can't work out why. There's nothing wrong with her feet or legs, I've examined them, but she doesn't want to walk."

Jabu cast his eyes over the bush. In the distance they could hear the throaty roar of a lion calling his females to come and hunt. From the water hole, they could hear the deep chortling laughs of the hippos, followed by the whoop-whoop of the scavenging hyenas and the dull, monotonous, croak of frogs.

"I've given this a lot of thought Grace. I don't know how long she was out in the bush on her own. I would think one of the reasons she survived was because she climbed up into the trees to protect herself from predators, she must know about the bush and its ways.

"If I'm right, then this would make the ground, somewhat full of danger. If she's up high she feels safe. This might answer your question. I think whilst she was up in a tree, she saw the lights of the lodge, and made her way here."

"Yes, that would make sense…but one thing puzzles me. How on earth did she survive out there? With all the predators?"

Jabu sighed. "We humans think we know all about animals in the wild. We study them, watch their behaviour, come to our own conclusions as to what they are thinking, their habits, why they do certain things. But we don't know how they think. Yes, we know they have to kill to eat. They have their natural prey, perhaps something on two legs is not to their palate. Maybe they sensed the child was no threat to them, she would have a different scent, looked different. Maybe, like humans, they would rather stick to what they know."

He looked again towards the shadowy bush. "They would have been curious; that's for sure. I don't have any answers to your question Grace. Perhaps they sensed she was like, for instance with any of the cat family, lions, leopards, cheetahs, she was like a vulnerable cub. I know lions will sometimes kill a lioness' cubs to gain control over the pride, but this little girl was not a cub."

He turned back to her. "Animals only kill to eat, to survive. I don't think they would have been interested in a small girl who offered no threat to them, there's plenty of their natural prey around, plenty. The only predator who can climb a tree, unlike in your country, is a leopard, but he will invariably have his kill with him, he climbs the tree so he doesn't have to share his dinner. A child high up in a tree would not be a threat to a leopard, he would leave her alone, more concerned about protecting his dinner.

"It's not unheard of, a child surviving in the bush, but not usual. Refugees trying to get cross the borders into South Africa from Mozambique or Zimbabwe sometimes became separated from their children. Of course, many of them don't survive. But there have been a couple of cases where a child did."

He glanced at his watch. "I heard about one child who hid in an abandoned termite hill, and he survived. And there have been stories of small plane crashes in the bush, where, against all odds, the passengers survived."

Jabu looked back to the lodge. "I must get back, we have a full camp tonight. Give her time, Grace, it won't be long before she gets her confidence back, begins to trust the ground beneath her feet, and the people who are trying to help her."

He turned to go then stopped and looked back at her. "It might be an idea to put a gate up at the entrance to your cottage, and always keep the patio doors closed if you're not with her. I think she's unpredictable at the moment and the last thing we need is for her to bolt off into the bush again."

"Good idea, Jabu. Would you arrange that for us?"

*****

Grace checked on her patient. Meggy was sleeping, the bear thrown on the floor. Melody's family bible lay on the bedside table next to her bed.

She made a mental note to get in touch with the American family who had been witness to the girl being carried in from the bush. They would want to know how the girl was progressing. Olivia, the English doctor, had promised she would keep in touch with the family – Grace would carry out this promise, and she would also, in a day or so, update Olivia and Doctor Delamere on how the child was coping with her new life at Infinity.

There were so many people involved in the story of the little girl they had chosen to call Meggy. She had a tentative new family here – but where was her own family?

*****

Grace awoke with a start. Meggy was calling for Jabu. She checked her watch; it was three in the morning.

Hastily, she made her way to Meggy's bedroom. "I'm here, Meggy, I'm here."

The night light cast a shadow over the child's face. She held up her arms, now a familiar enough sight.

"Come, it's alright. Sit on the sofa and I'll change the sheets."

When she returned Meggy to her bed, the child wound her arms around Grace's neck, refusing to let go.

Grace sighed. "Alright, let's bring Mr Teddy and you can sleep in my bed. Have you given your teddy bear a name yet?"

"Scusie," she said urgently. Lifting her hand to Grace's cheek she turned her face towards hers. "Scusie?"

"Are you saying excuse me?"

Once more the child's eyes flooded with tears, as she threw the bear angrily on the floor.

*****

Grace lay awake, the child sleeping restlessly next to her. Feeling the warmth of her body, Grace remembered her own children when they were young, when they would run through to her bedroom during a thunderstorm, seeking comfort and reassurance.

Her children didn't need her now, but this little girl did. Once more she was wanted and needed.

In the back of her mind, however, she knew once the child's family, or relatives, were found, her job here would be over.

She tried not to think about it too much. Right now, she had a purpose, she was back in her beloved Africa, her son was with her, and someone needed her. She was content.

Chapter Twenty-Nine

For the next few days Grace tried to interest Meggy in some of the games she had bought. Encouraging her to draw with the brightly coloured crayons. But Meggy seemed far away, and showed no interest in what was going on around her, silent tears sliding down her thin cheeks.

She lay on the sofa, sucking her thumb, her eyes following Grace, she barely whispered a word, and refused to walk.

Grace knew all about children with problems, she would have to be patient, eventually, like all children, this one would start to come out of her shell and, hopefully, start to talk.

*****

As darkness fell, after Jabu had made his usual call to say goodnight to Meggy, Caroline joined her out on the deck carrying two glasses of wine.

"How's it going Grace?"

Grace, smoothed her hair back from her forehead, looking at the spiritual tree in the distance. "I think we're making some progress, which I'm happy about. She's eating, not well, but she is sleeping through the night. No sign of any nightmares, no bed wetting any more. I wish she would take a few steps on her own. Once she does, she'll become curious about her surroundings.

She glanced at Caroline. "I think Jabu was right in his assessment. Meggy must have spent a lot of time in the safety of the trees, especially at night. She's definitely still in a state of shock but I think she's blocking everything out. At the moment I'm happy, if this is the case. The body heals a lot faster than the mind.

"I'm in contact with Doctor Delamere in Nelspruit, keeping him up to date, also Olivia in London. I promised her I would get in touch with the American couple, Melody and Chuck, who gave her their family bible. I'll do this in the next few days."

Caroline lifted her glass, twirling the stem in her fingers, watching the last of the sun turning the liquid to golden sun bursts.

"I've been in contact with the police, Grace, they haven't made any headway with their enquiries. The media seem to have lost interest as they don't know where she is, and with all the other horrible things going on in the world, well, they have other things to cover."

She looked at her friend who was staring off into the distance. "I know you've probably given a lot of thought as to what will happen when her parents are found."

Grace nodded but didn't say anything.

"I wanted to ask you something. You know how I like to make Infinity as different as possible. Trying to get the edge on the competition? Well, I don't know of a single game lodge with an on-site nursing sister. All the game rangers and managers are trained in first aid, but their knowledge is limited, especially if there's an emergency, like we had here."

She now had Grace's attention. "I think it would be a huge plus for our lodge if we had a full-time nursing sister on our staff, someone who trained in Africa."

Caroline tucked her hair behind her ears. "A good percentage of our guests are from the States. Not only are they always a little nervous about coming to Africa, no, make that extremely nervous. They also worry about their health, it's of the utmost importance to them. I think it would be a big deciding factor in choosing which lodge to stay at if they knew we had someone like you on the team. What do you think Grace?"

Grace smiled tentatively. "It would be one of the best jobs in the world, especially based here. Yes, I accept, thank you."

"You're right Caroline," Grace was suddenly serious. "Older people always worry about the *what ifs* when they're far away from their own doctors. If they know they could be treated for any ailments in the comfort of their own suites, it would certainly make a difference as to where they would spend their safari. I won't have to walk around in my nursing uniform I hope?"

Caroline shook her head.

Grace pulled her thick blond plait over her shoulder and twisted it. "I'll need to have a room to stock medical supplies and a fridge, of course. I'll make a list of what I need and perhaps you can put me in touch with the pharmacist in Nelspruit. Some of the things I'll need will have to be signed off by Doctor Delamere. After what Jabu told me the night he found Meggy, it would be a good idea to have some IV fluids in stock and some oxygen tanks."

Caroline stood. "Good, that's settled then. I'll organise for your medical supplies to be flown in from the pharmacy, once you've signed things off with Doctor Delamere, also the IV fluids and oxygen.

"I'm going to call Kia, now, and tell her to trumpet the news of our on-site personal nursing sister, to international tour operators, and the media. I want her to get it up on our web site immediately, with a brief bio of your background in Kenya, and a pic of you as well."

"Whose Kia?"

"Well, initially she was my interior designer, but she was into social media as well – which I'm not by the way. She's good with the mainstream media as well, they like her.

"Kia was pivotal to the launch of Infinity. The launch was so successful I offered her a full-time job, managing all our public relations and marketing, she's based in Cape Town. She handles all that side of the business for me, she's excellent. Oh, and she's Jabu's sister."

*****

Grace leaned back in her chair. For the first time in many years, she felt she had a future to look forward to. A place to belong.

Sensing something behind her she sat up and looked around. Meggy was crouched by the door leading out onto the deck.

Grace leaned back slowly in her chair and waited.

A few minutes later the child crept on all fours to the other chair, climbing up she drew her knees up to her chest and stared at the darkness in front of her.

"Well hello, Meggy," Grace said quietly. "Have you come to sit with me and look at the stars. I can tell you all about them if you like. They're clever, you know, they can even show you how to get home if you're lost, did you know that?"

Meggy stared straight ahead, looking out over the shadows of the bush, a soft sound, like a purr, came from her throat as she rocked back and forth.

Grace spoke softly. "A long time ago I lived out in the bush with my two children. We would lie outside on a mattress, when it was dark, and I would tell them stories about the stars."

Sucking her thumb, the child rocked back and forth, staring out into the black night, the odd sound purring in her throat.

"Let me go and fetch a blanket for you, it's getting chilly. I want you to stay in your chair and not go wandering off, okay?"

Swiftly Grace returned to the deck, relieved to see the child hadn't moved. She covered her up and returned to her own chair.

"So, now we are going to have our first school lesson. I'm going to teach you about the stars."

Half an hour later Meggy was asleep. Grace carried her back to her bed, well satisfied.

It had only been a few faltering steps, on her hands and knees, but the child had made them all by herself – perhaps this would be the beginning of finding her way back to where she had once belonged. Perhaps sometime soon she might smile.

*****

The next morning Moses brought their breakfast up from the kitchen, he went through to Meggy's bedroom.

"Good morning little miss. Today we are having the scrambled eggs with the bacon. Also, I am bringing some fruit for you, so you will grow big and strong. This, I am thinking, is what your small legs are crying for. These legs are much looking to be used again, for they will show you many things. But now, these legs have no job to do. For what good are two legs and feet if they are going to no-where? We must make these legs big and strong, so you can run and play."

She looked at Moses, then at her feet, and held out her hand. He led her through to the dining alcove.

Grace looked up a smile spreading across her face as she watched Meggy's tentative wavering steps as she held fast to Moses's hand.

"Appy."

"You are happy, little miss? Then I also am happy. Come, you must eat."

Grace sat across from Meggy, watching her pick at her breakfast. "Remember our story last night? About the stars, Meggy?"

The child stared at her, then pushed her plate away.

"Well, Caroline has a special place here. It's a room, high in the trees. You can lie on a big soft bed there and look at the stars and the moon. Would you like me to take you there one day? Jabu can come with us. I will be with you there and Jabu will look after us, he'll make sure we are quite safe. We don't have to stay there for long, only a little while. Would you like to do that?"

The child shook her head vigorously.

No.

"You can bring the bear with you. Why doesn't it have a name?"

Grace saw the child's eyes widen with terror. "Scusie, gone. Scusie gone!"

To make her point the child threw her teddy bear on the floor, and ran back to her bedroom, the door slammed behind her as she howled with obvious desperation.

Grace sat back in surprise. She stirred her coffee and thought back to their stilted conversation. "Excuse me, gone?" What on earth did that mean?

It had crossed her mind on a few occasions. This child understood English, therefore, she could speak it. Was it possible she had some kind of speech impediment? Autistic maybe? No, the doctors would have picked that up and there was no mention of it in their medical reports on Meggy. Maybe what she was trying to say had another meaning altogether.

It was also odd she kept saying "*Appy,*" when she so clearly wasn't, and saying "*excuse me*" when she didn't need to be excused for anything at all.

Chapter Thirty

Jabu tapped on the open door of Grace's cottage.
"Are you ready Grace?"

"Yes. I'm as ready as I'll ever be." She reached for the box holding her son's ashes.

"Caroline said she would come with us, if it's what you would like."

"Thank you, Jabu, but I want to do this on my own. I need to be alone with my boy."

Jabu stood there, holding Meggy. "I'm afraid that is not going to be possible. I will come with you. The old spiritual tree where you want to scatter Tim's ashes, is a fair way away from the lodge, even though we can see it clearly from here because of its blackened branches.

"It's not safe for you to do this alone, too many animals around. I'll drive you there. I'll try to give you as much space and privacy as I can, but I need to keep you safe. It's not negotiable, I'm sorry."

Grace turned to him, clutching her son's ashes to her chest. "Alright. I wonder if I might ask you to bring a shovel with you?"

Jabu looked at her, understanding her request immediately. "Of course, we always keep one in the vehicle."

Caroline tapped on the door. "Shall I come with you Grace?"

"Thank you, Caroline. This is my own private journey. But please stay with Meggy. She must never be left alone, under any circumstances. The last thing we need is for her to take off again into the bush."

"Of course, I will." She hugged Grace. "We're all part of your family now. I brought Tim back, but you're his mother. You must do what you feel is best for you and your son."

Caroline reached for Meggy, who turned her face into Jabu's neck. "Come on, Grace has something she must do, she won't be long, she'll come back. I thought we might try to do some painting."

Grace interrupted her. "It's alright. Let Meggy come with Jabu. It will be good for her to get away from the lodge for a while. He'll watch over her."

Jabu drove them towards the blackened tree. Grace, Meggy and Tim.

He parked near the tree. Meggy was looking around, her thumb in her mouth, her eyes never leaving Grace who was getting out of the vehicle.

Jabu, holding Meggy, reached for the folding green director's chair he had brought with him, along with the shovel. They walked together towards the base of the tree.

He stilled Grace with his hand on her arm. "You won't be scattering his ashes, will you?"

"No. I've changed my mind. I want to bury him here, so I can see him from the lodge, and know he's not scattered to the wind, but here, lying beneath this tree. It seems to me the right thing to do, what he would have wanted."

She reached out her arms. "Here, give Meggy to me. The hole doesn't need to be too deep, but as close to the roots as you can get."

Jabu dug the hole, as close as he could to the roots of the long dead tree. He wiped his brow and stood back, holding out his arms for the child, so Grace could be alone with hers.

But Meggy, surprisingly, rejected him and clung to Grace's neck. Grace looked at the child and saw something in her eyes.

"Alright. Shall we do this together then, Meggy?"

Jabu turned the vehicle around so his back was to the tree, wanting to give Grace the privacy she needed to say goodbye to her son.

Grace leaned forward, holding Meggy close. She placed the box carefully in the shallow hole Jabu had dug. "Here you are Tim, back where you belong, where I'll be able to see you each day – from afar, it's true, but we're together again."

The child slipped from her grasp and knelt at the grave. With her hands she scooped up the dirt and placed it over the box. Wiping her hands on her shorts, she turned to Grace, her face perplexed.

"Scusie. Bye, bye?"

"Oh Meggy, what do you mean *scusie, bye, bye?* I wish I could understand what you're trying to tell me. This is my boy, his name is Tim."

Grace sat in the chair Jabu had provided. Meggy crawled up on to her lap.

"Ace sad?"

"Yes. My boy has gone from me, but he'll always be here beneath this magical tree."

With both hands the child turned Grace's face towards her, dusting her wet cheeks with some of the dirt from Tim's grave. "Appy elp?"

Through her tears Grace smiled. "Sometimes it helps to be happy. I'll try to be."

The mother and the child sat beneath the towering dead tree. Meggy sucked her dusty thumb.

Grace allowed her tears to flow, thinking of all the years when her child was growing up, as a baby, a teenager, and then a man. Remembering him.

Meggy looked up. "Mommy."

"No, darling, I'm not your mommy," she said distractedly, "but we'll find her for you."

Jabu turned the engine of the car and left it running as he approached them both. "It's getting hot Grace. Are you ready to go back to the lodge?"

She wiped her eyes. "Yes, I'm ready."

Jabu reached for the child. "Come, little one. Time to go home."

Meggy shook her head, her arms around Grace's neck. "Ace, sad."

"Yes, she is. But we must go home now." He collected the chair and the shovel and put them in the back of the vehicle.

Grace, carrying Meggy, climbed into the vehicle. She had lost one child, and here was another who needed her. She looked back at Tim's grave.

Was it possible?

Chapter Thirty-One

Grace sat out on her deck. The sun was going down, the evening full of the sounds of nocturnal animals and birds. An owl hooted in the distance. A male lion gave a throaty, distinctive call to his females, calling for them to hunt. Moths fluttered around the gas lamp on the table next to her.

The magnificent sunset threw its molten gold and red colours over the darkening bush, like a shimmering furnace. A few stars were already beginning to peep through the darkening sky. In the distance she could see the spiritual tree.

She had phoned her daughter. Megan, had accepted she wanted to be where she called home, here in Africa.

"I was wrong to put pressure on you, Mommy, I wanted to have you near me, I miss you. But it was no good when I could see how unhappy you were.

"If you're happy now, then so am I, and," she had laughed down the phone, "hey, I also get to come back to Africa to visit you, which as you know I also miss."

*****

The little girl had been at the lodge for three weeks now. Her thin body had filled out slightly, but her appetite was poor. Her hair was starting to grow again, but she had shown no interest in the colouring books or crayons Grace had supplied for her. The only time she showed any animation was when Jabu visited her.

Mostly she sat on the sofa sucking her thumb, rocking back and forth, silently. That strange purring sound coming from her.

Grace made her way to the child's bedroom and sat on her bed. She was fast asleep.

"I know what you want," she whispered to the sleeping child, "you want your family. But how will we ever find them if we don't know your name, or where you come from?"

She made her way back to the deck and sat down. She needed to get inside the child's head.

According to Doctor Delamere the police had made no headway into their investigations, and it seemed to Grace if they were ever to find out how Meggy had arrived at the water hole, she, herself, would have to be the one to do it. She had to get the child to talk. Somehow.

*****

The next morning, after Moses had delivered their breakfast, she asked him to sit with them. Meggy watched them in silence.

"Can you draw a picture, Moses?"

Moses's eyebrows crawled up his forehead in surprise. He shook his greying head.

"Well, that makes three of us then. You see, Moses, I have all these wonderful drawing pads and pretty coloured crayons, but no-one wants to use them."

"*Eish*, Miss Grace, what good are these drawing things when no-one will use them, or see them?"

"Because, Moses, drawings tell stories. You know yourself your ancestors' made paintings inside hidden caves, you're a Griqua just like Jabu, you must know this?"

"These drawings told the story of your people, how they hunted, what they hunted, what their spears looked like, what they wore. The animals they saw. Without these drawings you would have no memory of your ancestors."

She glanced at Meggy who was watching them intently, sucking her thumb.

"*Eish*, this is true Miss Grace, but what good have these drawing in the caves made. I do not remember these people; it is today I am looking at. I am looking at my own children and grandchildren, I have no need of drawings on the wall in a cave. I will not see them there. I will see them here where they are."

Grace glanced again at Meggy, her anxious eyes now watching Moses's face.

"But you have seen these cave paintings Moses?"

"It is true, these I have seen. But these people are made of sticks and not looking like us."

"Yes, I know. But these stick people are many sizes, right?"

"Yes, they have the big stick people and the smaller stick people, these are the children of the big stick people I am thinking."

Satisfied, Grace pushed her plate aside.

"When you've finished in the kitchen, Moses, I'd like you to come back here. You see, today we're are going to try to draw some stick people, we need you to help us. Will you do this?"

Moses gathered up the plates and put them on his tray. He nodded, seeming to understand what Grace was asking of him. "I will try to draw these stick people for you, but the little miss must also have to try as hard as I will. Will you draw these things with me Miss Meggy?"

She stared at him, still silent, but she was eyeing the pile of crayons and drawing pads piled up on the desk.

*****

Moses arrived back at the cottage, having finished his duties. Grace had laid out the drawing pads and a tin bucket full of brightly coloured crayons.

Grace picked a yellow crayon and started to draw. Moses also picked up a crayon, a green one, and stared at the blank piece of paper in front of him.

He looked at Grace who nodded at him. "*Eish,* this drawing I have not done before. But, if my people can draw like this in the caves, then it must be in my blood. I am thinking if my ancestors could do this drawing thing, then I am able to do this thing also, but I am also thinking they have been using a porcupine quill for the caves, not these small soft sticks."

Grace and Moses bent their heads and began to draw. She watched out of the corner of her eye as the child tentatively reached out her hand for a yellow crayon...

Studiously avoiding her, Moses and Grace continued with their random drawing. Half an hour later, Moses held up his drawing for them to see.

"*Eish*, it is true. My ancestors can draw these things better than Moses. This is the paper I am drawing on. How would it be to scratch this drawing on a wall in a cave. I must speak to these ancestors and ask them how this is."

Grace held up her rough drawing of a field of yellow sunflowers.

Moses frowned at the bright colours. "Where is this place with the big yellow flowers, Miss Grace. It is a place far away from here?"

She smiled at him. "I have no idea, I've made it up, it could be anywhere. But a true artist, like a writer, only draws or writes about things they know. Now Meggy, let's see what you've drawn shall we?"

Meggy, who had been crouched over her drawing, lifted it up and held it to her chest, shaking her head.

"*Eish*, little miss, I have shown you my drawing. Where I am coming from it is the custom you must show me what you have worked so hard on. I am thinking your drawing will be better than mine."

Shyly, she passed her drawing over to Moses. He studied it for some time, then glanced at her.

"You have more people here than I have in my cave drawing. Is it so, you know more people than Moses does?"

Grace held her breath.

Meggy snatched the drawing back, then, with panic flooding her eyes, she ran from the room back into her bedroom. The drawing fluttered to the floor next to Grace's chair. Bending she picked it up.

"Thank you, Moses," she murmured, "you've been a great help."

Moses stood. "This child has drawn her family. The family which is lost to her. In our culture, our African culture, we keep our family close by. We have big families, many brothers and sisters, aunties and uncles, also the cousins, who may not be cousins, but wish to be cousins anyway. We are never lost, there is always being someone who will help, if help is needed, we are looking after our own always."

As Moses left, Grace studied Meggy's drawing.

Stick figures, it was true. Holding it in her hands, she now knew a little more about the child's family.

So where were they and what had happened to them?

Chapter Thirty-Two

Jabu, Caroline and Grace studied the drawing. The guests were all out on a game drive and they had met on the viewing deck overlooking the water. Moses was watching over Meggy.

Grace pointed to the stick figures. "Here are two children, one is Meggy I think. She's drawn someone with long yellow curly hair, see? This is her, or maybe her sister. I don't know, she might be the small figure or the bigger one.

"There are two bigger figures. Both of them she has drawn but, both of them she has scribbled out their faces. I think it has to be her parents."

Caroline took a sip of her tea. "Why would she have scribbled out their faces?"

Grace fingered the bracelets on her wrists. "I think there must have been some kind of split between the parents, a divorce perhaps. You see here." She pointed at the bigger stick figures, "Meggy has pressed the crayon into their faces their features flattened before she rubbed their faces out with a black one."

Jabu leaned forward in his chair. Lifting the drawing he peered at it. "I don't think the figure with the yellow hair is Meggy. Her hair was definitely dark brown before Olivia shaved her head. She seems to have drawn something else here, something in the sky. A dot of something, in a different colour. In the background there's also something else. It looks like a building of some sort, with a big sloping roof, and chimneys. I think these are two dogs she's drawn."

Caroline stretched forward and took the drawing from him. "She's also drawn some scrubby looking bushes, which spells Africa to me, but the long roof and chimneys, the big trees. This smacks of Europe or England."

Jabu's radio bleeped. He picked it up and listened. "I'll send her right way Mrs Bellingham."

120

He turned to Grace. "One of the guests is feeling unwell. Suite number five."

Grace stood quickly. "On my way Jabu. I'll grab my coat and medical bag."

Caroline held up her hand. "No, wait Grace. No medical type uniform, remember. Take your bag, of course. These guests won't want a medical type dressed person coming to their suite. They're living out their dreams, let's not spoil it with remnants of their normal life. Be who you are. They'll know you are a fully trained medical sister, it's on a small card in their suite. No need for the reminders of the life they are trying to forget for a while."

*****

Caroline looked out over the water hole, holding the child's drawing in her hands.

"What next Jabu. Where do we go from here?"

Jabu ran his hands over his head. "Remember I told you about Kia. The story. The person who put the story together?"

"Yes, of course. But what has it to do with anything now?"

"He's a journalist, he specialises in cold cases, his turf was the UK. He freelances for the UK newspaper, *The Telegraph*. He's based in Franschhoek now."

Caroline frowned. "But this is hardly a cold case, is it."

"No. But he has an uncanny knack for digging around and finding the truth. I think we should get in touch with him."

Caroline shook her head vehemently. "No. This is what we have tried to avoid all along. No journalists, no media! We have to protect Meggy. That's what we agreed, remember."

"Caroline, I know him. If we want to find out what happened to her, then we have no-where else to turn. We're getting nowhere with trying to locate her family, and we must. I trust him. We need help."

What's his name then?"

"His name is Jack. Jack Taylor."

Chapter Thirty-Three

Jack Taylor stepped out onto the deck of his rented home in Franschhoek and breathed a sigh of utter contentment.

After chasing a story in South Africa, two years previously, he had decided to leave his rabbit hutch of an apartment in London and live in the country he had come to love. This one.

His whole career in London had been built on closing cold cases. He had worked for *The Telegraph* as a cub reporter and worked his way up until he became one of their top, and most respected, journalists.

His last cold case had brought him to the Eastern Cape where he had chased a twenty-year-old story and brought it to its astonishing conclusion.

It had been a major turning point in his life. An Englishman, through and through, he had never imagined living anywhere else other than his country of birth.

But having travelled through South Africa, following his story, he had been overwhelmed by the majestic beauty, the spectacular coastline, breath-taking landscapes, the glorious weather and the friendliness of its people. He loved the fascinating and varied cultures, the turbulent political histories and the curious sense of timelessness that was Africa.

With the case solved he had returned to London, but found it hard to settle back. One day he had left his tiny flat and battled his way through the grey and black clothed crowds, and the even greyer and black heavy clouds, the rain pounding against his umbrella, the wind threating to turn it inside out. He'd squashed up next to his fellow travellers on the overpacked tube train and felt his spirit's plummet.

Arriving at the newspaper's offices, he had hung up his soaking raincoat, run his hands through his untidy wet hair, then slumped at his desk.

Although he loved the buzz, the energy, of the newspaper's office, his fellow journalists and the challenging stories which made his blood fizz, something had been missing.

He had tasted a different life, seen a brighter life. He wanted more of it, Jack had fallen in love, and not just with the country.

Harry, his editor, had been sympathetic to his top journalist's vision of a different life, almost envious, Jack had thought.

He had resigned. Harry, stretching his famous navy-blue braces had refused to accept the resignation. Instead, he had offered Jack a freelance position, which he could do, based in South Africa.

"They say the South of France is the place to go for shady people in shady places. I reckon you can churn out some good stories from a place which has little shade and plenty of shady people. A lot of them who have escaped to South Africa from all over Europe and the UK. Who knows what you might dig up?"

Harry grinned at him. "It doesn't have to be cold cases anymore, Jack," he had said. "There have been some pretty startling court cases coming out of the country. Oscar Pistorius for start. From glory to gloom. A crime of passion, as the French would say. Or cold-blooded murder as it turned out.

"The Diwani case. Another crime of passion, or maybe another cold-blooded murder it would seem. A British man gets someone to knock off his young bride in Durban.

"The wealthy wine farmer whose son ran amok one night and killed his parents and older brother with an axe.

"A cosy week-end conference and a high-profile property mogul, who finds his wife hanging in the bathroom of their fancy suite. But who did the hanging?

"Oh yes, my boy, there are many stories coming out of there. It should keep you busy. Our readers will be enchanted as they gaze across the seas from their predictable safe, and routine life. They'll lap it all up over their breakfast cornflakes."

Harry had hooked his thumbs into his navy-blue braces as they strained across his considerable stomach. "I want the stories Jack, plus a column once a week for our Sunday supplement, describing the quirks and quiddities of an Englishman abroad. We'll put you on a retainer, of course, with a generous expense account. But I expect great stories, you hear?"

He had rubbed his hands together gleefully. "I like this. Off you go then. Sort things out with our legal chaps and start filling my column inches."

Chapter Thirty-Four

Jack looked at his thirty-eight year-old brown legs, clad only in shorts, his feet bare, his untidy hair blonder now with the caress of the sun.

He reached for his cold beer and thought about what it would be like if he was still living in London. His face and body would be so terribly white, blue veins showing through the skin, his face grey and pinched from the relentless weather, and weighed down with clothes to keep out the cold and the rain.

Yes, England could be beautiful, stunning in fact, in the summer, but it seemed to be so short lived, with not much time to get out and enjoy it all.

Despite his job, moving in the dark underbelly of crime, he had begun to lose the stomach for it. A person could only absorb so much horror, murder, tortured bodies, and young people cruelly cut down in the prime of their life.

He had seen enough depravation of what one person could do to another to last him a lifetime. The gut-wrenching grief of the parents, sisters, brothers and other family members left behind to try and deal with the horrific truth of what had happened to their loved ones in their final hours. The young children who had gone missing and never been found, leaving only a gaping hole and lots of question marks.

Jack topped up his glass and gazed out over the slate grey mountain range, shielding the verdant wine growing farms from the harshness of inclement weather.

Franschhoek. The food and wine capital of South Africa. It had produced international award-winning wines and was famous for its exquisite restaurants.

The ancient vineyards marched straight and tall across the valleys in front of him shimmering in the October heat, rose bushes planted at the end of each row which would reveal any disease before it penetrated the precious vines.

A vintage tram, with two open carriages', wound its daily way through the valley, loaded with tourists, stopping at vineyards, for a wine tasting, or lunch at one of the many acclaimed restaurants. He'd even taken the trip himself.

The town had a definite French feel to it, inherited from their forefathers, the Huguenots, who had strong French blood running through their veins. So much so every year, Bastille Day, the 14th July, was celebrated with all things French.

Jack never tired of driving through town, delighted South Africans drove on the left-hand side of the road, the proper side, as they did in the UK.

With its backdrop of majestic mountains, towering oak trees and exquisite vineyards, one producing a label called Angel's Tears, well, as far as he was concerned it didn't get much better, or romantic, than that.

The town was awash with elegant restaurants, and outside bars fringed with umbrellas to ward off the harsh sun in the summer months. Family run farm stalls, antique shops, cafés, art galleries, chocolatiers, and boutique clothing shops. There was a brief nod to the small chain supermarket, the obligatory petrol station, although a little out of town, and the popular steak house for the more robust palates.

Jack who appreciated all thing *haute cuisine*, liked nothing better than to sink his teeth into a thick steak accompanied by crispy golden fries and crunchy fried onions at his local steak house.

A lasting memorial to the good folk who, along with the French forefathers who had founded the town, stood stoically tall, reaching for the sky, and, as elsewhere in these smaller towns in South Africa, the glorious white spired Dutch Reformed Church, which epitomised the indomitable spirit of the people who had come here over the past three centuries, their roots deeply embedded in the soil.

Jack could see the classic Cape Dutch architecture in abundance, from modest houses in the town, to the majestic manor homes on the wine farms.

The curvaceous, ornately rounded gables, trimmed thatched roofs, thick white walls to keep the heat out and the coolness in, dark green mahogany wooden shutters, with immaculate gardens gracing the rolling lawns in front.

On returning to South Africa, Jack had lived in Cape Town, hopeful his fledgling relationship would blossom and lead to something more permanent.

Circumstances had dictated otherwise and after two months he had chosen to live outside the city. Franschhoek was the perfect place, only an hour from the city, and an easy and pleasant drive when he needed to be there for his work, or meeting up with fellow journalists at one of their famous watering holes. The Mount Nelson being a particular favourite with its endless stream of the rich and famous from all over the world.

Jack sipped his beer and stroked the head of the dog who had adopted him.

He'd been walking through town when a squat, scruffy looking dog had decided to join him. Its coat the colour of cappuccino coffee. Its little brown ears bent over big brown eyes, fringed with white eyelashes.

The dog had followed him home and, Jack thought, liked the place and thought he would like to live there too.

With no collar Jack had no idea who the dog might belong to. He took a photo of him, had some flyers printed out and handed them around town. No-one claimed the little fellow. He liked dogs, although his idea of a proper dog was a Labrador or a Retriever. He had grown up in the country where his parents always had working dogs.

When he had moved to London a dog had been out of the question. His rabbit hutch of an apartment was too cramped for him, let alone a dog, and his job had him travelling all over the country as he chased his stories.

But this little chap had a lot of appeal and so Jack adopted him and called him Benji. He'd taken him to the local vet for his shots, and to check if he was chipped, which he wasn't. He had bought him a collar and a tag, a dog bed, which he never used, preferring his new owner's bed, it was comfortable and he could spread himself out more. Benji stayed.

Jack fondled his brown ears as they both stared out over the vineyards in the distance in compatible silence.

Jack had uploaded his latest story to Harry, his editor. There were a few other intriguing stories he was keen to follow up, nothing particularly inspiring and he was anxious to find something more exciting, other than writing his regular Sunday column.

The God of news must have heard him. His phone vibrated on the table.

Unknown caller.

Jack snatched it up. "Jack Taylor here."

Her voice was strong and business-like. "Ah, Mr Taylor. My name is Caroline Gordon. I was given your name by my manager Jabu. I think you know him?"

Jack smiled into the phone. "Indeed, I do. How is he, it's ages since I saw him last."

"Quite well, thank you. Mr Taylor, I own a lodge called Infinity, based in the Sabi Sands near the Kruger."

"Yes, I've heard of it, and please call me Jack. Your lodge has been featured in many magazines, it's hard to miss. It looks quite something."

"Jack, if you have some time, I'd like you to come and spend a few days here."

Jack was taken aback. He'd never been on safari and like so many people, he was keen to go on one. But even on his generous retainer from the newspaper, and his expense account, the prices of staying at any of the top lodges, Infinity being one of them, made his eyes water, especially as the rates were quoted in American dollars because of the weakness and fluctuation of the local currency. He knew Harry would have a heart attack if he were to put something like that on his expense account.

"Well, Miss Gordon, it's a most generous, and may I say, unexpected offer. But why would you want to invite me, if I might ask?"

*****

Caroline smiled into the phone. Mr Jack Taylor was interested. All she had to do now was reel him in and she knew what she said next would have him booking his flight.

"Please call me Caroline, Jack. A few weeks ago, a child was found at our water hole, she's probably around six years old. The thing is no-one knows where she came from, who she is, or where her family is. The authorities, and her doctors, have allowed us to keep her here and only here. We were wondering if perhaps you could help us trace her family. You'll have to come here to do that. I'll cover all your expenses, of course."

"Have you offered this to any other journalists Caroline? A private detective perhaps?"

"No. It was Jabu who suggested I contact you. No other journalist knows where the child is living at the moment, and certainly we haven't hired a private detective."

*****

Jack placed his phone back on the table and rubbed his hands together. Now here was a story he could get his teeth into with the bonus of staying at one of the most famous game lodges in South Africa, if not the whole of Africa. A lodge he knew a little about except the prices and the photographs in the many international glossy magazines.

Like all the other journalists here he had heard about the child who had appeared out of the bush in a bad condition. He had been intrigued and keen to follow the story. But the child had been whisked away to a hospital, heavily guarded to keep the media out, then disappeared from the hospital without a trace. No-one had any idea where she had been taken to.

It was assumed her family had been found and were keeping a low profile after such a traumatic event, with no story to follow the media lost interest.

Jack felt the familiar sizzle coursing through his veins. It looked like an exclusive for him, something he would insist on. He was now the only journalist who knew where the child was.

He picked up his phone and scrolled through the few airlines that flew to the area where the lodge was situated. Within minutes he had booked his flight, then he sent a text to Caroline giving her the details.

With Benji following he made his way to his computer to find out as much as he could about what happened on the night the lodge had received its unlikely visitor.

There was precious little information. The police had kept a tight lid on the case. A photo had been circulated showing an emaciated child, the eyes and cheeks sunken, the head completely shaved. He doubted whether the child's mother would even recognise her.

But the mother and father had to be out there somewhere.

Benji watched him, blinking anxiously, as he threw his clothes into a leather bag; shirts, shorts and trousers in muted tones, khaki, olive green and cream. Although he'd never been on safari, he had seen enough wild-life programmes to know bright colours were out, one had to blend in with the colours of the bush and not spook the animals.

He bent and patted the dog who was now lying down looking despondent. "Don't look so worried Benji. I'll only be gone a few days. Daisy will look after you until I get back. By the way do you understand English, Benji? Or only Afrikaans? It could go a long way in helping to understand why you look so puzzled all the time, and don't take a blind bit of notice if I give you any instructions on acceptable behaviour."

The dog looked up with slitted eyes then closed them again.

Jack smiled to himself. He had only been in the cottage a few days when there had been a rapid knock at the front door. Standing there was a short wiry woman of an indeterminate age, a white scarf covering her hair and tied behind her neck. Her wrinkled face the colour of an old walnut.

Grinning at him, with hardly a tooth in sight, she had announced her name was Daisy and she was going to come and work for him and look after him.

She had edged past him and surveyed the somewhat chaotic sitting room with its empty take away cartons, unwashed glasses and clothes hanging over the backs of chairs. Newspapers and magazines were strewn everywhere.

With her hands on her hips she had, clicked her tongue with disapproval. "I start here, there is much cleaning to be done, Daisy will be doing these things."

Benji had rushed up to her his tail wagging enthusiastically. Bending down Daisy had patted his head. "What is the name of this scruffy dog?"

Taken aback Jack had muttered his dog's name. The woman was like a mini tornado.

"Where is kitchen, sir?"

Jack had run his hands through his untidy hair and frowned at her.

"How do you know I don't already have someone to look after me Daisy?"

She had thrown her head back and given a surprisingly loud and hearty laugh, given her size.

"This is small town. We people know everything. You have no-one. Hah, but now you have Daisy. Kitchen?"

He had taken her on. Now his home was immaculate. No more dust, everything gleamed, his clothes washed and ironed. His shopping done, his evening meal prepared for him.

Sometimes he had to pinch himself, this certainly was a giant step away from his tiny flat in London. He had never had a housekeeper of his own before. His parents had had someone who used to come in once a week and "do" for them, but that was about it.

Moving to South Africa had given him an elevated lifestyle his friends and colleagues could only dream about, and envy.

Jack snapped his bag shut, fed Benji, retrieved his dinner from the oven and took it through to the patio where Daisy had laid the outside table for him. He sat down, watching the sun slide down over the mountain range, throwing the vineyards into sharp relief.

Jack was a happy man, despite his failed relationship. Tomorrow he would be off chasing what promised to be an intriguing story, meeting the mystery child who had disappeared from the headlines, and finally realising a dream of staying at an exclusive game lodge in the middle of the bush.

After dinner he would make a call to his editor Harry in London. Harry was going to like this potential story. It had all the ingredients he loved.

Chapter Thirty-Five

Jack's flight made a rather ungainly landing at Skukuza airport before making its way to a flat-topped building. A wind was blowing, the temperature in the mid-thirties. November was a hot month.

Unlike the UK where the shops would already be hanging out the Christmas tinsel, playing the Carols, their shelves bulging with glitz and glitter. Here there was no sign of it at all.

Jack looked around with interest as he and the other passengers made their way to the arrival's hall. It was unlike any other airport he had been to. It had the feel of a bush airport, a tantalising introduction to what lay ahead. The hot summer wind blew his hair around, the heat instantly drying the skin on his face, stretching it across his cheeks.

Formalities were efficiently completed by smiling officials, and he made his way to the flapping skirts of the carousal to collect his bag. There was an air of excitement with all the passengers, many of them, judging by their accents, from different parts of the world. This was the moment they had been waiting for, their long-planned safari, their trip of a life time, was about to begin.

Tour guides and game rangers, appropriately dressed in khaki safari clothes, held up name boards waiting to greet their clients.

Jack spotted Jabu and made his way through the excited chatter of his fellow passengers.

Jabu, a broad smile on his brown face, lifted his arm when he spotted Jack. They shook hands enthusiastically. "Good to see you again Jabu. Been a while. How are you?"

They exchanged pleasantries as Jabu led him out to the four-wheel drive safari vehicle, with the brass *Infinity* logo discreetly running along the door.

Jack threw his bag into the seat behind and climbed in next to Jabu.

Jabu handed him an ice-cold bottle of water which he drained eagerly. "Phew, thanks. A lot hotter up here than I expected for this time of the year."

He pulled his sunglasses out of his shirt pocket and put them on, then jammed a khaki baseball cap on his head.

Jabu started the engine, using the heel of his hand against the blistering heat of the steering wheel. "Yes, it's pretty hot today. The lodge is about half an hour's drive from here. Might be a bit of a game drive, en route, although most animals will be dozing in the shade, it's a bit too hot even for them to be out at the moment.

"But we'll see kudu, impala, buffalo, giraffe, zebra etc. The big cats will be resting up before going out tonight to scare the hell out of their dinner."

Signs were clustered together as they left the dusty airport, pointing to all the various game lodges in the area.

"I don't see any signs giving directions to your lodge Jabu?"

"No, you won't. It's not that kind of lodge. All our guests are collected personally either by me or one of the other rangers. No-one drives in with their own vehicle, but they can fly in by private charter to our private landing strip. Caroline's rules."

"She sounds, um, quite strong willed, judging by our telephone call."

Jabu laughed. "She's strong willed alright. A tough business woman, but soft as a kitten inside, or should I say cub. She's passionate about her lodge and it's infectious. Between us we've put together a dynamic team. Best move I ever made, coming to work for her."

He turned left down a dirt road as they made steady progress towards the famous lodge. Jabu slowed as three giraffe made their regal way across the road in front of them. They stopped and gazed haughtily down at the vehicle and two passengers. Jack was silent as he caught his first ever glimpse of these wild animals in their natural habitat. Jabu turned off the ignition and waited for the giraffe to move on.

The only sound was the ticking of the engine as it started to cool, the smell of sage assailed Jack's nostrils, obviously wild he thought and not out of a packet, he breathed in deeply.

"Magnificent," he whispered.

Jabu smiled. "Wild animals in their own environment always have this effect on people who are seeing them for the first time. Like children opening Christmas presents."

The giraffe moved slowly on with their sloping swaying gait, stopping to pluck a leaf or two from some of the tall trees, then, as suddenly as they had arrived, they disappeared into the dense bush.

Jabu started up the vehicle and they carried on. He pointed out a herd of kudu, the males displaying their majestic curling horns. Impala startled by the appearance of the vehicle, moved away in alarm, leaping gracefully into the air, a choreography of dance which would have put any ballet dancers to shame. They settled some distance away and carried on grazing, their short white tails flickering, or tucked neatly between their back legs.

Eight warthogs marched in single file a short way in front of them, looking important, their stiff tails standing straight up like periscopes, as though they were on their way to a business meeting.

Jack took a sip from his bottle. Lost for words at the beauty surrounding them. Jabu gave him his moment, not saying anything to distract him from his first visit to the bush and the sightings of the game around them.

The wide gates of the lodge were ahead of them. The distinctive logo displayed on the curved stone walls either side of the gate. The guard came around to Jack's side of the vehicle and handed him a clipboard. He saw his name and hesitated.

"It's a formality in case you get eaten by a lion Jack," Jabu said laughing. "It's an indemnity form. Caroline hates them, but each guest must sign the form before entering a private game lodge. It's a legal thing."

Jack signed next to his name with the date and time. He handed the board back to the guard who touched his cap and swung open the wide gates.

The lodge loomed ahead in front of them. Jabu brought the landcruiser to a halt in front of it.

"Before we go in Jack, I must tell you that Caroline knows the story of my family. I had to tell her before she went to Cape Town to interview interior designers for the lodge before it was built. Kia was one of the people she interviewed – she got the job. She rarely comes to the lodge now, so you won't bump into her. But she still works for Caroline out of Cape Town. I know things didn't work out for you both, of course Kia told me what happened. I'll leave you to decide how you want to play it with Caroline."

Jack nodded but didn't say anything.

"So here we are Jack. Welcome to Infinity. Follow me and I'll show you to your suite. Let me take your bag."

Jack whistled softly. This was luxury beyond even his vivid imagination. Two bronze life-sized leopards stood guard at the front of the lodge; soft white curtains fluttered either side of them.

Jack noticed the cool white flagstone floor, the Arabian style bed along one wall, the apothecary's chest with its gleaming brass handles, with an ancient typewriter and adding machine perched on top.

Jack looked around for the check-in desk, and not seeing one he trotted after Jabu.

Walking down the immaculately treated wooden decks he glimpsed glass suites nestling between the tall trees. Infinity pools glinting in front of each one.

Jabu waited for Jack to catch up. "Caroline has put you in our star attraction."

Jack looked at him puzzled, but unable to keep the wide grin off his face.

Jabu pointed up into a tree set a short distance from the main suites. "It's the star bed suite. The only place available tonight. It's reserved for our guests if they want to spend a night under the stars. It has all the necessary facilities," he looked at Jack innocently. "The only thing missing is a roof."

Jack looked up, then took off his sunglasses. "Looks like it's floating to me. How do you get up there?"

"There's a wooden stairway around the side, that's how you get up there."

Jack hesitated. "No roof you said?"

"Nope. After dinner one of the rangers will escort you here, then leave you. But, don't worry, you'll be quite safe. There's a guard who will stay all night. He'll make sure you'll be alright."

Jack took off his cap, running his hand through his slightly damp hair, then wiped his face, before putting back on. "Okay, well if you say so."

Jabu dropped his bag at the bottom of the tree. "Someone will take your luggage up. Let's go and find a spot for a glass of home-made lemonade and some lunch, shall we. Caroline will join us," he checked his watch, "in about fifteen minutes."

Once again Jack followed him down the wooden walkways and into the dining area where guests were enjoying their lunch. He nodded at the ones who looked up as they walked by.

"Hey, Jabu!" some of them called out, he lifted his arm and smiled at them. Clearly a popular host with his guests.

Chapter Thirty-Six

Jabu indicated Jack should take a seat with the view across the expansive waterhole. A few impala were drinking at the far side and a small herd of six elephants. A troop of baboons paraded arrogantly by, eliciting a sharp bark at anything they didn't like the look of, before perching on an untidy outcrop of rocks near the elephants.

Jack was still grinning. "Not a bad place for a spot of lunch. I'm impressed Jabu, seriously impressed. I've never seen anything like this in my life."

Jabu waited until the waiter had brought them a jug of lemonade, packed with ice cubes, a few sprigs of mint and two tall glasses. He poured their drinks then padded away.

"One thing Jack. Caroline knows the story you followed about my family. That's all she knows, the hard facts that anyone could read up about. But nothing personal – nothing about you and Kia. I'd like to keep it like that. Can we agree on this?"

Jack nodded and sat back. "Right. Let's get to work. Tell me about the girl. Where did you first see her?"

Jabu pointed to the far side of the water hole. "Over there, where the elephants are. It was dark, but the water is discreetly lit at night, so as not to disturb the animals. She appeared out of the bush, tiny little thing, then she collapsed near the water hole."

He continued the story, telling Jack how he had carried the child back to the lodge, the long night with Olivia as they fought to save her life, and the helicopter and medics who had whisked her away to hospital the next day.

Jack made notes in his book, which he always carried in his shirt pocket.

Jabu stood up. "Ah, Caroline. This is Jack Taylor."

Jack hastily pushed his chair back and stood. "Jack, this is Caroline Gordon."

Caroline shook his hand and he found himself looking into a large pair of intelligent brown eyes, fringed with dark lashes. A spattering of tiny freckles spread across her tanned cheeks. Her mouth was devoid of any lipstick, wide and smiling, displaying even white teeth. Her straight dark blonde hair skimming her shoulders.

"So, I finally get to meet the famous Jack Taylor. Welcome to our lodge. Thank you for coming so quickly. We need all the help we can get at the moment."

Jack took off his sunglasses. "And I'm more than happy to help Caroline, but there is just one thing before we proceed. As you know I wrote the story about Kia and Jabu. There were a lot of people involved. When it was all over Jabu's family and I agreed that we would not discuss the story with anyone in the future.

"I made that promise. I would like to concentrate on what we need to do now, with the little girl. That's what I need to focus on, not any other story. That's how I work."

Caroline gestured for him to sit. "Of course, I understand. Now, shall we eat?"

The waiter spread their lunch on the table, alongside crisp white linen napkins and delicate square white plates.

Caesar salad drenched in its creamy dressing, a platter of shelled prawns, with a garlic or mayonnaise dip, thinly sliced avocadoes drizzled in olive oil, a crisp golden baguette, sliced to perfection and some dressed crab.

"Dig in Jack, I expect you're hungry. Airline snacks leave much to be desired, so I hope you'll enjoy your lunch." She cast a critical eye over the food. "You're not allergic to shellfish, I hope?"

He shook his head eyeing the food.

Caroline rolled her eyes. "You have no idea how careful we have to be with people's fussy eating habits these days. Everyone seems to have an allergy, or an intolerance to something, can't eat this or that, because of whatever. It can be a nightmare for the chefs."

Jack rubbed his hands together in anticipation of the feast laid in front of him, then spread his napkin over his knees.

"I can eat anything Caroline, you won't have any trouble with me. But if I should break out in a rash, I believe you have a fully qualified nursing sister lurking in the bush who can fix anything, right?"

Caroline laughed, then blew her fringe away from her eyes. "I see you've done your homework. Grace is our nursing sister, brought up in the Kenyan bush so nothing much she can't fix, I can tell you.

"We employed her to get Meggy released from hospital. The doctors and authorities insisted we had someone with a medical background to look after her, otherwise the child would have been fostered out, and we weren't going to have any of that were we Jabu."

Jabu shook his head. "No way. We've all become attached to our girl, she's not easy, but there's something about her…"

*****

The waiter came and took away their empty plates. Jack dabbed at his lips with his napkin and sat back, well satisfied.

He reached into his pocket for his note book again. "Meggy? Did she tell you her name?"

Caroline shook her head. "She barely speaks, sort of whispers. Grace thinks she's blocking things out, unable to face or verbalise what happened to her. She cries a great deal, it's heart-breaking. The only person she reacts to is Jabu, she's not hostile or angry when he's around."

Caroline went on to explain her fear of walking, her need to be carried everywhere initially, her constant insistence she was happy.

"So, she didn't tell you her name. You gave her one."

"Yes. Well, we had to call her something." Caroline said, raising her eyebrows.

"She seems to trust Jabu. Grace thinks it's because somehow she knows he rescued her and looked after her, with Olivia."

Jack frowned as he made more notes. "I'd like to speak to Grace, of course, and meet Meggy."

"Absolutely. Grace knows you're arriving today and she's anxious to talk to you."

"Good. I'd like to observe her whilst she's with Grace. I think it would be useful if Jabu was around as well for that. I'll need to take some photos of her. Obviously, the child trusts Jabu and may open up a bit more if he's around. I don't want to be too obvious in case she clams up. After all I'll just be another stranger to her."

Jabu nodded in agreement. "Good idea, a one on one with you would definitely make her clam up and if she did, she will suck on her thumb and stare at you with those big eyes of hers. It can be a little disconcerting."

Caroline stood, followed by Jack and Jabu. "Let me have a chat with Grace and see how she wants to play this. Make yourself at home

Jack. If you need anything a member of staff will be in attendance," she paused.

"I want you to give me your word nothing will be leaked to the press about Meggy being here."

"You have my word, Caroline. However, if we solve the mystery of her past, there will be a story, and I need your assurance it will be mine exclusively. Deal?"

Caroline put out her hand. "Deal."

Jabu made to leave. "I must get back to work and make sure my guests are all happy, don't want anyone to find a ten-foot python wrapped around their bath tub."

Jack blanched. "You're kidding right. I don't mind facing an axe wielding killer, but snakes freak me out – can't stand them. If I see one on television, I immediately change the channel. If I'm sleeping somewhere with no roof…"

"Relax Jack, I'm only kidding. Snakes are more scared of us than we are of them. I've never seen one at the lodge, well one or two, smallish ones."

Jack lowered himself back into his chair as he watched Jabu walk away, his shoulders shuddering with laughter.

Jack liked a laugh as much as anyone but snakes? He shuddered, hoping Jabu had been teasing him.

He took out his notebook and spent the rest of the afternoon writing notes, and questions he needed to ask. Contact numbers and names of all who had come into contact with Meggy since she arrived at the waterhole, especially Doctor Olivia Hamilton who was now back in London where she lived and practiced.

He looked across the water, glinting in the afternoon sun. The lodge was now quiet and he assumed guests were having a nap before going out on an afternoon game drive.

More elephants had appeared, bringing their babies with them. He watched them unable to believe where he was.

Occasionally, feeling brave one or two would dart out on wobbly legs and splash into the water, squealing and waving their rubbery trunks around, before running and skidding in the mud, tripping over their feet, some falling over, then back to the protection of the herd and their mothers.

Jack could hear the herd rumbling to each other, communicating, the sound coming from deep within their massive bodies, reminding him of an impending thunder storm, or the distant approach of an underground train.

He looked out over the thick bush with its high trees, the rolling hills, and the distant range of mountains, shimmering in the heat of the day, but didn't allow himself to relax and absorb his surroundings. He would need someone to fly him low over the area surrounding the lodge. The child had not walked into the bush by herself from the nearest town. He would need a detailed map of the area. Jack loved maps. His fellow journalists laughed at him, telling him maps were obsolete, but he doggedly purchased them, when necessary, always confused by how neat and compact they were when he bought them, but how it was impossible for him to return them to their original shape once opened.

He needed to visit any towns outside of the private reserve, speak to the locals, see if anyone remembered the little girl, although remembering having seen her photo, in the newspaper, he had his doubts. But maybe a more updated photo of her would help.

He also needed to speak to the police officers who were handling this case, but doubted, as a journalist, they would discuss it with him.

His mind wandered back to Detective Piet Joubert, the now retired police officer who had been involved in what had turned out to be his last, and most spectacular, cold case. Perhaps, with his thirty-year-old network of contacts in the country, Piet would be willing to help him.

He smiled at the memory of Joubert's scruffy office, the bad-tempered cat and possibly the most uncomfortable chair in all of South Africa.

The cat had been called *Voetsak*. At the time he had been puzzled by the number of dogs and cats in the small town of Willow Drift who had the same name, and why they'd all run off when being called.

Joubert had nearly fallen off his chair laughing, when Jack had asked him.

"*Ag*, Jack," he had said. "You Englishmen know nothing of us here in South Africa. *Voetsak* means *fok off.*"

Jack was glad of the explanation, otherwise he might well have called his recently acquired dog the same name. With eleven official languages in the country, he wasn't even sure what language Benji understood. However, his companion was smart, he would answer to anything as long as there was food around and a comfortable bed to lie on, his as it turned out.

He pulled out his phone, he would check in with Daisy and see how the dog was and if all was well at the cottage.

"Mr Yak." Daisy's loud voice, with its sing song lilt, travelled over the bush in front of him. "Benji is fine, eating his dinner, sleeping on your bed. But he is sad without you, but, hey, we make a plan. I take him for his walk in the evening.

"Tomorrow Daisy is cleaning all windows. Also, my cousin is coming to fix your garden, it is a big mess."

Jack smiled and said goodbye to her. It amused him how some of these people in the more rural areas could never pronounce his name. He was destined to be Mr Yak to all of them.

A waiter sidled up to him, delivering a note on a silver dish. He opened the envelope. It was from Caroline.

"Jabu will be coming to Grace's cottage to say goodnight to Meggy at about 6. Grace, of course, will be here. She feels this would be a good time for you to meet Meggy. She would have had her supper and be ready for bed. Jabu will pick you up from the star suite.

The waiter waited patiently whilst he read the note. "May I show you to your suite Mr Yak."

Jack smiled as he gathered his notes and phone. "Thank you. I need to change and freshen up a bit. Please tell Jabu I'll meet him out on the deck where we had lunch."

Jack followed the waiter as he led him back along the wooden walkway, finally stopping at the bottom of the tree. He indicated Jack should ascend. Taking a deep breath Jack mounted the short flight of steps. When he reached the top, his mouth dropped open. The sliding glass doors were open, a vast bed lay in front of him, festooned with billowing white mosquito nets. His clothes had been unpacked from his safari bag and laid out on a leather trunk at the end of the bed.

He looked at the sky above. The air was unwavering, the leaves of the tree still. A dove called; its mate answered.

A curved wall indicated a possible bathroom. Jack poked his head around and found an elegant shower, with a head the size of a frying pan, open to the skies above. A carved branch held a bar of soap, shampoo, conditioner and some body lotion, and his shaving kit. Two large white fluffy towels were hung over another carved branch and a thick towelling gown. So far, no snakes.

Unable to resist, after his long journey and hot afternoon, Jack peeled off his dusty clothes and stepped into the shower. The water cascaded over his body as he reached for the soap. Wiping the water from his eyes he looked at it. Embedded in the soap was a perfectly preserved flower, its delicate white petals surrounding its yellow centre. He rubbed the soap over his body inhaling its exquisite fragrance. He had seen this flower before on his travels through the country. Frangipani.

Jack shampooed his hair vigorously then rinsed it, stepping out he reached for one of the towels. Wrapping it around his waist he made his way back to where his clothes were laid out. As he dressed, he looked at his room with no roof.

Already he was feeling the magic of the place - it was another world. A world people could only dream about, unless they were extremely wealthy.

Changing into long beige trousers and a loose white shirt, he rolled the sleeves back to his elbows, slipped his feet into his safari boots then reached for his comb. His hair lay quite neatly whilst it was wet, but he knew once it dried, which would be minutes in the hot air, it would spring back to its usual unruliness.

Descending the steps, he made his way back to the seating place at the water hole. He checked his watch. Ten minutes before Jabu was due.

The same waiter who had shown him to his suite sidled up, appearing from nowhere. "Something to drink Mr Yak?"

"Not right now, thank you." He glanced at his watch, "Jabu should be here any minute."

"He is on his way, Mr Yak, he will be here shortly. I have told him you are waiting here."

Jack looked out over the dusky bush. A large black and white bird hovered over the water. He squinted trying to identify it. Ah, yes, a fish eagle, it's haunting cry, leaving him in no doubt. He waited and within seconds the bird had plummeted into the water, emerging with a wet silver fish, wriggling between its talons, before flying off to enjoy his dinner.

"Hey, Jack. Let's go and meet Meggy, shall we."

Jabu led him through the camp and a little beyond where a cluster of cottages, with thatched roofs, nestled amongst the trees, almost hidden from the main lodge.

A tall woman, her hair pulled back, stood on the deck of one of them, waiting to greet him. "Hello Jack, I'm Grace. Come and meet Moses and Meggy."

She turned and Jack saw the fat blonde braid of her hair snaking down her straight back. Both her wrists sporting colourful bead bracelets, a single brown and cream one enhanced one of her ankles.

Jabu went ahead of them. Jack heard the voice of the little girl. "Abu, Abu!"

Jack watched as he swung the girl around before carefully putting her on the sofa. "Hey, little one, this is a good friend of mine, his name is Jack."

Jack looked at her. She was slight, and quite tiny. Her big blue eyes turned towards him; her thumb immediately went to her mouth. Her hair was gone, but a small fuzz of light-coloured hair was growing back.

Grace introduced him to Moses. "It is a good thing you are here Mr Yak, you are most welcome." He cupped his hand to his elbow as a mark of respect.

Jack shook the old man's hand, then turned and spotted a chair a little way from the sofa where the girl was sitting, watching him.

Grace sat at the round table where books and drawing pads were stacked, in a small tin bucket a kaleidoscope of bright crayons were clustered.

"Now Meggy, I'm going to show our visitor the beautiful drawing you made for us, would you like that?"

She shook her head. "Appy, no," she whispered.

"Alright then, let's not do it, if it will make you unhappy. Moses is going to have his dinner now. Jabu and Jack are going to stay whilst I read you a story."

Grace settled next to the child on the sofa and opened a book. The child glanced at the book then stared at Jack again.

Jack, being an expert at body language after studying some of the worst criminals in British history, adults and adolescents alike, and yes children, watched her closely.

He could see the pent-up anger in her body, or perhaps the denial of who she was now. For a so called six-year-old, her vocabulary was almost non-existent, but the odd word she had whispered was perhaps with a trace of a lisp.

He had often dealt with children who had gone through traumatic situations in their young lives. He studied her closely. Caroline had told him the child cried a lot, could erupt into a temper tantrum, throwing her teddy bear and story books across the room in a rage.

144

Jack understood this. A normal child was given to tantrums, everyone knew this. But a six-year-old would only display those feelings if she, or he, was misunderstood or frustrated. Unable to communicate how they felt.

He watched and waited until the story was finished. Grace closed the book. Jabu stood, glancing at his watch. His guests would be returning from their game drive, and he needed to be there when they did. Dropping a kiss on the child's shaven head he left.

Grace shook her head, looking frustrated. The child continued to stare at Jack, sucking her thumb, rocking back and forth.

Jack stood. "It was nice to meet you Meggy. I enjoyed the story, did you?"

She let go of her thumb. "Appy," she said, angrily, "appy, appy, appy!" She ran to her bedroom where they both heard her howling and screaming with rage.

Grace crumpled in her chair, rubbing her forehead. "Sorry Jack, she wasn't at her best this evening. I sometimes think I'll never get through to her. It's hard to deal with a child full of rage – very hard. So difficult to get close to someone so full of anger. She keeps saying she's happy but she so clearly isn't."

Jack put his notebook back in his pocket. "Grace, I'm going to help in any way I can. I have a lot of contacts. I'm used to dealing with children traumatised by life, not caused by them but by others. Don't give up on her. She needs you."

He was surprised to see the exhausted tears in the woman's eyes, flooding the blueness of them.

"Come on Grace, together w*e can* do this. If we don't find her family then the authorities will have no choice but to take her away from you and place her with foster parents. It would be the worst thing that could happen to her right now.

"I'll find out what happened to her, I'm good at what I do. But I need you to help me. I need you to stay with her, to keep exploring her mind, you're the only one who can unlock it."

Grace swiped her hand across her eyes. "I know what you're saying is right, but she seems so furious all the time. She cries so much. I can't get her to talk to me. She keeps telling me she's happy but she isn't."

Jack stood. "Look I don't know how things work here, but how about we have dinner together later. Maybe Moses can come and look after her. We need to talk all this through, I need as much information as you can give me, from a medical point of view."

Grace stood up. "I'll help as much as I can. Jabu will be able to find us a table in the dining area, away from the other guests. I'll organise it."

Jack turned to walk away. Then he stopped suddenly, and turned back. Thinking, with various accents, how words and names sounded different.

He heard the voice of Daisy, her inability to pronounce his name and all the others who had struggled.

He looked at Grace. "May I?" he inclined his head towards the child's bedroom. She nodded frowning slightly.

Meggy was curled in a foetal position, her thumb in her mouth, her face to the wall. She didn't turn when he sat on the side of her bed.

Grace watched anxiously from the door, her hand to her mouth

Jack turned the rigid child towards him and gently pulled the thumb from her mouth. She looked at him, anger, frustration, and hopelessness in her swollen eyes, before scowling and turning away from him.

Using his hand he turned her face back to him again, and held it there. "I know who you are. Your name isn't Appy is it? That word you use all the time?"

"Your name is Gabby."

She shook her head – no.

"Then I think your name is Abby."

The child threw herself into his arms.

Chapter Thirty-Seven

Over dinner Grace talked to Jack about Abby.

"So clever of you Jack, to figure out her name. Now so many things are beginning to make sense. All the tears, tantrums and rages were because she was so frustrated, we couldn't work out she was telling us her name, not that she was happy.

"Oh, her face when you said her name. It's something I'll never forget."

"Not clever, I know so many of the locals here can't pronounce my name, so I worked my way through the alphabet to see what name came close to Appy. It had to be Abby or Gabby."

Jack brushed a moth from the tablecloth. "Is there another word she uses on a fairly regular basis?"

Grace finished the last mouthful of her kudu steak, dabbed at her mouth with a napkin, and sat back in her chair.

"There is another word, or two. She often says *scusie*. But not in the right context. I think she's saying *excuse me.* But there's really nothing to excuse her for.

"The teddy bear Caroline bought for Abby? She seems to hate it. Now I'm wondering if it might be because we can't call it the name, she wants us to call it."

"Could be. I'll give it some thought."

Grace looked at her watch. "I must get back and let Moses get some sleep. So, are you going to take Abby's case on, try and find out who she is?"

Jack smiled at her. "Of course, that's why I'm here. I'll be depending on you a great deal to feed back any new words Abby might come out with. Make a note of them, no matter how they sound, write them down phonetically."

Grace fiddled with her braid. "I'm not sure she's able to speak Jack. She understands what we're saying but seems to struggle with her own words. The mind is complex. Shock, as I'm sure you know from your experiences, can render a person speechless.

"In fact, it's called *speechless terror* where a patient can't articulate their feelings. I think this is what has happened to Abby."

Jack waited as the waiter cleared their plates away. "I think you're right there. It was seen often after both the great world wars and the others that came after. Soldiers came back in a state of shock and refused to speak about their experiences, shell shocked they called it then, post-traumatic stress is what they call it now. I guess they felt if they didn't talk about it, then it hadn't happened, or perhaps the nightmare of what they had seen would go away.

"My job will be to find out what happened to Abby. She might have come from Zimbabwe, Mozambique or even Botswana. All those countries are fairly close by. One thing is for sure. She could only have come into this area either by boat, a vehicle or a small plane, therefore she had others with her, her parents and possible siblings, and a pilot, if she came by plane. Perhaps one of her parents was the pilot. But where are they?"

Grace shook her head. "No-one leaves a child on her own under any circumstances. My gut feel tells me there was some kind of accident and Abby was the only survivor."

Chapter Thirty-Eight

Jack was escorted back to his star suite by Jabu.
"Sleep well, Jack. See you in the morning. Oh, by the way, the star suite is booked tomorrow. I'm not sure how long you need to be here, but we'll be moving you into one of the cottages near to Grace and Abby."

"No problem. I'd like to spend another day with them. Then I should head back. I need to do a lot of research and use some of my contacts, see what I can come up with.

"I'm going to base myself in Hazyview, initially. It seems a good place to start. A decent sized town and close to all the reserves. I'll also work my way through some of the surrounding towns, see what I can come up with."

Jack slid open the glass doors then climbed into the sumptuous double bed. He lay back on the mountain of soft pillows and looked up at the sky.

The stars were glorious against the deep navy sky. Having lived all his life in England he had never seen anything quite so spectacular. He felt as though he was floating high above the earth in another universe.

The sound of frogs and cicadas burped and chirped all around him. In the distance he could the rasping throaty call of a lion, a primitive noise, making the hair on his arms stand up.

Then the eerie *whoop whoop* and disturbing high-pitched cackle of giggling hyenas, was followed by the deep sawing cough of a leopard. An owl called to his mate, a lonely haunting sound.

At the water hole he could hear the grunting belly laughs of hippo, the splashing of water as they made their way onto land where they would browse through the night. A male baboon gave an agitated warning bark, then another, alerting his troop to predators.

There was a rustling in the trees and Jack looked around nervously. A small monkey with a black face and light grey body fur was sitting on a branch watching him.

Jack sat up wondering if the furry creature was planning on spending the night with him. The monkey bared his teeth and Jack hoped he was smiling and not cross.

"*Voetsak,*" he hissed. The monkey stared blankly at him then scampered back through the trees, the shawl of leaves shuddering in its wake.

Jack smiled. Good word. It seemed to work with not only dogs and cats but monkeys as well.

He turned off the lamp and lay back, mesmerised. Wondering if he would ever get to sleep with all the night sounds around him, the stars above were soporific and he felt his eyes closing, the lullaby of the warm land all around him pulling him into sleep.

The whisper of a little girl's footsteps following him into his dreams…

Chapter Thirty-Nine

Jack took numerous shots of Abby with his phone, as she lay on the sofa sucking her thumb, or drew rough pictures with her bucket of crayons at the table.

Caroline had arranged for a private Cessna and bush pilot, Toby, the one she knew and trusted not to mention the child or the flight to anyone else, to fly Jack over the area where Abby was found.

At Jack's request, Caroline had asked Toby to bring the best map he had of the whole of the Kruger Park and Sabi Sand area, showing as much detail of the vastness it covered. She had told him it needed to show all the camps, lodges, the entrance gates, roads, routes, private air strips and surrounding territories. Jack had also requested the pilot go into the gift shop at the airport and see if he could find a soft toy of a giraffe.

Toby, complete with an impressive map and a wobbly toy giraffe, had landed at the airstrip at Infinity and collected Jack.

They shook hands. Toby was probably in his mid-thirties, blond hair cut short, dark brown eyes creased by hours of flying in and around the harsh sun, his slim frame encased in khaki shorts, safari boots, and white shirt sporting his pilot's wings.

The bush below was dense, with trees offering respite from the burning sun, and the perfect camouflage for all the animals of various sizes seeking to evade predators. Dotted around were the many game lodges, some barely visible, others displaying thatched roofs or green tented tops.

The Kruger Park itself was easily identified by the tarred roads running through it. Visitors had to drive on the tarmac, he now understood, and were not allowed to go off-road, unless they were with a Parks Board ranger driving his own registered land cruiser.

Occasionally he glimpsed the outline of safari vehicles, loaded with tourists, wending their way slowly through the bush.

He saw buffalo, elephant, a few crocodiles, endless herds of kudu, zebra, impala and other buck, rhino, and many giraffe, all looking like children's toys below him.

With the map spread out on his knees, Jack indicated certain areas below, Toby located them and pointed them out on the map where Jack circled them. At Jack's request Toby had widened the radius, trying to work out between them how far a child could have walked in maybe a week or so, or a matter of days.

The wide Sabie river meandered its way through this vast landscape, Jack could see it glinting and flashing in the sun below.

Following the river with his finger he stared down, noticing dead trees caught and trapped. He looked at Toby and pointed them out.

"Debris from the floods." Toby said through the mouthpiece.

Jack nodded. He would have to find out what the weather conditions were in the days before the storm had hit.

Toby had taken him back to the landing strip at Infinity. As they approached, Toby pointed out a pride of lions, dozing in the afternoon heat under the shade of a tree, lying on their backs with their bloated cream bellies exposed, their great paws suspended in the air.

They landed with a bump and rumbled down the airstrip before coming to a halt.

Jack thanked Toby for all his help, watching as the pilot made his way back down the dusty strip, before turning and at full throttle took off, leaving a cloud of dust in his wake.

Jabu was waiting for him, as he tried to fold his map back into some kind of order. Giving up he folded it any way he could.

"Good trip Jack?"

"Excellent. You get a different perspective altogether from the air, the vastness of it all. How a child survived down there must have been a miracle."

He wiped his brow with his sleeve. "Mind you, there have been documented accounts of other children who have survived out in the wild, against all odds. Maybe not so much in Africa but certainly in other parts of the world."

Jabu looked out over the still bush. "It's happened here before. Families crossing illegally into South Africa, on foot. I heard one story of a child who became separated from his mother and got lost. He was found ten days or so later. So, it is possible. Poachers, unfortunately find their way as well, undetected."

Jack slid into the passenger seat of the vehicle. "I'll need your help now Jabu. I need some contacts from the various airports used to get guests to their game lodges, also private charter companies," he shook his head, "I didn't realise how massive the area was."

Jack sipped thirstily from the bottle of cold water Jabu had given him, took off his sunglasses, then splashed what was left over his face, neck and hair, wiping away the dust.

"I need to find some way of working out what the weather was like a week or so before the storm. Where would I start with this?"

Jabu grinned at him, and tapped his chest. "Right here with me. I keep a daily log of the weather conditions, wind, rain, sun, temperatures, animal sightings etc. I can help you there. Toby will be able to help you with where the various charter companies can land in the area, and where they come from."

They pulled up at the lodge and Jack gathered up his map, his notes, his binoculars and the toy giraffe.

"Thanks, Jabu. Did you manage to book my flight back to Cape Town? I need to get some of my gear before coming back and getting to work."

"All done. I'll drive you to the airport tomorrow morning. Caroline and Grace would like you to join them for dinner tonight, to see if you need anything else for your search. If you come with me now, I'll make copies of the weather conditions you were asking about.

"Oh, by the way if you'd like to go out on a game drive, the vehicles leave at four."

"Thanks, but I've just had a fantastic aerial game drive, it was amazing to have an elevated view of all the animals. As I'm leaving tomorrow, I'd like to spend some more time with Abby."

He held up the giraffe. "I have a present for her. I don't think she likes her teddy bear."

Chapter Forty

Jack walked from his cottage over to Grace's, her door was open. She was sitting on the deck looking out into the distance. Abby was drawing inside dressed in her pyjamas.

"I thought I'd come and say goodbye to Abby, before she goes to bed. I've brought her something."

Grace motioned her head, wearily, to Abby. "Go right ahead Jack."

Jack sat at the table. Abby didn't look up. "Hello Abby, what are you drawing. May I have a look?"

She shook her head. No.

"I've brought you a present Abby. He placed the giraffe on its wobbly legs on the table. "His name's Tom, so you can't call him anything else, okay. But you can talk to him and tell him anything you like, because he won't tell anyone."

Abby looked at him and scowled, then she picked up the giraffe and held it close. "Scusie gone," she whispered, her voice breaking as she reached for his hand. "Yak find Scusie. Peese?"

Jack looked at her big blue eyes, ringed with dark lashes, which were rapidly filling with tears. He held her hand in both of his. "Tell me Abby, is Scusie your sister?"

She dipped her head as the tears splashed onto her pyjama top, clumping her eyelashes together.

"Is your sister's name Susie?"

Relief spread over Abby's face. As she smiled through her tears. "Scusie!"

She hugged the giraffe to her chest. "Scusie…" she whispered.

"Do you know where Susie is, Abby. Was she with you when you were lost?"

Abby buried her head against the giraffe and howled. Grace hurried in. She scooped Abby up and held her close. "She seems extremely agitated, Jack, I'm going to give her something to calm her, then I think she should go to bed."

Jack waited whilst Grace settled the child. Twenty minutes later she was back. "What happened?"

"Abby has a sister called Susie, this is what she was trying to tell us, not Scusie, not *excuse me*. It's why she kept throwing the teddy bear across the room, because no-one understood what she was trying to say."

He ran his finger across his bottom lip. "There must have been some kind of accident and they were left alone. I think Susie must have been injured in some way and Abby went to find help."

Grace lowered herself into the chair next to him. "Oh God Jack."

She put her hands to her cheeks. "You know what this means? It means her sister was left out in the bush on her own. She *must* have been injured, or they would have stayed together. Her sister could not have survived, not after all this time, especially with the storm and the floods afterwards.

"How did they get there?"

She twisted the bracelets around her wrists. "There couldn't have been anyone else with them. Otherwise, he or she would never have allowed Abby to run off on her own to look for help."

Jack nodded agreeing with her. He closed his eyes imagining a terrified girl, all alone, as she tried to stay alive. Swept away in the raging torrent of the flood waters. Her long curly hair unfurling and straightened with the might of the river. Sweeping it across her face as swiftly as the water carried her away, her arms flailing, her screams for help drowned by the thundering roar of water.

Grace pulled her plait from behind her neck and wound it through her fingers. "This child needs psychiatric care, Jack. What did she see? What did she go through? It's selfish to keep her here now. She needs more help than I can ever give her."

"No, Grace. Putting her into care now will do more harm than good. Keep her here, work with her and encourage her to draw. She feels safe with you and Jabu. Don't take that away from her. I have both the sister's names now, it's a good start. I have a lot of work to do to try to figure who they are, and what happened to them both."

"Will you go to the police handling this case and update them?"

"No, not yet. Let's keep things as they are. I promised Caroline, gave her my word, I wouldn't involve anyone until I have the full story. The police, and other authorities, may insist the child goes into care and none of us want that. I want to put all the facts together, do a lot of research, make some calls etc. I'll find out what happened to her, I promise."

He smiled at her. "You're doing a great job Grace, you're exactly what Abby needs now."

He paused. "I was watching her as she was drawing. Another family picture but with both girl's hair a dark brown. Abby doesn't have dark hair, Grace, she's blonde, I know she only has a little fuzz at the moment, but it's definitely not dark brown. Remember the first picture she drew with Moses, the one you showed me? Both children had blonde hair."

Grace nodded in agreement.

"I'd like to make a copy of her first drawing. I have a good friend who's a child psychiatrist, she might be able to read a lot more into it than we can."

Grace stood and retrieved the drawing. "I'll make a copy for you. Why on earth would any mother dye their children's hair dark brown?"

Jack shook his head, keeping his tenuous thoughts to himself.

Chapter Forty-One

Back in Franschhoek, Jack sat at his kitchen table and spread the map out in front of him, Benji sitting close to his leg.

"Okay, Benji, where do we start. There are a few towns close to the game reserves. White River, Sabie, Graskop, Hazyview, Malelane and Pilgrim's Rest, even a place called God's Window."

He laughed. "Sound a bit more exciting than places back home called Piddle, Slackbottom, Giggleswick and Splatt. Far more dramatic if you ask me."

For the next two hours he circled more places on the map, made notes, checked the weather conditions, given to him by Jabu, around the time of Abby's appearance at the lodge, and made a list of the people he needed to contact.

He checked the time and called Caroline. "A question for you. The land on the private reserves, the buildings, are they all game lodges. All privately owned?"

"Yes. All the land is privately owned, has been for decades, and not necessarily has a game lodge built on it. Some lodge owners might have a couple of separate private homes near the lodge, not all of them live in the actual lodges. They have friends and business associates who use them for a bush break when they want to get away from wherever they work, like Johannesburg or Cape Town.

"To traverse a private reserve, you must have a vehicle registered to the lodge with the name of the lodge clearly visible. Friends are allowed to drive themselves but they must register at the entry point to the reserve and state where they're staying, lodge or lodge owner's private accommodation, and be able to prove it.

"Under no circumstances are visitors allowed to drive a game viewing vehicle."

Jack scribbled another note. "Abby must have spent time in the bush as she was growing up. She must have been taught about what berries or fruit were safe to eat and what was not. Therefore, she either lived in a town near a reserve and was taken there for holidays, or maybe to one of the owner's private homes."

He could hear her tapping on her computer. "It's going to be nearly impossible to find out which private home belongs to whom, Jack. My suggestion would be to get talking to the locals in the various small towns surrounding the Kruger. Maybe find out where the pilots hang out. Jabu tells me you are going to base yourself in Hazyview. That's a good place to start."

Caroline continued to answer the questions he had put to her. "It's more likely friends would have flown in from the city and used a private pilot to get them to an owner's home. Some of the pilots might remember someone if they were frequent visitors. They would have had to have landed on a private airstrip."

He heard her sneeze then blow her nose, before she continued.

"On the other hand, friends might have been picked up by the lodge vehicle and taken to the owner's home, or as I mentioned, driven there themselves.

"If this was the case then there's no way of finding out, unless you went to each lodge, and there are many of them, and asked the owner who his friends are. Something I don't think they would like much, besides you wouldn't be allowed to just drive where you wanted, regulations about movement in the reserves are extremely strict because of poaching.

"I'll ask around with the pilots I know. Toby, our pilot, will probably be able to give us some information."

Jack consulted his notes. "Are there any other vehicles allowed on the reserve, over and above tourists and land owners?"

"Oh yes. There are delivery trucks who bring in goods for the lodges, tractors and other vehicles to do bush clearing, or maintain the dirt roads leading to the game lodges. Oh, and the anti-poaching units. Poaching as you probably know is a huge headache in this neck of the woods, hence the strict rules and regulations governing who can be in the reserve at any given time. All closely monitored."

"Okay, thanks Caroline. How is everyone, especially Abby?"

"All well. Abby seems more withdrawn since your visit, but Grace stays close to her, encouraging her to draw, she's trying to get her to read, but not having much luck. The child is hardly saying anything now.

"Grace is beginning to think she hasn't had much of an education, which means her sister Susie probably hadn't either. Maybe they were home schooled somewhere remote. This would give some weight to your theory that perhaps they were brought up in the bush somewhere. If they had lived in a town, they would have gone to school. But who knows, we're only guessing at the moment."

Jack thanked her again and rang off. He scrolled through his list of contacts and found the one he was looking for.

Ex-Detective Inspector Piet Joubert grunted into the phone, speaking Afrikaans.

"Hey, Piet! You're sounding as grumpy as ever, even in your own language which as you well know I don't speak. Well, except for one word you taught me – *voetsak*. Tried it out on a monkey and it worked a treat."

He heard Piet give a short bark of laughter. "So, you're back Jack Taylor. Must be if you can find a monkey to swear at. What are you after this time?"

"Yeah, I'm back Piet. In fact, I live here now, have been for the past two years, in Franschhoek. Been meaning to call you but, well, you know how it is. I still work for the London newspaper though."

Piet sounded suspicious. "*Ag, man,* better have your paperwork in order otherwise the Government will kick your butt out as being undesirable, or whatever other label they want to give you."

Jack laughed. "No worries there, remember I told you my grandfather and my mother were born in South Africa? Well, it gives me the right to live here. Never been happier in my life Piet."

"*Ag, man,* as long as you can live with the *bleddy* power cuts, the politics, the corruption, the crime and all the other bad things going on, well, there's no other place on God's earth like this country."

Jack interrupted him; his voice serious. "Listen Piet, I need a favour. I'm following another case, not a cold case this time. But I need some information from the police in Nelspruit. I know it's a long way from the Eastern Cape, and Willow Drift, but maybe you'll have some contacts there?"

Piet grunted. "I was born not far from Nelspruit Jack. Most of my contacts have retired but I still know a few people in the right places – what do you need to find out. What are you following now?"

Jack explained the situation with Abby.

"Yes, I heard about the girl. Then someone slammed the lid on the story and that was the end of it. So, you have her hidden away somewhere, hey?"

"It's for her own protection until we can find out who she is and where her family are. I know the police won't tell me anything, as a journalist. I need to know if they have any further information and who's handling the case. My newspaper is prepared to pay you for your time."

Piet's voice seemed to brighten with interest. "Leave it with me, Jack. You say the police don't know the girl's name and you haven't told them? But they do know where this Abby is staying and gave their permission?"

"Yes, they agreed on the recommendations of the girl's medical team."

Piet grunted again. "Well, my friend, if they haven't checked up on her then I doubt anyone is working hard on her case. Unlike the old days when I was a detective, we worked *bleddy* hard on every case.

"The police in this new South Africa are too busy toeing the party line and making sure they get their share of the pickings. I'm not saying all of them, but plenty of them are as corrupt as our politicians. Few of them would be interested in a white girl pitching up at a fancy game lodge – only if she was dead."

Piet sighed down the phone. "The cops have enough on their plates these days with all the crime, hijackings, corruption and murders, and so on. Prisons are bursting at the seams with these *skollies*."

Jack's heart sank. "So, will you help me out Piet? I need to know if anyone has come forward. I know the cops put out a picture of Abby in the newspapers. Someone, somewhere must know who she is, someone must be looking for her. As I told you, she had a sister. No sign of her though."

"*Ja*, okay. Give me a couple of days, so long. Now where do I send my bank details and how much is this English newspaper of yours prepared to pay for my services, hey?"

Laughing, Jack put his phone down, then laid out Abby's drawing of what he thought might be her family, with the blacked out faces of what he also assumed were her parents, then took a couple of shots and sent them through to his psychiatrist friend in Cape Town with a brief precis of what he was dealing with.

Within two hours his psychiatrist friend called him back.

"This is not good Jack. You are dealing with a seriously damaged personality here. A young child with extremely strong emotions. It's disturbing to see how she has blacked out the two faces of the older figures in the drawing.

"If we assume they are her parents, then something went badly wrong at some point. To me it looks as though her parents might well be dead, and they died under unusual circumstances, I don't think it was a divorce, she's angry with them for some reason. This is all I can gather so far. If I figure anything more out, I'll let you know."

Thanking her profusely Jack rang off and tapped his pen on the table.

That had been his gut feel as well. Something horrible had happened to Abby's parents, something which had angered her so much she had drawn their faces then blacked them out with a few angry strokes of her black crayon.

If he was right then where had this happened?

Either the girls didn't come from South Africa or they were brought here by someone. Someone they must have known, who had brought them to the game reserve and hidden them away from any prying eyes.

But why? He had no idea whatsoever. But he was going to find out.

Chapter Forty-Two

Jack made arrangements for Daisy to come and stay at his cottage.

"I don't know how long I'll be away, Daisy. I have some work to do out of town. I don't want to put the dog in the kennels, he'll think I've deserted him."

He thought briefly of Abby. "I'd like you to come and stay here whilst I'm away. Keep Benji company. I don't want to disrupt your own family life though. Would you be able to do this for me?"

Daisy looked up from her ironing and gave him her big gummy smile. "*Ag,* Mr Yak. I have a big noisy family, too noisy, always wanting food, always fighting. Daisy will stay here and look after your house and the scruffy dog."

*****

Jack landed at the airport in Nelspruit and collected his hire car. He opened the windows and looked at his map, smiling at some of the names, Robber's Pass, Long Tom Pass…

He was heading for a place called Pilgrim's Rest, an ancient mining town and fairly close to the Sabi Sands reserve. He planned to start here and then work his way around the few other places he had marked on his map, White River, Sabie, Graskop, and Malelane.

Pilgrim's Rest had had its heady days of pioneers streaming in looking for gold, he decided, as he drove down the short road. He imagined garter snapping barmaids with fish net stockings, highway robbers, good time gals, pubs, brothels, and the feverish, heady, atmosphere of the old gold rush days.

Now it resembled a ghost town. Most of the shops had closed down but he found the Victorian style Royal Hotel with no problem.

Perched on the side of the road with its red tin roof, it was not easy to miss.

He checked in and was shown to his room. Dated was the word which sprang to mind, tired would be another way of describing the slightly peeling wallpaper with a few damp patches.

He made his way to the pub which apparently had once been a small chapel. The place was deserted although the African barman perked up immediately when he saw his one and only customer.

Jack sat on the hard wooden stool and hoped some of the locals might arrive and he could ask a few questions.

After two hours he realised this was highly unlikely to happen. Only one car had driven down the road outside.

He ordered another beer and something to eat from the pub menu.

"Bit quiet around here isn't it," he peered at the barman's name badge, "Titus."

"Always quiet here, sir. No-one lives here anymore it's a ghost town, didn't you know? Only tourists now and again. I'll go and see if there is anyone in the kitchen to make your food."

Jack mentally ticked the town off his list, devoured his limp sandwich, and equally limp potato crisps, he then called it a day. Disappointed he would learn nothing here.

The next morning he set off, the town was indeed a ghost town. Its former glory leaving only an eerie feeling of persons and activities long departed. He imagined he could hear the sound of a honky-tonk piano, the raucous laughter of miners, the double doors of the drinking salons squeaking as they were pushed open by customers seeking some respite from a day panning for gold under the brutal sun.

Having visited the other towns on his map, and learning nothing, he decided to head for Hazyview. As he entered the town his spirits lifted. This was more like it.

There were plenty of safari vehicles parked, dark green and sand coloured, displaying their lodge logos, and moving through the town, which was only twenty minutes away from the Kruger Park, and close to the private reserves. Various shop fronts offered day trips to the Kruger or safaris to private lodges, and plenty of shops stocking safari clothes.

The hotel he had chosen and booked into was called simply, The Inn. It was once, he understood from his research, a private homestead which the now owner had turned into a hotel, adding rooms and public areas.

Judging by the vehicles parked outside it was popular even in the early afternoon, he recognised the local number plates, this was exactly what he was looking for. Locals.

He checked in and was shown to his room which was large, bright, airy and comfortable, with a private patio outside overlooking the lush gardens. Jets of fine mist swept across the lawns from the clicking water system. Brightly coloured birds dipped in and out of the spray.

Jack took a quick shower and changed his clothes. He checked his emails and spent the next hour answering them. His phone chirped next to him.

Piet Joubert.

He snatched it up.

"Hey Jack," he said grumpily. "I'm not going to make much money out of your newspaper. I've been in touch with some buddies from the old days. One of them knew a senior police officer in Nelspruit, I talked to him.

"They've pretty much put the case of the kid on the backburner. As far as they're concerned, she's alive and it's about as much as they care about. No-one has come forward with any solid information, only a few nut cases, of course, but that's normal.

"Over the past couple of months no-one has reported any two girls missing. No parents killed in an accident, or murdered, who had two girls and left them orphans. I'm thinking they must have been tourists who found themselves in trouble out in the bush. Even so, if this was the case, it would have been all over the newspapers – but nothing, hey.

"Trail's gone cold, my friend. Where are you?"

"Hazyview. Just checked into a place called The Inn. It looks lively, lots of locals here. I'm hoping to make some headway with my investigation. Didn't have any luck, or come up with anything interesting from the other places I visited. White River, Sabie, Graskop, Malelane, everyone I spoke to had heard the story but I didn't get any leads from anyone. Hazyview, I figured, would be the best place to base myself. Anyway, thanks Piet. Maybe one of your contacts will come up with something later."

"*Ja*, they know what I'm looking for. Watch out for those wild safari types, my friend. It's Friday night. Party time in those bush towns, hey! If you're going into the bush don't forget to take your malaria tablets, you Brits seem to be a big attraction for our mosquitoes, they have no taste, only for blood. Just sayin'…"

He chuckled and rang off.

Jack checked the time. Five thirty. Time to hit the bar and see what he might come up with.

*****

The bar was heaving with people and noisy, like a million angry bees punctuated by barks of laughter.

He made his way through the crowd. The smiling stocky man behind the bar, wearing cut off frayed shorts, no shoes, and a loud shirt, lifted his hand in greeting.

"Jack Taylor? You're staying with us. Only guest checking in today so it must be you. Reception told me to look out for a tall good-looking Englishman with wild blond hair. Has to be you right? Welcome to the noisiest bar in town. My names Hugo Butler. I'm the owner."

Jack leaned over and shook his hand. Hugo looked as though he were permanently amused, either that or he was supremely happy with his lot in life. "Another Englishman?"

Hugo laughed, wiping his brow with his shirt sleeve. "Yeah, but it was years ago. Where are you from?"

"London, but I've been living here for the past two years, in Franschhoek."

"Lovely spot Franschhoek. Though damn hot in the summer. I'm also from London, which is a distant memory now. What can I get you?"

Jack ordered a beer and looked around. Nothing like the subdued voices in an English country pub, the place was lively and buzzing. The staff behind the bar serving drinks and snacks looked as happy as the patrons and owner.

At around six the rowdy crowd started to disperse, leaving only a handful of people at the bar. Suddenly the lights went out and a groan went up from the ones who were left.

"No worries, guys," shouted Hugo. "Eskom strikes again. Drinks on the house!"

The deep shuddering growl of a generator rumbled through the hotel grounds.

Hugo slid another beer towards Jack. "So, Jack, how are you enjoying life here, aside from the never-ending power cuts that is."

"Best move I ever made. Love it. Power cuts don't bother me, I've learned to live with them. It's a challenge, trying to beat the system, although I have to admit dinner by candle light is fast losing its appeal."

Hugo wiped down the bar. "So, what did you do in London and what are you doing here. Going on safari?"

"No, I'm working on something. I'm a journalist, used to be based in London with *The Telegraph*. Came here following a cold case, fell in love with the country. Now I freelance for the paper, look for interesting stories, and also write a weekly column on life in sunny South Africa."

Hugo grinned at him. "When I lived in London I worked for a top tour operator, specialising in trips to South Africa. I came here regularly, checking out the hotels and game lodges, then worked out I would rather be here myself, rather than sending people here. Best thing I ever did. I used to come to this hotel often when it was only a small place with a couple of rooms. I decided to buy it, been here twenty years. Now we have thirty rooms."

Jack saw the opportunity and went for it. "I guess you know almost everyone in town?"

"Well, I did at one point, but over the years the town has grown from a sort of frontier town to a vibrant portal to all the game lodges in and around the Kruger, and the Kruger Park itself. But we still have the same old crowd one way or another. This is their favourite local pub as you probably gathered.

"Are you following a story or doing a piece on the area?"

Jack took a sip of his beer. He leaned over slightly and lowered his voice. "I'm quite intrigued with the story of the child who was found at a water hole at one of the game lodges."

Hugo eyebrows shot up with interest. "Oh yes, we were all quite fascinated with that story, as was the media. But they couldn't get anywhere near her. She was in a hospital in Nelspruit, then completely disappeared. No-one has a clue where she is now.

"Rumour has it the parents came forward and whisked her away to recover somewhere, out of the country maybe, and it seemed to be the end of the story. I don't think you'll get any more mileage out of it Jack."

Hugo put a small plate of crispy garlic prawns in front of him.

Jack bit into one of the prawns and closed his eyes, butter, garlic and prawns…

"Tell me something Jack. Is Harry still with the newspaper? He used to give us tour operators some good coverage in his Sunday supplements. Of course, we had to spend a good deal on advertising to catch his attention."

Jack smiled at him and wolfed down a few more prawns. "Yup. Still there, sporting his signature navy-blue braces. I work directly for him now. Nothing he likes better than a good story out of Africa."

Hugo clicked his fingers. "Hang on a minute I remember your name now. You chased a story a couple of years ago. Down in the Eastern Cape. Am I right? Something to do with an ambassador's daughter?

"I might love my new adopted country but I still have a hunger for a good British newspaper. I get the *Sunday Telegraph,* couriered to me each week. I followed the story you wrote in it.

"What happened to the girl, what was her name now…ah, yes, Kia. Unusual name that's why I remember it."

Jack hesitated slightly. "I'm not sure, once the media got hold of the story again, she went into hiding. Didn't care much for the mob of photographers camped out in her front garden."

Jack helped himself to the last prawn. "But, yes, it was me, I wrote the story."

Now knowing Hugo's connection with Harry, Jack took a chance.

"The thing is Hugo, I think there *is* a lot more to the story of the girl who was found at the water hole. I want to find out how she ended up there, who her parents were, where they came from. I need someone I can trust who won't alert the media to the fact I'm doing a follow up. I need some information. You see it's possible there were two girls, not just one."

Hugo looked shocked. "I'll help you any way I can. The key to running a successful bar, like this one, is the ability to listen to the customers who want to pour out their life stories, or their personal problems to you, and respect their confidence. Whatever you tell me will remain absolutely confidential.

"Two girls you say? Surely the other one must have known what happened?"

"We think she must have been injured, otherwise they would have looked for help together. There was a vicious storm the night the girl was found, her sister could not have survived out there alone. We think she must have died out in the bush."

Jack patted his mouth with a linen napkin. "Okay, here's what I'm surmising. There must have been an adult involved. I'm only guessing this, but I'm putting my money on a man. Someone who knew the bush well, knew the area well. A man who was trying to hide the fact he was there with two children."

"Why?" Hugo asked.

"He was obviously not supposed to be where he was, given all the strict rules and regulations governing the private reserves. Or, he was hiding out in clear view with a bolt hole either owned by one of the landowners, or rented from them."

Hugo pursed his lips and nodded. "It's possible but highly unlikely, go on."

"Whoever he was he would need to go to town for grocery shopping, which, to my mind puts him in the category of living on the reserve, hidden, perhaps protected, or otherwise."

Hugo glanced around the bar and back at Jack. "A bit of a wild theory."

"Wherever he was staying with the two girls, well, someone must have known all about him and given him refuge from whatever he was running away from."

Jack took a sip of his beer and continued. "Now, here's the thing. A man needs to buy food to feed his kids. What else does he need, Hugo."

Hugo raised his eyebrows, he polished a glass vigorously, getting caught up in the story.

"A doctor? A dentist? A pharmacist? A woman, if he didn't have one of those stashed away with the children."

Jack patted his unruly hair. "No, none of the above."

"What then?"

"He would need to get his hair cut."

Hugo smiled at him. "Not necessarily. He might have had a wife, or woman, stashed away in his hidey hole. Maybe she cut his hair. Or maybe he wore it in a ponytail."

"Nope. There can't be a woman, a mother involved with this. If the mother of the children had found them missing, she would have been howling at the moon to find them, so would a father come to that. No, this man lived alone with the children, whoever he was."

Jack glanced around the now crowded room. "He would have found a small, non-descript place to have his hair cut. No fancy salon where they would give him a Brazilian head massage, or tossed hot stones down the back of his shirt to help him relax, with prices to match. No. My man would have found somewhere where he could zip in and out with as little fuss as possible. Somewhere low-key where he wouldn't have to talk to anyone, or sit with a load of women, complaining about their husbands many shortfalls, or possible lovers."

Hugo shook his head. "Maybe he was bald, didn't have any hair?"

Jack smiled. "Come on Hugo, gimme me a break. I have to start somewhere."

Hugo frowned then smiled. "I know of only one place in town with the traditional red and white pole outside her shop. Good place to start with your somewhat wild theories."

He wiped the bar in front of him. "The other sister? God, it's too horrific to even think about, poor little mite, didn't even get a chance at life."

He shuddered as he threw the towel over his shoulder. "The bush can be a magical place, but it's unforgiving as well. Well, the predators have a good time, but the other poor buggers are always looking over their shoulders for trouble.

"As for a child alone out there – well, it doesn't bear thinking about, does it."

Chapter Forty-Three

Armed with the name of the barber's shop in town, *Elly's*, Jack drove through the town, nursing a slight hangover.

He found what he was looking for, wedged between a bakery on one side and a second-hand book shop on the other.

A bell pinged as he entered. A young woman with choppy pink hair and studs in her ears and nose looked up from her magazine, and smiled at him.

"*Howzit*. You look as though you might be needing some help with your hair." She closed her magazine and stood up, making her way to the appointments book at the front desk.

Jack smiled at her. "Only a trim, nothing drastic, can you fit me in?" He looked around the empty shop.

"*Ja*, no problem. Can I have your name."

"Jack Taylor."

She wrote it in the book then looked up at him. "Come, sit here. My name's Elspeth."

Jack grinned at her. "That's clever then, the name of your salon? Your name's Elspeth and you work close to where the elephants roam. It's a good name for it."

She chatted away to him as she washed his hair, then draped a black nylon cape around his shoulders and went to work.

"*Jeez* like, you have a *lekker* head of hair - how much shall I take off?"

"As little as possible, Elspeth, maybe tidy it up a bit."

"So, where you from? Not here I'm sure, I would have noticed someone like you around town." She nudged his shoulder playfully, clearly flirting with him.

"I live in Franschhoek, but before then in London."

She snipped away. "*Ja*, plenty English people hereabouts in Hazyview, but they don't speak like you. You sound like that Prince person. He was married to Princess Diana, um, Charles, *ja*, Prince Charles. *Ag, man,* shame what happened to her, hey."

Jack refrained from nodding in case her scissors slipped.

"Only heard one other man speak like him. Lived out in the bush with his family."

Jack felt the familiar sizzle of a story pulsating down his spine. "Have you seen him recently then?"

"*Nah*, not for a while now, probably left for somewhere more exciting."

"Do you remember his name? I lost touch with a good friend of mine. He was English with a couple of kids. I heard he'd come to live up here somewhere. It's why I'm here - looking them up, and his wife of course, but, sadly, I can't remember her name, probably because I never met her."

Elspeth whipped the cloak from around his shoulders and studied her work.

"There you go, all done. *Nah*, can't remember his name but I can look back in the appointments book, so long, and see if I can find it if you like?"

She went to the front desk and flipped through the pages of her book, frowning. Elspeth paused for a second, looked at him quickly, then back at her appointment book.

"*Ja*, here he is. Mr Phillip Fletcher-Jones. Funny how these English people have so many names. We Afrikaners only have two, Christian and surname. Is this the name of your friend then?"

Jack smiled. "Yes, it's him. Did he have a phone number?"

She shook her head. "I remember asking for it in case we had to change his appointment but he said his phone didn't work out in the bush. He didn't say much, one of those silent types. Not friendly like you, hey."

Jack paid his bill and added a generous tip. "Thanks. I wonder how those girls are, it's a couple of years since I saw him last."

He handed her his card. "If you remember anything else, please let me know, won't you."

Jack had had one of his contacts in the digital world to take the recent photograph of Abby and enhance it with a full head of blonde curly hair.

"Oh, hang on, just remembered something."

He scrolled through his phone until he found what he was looking for.

"Have you seen this girl before maybe with Fletcher-Jones?"

Elspeth looked at the photo, then at him. Her bright smile suddenly gone, her face white. The friendliness, and flirtatiousness, in her voice now absent. "Why are you asking all these questions if you know the family. Are you with the police or something?"

"No, not at all. Do I look like a policeman? Look, I'll be honest with you. My friend and his family seem to have disappeared, I'm trying to find them, I'm a journalist. I want to help the family relatives locate them."

Elspeth twisted the stud in her nose. "*Ag*, man, they probably went back to where they come from in the beginning. I can't help you there."

Then she turned sharply and stared at him, her eyes narrowing. "Is this about the girl they found in the bush? Are you thinking she might have been Mr Fletcher-Jones daughter?"

Jack knew he had misjudged her intelligence by her bright and breezy conversation and distinct Afrikaans accent.

"Look, Elspeth. I don't know about a girl found in the bush; I'm just passing through here trying to find my friend. But thanks for your help and the haircut."

*****

Elspeth watched him from the salon window, as he got into his car.

The Englishman had not been telling her the truth. There was no way he could have ever heard of Mr Fletcher-Jones.

She looked at the card he had given her. She remembered the story of the girl. Hazyview had been buzzing with speculation about who she was.

Elspeth thought back to that night. The soft knock on the back door. It was a Monday. The salon was always closed on a Monday.

He had been standing there. She had been expecting him.

Now she shook her head. Her Ma had always told her, her endless chatter would one day get her into trouble, and now it had.

She had given the Englishman, called Jack, a name, desperately trying to retrieve the situation. But he was a journalist, and he was asking questions. She had kept her wits about her, fumbling through the names in her appointment book and picking randomly on one.

Elspeth flipped the sign on the door to closed, then punched in a number on her phone.

"It's me. I think you might have a problem. There's a journalist sniffing around…I've tried to head him off."

*****

Jack stopped at a small restaurant and sat outside, watching safari vehicles, tour buses and busy tourists aimlessly milling around.

He stirred his coffee and thought about the conversation with the hairdresser. It was a tentative start.

He had immediately picked up how she had gone from chatty to being subdued, looking edgy and nervous, her smile taut and not reaching her eyes.

It was time to start showing the enhanced photo he had of Abby around. It had certainly evoked a reaction from the hairdresser called Elspeth. A strong one.

Chapter Forty-Four

Jack pulled up outside the hotel. Many more cars than yesterday, then he remembered there was a big rugby game on this afternoon. Nothing South Africans loved more than their rugby.

He went to his room and spent the next two hours searching the internet for Mr Phillip Fletcher-Jones and came up with nothing.

He made a call to Harry, his editor.

"Hey, Harry, I'm making progress, but it's slow. I'm up near the Kruger Park in a place called Hazyview. Like the wild west here. A real safari town. I need your help with something. I think I have a tentative lead on our story."

He filled Harry in on what he had so far, including his visit to the barber shop.

"Good start Jack, sounds promising. Hope you're wearing your sun hat, hot as hell there from what I can gather."

Jack heard him sigh and could swear he could hear the rain thundering down in London, even at this distance. "Weather's bloody terrible at the moment," Harry continued. "Could do with a dose of sunshine myself. Now what do you need from me."

"I've drawn a blank on this Phillip Fletcher-Jones. Can't get a sniff of him on the internet. Maybe you could use some of our network over there and see if you come up with anything. A marriage certificate would be useful and birth certificate for the two girls, now we know their names. If indeed, we have the right family. Well, at least I can eliminate them from my search if the girl's surname is wrong."

"Leave it with me Jack. I'll see what we can come up with. I have a South African journalist working for me, he's showing a lot of promise. His name's Stefan de Villiers. I'll use him to do a bit of digging."

Jack made his way to the bar. A huge screen was broadcasting the rugby match. With all eyes glued to the screen he had no trouble in catching Hugo's eye.

"How did it go today, Jack. Beer?"

He nodded. "Have you ever heard of someone called Phillip Fletcher-Jones, Hugo. He had two children apparently."

Hugo put his beer in front of him. "Fletcher-Jones? The name rings a bit of a bell, let me have a think."

Jack told him about his visit to the barber shop.

Hugo glanced at the rugby score. "A few wealthy Brits, South Africans, and Europeans own bush homes around here, but not in the private reserves. Some of the properties there have been in the same family for generations. It's strictly controlled. Can't just pitch up, build a house, stick some bleached buffalo horns on the entrance and call it home.

"They keep their lives private and rarely venture into town, certainly most of them don't socialise. They come to the bush to escape from whatever they need to escape from," he grinned, "avoiding places like this."

A roar went up from the crowd in the bar. South Africa had scored again. Hugo raised his eyebrows. "I think another round is called for. I'm going to give my guys a hand."

Jack watched the final twenty minutes of the game as he nursed his beer. Another win for South Africa. Phew! Those guys were good. Better than the Brits by far, and the Australians. Their greatest opponents were the New Zealanders, the All Blacks, but they had thrashed them a couple of times as well. No one in South Africa would forget the heart stopping moment when they had won the world cup over twenty years ago, they remembered it as if it were yesterday.

Jack glanced at the huge photograph on the wall behind the bar. Nelson Mandela and the Captain of the Springboks raising the mighty gleaming cup to a hysterical, elated crowd. A turning point in the tentative, but hopeful, future of the country under its new government.

Hugo edged his way back to Jack. "I do remember someone called Fletcher-Jones. Phillip. He only came in a few times over the past few years. Nice guy, very British. He has a bush home here somewhere. Came out from the UK each year. Not chatty, but nice enough. Only used to have a beer or two then leave.

"If he had children, he never mentioned them. He was in the wrong age group to have young children, but these days you never know, what with trophy wives and all that."

Chapter Forty-Five

Jack finished his drink and went out to his car. He wanted to visit another bar which, Hugo had told him, was a favourite watering hole for the local bush pilots.

He pulled up at what could only be the place. An old Cessna decorated the roof. The bar was called The Last Drop. Slightly ominous he thought to himself.

The place was relatively quiet for a late Saturday afternoon, the large television was on mute as sporting experts held a post mortem on the game the Springboks had just won. The rugby crowds had departed.

Pilots, sporting their uniforms, and their wives or girlfriends were gathered at small tables, a handful were propping up the bar.

Jack found a seat at the bar and ordered a beer from the smiling barman. "I'm looking for Toby Johnson, have you seen him around?"

The barman pushed his beer towards him. "Normally comes in around five, if he's not flying. Ah, there he is chatting with one of the other guys."

Jack waited until Toby had ended his conversation then raised his arm as he saw him heading for the bar.

"Hey, Jack. What are you doing back? Or have you been here all the time."

They shook hands and Toby slid onto the bar stool next to him.

"No, I went home and arrived back a few days ago. Good to see you again."

Toby took a long drink of the beer he had ordered, smacked his lips and gave Jack a roguish smile. "No flying until tomorrow afternoon," he explained, wiping the froth off his top lip.

"Did the map I found for you help with your search?" He looked around and lowered his voice. "For the little girl."

Jack sighed. "I've narrowed down the area where I think she might have come from. It has to be a town near the Sabi Sands, somewhere like here. But of course, she couldn't have walked from Hazyview, so it was by plane which must have crashed, a land cruiser or a boat, there's no other explanation."

Toby shook his head dismissively. "Couldn't have been a plane, we pilots would have heard about it. As for a land cruiser? You can't drive around the Sabi Sands on your own, unless you're an incoming guest at one of the lodges. If you are, you have to follow the rules. You have to have proof at the entry point of the reserve of your reservation."

Toby took another sip of his beer. "No getting out of your vehicle, you must observe the strict speed limit, and animals have the right of way. So, no paddling up or down the river. I think you can cancel a boat out as well.

"Since Caroline told me about the child, Jack, I've been giving it a great deal of thought. I can't come up with any feasible answer."

Jack scratched a mosquito bite on his leg. "That might be so, but from what I can gather there are poachers out there. They move in and around without any problem, in the dead of the night. So, it *is* possible to move round the reserves undetected, clearly they do."

Toby shrugged. "That, I'm afraid, is sadly true, despite all the sophisticated equipment, dogs, infra-red cameras, and helicopters etc, used by the anti-poaching units. The security is pretty impressive, but the poachers still manage to move around and kill the animals. Bastards."

Jack signalled to the barman for another round. "There's another theory I have. Supposing this family lived in a private home in the Sabi Sands. Maybe there was an accident of some kind and the family were split up. By the way, there are two girls involved. Abby, that's the one who was found, always draws pictures with two girls, the other girl is her sister, Susie. We think she may have died during the floods, otherwise the girls would have been together. It's possible, but only faintly possible, the family name was Fletcher- Jones. Heard of them?"

Toby shook his head, but looked impressed. "You must be damn good at what you do Jack. That's quite a bit of information you've gathered. How the hell did you put it all together."

Jack lifted his hand. "It's what I do. Been doing it for years, following my gut feel, my instincts, and chasing stories. I look beyond the obvious to the overlooked. Tracing something back to its unknown origins and working out the steps along the way. Looking for something that's not there, working with what little I have.

"Anyway, what do you think about my theory that the family may have lived in the Sabi Sands"

Toby scratched the stubble on his chin. "It's possible. Besides the lodges there are a few homes built on privately owned land. I've flown a few families in but I haven't heard the name Fletcher-Jones before."

Jack pulled out his phone and scrolled to the photo of Abby. "This is the little girl called Abby. We've enhanced the picture and given her a full head of hair, one with blonde hair the other with dark brown hair. Do you recognise her. Did she and her family ever fly with you?"

Toby studied the photograph and frowned. "I can't be sure, but I think I would have remembered two little girls. Most private friends of the owners of the lodges rarely bring children, most of them are pretty much retired. Nope, sorry, can't say I recognise her."

He drained his beer and stood up. "Better be on my way, taking my girlfriend out for dinner. Good to see you again Jack. Look, here's my card, keep in touch, let me know if I can help you with anything, and, don't worry, no information concerning Abby, or her missing sister, will pass my lips. I have great respect for Caroline, she trusts me, and I value that trust," he grinned, "and also all the business she gives me."

He shook Jack's hand. "I'm her go-to pilot, pretty much work for her full time now, ferrying her guests back and forth, so if you're ever looking for a lift to the lodge and I have a spare seat, you're welcome to hitch a ride. Much quicker than driving as you probably know, and more comfortable.

"I'd like to help with the search for the little girl's family, try and do my bit. Maybe getting you back and forth to the lodge when you need to be there can be my contribution. See you around Jack."

Jack mulled over his other follow ups for the next few days.

Tomorrow he would visit a couple of the top estate agents in the area who specialised in selling, or renting out, bush homes in the area.

Chapter Forty-Six

Jack phoned Grace at Infinity.
"How's Abby?"
He heard her sigh down the phone. "Withdrawn. It's clear she's never been to school, she can barely read or write, so I'm teaching her. What progress have you made?"
Jack filled her in with the information he had gathered. "I'll leave you to introduce her surname to her, if it is her surname. If she recognises it, then I'm on the right track."
"I'll have to pick my moment, Jack. I don't want to tip her over the edge. She's physically getting much stronger, although we don't allow her to stray from the cottage. It's her mental state that's of great concern."
"Grace, I know she feels safe with you, and with Jabu. But she does have this different sort of empathy with him. Maybe Jabu could pick his moment and perhaps he could suggest her surname may be Fletcher-Jones. I don't want to push it. You know how much she can, or cannot, take. But this is the one thing I need to know now, as soon as possible."
"I'll speak to Jabu. See what he thinks. I'll let you know."

*****

Jabu sat with Abby on his knee, down at the waterhole. All the guests were out on their game drive.
He was looking at all the pictures she had drawn. "These are good, little one. What will you draw tomorrow?"
Abby played with the beaded bracelet on Jabu's wrist. She pointed to the herd of impala drinking at the water.
"Such gentle creatures aren't they," Jabu said softly. "So pretty with their big eyes, big ears and black shiny noses."

Abby sucked at her thumb and leaned back into Jabu's arms.

Jabu spoke to her in his mother tongue, which he knew relaxed her. Then spoke to her in English.

"Once the brave impala who are drinking at the water hole feel safe, they fetch, er, fetch, er, the others to come and join them. They don't have phones you see."

The child turned in his arms. "Fetcher. Owns."

"Do you know these words, little one?"

Chapter Forty-Seven

Jack held his breath as he listened carefully to Jabu.
"I applied your magic trick about phonetics, Jack. Her name is not Abby Fletcher-Jones. There was no reaction at all. Either that or she can't, or doesn't want to remember it.

*****

Jack pulled up outside an estate agents office in the middle of town. He perused the window looking at the properties for sale in the area.

Patting down his hair he rang the buzzer on the security gate, it swung open and he was confronted by a receptionist, a blast of air conditioning, and four agents who looked up expectantly at him.

The receptionist smiled warmly at him. "May I help, sir?"

"Yes. I'm interested in buying a property, not in town but out in the bush. I see you have one advertised in your window."

A tall, heavily made-up, middle-aged woman stood with one fluid movement and bustled over to him. "Hi, my name's Zelda. If you'd like to sit?" She indicated for him to take a seat then went the other side of the desk and lowered herself into her chair, smiling brightly at him, a hint of her red lipstick smudged on her teeth.

"Now what did you have in mind? There are a limited number of homes available to purchase in the bush."

"An old school chum of mine bought a place in the Sabi Sands, some years ago now. Ever since I saw his home, I've dreamed of owning a place in the Sabi Sands myself. Nothing fancy, something modest and comfortable."

Zelda shook her head and raised an eyebrow which didn't match its partner. "There is nothing available in the Sabi Sands. All the land is privately owned. Your friend couldn't have owned a property there unless he bought a game lodge? I think you must have made a mistake.

"However, outside the reserves there are properties available. Would you like me to show them to you?"

Jack stood up, feeling the icy air conditioning on his face, and her now icy demeanour. She looked as though her face had been embalmed, with her cold expression and heavy make-up.

"No, I specifically wanted something in a private reserve, but, as you say, it won't be possible, unless I buy a game lodge which would be a bit out of my budget."

He smiled at her. "Let me have a think and I'll come back to you. My old friend's name was Fletcher-Jones. Did he, by chance, purchase a home from you?"

Zelda's face hardened even more, if it were possible. "If he did, I wouldn't discuss it with you. We're not given to handing out personal information about our client's, sir."

*****

Zelda watched him walk back outside. The good-looking Englishman with his British accent, and gorgeous brown eyes, would not be back, of this she was quite sure. She had never heard of anyone called Fletcher-Jones, although it wouldn't take her long, to track down an agent, from the other agencies, who had sold him a property in the area.

But there would be nothing in it for her, or her agency. It wasn't a property he was looking for; it was something else entirely.

She had met some shifty types over the years, looking for places to hide out. The Englishman didn't look exactly shifty, but he was definitely looking for information. He had the look of a journalist about him.

Chapter Forty-Eight
London

Harry drummed his fingers on the side of his desk, then put his thumbs under his navy-blue braces as his office door opened.

"Ah, Stefan, there you are at last. I have a story I want you to chase. Jack, our man in South Africa, needs to find out all he can about a man called Phillip Fletcher-Jones, and you're going to do the digging. We've found out he lives down in Cornwall, in St. Ives, but unfortunately, we don't have an address, or a phone number.

"Jack seems to think he may well be involved in a case where a kid pitched up at a water-hole deep in the bush, half dead by all accounts. But she's now recovered and Jack is trying to find any known relatives of hers. So far, the police over there have come up with nothing. He needs our help."

Stefan rubbed his hands in anticipation. "Cornwall? I hear it's nice and warm there, warmer than London. Could do with a bit of sun."

"Don't get your hopes up, son, it is late October after all. Now, get hold of Jack and he'll give you the run down on the story and who, and what, he's looking for. Reception will have his number."

Harry looked out of his window, it was only four in the afternoon and already getting dark. He sighed. "Small enough place, St. Ives, shouldn't be too difficult to engage this Fletcher-Jones in conversation, if you can find him, that is. Hopefully he's not trying to dodge this bloody awful weather and flown off back to the bush."

Stefan raised an eyebrow. "How come you think he'll talk to me then, if he's there that is?"

"Because, son, he seems to have a bush home in your country, somewhere near a place called the Sabi Sands. Do you know it?"

Stefan nodded. "Heard of it, of course, but never had the pleasure of going there."

Harry continued. "Fletcher-Jones travels there on a regular basis, or used to. Once he finds out where you come from, I guarantee he'll open up. Works every time when you've been to a country which someone else has a connection to, it's natural to chat about it. Trust me."

Stefan smiled at him. "Wasn't always like that, Harry. Before, when I mentioned I came from South Africa, it had the same effect as throwing a skunk in their midst. I could clear a room in seconds, back then. But it was a long time ago now. Right, I'm onto the story, I'll go check with Jack, and do a bit of my own research."

"Watch your expense account Stefan. Cornwall is not cheap, no staying at five-star hotels, afternoons at the Spa with some gorgeous girl spreading mud all over your body, and no fine dining, okay. Don't come back 'til you find out everything you can, you hear me?"

Harry watched Stephen as he left the office. In his experience he had always found the South Africans easy going, good natured, mad about rugby and damn hard workers. As though they were carrying the weight of the history of their country on their shoulders, and wanted to prove to the world they were worthy of a second chance with their turbulent and brutal past.

He had high hopes for young Stefan with his easy-going smile, and warm personality. He was a nice-looking kid, well hardly a kid at thirty-three, but he looked like one with his dark floppy hair and grey eyes. People found him easy to talk to – the key component and a great asset for any journalist after a story.

Stefan and Jack would make a good team, each of them living in the other's country.

Chapter Forty-Nine

Stefan de Villiers boarded the train at Paddington Station, his journey would take five and a half hours. Plenty of time to do a little more research and read through Jack's emails and reports to Harry.

He was as intrigued with this girl from nowhere as Jack was. He knew the bush – it seemed impossible to him a child could have survived, but she had.

When the train pulled into St Ives it was already dark and had been since four o'clock. He had enjoyed the journey, passing through country towns with their brightly lit pubs and houses; a welcome sight from the bare, twisted branches of trees, bereft of their leaves, and the endless frost hardened fields, sometimes with only a lone stately manor house for company, shrouded in sweeping fog and drizzle.

Used car lots with their drooping bunting and the occasional glimpse of a red telephone box, or post box, relics from the past, flashed past his streaming window. Houses huddled together like a rugby scrum under the dark skies.

As he often did, he wondered about the lives of the people who lived in those small houses, what secrets they held, what stories lay within.

Following the signs, carrying his overnight bag, he took the ten-minute walk into town and found the bed and breakfast he had booked the day before.

The receptionist greeted him warmly with his soft Cornish lilt and showed him to his comfortable looking room. Stefan, who had the solid build of a rugby player, ducked his head to avoid concussion by colliding with the low wooden beams as he entered the room.

It was clean, and small, but best of all – it was warm. If he bent his knees in the bed, he would probably be able to manage a good night's sleep before he set out on the trail of Mr Fletcher-Jones.

Stefan took a quick shower, squeezing himself sideways, into the tiny cubicle which housed the facility. Then, dressed warmly, he made his way down the dark cobbled street until he found a modest restaurant which, according to the board outside, specialised in freshly caught fish from the harbour.

The young waitress bustled over, her pen poised over her order pad. He scanned the menu then looked up. "It all looks good, what do you recommend?"

She looked at him and smiled. "You look like you have a good appetite, the cod is highly recommended, almost jumped out of the sea and into the frying pan this afternoon. That with a healthy dose of our famous golden chips and mushy peas should do the trick."

Stefan polished off the rounds of bread in the basket and then made short work of the excellent meal.

The waitress brought him his bill. "There we go, sir, I trust you enjoyed your meal."

"Great, thank you. Good recommendation." He reached for his credit card.

"Are you here on holiday, sir?"

"No, a bit of business. Only staying for a couple of days."

She tore the receipt from her machine and handed it to him. "Where are you from?"

"Well, at the moment I live in London, but originally from South Africa."

She beamed at him. "Yes, I thought so. We have quite a few South Africans here, I think they prefer our weather, and our surfing, to other parts of the UK. If there's a rugby match on anytime soon, you'll find them at The Fiddler, in the middle of town. Noisy lot if their team is playing."

Stefan tucked his credit card into his wallet. "I'm actually trying to track down an old buddy of mine, I heard he lived here in town. Name of Fletcher-Jones. Do you know him? I'm sure he must have eaten here judging by the calibre of the food. Always did like his food and eating out."

The young girl shook her head. "Maybe, but I've only been here three weeks, it's a temporary job until I go to Uni. I don't remember any credit card with that name, sorry."

*****

Stefan returned to his lodgings, stripped off his clothes and wedged his body into the bed.

The Fiddler would be his first port of call after scouting out the town the next morning. Tomorrow was Saturday, if there was any rugby on, The Fiddler would be a good place to start with his investigation as to the whereabouts of the elusive Fletcher-Jones.

Besides he had a longing to hear the voices of his homeland with any fellow South Africans who might be watching a game.

*****

Stefan woke early, it was still dark but he was keen to explore the town. After a substantial breakfast he set off. A faint promise of sun started to gild the sky.

St Ives was a pretty fishing village with narrow cobbled streets, independent shops, white washed fisherman's cottages and a wide sweeping bay with sandy beaches. Tall lush palm trees rattled in the stiff breeze and Stefan was instantly reminded of Cape Town, Camps Bay in particular, without the howling wind whipping the sea into a broiling frenzy.

He walked around the town for a couple of hours, enjoying the fresh sea air, a pleasant change from the choking polluted air of London, and the slower pace of things.

Stefan sat on one of the hard benches straddling the curve of the bay, an enormous seagull eyed him greedily, hoping, perhaps he might whip out a bag of chips. The colour of its wings matched the white and grey clouds now rolling in. He checked his watch, time for an early pub lunch. Time to get to work.

The Fiddler sat straddled between a fishmonger and a shoe shop. He pushed open the door and went in.

A large screen took up most of one of the walls, tables were grouped together and a long bar with leather backed stools ran the length of another.

He propped himself at the bar and ordered a glass of cider and a crab sandwich, chalked up as the special of the day, on the bar menu. Someone had left what looked like a local newspaper on the seat next to him. He picked it up.

Stefan knew if you wanted to know more about a place and the people who lived there, the local rag was the way to go.

188

He flicked through the ads, read a few of the articles, skimmed through the announcements for sporting events, mostly water borne, times of church services, the date of the next village fete, a local funeral, and other village happenings. He made a mental note of the address of the newspaper, folded it up and finished his sandwich.

A young man two seats away from him turned and smiled. "Not much going on in this town, hey."

Stefan returned the smile, recognising the accent immediately. "I'm sure the locals who live here like it exactly the way it is. Where are you from then?"

The young man laughed. "Durban, and you?"

"Cape Town, but I live in London now. Do you live in St Ives?"

The young man held out his hand. "Marius Steenkamp. No. Way to quiet for me. I'm taking a break for a couple of days. I try and get down here at least once a year. I live in Manchester, lots of South Africans there, I supply them with all they need.

"I own a small shop and stock all their favourite brands from back home, I also make my own biltong, boerewors, *braai* sauces, droewors, and import Ouma's Rusks, all those sorts of things. You'd be amazed what people miss from the old country. And you?"

"Stefan de Villiers. I'm a journalist with *The Telegraph*."

"Oh yeah, what are you doing here then. Following a story or interviewing someone?"

Stefan took a mouthful of his cider. "I'm following a story which, strangely enough, has its beginning up near the Sabi Sands, near the Kruger."

Marius looked incredulous. "How does a story start near the Kruger and lead here to St Ives?"

"I'm trying to find someone who might be able to help with the identity of a child who went missing in the bush. It's a long shot but the only one we have at the moment."

Marius tugged at his earlobe. "Haven't heard anything about this story. Who are you looking for? I don't know a lot of people here but my mate, who I'm staying with, has lived here for years. He owns a rather fine wine shop in the centre of town. Maybe he could help."

Stefan's face brightened. "The guy I'd like to chat to is called Fletcher-Jones. He used to have a bush house in the area where the child was eventually found. I'm not saying he was involved, not at all, but he might be able to help us find the kid's family. No-one's came forward to claim her, but it's possible Fletcher-Jones might have known her parents, or possibly be related."

"Give me your number, Stefan. I'll ask my friend if he knows him. With a posh name like his, it's possible he might enjoy a bottle of fine wine or two and frequent the shop."

Stefan slid his card across the bar. "Appreciate any help you can give me. Here, let me buy you a drink, then I'll be on my way."

Chapter Fifty

Stefan made his way back to the guest house, already the evening was closing in and he was no-where near finding his man. He had been loath to ask too many of the locals if anyone knew him. A few of the shop owners had regarded him suspiciously, as if they had rumbled he was a journalist. In a small place like St Ives, it wouldn't take long for word to reach the person he was looking for, if indeed he was in town.

If Fletcher-Jones was somehow involved in the case of the child, he might go to ground. If he had something to hide.

Stephan spent the next hour checking Jack's reports again, searching for any other clues which might have been missed. Looking for anything he could follow up.

His phone vibrated on the table next to him.

"Stefan? Marius here. I spoke to my mate. He does know Fletcher-Jones, he's a good customer of his, and he's currently in town.

"From what I can gather he's a bit of a loner, doesn't mix much with the locals. His favourite watering hole is called The Tinners Arms which is about a forty-five-minute walk from town. One of the oldest pubs in the area. Good luck."

*****

Stefan again squeezed himself into the cubicle of the shower, then changed, pulling on a fresh shirt, a thick sweater and his coat, before heading for the reception desk downstairs and ordering a taxi to take him to The Tinner's Arms.

Apparently, the pub was at least seven hundred years old, a favourite haunt of long-gone poets, artists and writers; D.H. Lawrence being one of them.

Stefan ducked through the entrance and made his way past the crowded tables and wooden benches, stacked with plump cushions.

Easing off his coat he found a table near one of the roaring fireplaces, then removed his sweater, before heading to the long-pitted wooden bar, which certainly looked a few hundred years old, to order a drink.

He returned to his seat, clutching a glass of wine in one hand and the menu in the other.

The Tinners Arms was a quiet subdued place, no loud music, no massive television screens, only groups of people talking quietly amongst themselves, a large dog was stretched out near one of the fires. This was a local place for locals, especially at this time of the year, when all the tourists had returned home.

He ordered a rare steak, which, according to the menu was from herds reared on the local pastures, and had been hung for twenty-eight days.

His meal arrived and he tucked in, closing his eyes with pleasure as he bit into the steak with its baked potato and onion accompaniments, it truly was a feast for the senses. Mopping up the last of the steak juices with a crusty roll he sat back, satiated.

The waitress removed his plate and whisked away the basket of bread. Feeling pleasantly full and having thoroughly enjoyed his dinner, Stefan scrolled through the messages on his phone, unaware of the person standing in front of him.

"I hear you've been asking around town about me."

Startled, Stefan looked up. In front of him stood a tall man, expensively dressed and sporting a full head of hair, tinged at the edges with grey, as was his neat beard, and with a pair of startling blue eyes set in a face which looked as though it were made of granite, sixty or so years of it.

"What do you want. I don't like people asking questions about me."

Stefan carefully put his phone to one side. There would be no messing around with polite conversation with the man in front of him. The wine merchant had clearly tipped him off.

He half rose in his seat and extended his hand, which was pointedly ignored.

"Mr Fletcher-Jones?"

"Maybe. We don't like strangers asking questions around here."

Stefan sank back into his chair. "My name is Stefan de Villiers. Perhaps you'd like to join me and I'll explain."

"I know who you are. A South African journalist. I don't have a lot of time for journalists, scum of the earth as far as I'm concerned, always out and about, trying to dig up dirt on someone's personal life. Well, believe you me, it's not going to work with me. Why, exactly are you looking for me, may I ask?"

"I'm trying to help a little girl who seems to have lost her parents."

Fletcher-Jones raised his eyebrows. "What has that got to do with me?"

Stefan held up his hand. "We need your help, sir. I understand you visit South Africa quite often, and you have a bush home there?"

"That's none of your business, or anyone else's."

Stefan narrowed his eyes, his voice hardened. "A little girl was found up near the Kruger Park. Someone suggested you might be able to help us. Perhaps you might know her parents having lived in the same area, or close by. The child needs help, sir. We don't know who she is, her sister is also missing."

Fletcher-Jones granite expression didn't soften. "How did my name come into this story?" he asked abruptly.

"We have a journalist following the story in South Africa. He was in Hazyview, your name was mentioned."

Fletcher-Jones shrugged off his coat and lowered himself into the seat opposite Stefan. "Oh, so now there are two lost little girls, eh. And you think that I'm involved in this?"

Stefan stood his ground. "We need to find the truth and if you can help us in any way, we'd appreciate it."

"Let me make myself quite clear. If my name is mentioned I will sue your newspaper." He shrugged. "But I'm a reasonable man, De Villiers, with nothing to hide. A lost child, or, as it would appear, two lost children, gives cause for concern. I can't imagine what the parents are going through, I have a niece and nephew, so I do know a little about families with children."

Stefan lifted his phone and scrolled to the photograph of Abby.

"This is the little girl called Abby, sir. Did you ever see her around the Sabi Sands area?"

Fletcher-Jones stared at the photograph. "No, I've never seen her before. These days one doesn't go around staring at little girls, or boys for that matter. I don't need to explain to you why. The world is a different place to the one I grew up in. Quite different. People are quick to point a finger these days, wrecking reputations in the process. Reputations which are hard to build up again." He glowered at Stephan. "The consequences can be disastrous, as you no doubt know being a journalist. The media have a lot to answer for."

He handed the phone back to Stefan. "To set the record straight, I don't have any children. I'm sure if you check the official records this will become blatantly clear. I have never been married, and don't intend to change the situation any time soon. Yes, I have a bush home near the Kruger Park, but I haven't been there for a year or so now.

"I don't know how my name has come into all of this, but you can be damn sure I am going to clear it, one way or another, especially as it involves two little girls. That's the kind of story the media love, it implies all sorts of despicable things. Once someone is suspected of being involved with small children, well, it destroys his standing in any community. A hard label to shake off, even though one's name may be cleared."

Stefan smiled at him, hoping to soften the angry expression on the man's face. "Rural towns are a breeding ground for gossip, involving all sorts of speculation. Someone has obviously made a big mistake by introducing your name."

Stefan glanced at his phone. "I shall make it quite clear to my editor, and to our journalist in South Africa, Jack Taylor, that you are no way involved in any of this, based on what you've told me."

Fletcher-Jones sat back in his chair and seemed to relax slightly. "I want the name of your source in Hazyview. The name of the person who said I was involved with the two girls. I'm going to sue them. You can be sure of that. These are serious accusations De Villiers."

He glanced around the bar before turning back to Stefan. "Now, tell me what this is all about, the whole story. I didn't venture into Hazyview much. I went to the bush to write my memoirs, to get away from people. The sounds of the bush are cathartic, I enjoy my time there, I'm not sure I will in the future, though. Given your story there might be a cloud over my head with these girls."

Stefan extended his hand across the table, and this time the greybearded man shook it reluctantly. "Nothing in our newspaper, and we have the exclusive on this story, has connected you with this, nothing has been published. Only one person gave Jack your name and apparently, she wasn't a reliable source. I'm sure he will re-visit her with his own questions."

Fletcher-Jones raised his eyebrows. "A female? Highly unlikely. I don't know any females in Hazyview. I rarely went into town as I told you."

Stefan chose his next words carefully; the man had become less aggressive with his conversation. "I think, perhaps, you had your hair cut now and again, in town."

Fletcher-Jones looked astonished. "You and your fellow journalist have been digging deep. Yes, I did have my hair cut once or twice in a place on the main road. Are you telling me the girl who cut my hair gave you this information about me and these girls?"

Stefan nodded. "We'd appreciate it if you didn't set your lawyers on her, sir. Jack is following any lead he can lay his hands on. If this hairdresser is in anyway involved, we don't want her to disappear."

"But why would she use my name, for goodness' sake?"

Stefan, shrugged and shook his head. "I don't know but we'll find out."

He reached into his shirt pocket. "Here's my card. Feel free to call my editor, Harry, I'm sure he'll give you all the reassurance you need that your name will not be mentioned in any stories we're following."

Fletcher-Jones stood up and reached for his coat. "I will indeed call him. I'm the local Magistrate here, just so you know." He paused for a moment. "Well, one thing you have achieved, young man, is this. I now have no desire to return to my bush home, which was a place of great joy to me. Your story has tainted it for me.

"I've been thinking of selling it anyway. I don't like the way the Government there is looking to reclaim land, farms or otherwise. It would appear some old goat farmer whose ancestors farmed the land a hundred years ago, and whose goats nibbled on a bit of grass now and then, is able to claim the land as his own."

He tugged at his beard then smoothed it down. "Much as I love Africa, South Africa in particular, I don't need those sorts of problems in my life, and this latest bit of news which you have imparted to me, makes me quite sure selling the place would be the best thing to do."

He stroked his beard. "It seems to me," he mused, "even now, after all this time, there's a certain resentment to English born people buying homes in your country. I always felt it. Not quite belonging, not quite fitting in."

He eased on his coat. "You see, we English, French, Germans or Belgians, or wherever else people come from, have a choice. If things don't work out in Africa we can come home. You, on the other hand, don't have those choices, do you?"

Stefan narrowed his eyes. "What you're saying is quite true. Unless we have an ancestorial history in another country, and can become a citizen of one of these countries, then we have no other choice but to fight our way through the various situations developing in South Africa, and despair at the destruction of our homeland. But it is our land, our home - and the roots are deeply embedded."

He felt the anger, the injustice of it all, now souring his stomach, ruining his dinner.

"You may not have a high opinion of South Africans, sir, and yes, our history is raw and new compared to yours. However, if I recall from my history lessons at school, the British did their fair share of plundering and pillaging. Taking foreign countries and ruling them without the consent of the people living there, people who were born there."

Stefan tried to keep his temper under control as he continued. "Enjoying the lifestyle, the cheap labour, the bevy of servants at their beck and call, the exclusive country clubs and elegant social life.

"Your own history is not without blemish, the same with America, Australia, and many other European countries, they also carry the burden of guilt with their past.

"And, let's not forget the Chinese. They resented the imperious way foreigners treated Shanghai as their own port city and governed her by their treaties and laws, speaking pidgin English to some of the Chinese whose English was as refined as any English Lord's.

"As for the Opium trade…well, you British did well out of it if I recall."

Stefan's pent-up resentment, and the unfairness of some of the treatment he had experienced since arriving in this country, bubbled to the surface.

"Funny how history manages to brush it all under the carpet isn't it?"

He gave Fletcher-Jones a tight smile. "Even today, the slightest whiff of racial discrimination in South Africa, and the world comes down on our heads. I think there is envy in the way we live, our glorious weather and elevated lifestyle, which, by the way, is enjoyed now by all races. There will always be the great divide between the poor and the rich, but, then it would make us equal to almost every other country in the world, wouldn't it?"

Fletcher-Jones wrapped his scarf around his neck, a faint smile hovering on his lips. "Good luck, De Villiers, I admire your spirit. Never give up with what you believe in. We British fought two deadly, destructive world wars, and a few others after that, for what we believed in. It was our love for our country, that pulled us through. Our passion for what was right; our passion to endure. It's who we are today."

A smile flickered across his face. "It's what your people can be tomorrow."

He paused as he buttoned up his expensive looking coat. I'll speak to your editor tomorrow. This whole thing smacks to me of mistaken identity. A foolish young woman who gave your Jack Taylor the wrong name."

He rammed his hat on his head and stomped out of the pub.

*****

Stefan curled up on his bed and pulled the duvet up under his chin, feeling the warmth seep through his bones, although his feet were sticking out at the end of the bed. He stared out of the window, going over his conversation with Fletcher-Jones, hoping his outburst hadn't messed things up for Jack and Harry.

A lone car splashed through a puddle outside. The yellow street light was wreathed in a filmy shroud of fine rain, then there was utter silence.

He reached for his phone from the night stand and called Jack.

"Fletcher-Jones is not our man, Jack. Too old to have two small daughters. Bachelor through and through, and the local bloody magistrate to boot. Harry might have to do a little massaging to cool the guy down – he's not happy."

He rubbed his feet together trying to warm them. "I think Harry might be in for a rather expensive lunch next time Fletcher-Jones is in London, which, if I'm not mistaken, might be in the next few days. He was furious to say the least, thought we were hinting he might be a paedophile or something."

Jack laughed. "Don't worry, Harry is the master of diplomacy, it's why he's where he is, top of his game. They'll be the best of mates after a long, expensive, liquid lunch, at Harry's club."

Stefan stifled a yawn. "So, Jack, what do we do next. Where are you with the story."

Jack brought him up to date. "I'm beginning to think these two girls were not from South Africa, it's the lead I'm going after now. Maybe they came over one of the borders. I think they lost their parents in some kind of accident, otherwise the parents would have come forward by now.

"I'm working with Piet Joubert, my grumpy old retired detective who lives in a small town near Port Elizabeth. He might be grumpy but he's pretty smart. He's following a few other leads for me; I've worked with him before."

There was a pause at the end of the line before Stefan spoke.

"You think these girls may have come from a different country? I might be able to help you there. There's a shop in London called *Vintage Africa*, have you heard of it?"

"Yeah. It was part of the story the newspaper covered about the two sisters who lived in Kenya in a place called Mbabati. You obviously know it, Stefan?"

"Of course. I don't go there often but it's where a lot of ex Kenyan's, Zimbabwean's and South Africans hang out once a month. They have a sundowner evening there – hugely popular.

"New owner now, but it still has the buzz, a real melting pot of people who all seem to be related or know someone who knows someone from what they call the old days. It's extraordinary, history has changed everything, but these folks all seem to have a connection, difficult to explain to someone who has never been brought up there."

Another lone car splashed through a puddle outside, then there was silence again. "I'll be back in London tomorrow, Jack, I'll drop by *Vintage Africa* and see what I can pick up – someone may know something, may have heard of something. I'll let you know what I find out."

Chapter Fifty-One
South Africa

The next morning Jack dressed quickly. Outside, the hotel gardens and trees were bathed in a fine film of rain. A brisk wind blew leaves haphazardly across the normally immaculate lawns. The dark green sun umbrellas usually shading small tables, had been lowered and tethered to their poles.

Surprised at the dip in temperature at this time of the year, Jack reached for a warm jumper, shoved his feet into his safari boots and made his way to the dining room for breakfast.

As he tucked into his bacon and eggs, he mulled over the conversation he had had with Stefan the night before, glancing at the notes he had made. It seemed Fletcher-Jones was a dead end after all. Harry would not be happy with the expense of that trip which had come to nothing, except they could eliminate Fletcher-Jones as someone who was involved with Abby's story. So not a complete waste of time. Although by the sounds of it he had given Stefan a hard time.

Harry wouldn't be happy about the expensive lunch he was going to have to pay for at his club either.

Perhaps Stefan would come up with a few leads after his visit to *Vintage Africa*. Jack had a good feeling about that. From experience he knew that although a huge continent, Africa seemed quite small when looking for information. Everyone, it seemed to him, knew someone who knew someone. The network was extraordinary.

After two cups of strong coffee, Jack was ready to get on with the day ahead.

*****

Jack looked at his watch as he cruised down the main street of the town. The barber shop wasn't open yet, it was only eight o' clock.

The shades of the shop were down and a *closed* sign hung listlessly over the door.

He parked his car a short distance away and settled down to wait. The light rain was still falling and he used his wipers to clear the screen so he had an unimpeded view.

An hour later the shops and cafés started to open up, but the barbers shop stayed closed.

Jack scrolled through his phone, found the web site for Hazyview which listed many of the businesses in town and what time they opened.

The hairdresser with the pink hair was no-where to be seen and the shop remained stubbornly closed. He rang the number listed then gave up after six rings.

Jack locked his car and made his way across the road, dodging the puddles. He peered through the windows of the barber shop, using his sleeve, trying to see around the closed shades, pondering his next move.

Giving up he took refuge from the rain in a second-hand book shop next door.

The older man behind the till, who he presumed would be the owner or manager, was sporting an impressive beard and stomach, his khaki shirt pulled tightly across it. He lifted his head when he saw Jack and gave him a big smile displaying uneven, tobacco-stained teeth.

"Morning. Feel free to browse around," he looked out of the window. "Good day for it, looks like the rain is here to stay for the day. But, hey, tomorrow the sun will be out again, and everyone will be complaining about the heat," he said cheerfully.

Jack nodded to him. "Thanks, I'm not looking for anything in particular, but I might find something…"

The big man gestured around the shop. "Fiction on the right, non-fiction at the back. Local authors over there, although most of the books are in Afrikaans which you might struggle with unless you speak the language."

Jack glanced around the shop. "You don't by any chance have some old maps of the Kruger Park and Sabi Sands area, do you? I'm a bit of a collector."

"*Ja,* I have a few, over there in the corner in the top right-hand drawer of the cabinet."

Jack soon became engrossed in a world long gone, the maps he perused were basic to say the least. All hand drawn but offered an insight into the magical untouched kingdom of the wild before man started to intrude and turned the area into the spectacular, world famous, tourist destination it was today.

More careful than he usually was, he folded one of the maps up, delighted it was a simple exercise and folded nicely, unlike the ones he normally had to do battle with.

He made his way back to the front of the shop to pay for it. The man with the big beard nodded at him. "*Ja,* this is a good piece of history to add to your collection." He scratched his beard and dislodged what looked like a few crumbs of bread. "But it's not cheap, hey."

Jack handed over his credit card. "No worries, just ring it up."

Jack peered out of the window. "I was hoping to get my hair cut next door, but the place seems to be closed up. Any idea what time it might be opening?"

The book shop owner slipped Jack's map into a paper bag and handed him his receipt.

"You mean Elspeth's place? Haven't seen her for a few days. Maybe she's gone on holiday somewhere, or gone to visit her family in the Eastern Cape. But plenty of other places in town you can get your hair cut."

The man scratched his beard again and dislodged a few more crumbs. "Well, who knows where she is. She might be up in her flat and not feeling so good. She lives on top of the shop."

Jack thanked him, slipped the paper bag into his top pocket under his jumper and left. He looked up and located where her flat might be.

He made his way to the corner of the block and found the steps leading up to what he presumed were the flats above the shops.

A young African woman was enthusiastically beating a mat over the edge of the railing outside one of the flats.

He smiled at her. "Morning. I'm looking for Elspeth. Can't remember the number of her flat though."

The young woman smiled at him, revealing perfect teeth. "Number eight, mister."

He thanked her and made his way to flat number eight. He paused then rapped lightly on the door.

There was silence from within, he tried again. Still nothing. The African woman was looking at him. "She's there, mister, I saw her yesterday. Here, let me try."

She rapped hard on the door. "It's me Elspeth, Agnes" she shouted. "You alright?"

Jack heard the keys turning in the lock. Elspeth appeared with a smile on her face which quickly turned to fear when she saw who was standing outside.

She tried to close the door but Jack was ready for her, and held it open with his arm. "It's alright Elspeth. I only want to talk to you.".

Agnes looked curiously from one to the other, then went back to beating her mat.

"May I come in Elspeth. We need to clear something up. I need your help."

Elspeth seemed to shrink in front of his eyes, as if all the puff had gone out of her. The bright, breezy, friendly and confident girl now seemed to be cloaked in something else. Warily she stood back from the door and reluctantly let him in, her face white with apprehension.

She sank down on a pink sofa. In Jack's eyes, everything around Elspeth seemed to have a pink tinge to it. She put her face in her hands.

The flat was simple, a modest open plan area which encompassed the living space, the kitchen, and a tiny two chair dining room alcove with a table.

He lowered himself into the single chair, covered in a pink nylon throw.

"Why did you do it Elspeth. Why did you randomly pick a name out of your appointment book and tell me Fletcher-Jones was the father of the two children. Because, as you well know, he isn't. We have proof of that now."

Elspeth looked up, pulling a tissue out of her sleeve. She dabbed her eyes. "I had no choice, you see. I gave you the wrong name, it's true."

He paused, watching her. "Why?"

Elspeth twisted the tissue in her hand, avoiding his eyes. "It was when you mentioned the girl, the one they found at the game lodge. I didn't have time to think it through. I panicked."

Jack leaned forward and spoke to her softly. "Elspeth, I'm not here to hurt you or get you into trouble. I'm trying to find the parents of two girls, one was called Abby, her sister's name was Susie. One has been found; Susie is still missing. It's unlikely she would have survived out there in the bush on her own, if she was on her own that is."

He leaned towards her. "I want to find out what happened to them. How they both ended up in the bush by themselves. It's impossible. They must have had an adult with them. I need to find their parents, and I think you know something about the girls."

Elspeth rubbed her eyes. "Their parents are dead, they died somewhere in Zimbabwe," she whispered desperately.

Jack took a deep breath. "Were they relatives of yours. Family? Where in Zimbabwe did this happen and when? What was the family surname, you must know it?"

Elspeth shook her head. "No, they were not my family. I don't know when it happened or where, or what their surname was."

"So, they were not your family. Okay, but perhaps someone in your family knew the girls' family, would I be right?"

She looked at him suspiciously, then dropped her eyes from his.

Jack tried again. "How come you know so much about this family but you're telling me nothing, and that you didn't know them. Someone must have told you the girls' parents were dead. How do you know they came from Zimbabwe? Come on Elspeth. Help me out here."

She stood up, the crumpled tissues falling to the floor next to her chair. "I can't talk about this now. I need to think about things, talk to someone. Come back tomorrow, and I'll try to help you, okay?

"Maybe I can bring you someone, just now, who will help you."

Jack frowned. "Just now? I thought you said come back tomorrow."

Despite her obvious distress, Elspeth managed a shaky smile. "It's what we say here. Just now can mean, well, just now, or tomorrow, or next week or next month."

Jack shook his head in frustration. "So, what's the time scale here then? Tomorrow, next week, or when?"

"Tomorrow. I'll bring someone tomorrow. In the afternoon."

Jack had enough experience to know he couldn't get anything more from her, and reluctantly he left.

*****

Elspeth closed and locked the door behind him, then slid down the wall and nibbled at her already bitten nails. She was in big trouble.

Getting unsteadily to her feet she reached for the phone and punched in the number of her contact.

"The girl they found at the water hole," she whispered, "it was Abby. But they only know her Christian name."

Tears flooded her eyes. "Susie is missing," her voice rose with each word. "She could never have survived the storm.

"What happened to *him*! Tell me!" she screamed.

"Oh God, what a terrible mess, why didn't you tell me about the girls. How could you *not* tell me? The English journalist is super smart, he won't let this story go. Then the police will get involved.

"And where will it leave me, hey?" She was sobbing with fear now, her voice breaking.

"In big trouble, that's where! I have to disappear for a while and hope this nightmare will go away. The police will come for you as well. They'll find you, and what will you tell them?"

The phone went dead in her hand.

*****

Jack unlocked his car and slid into his seat. Elspeth was the key to many of the questions he was looking to find answers for. She knew the girl's family, or something about them.

He would return the following afternoon and meet whoever it was she wanted him to meet.

If Elspeth was telling him the truth, then the two girls must have come across the border from Zimbabwe.

But who did they come with if their parents were dead?

They would have needed passports, visa's, whoever brought them here would have had to have had the permission of the deceased parents.

Therefore, he concluded, it must have been a relative.

Elspeth?

The other thing he had noticed was a map tacked to the wall in her flat – it was the same as the one Toby, the pilot, had sourced for him…

Chapter Fifty-Two

Jack had a feeling Elspeth, and her friend, whoever it was, would not be there when he pitched up at her flat after lunch. He had more than likely frightened her off. He knocked on the door and waited.

He looked around to see if the carpet beater and her warm smile was anywhere around, but she wasn't.

Giving up, Jack, went back to the book shop. The big Afrikaner smiled at him as he handed a book and sales slip to a customer, before turning to him.

"So, my friend, you didn't manage to get something done with your hair."

Jack smoothed his hair. "No," he said sheepishly. "The shop is still closed and it seems Elspeth is nowhere around. I tried her flat but there was no response. I was supposed to meet her there this afternoon."

"Ja, you'll have to find another place for a haircut. Elspeth left this morning. Dropped the keys to the salon off here. Said she was going to see her family. Some personal problems."

Jack cursed under his breath. "Any idea where she went? Where her family lives?"

He frowned at Jack. "Why are you so interested in our Elspeth? Not your type, I would think. Plenty other places for getting your hair fixed."

Jack sighed. He would have to level with this guy if he wanted more information, the man, he could see, was already suspicious of his motives.

He leaned on the counter. "My name's Jack Taylor. I'm a journalist. I'm following the story about the girl who was found in the bush. Do you know the story?"

The big Afrikaner stretched out his hand, the size of a side plate. "Gert van der Westhuizen. Yes, of course, I know the story. Everyone knows the story. But how is Elspeth involved in this. She's a hairdresser?"

"How long have you known her Gert?"

Gert scratched his beard, dislodging a crumb or two. "Over a year maybe. Quiet as a mouse when she first arrived, but she changed a bit after a year here. Took to drinking in the local bars, loved to party, yes, she changed…"

"She changed?"

"Yes. From quiet, to not so quiet. Sometimes the salon would be open, then closed for a day or two, sometimes three."

"So, Gert, who owns the salon? Who employs her?"

Gert moved some books around on the counter. "Well, I own the whole block here. Elspeth took over the salon. No-one was interested in a barber's shop. Not fancy enough for the tourist types. The previous owner ran it down. Elspeth revived it, and did quite well. Paid the rent, took the flat above the shop. I didn't ask any questions. She paid both rentals in advance."

Jack scratched his head. "Did you ever see her with a man, a boyfriend, any family members?"

"No, never. But what went on in the salon, or her flat, after hours was none of my business, like I said, she paid both rents on time."

"Okay Gert. Can you give me her surname? An identity number, which I know everyone must have in this country?"

Gert shook his head. "No. I was happy to have someone take over the salon and one of my flats. I didn't ask for an ID number. *Ag*, Jack, it's how it is here, out in the bush, we don't ask questions, we don't have hard and fast rules. We like the look of someone, they pay their deposit, we do the business."

Jack bit the corner of his lip. "But surely you have to file your business dealings with the tax authorities. You must know her surname to do this, have her identity number. There must have been a lease of some sort, which would require an identity number. I know this from my own experience here."

Gert snorted. "We Afrikaners can be creative when we need to be. The government has taken enough from us. Our national anthem, our language, our flag and just about everything else. Our loyalty lies with our people now. We do what we need to do, to survive.

"So, no, I can't remember Elspeth's surname, she probably told me but I've forgotten what it was, although I'm sure she has an identity number, like we all have to have. But this, my friend, I cannot give you because like all of us, our Elspeth flew under the wire. There was never a lease signed between us."

Jack nodded and shook the man's hand. "Thank you, Gert. I don't suppose you would let me have the keys to Elspeth's flat. See if I could find a bit more about her perhaps?"

Gert shook his head vehemently, his eyes suddenly hostile. "No. Absolutely not. As I said, her private life is her private life. We Afrikaners respect this. I'm sorry I can't help you."

Disgruntled and angry with himself that he had let his one lead escape, he left the bookshop. There was only one person he could turn to for help. Someone who knew these people far better than he did.

Piet Joubert. He was an Afrikaner; Gert was an Afrikaner and so was Elspeth.

Chapter Fifty-Three
London

Stefan de Villiers dodged his way through a canopy of a steady stream of black umbrellas as he headed for the shop, *Vintage Africa* in Mayfair. Although only five in the afternoon it was already dark on a bitterly cold, and wet, late October day.

He ducked under the dark green canopied entrance and let himself into the shop. It was the legendary Sundowner evening, and the place was buzzing. A melting pot of different cultures and ages, blending happily together.

Wafting lazily in the warm air were the old flags of East and Southern Africa, standing defiantly alongside all the vivid colours of the new ones.

Stefan made his way through the crowds, noticing the old trunks made from wood, canvas and tin piled up along one wall of the room, their sides stencilled in ghostly white, giving names of long-forgotten people who had journeyed by sea looking for romance and adventure.

Displayed on another long trestle table were various items made of solid silver. Candlesticks and cutlery, napkin holders with worn and illegible engravings, some with crests of long-dead aristocratic families. Objects which had probably graced elegant tables in places far away from England and Europe, he thought to himself.

Each item with its own story, as lost now as their long-ago owners. Things which would have brought a sense of continuity, a sense of place, to lives in an unfamiliar land, a touch of home left far behind.

Stefan made his way past hundreds of books which lined another wall, having survived the hot and sometimes humid conditions, the ants, the moths and silver fish. Medical, farming, and cookery books. Legal tomes with faded red covers and cracked spines, hunting books, and memoirs of the old pioneer families and their children. All gone now.

But their names lived on through their writing. Stefan found that thought strangely poignant.

Campaign furniture, which he knew was very collectable now, filled half of the shop, exquisite pieces which could be packed away and carried on mules and horses through the sometimes hostile, and unchartered terrain, so many years ago.

Stefan thought about the young men and women from England and Europe, who had set out from their own secure countries and gone on their great adventures to Africa and India, determined to map it all out. Setting up their camps as evening fell, surrounded by their hired porters who created a touch of comfort in the middle of the wild, with standards to be adhered to come what may.

Chairs, camp beds and cooking pots, along with candlesticks and silver cutlery would have graced their tables, as they diligently wrote up the days experience and discoveries in their diaries, dipping their nibs into ink pots, swatting away the mosquitoes and moths as they fluttered and collided with the hissing hurricane lamps.

Stefan lifted his hand, acknowledging some of the people he recognised, before helping himself to a beer from a makeshift bar, and dropping some coins into a battered silver champagne bucket sitting in a hollowed-out elephant's foot.

Then he spotted Marius, the purveyor of all things South African, whom he had met in Cornwall.

"Hey, Stefan, good to see you again. How was the rest of your trip in St Ives? Did you find your man?"

Stefan nodded. "Yes, I did, thank you. Not warmly received I have to say. What are you doing in London, Marius?"

"Stocking my London shop. I always try to drop in here," he waved his hand around the crowd, "always a lot of contacts, and it gives me a taste of home, instead of me giving everyone else the same thing. But I'm off back to Manchester tomorrow. How's the story going?"

"We're following a few things. It seems one of them might lead to Zimbabwe, a tenuous link but one we need to follow up."

Marius took a long pull from his bottle of beer then waved it around the room. "Well, I'm sure you'll find someone in this crowd from Zimbabwe. What are you thinking here? The girl who was found might have come from across one of the borders? It's very possible. The so-called winds of change blew many a family to South Africa, all looking for a new life."

Marius narrowed his eyes and looked around, then lifted his beer and beckoned to someone across the heads of the crowd. "Hey, Rob," he yelled, "someone I'd like you to meet," he waved the man over.

"Have a word with Rob. He's a third generation Rhodesian, or Zimbabwean, he knows what's going on there. Still lives there."

A man pushed his way through the knots of people. "Hey Rob, how are you? I'd like you to meet a friend of mine, Stefan de Villiers. He's a journalist. Maybe you can help him."

Stefan and Rob shook hands as Marius introduced them, then he wandered off to meet up with more of his mates and, hopefully, some new customers, leaving them to talk.

Rob watched him go then turned to Stefan. "So, another journalist chasing yet another story about the rise and fall of Zimbabwe. Which newspaper are you with?"

"The Telegraph, I'm based here in London."

Rob had the healthy look of a man in his early fifties who had spent most of his life under the merciless sun of Africa. Deep white lines fanned from his eyes from years of squinting into the far horizons, his skin baked dark under the same sun.

"You still live in Zimbabwe Rob?"

"Yeah, it's my home. I'm visiting my uncle; he wants me to come and live here. But it's impossible." He lifted his shoulders looking out at the darkening sky. "I don't know anyone here. I don't know how things work. I don't like the bloody weather either. I couldn't live anywhere else but my own country."

He raised his hand to acknowledge an acquaintance. "I rent a flat in Bulawayo. We lost our farm, it was taken from us by the government, but I can still get into my *bakkie* and drive out into the bush, that hasn't changed.

"The sun rises, and it sets, in this land of mine. Politicians can't screw that up, however hard they try. The animals are still there, doing what they do. The landscape is the same and the sun still shines. Despite everything, I'm blessed."

Stefan took a sip of his beer. "Can't have been easy. We're seeing the same in South Africa, not on the scale you saw, but farm murders are escalating and the government are doing nothing about it. White farms which have been in the families for generations, razed to the ground, families slaughtered, even babies and children. Those thugs show no mercy, it doesn't matter what colour you are."

Rob wiped his sleeve across his eyes, took another pull at his beer and gave a despairing shake of his head. "So, what did you want to talk to me about?"

Stefan told him about the girl at the water hole and the missing sister. "It's possible they may have come across the border with someone. A family member perhaps. It seems their parents died somewhere in Zimbabwe. We have no idea where in the country it might have been. Possibly a farm somewhere, it seems the little girl knew her way around the bush, must have done to have survived. Someone took the two girls, across the border, legally or illegally, and hid them away somewhere in the Sabi Sands game reserve."

Rob sighed and tugged at his ear lobe. "My country is in chaos, Stefan. No records are kept of which farms have been taken, or who has taken them, it happened all over the country. Farmers are still being murdered or badly beaten up, their livestock slaughtered, their homes destroyed.

"You're looking for a grey hair on a beach unless you have some hard facts, which it would seem you don't have. Not even the surname of the girls' family. Surely this child can speak and tell you something. Her name?"

Stefan shook his head. "Apparently, she's so severely traumatised she hardly says a word. We know nothing about her. Only that her name is Abby and her sister was called Susie. That's it, no surname."

Rob frowned. "Look, we try and keep track of what's happening in my country. We're a tight knit community, we look out for each other. But unless you can give me a surname, the name of the farm, which part of the country it might have been in, I doubt I'll be able to help you."

Stefan ran his hands through his damp hair. "Surely, if you're such a tight knit community, you must know of family tragedies in the past couple of years. It may be that the parents of the girls died together, a car accident, or even a farm attack. At this stage we know so little."

Rob put down his empty bottle of beer and reached for his coat draped over a chair behind him. "Give me your card, Stefan, I'll see what I can find out, to try and help you. But it will be nearly impossible without a surname, I can tell you that."

Stefan handed him his card. "Jack Taylor is our journalist in South Africa, following this story. His details are on the back of my card. If you come up with anything I think you should contact him direct. I don't think there's anything more I can do from this end. Appreciate it, Rob, thanks for your time."

Stefan watched Rob leave the shop, his shoulders hunched against the weather. The man clearly loved Zimbabwe, and would never leave, no matter how persuasive his uncle might be.

It was his home and he wanted to stay there.

Chapter Fifty-Four
South Africa

Jack punched in the number for ex-detective Piet Joubert, then sat back in his cane chair. A short burst of rain followed by the sun lit up the wet landscape, which now glittered like jewels scattered in the trees and through the grass.

"Hey Piet. How are you. Any news for me?"

Piet grunted into the phone. "What are you Jack, some kind of psychic? I was about to call you."

Jack sat up straight, the newspaper sliding from his lap, landing in an untidy heap on the floor. "You have news?"

"*Ja*, I have news for you. My old buddy from the force, the one based in Nelspruit? He had a call from one of his colleagues in Hazyview, a guy called Enoch. As it turns out Enoch's father was one of my detectives in the old days. Good start, hey? I called him straight away.

"The missing kid's file has been moved from Nelspruit to Hazyview, where it's been gathering dust – that is, until this afternoon."

Jack felt the familiar fizz snake down his spine, he could feel the first crack in the case coming his way. He held his breath.

"*Ja*, some village kids were playing in the river and found a small *rugsak,* tangled in the branches of a rotting tree, nothing in it apparently, but who knows?"

Jack ran his hands through his hair. "That's a kind of rucksack, right."

"*Ja*, Jack, I'll have you speaking our language before you know it. Anyways, the village headman insisted the kids hand the rucksack over to the police. My new mate, Enoch, thinks it must have travelled a few hundred kilometres', carried down the river by the storm. But, here's the thing. Village kids don't carry these kinds of bags, only if

213

they are going to school, but their bags are functional, to carry books, you hear what I'm saying?

"My buddy thinks it belonged to a white kid. You know how they like their bags with glitter, bright colours and so on, this one was pink, so long.

"It's only a hunch but maybe it belonged to the kid found at the water hole in the fancy game lodge where you're hiding her. It would be good if she could identify it, not so? Same river."

Jack grabbed his notebook from the table. "How can we get hold of the rucksack Piet?"

"We can't, or at least you can't. But maybe I can make a plan here. A few expenses involved though…" he said gruffly.

"Not a problem, Piet, I need to get my hands on the rucksack, it might give us a clue as to who it might have belonged to. If it has sparkles and glitter on it, the chances are it belonged to a young girl. We have to get hold of it one way or another and show it to Abby."

"So, my friend, what do you want me to do next?"

"You know what I need you to do next…"

There was a short silence at the end of the phone. "It's possible I could go to Hazyview," Piet muttered, "come see you there. It's also possible I might be able to retrieve this rucksack, through Enoch, but I won't be able to hand it over to you, Jack. It would be going against all the rules of friends in high places. It's police property now."

Jack chuckled. There were no flies on Piet Joubert. "Okay, I understand. Here's a plan. I'll book you into the hotel where I'm staying here in Hazyview. You collect the rucksack and both of us will go out to the game lodge, it's called Infinity, and take it from there?"

"I'll see what I can do Jack," Piet said grudgingly. "This game lodge, Infinity, it's a bit fancy for the likes of me, I've seen it in magazines. Do I have to dress up like a performing monkey, black tie an' all?"

He growled down the phone. "Never did understand why people pay more than I was paid in a month for a couple of nights at some fancy lodge with a fancy name. The bush is the bush and the animals are the animals – all for free."

"*Nah*. Give me a small fire out in the bush where I can wear my shorts and *takkies*, and see all the animals for free, and retire to my sleeping bag, after a *dop*, or two, when I'm good and ready."

Jack snorted, trying not to laugh. "No. You don't have to meet any of the guests if you would feel uncomfortable, but I can assure you, you wouldn't.

"Caroline, the owner, and Grace, who looks after the child, have their private quarters some distance away from the main lodge. There are a couple of other cottages they use for pilots who overnight, or friends. You could stay in one of those."

Piet roared with laughter. "*Nah*, Jack, I have a good expense account with you, I think I'll make an exception in this case. I want to try one of those fancy bedrooms I've seen in the magazines. Only chance I'll ever get on my paltry pension, also some of the food which looks as though it's been painted on a plate and only enough to feed a small kid with no appetite…"

Jack laughed out loud. "Okay, whatever you want. Let me know your flight details and I'll pick you up."

He paused. "Oh, and another thing, Piet. I have a lead here. An Afrikaans girl. I don't have her surname, no-one will give it to me. But there is a bookseller in town, he's Afrikaans, he knows her. She's a hairdresser here in town, rents her shop and flat from him. She left town in a hurry. I'll tell you all about it when we meet. I think you might have more luck with the bookseller and the hairdresser, if we can find her, than I did."

"I'll give it a go Jack. The Boers have a long memory, especially with *yous* English folk. But, hey, I like you well enough. We can work together, not so?

"Oh, and by the way. I do know about the super-rich and their ways. Murder is not exclusive to the masses, or ordinary people. In my former life I dealt with the rich and the famous. They never impressed me with their wealth and their lifestyle. I've seen their homes, their playgrounds. But murder is murder, it doesn't matter who you are. Whether it's a shack in a village or a palatial home with ten bedrooms. In the end it's all the same. A dead body or two. Life in extremis. Ah, yes, human nature – it's not exclusive."

Piet cleared his throat. "I want to meet the kid anyway, make up my own mind about her. I'll send you my flight details. Make sure they give me a decent room, okay?"

Jack heard a dull thud and presumed the bad-tempered cat had left the building.

"Don't go booking first class, Piet, I don't want you getting used to the finer things in life."

He rang off hastily, before Piet could respond.

Chapter Fifty-Five

Jack checked in with Daisy to make sure his dog was being well looked after.

"Benji is fine, Mr Yak, I think he loves me more now than he loves you. When you coming back, hey? We already forgetting what you look like."

"It will be a while yet, Daisy. I may have to make a trip to Zimbabwe. Keep the home fires burning, okay."

He held the phone away from his ear as she roared with laughter. "You want me to set fire to your house, Mr Yak? What good will this do. I am liking living here with the scruffy dog.

"You go off to Zimbabwe and watch out for the roads with the big pot holes and the bandits, hey?"

Smiling he rang off. His next call was to Grace.

"How is Abby, Grace?"

Grace sounded more upbeat than the last time he spoke to her.

"She's still not saying much, to us anyway. But Moses brought his grandson to visit her. Abby became the little girl she should be. She played with little Zuzu, they seemed to understand each other. Even though he's only four and doesn't speak English yet.

"Abby speaks an African language, I'm not sure which one, neither is Moses. They play and talk to each other, though I'm quite sure neither one of them understands each other.

"Jabu takes both of them out when he has the time and teaches them about the plants, healing herbs, roots and berries. They both love their time with him."

He heard her whisper something, presumably to Abby.

"Caroline has a map of the world tacked behind her desk and she shows Abby the different places she's travelled. Abby's getting the best geography lessons in the world."

She laughed. "I do the dull things – the English and the arithmetic. But I'm pleased she has a little friend.

"Having said all this she barely speaks English, if at all. But I'm encouraged with her progress, as are the authorities and the doctors. Of course, I'm in touch with them every week."

He heard the rattle of a teacup, then she continued. "Once little Zuzu goes home with Moses, she reverts to being silent again. I see her looking out over the bush and her face crumples and then she cries.

"Anyway, how are you doing Jack. Are you getting anywhere with what happened to her family?"

Jack sighed heavily down the phone. "I need her surname; without it I can't make any progress. Has Jabu managed to get an inkling of what it might be?"

"No, sorry Jack. I think she's blocked something awful out of her mind, and then to have to contend with what happened to her in the bush, well, it would be too much for even an adult to deal with. She's only a young child, and she seems to have lost her entire family. Of course, there may be relatives scattered around, but without her surname it seems almost impossible we will ever find them, doesn't it?"

"The thing is, Grace, someone must have brought those girls into the Sabi Sands, and whoever it was must have known them, was maybe related to them."

The raucous screech of birds halted his conversation, as he looked up. "Those bloody great birds. Why do they make such a din when they fly?"

Grace laughed. "They're called Hadadas, I can hear them from here. They scream like that because they don't like flying."

"Is that true?"

"Well, not really, but why else would they make such a racket. Where were we before being so rudely interrupted?"

Jack picked up the thread of their conversation. "Look, I worked with an ex-detective on my last cold case here. He's found something which may relate to Abby. A rucksack was found in the reeds of the river, in the roots of a tree, a long way from the reserve. It's the sort of thing girls like, covered in glitter and sparkles, and pink, of course.

"It was handed into the police. We're working on trying to get the rucksack to show to Abby. If we can do this then I'd like Piet Joubert, that's his name, to bring it to the lodge. It's police property now, so he's the only one who will be able to help us and he can be trusted. I trust him, even though he can be a grumpy bugger at times.

He has excellent instincts, doesn't mess around with unnecessary words. He might be able to help with a couple of other things I'm following as well.

"He also has a connection to Jabu. Too long a story to tell you now. Can you arrange to put us both up? I'll let you have definite dates, depending on flights for Piet."

"Of course, I'll clear it with Caroline and Jabu. We can put your detective friend up in one of the suites. We have a couple of them empty this week, if you want to come then, two couples had to cancel."

*****

Grace put the phone down, her gaze wandering to the spiritual tree, in the distance, as it so often did.

Then she turned and went to check on Abby.

That one phone call would change everything in what she had hoped would be a more predictable world.

Chapter Fifty-Six

The following afternoon Jack waited in the arrival's hall for Piet. He spotted him immediately as he stomped across the terminal floor, wearing, if Jack recalled correctly, the same battered baseball hat he had been wearing over two years ago when Jack had seen him last.

He hadn't changed much at all. His short hair perhaps more peppered with grey at the temples, his eyes surprisingly blue and alert, fanned by dark eyelashes. For a man in his mid-fifties, he was in good shape, his body lean and as hard as a man half his age.

Piet scowled as he scanned the crowds in front of him, then he saw Jack and his face broke into a wide smile.

He pumped Jack's hand with gusto, making him wince. "Good to see you again, my friend! I see you still sport the same hairstyle. I guess the only hairdresser who could handle your mop was the one who left town in a hurry. Come on, let's get out of here. I hate crowds and I hate flying."

On the drive, Jack brought him up to date with his investigations so far. Piet listened, then went quiet until they pulled up at Jack's hotel.

They arranged to meet in the bar after Piet had freshened up and unpacked his old battered leather bag.

*****

Piet wiped his hand across the foam on his lips, then took another long drink.

"Nice place this Jack. I even have a decent room with a fancy dressing gown and nice soap. What's the food like here? Any good?"

Jack nodded. "Food's very good here, not too fancy for your delicate palate. I can highly recommend the steak and mushroom pie."

Piet's eyes darted around the bar. "I need food. I haven't eaten anything all day apart from the bag of peanuts in economy class." He scowled accusingly at Jack, putting the blame squarely on his shoulders.

"Still as grumpy as ever, I see. Do you still have the bad-tempered cat in your office?"

"Nope. Not only do I have an ex-wife, I also have an ex-cat. It buggered off and found somewhere else to live. Like my ex. Must have been a female, is all I can think. Ungrateful. Waste of time that cat, and ugly as all hell."

He downed the rest of his beer, picked up his baseball cap and stood up. "Come on, I'm ready to attack the steak and mushroom pie, then we can go over the case again and I'll tell you what you missed."

He slapped Jack on the back almost knocking him off his stool. He hastily drained his glass and showed Piet the way to the dining room.

Piet, as usual, scanned the restaurant, missing nothing. It looked friendly enough to him. Tables spaced nicely apart, but not so far apart you couldn't lean over and have a chat with your fellow diners.

Candles were lit on each table pre-empting any plans the electricity department might have in store. Red tablecloths and white napkins, nothing too intimidating to make you lose your appetite.

They ordered their meal and enjoyed a glass of red wine before the food was delivered by a smiling waiter.

Piet attacked his pie with enthusiasm, stabbing his knife at the crisp golden pastry watching the thick creamy gravy spill over onto his plate and seep into the mound of buttery mashed potatoes. He removed the sprig of parsley with a look of disdain. The broccoli didn't seem to hold his interest either, as he shovelled it to the side of his plate.

During mouthfuls, he fired Jack with questions about the mysterious appearance of the girl and what had happened afterwards.

Jack in between his own mouthfuls of perfectly cooked fish and chips, with parsley sauce, answered as succinctly as he could.

Satiated, Piet sat back in his chair and sighed. "Damn good pie, enjoyed every mouthful, how's the fish?"

"Excellent. You have gravy on your chin, Piet. You'll have to up your game when we get to the fancy game lodge, no steak and mushroom pie there. Probably food you won't even recognise…"

"*Ag*, Jack, I was hungry. I know my manners when called for, I scrub up good if I have to. I can do fancy when necessary. Haven't spent all my life in steak houses, if that's what you think. I know what's what on a menu unless it's in a foreign language."

He grinned at Jack. "Now here's what I'm thinking. Tomorrow I take the car and go to the police station, see what I can do there with my new mate, Enoch. I'll find out as much as I can and, hopefully, borrow the pink rucksack for a day or two. Then I want to meet the kid, see if maybe she speaks Afrikaans. Or whatever other language she might speak.

"I have my identity book, of course, which clearly states my profession as a policeman," he shrugged, "well, ex policeman, but I have another document which confirms I am also a registered, licenced, private detective. This will help to open any doors, especially with the reluctant bookseller who seems to have difficulty in recalling the surname of a certain hairdresser called Elspeth. I don't think I'll have a problem there. I'll speak to him in his own language."

He paused until the waiter had removed his plate before continuing.

"As you did, I need to fly over the area where the kid was found, but make it a short trip Jack. I don't like flying at the best of times, and those small planes are not my favourite way of moving around. I'd prefer a donkey and cart."

He nibbled at a crusty roll, heaped with butter. "Then I'll walk around town, nearby where the hairdresser had her shop and talk to a few of the old timers. They might be old, but they sometimes see things others miss, simply because they sit on their *stoep* all day with nothing else to do but watch the passing crowds."

He reached for another roll and smothered it with the remaining butter and a sprinkle of salt.

"*Ja*, when you pointed out her shop to me on the way to the hotel, I noticed a couple of old cottages on the opposite side of the road. Someone over there may have seen something unusual, day or night, which might have not meant much to them but could give us invaluable information.

"Now, let's take a look at the map you brought with you. Show me what we're dealing with."

Jack pushed the wine glasses aside and spread out his map, anchoring the edges with the cutlery and salt and pepper pots.

He glanced up to see if Piet would be grinning at him, but he wasn't.

"Nothing wrong with doing things the old ways, Jack, worked for people then, why shouldn't it work for us now. What have we here?"

Piet fumbled in his top pocket for his glasses, put them on then threw them on the table in disgust. "Can't see *fok* all through these. Waste of time."

Jack reached over and picked them up holding them up to the light. "Helps to clean them now and again, Piet, there's even bits of cat fur stuck to them."

Piet scowled at him. Jack used the tail of his shirt to vigorously polish the lens, before handing them back.

"*Bleddy* cat..." Piet put the now clean glasses on and grunted.

For the next hour Jack pointed out the places he had circled with Toby, the pilots, help. Showed him the various game lodges, both great and small, scattered around the huge area, the game reserve's entry and exit points, and the thread like dirt roads which traversed through the entire area. Making its way through all of this was the mighty Sabie River which Piet studied with great interest. Tracing where he thought the pink rucksack might have floated, only to become entangled in the rotting branches of an old tree.

At eleven they called it a day. Piet tried to smother his yawn, then gave up and let it happen.

"Time for me to hit the sack, Jack. See you tomorrow at seven. Hopefully I'll be able to enjoy a full English breakfast, something *yous* countrymen have contributed to our country, not much, but we are grateful, I suppose. The European breakfast of nuts and fruit, cold cheese and ham, doesn't cut the mustard with people like us. Prefer a steak myself."

He grinned wolfishly at Jack, rammed his baseball cap on his head and marched out of the restaurant.

Jack folded up his map, messily, then ordered a coffee.

Despite being protective of his story, and the little girl in particular, he was glad to have involved Piet Joubert. The grumpy detective would be able to unlock doors an English journalist would find it impossible to do. He picked up his phone.

He would ask Grace to check if they had guests flying in tomorrow and if they could hitch a lift with Toby.

Chapter Fifty-Seven

Piet and Jack met for breakfast the next day. Piet ordered a full English breakfast and a steak to go with it, Jack settled for scrambled eggs and bacon.

Now ready for the day ahead they walked out to where the car was parked.

Jack handed over the keys and watched Piet drive off in the direction of town. Then he went back to his room and called Harry in London, bringing him up to date on what had happened and what might happen next.

Two hours later Piet was back carrying an object in a plastic shopping bag. They found a secluded spot in the corner of the spacious hotel veranda and ordered coffee.

Once the coffee had been delivered, Jack reached for the bag. Pulling it out he examined the rucksack closely.

It was bright pink with a cartoon picture of a cat, its whiskers and face peppered with sequins and "Hello Kitty." emblazoned on the side. He unzipped it and peered inside. The river had not been kind to the little rucksack. Bits of slimy reeds were stuck to the inside; the elements having dulled the outside and its playful picture of a cat.

Jack opened the side pocket. There was nothing to indicate who the object belonged to. An empty plastic bottle was all that was left of the previous owner, the label faded, the brand indecipherable.

Piet lifted his shoulders, seeing how disappointed his friend was. "The police have come up with nothing, Jack. They're no closer to finding out who the kid is than they were over six weeks ago."

Jack slumped back in his chair and sipped at his coffee. The sun was high overhead. The bag sat forlornly on the table, its sequins glinting dully in the spiked rays of sunshine spreading across the table.

"It's a long shot, Piet, but Abby might recognise it. It's a chance in a thousand, but we have to do it. In my experience girls, with the cases I have followed in the past, always stamp their identity on things like this," he indicated the rucksack. "But if whoever owned it had, well, it's been washed away by the winds, the water and the sun."

"Not quite, my friend, not quite." Piet said softly as he leaned forward and pointed at the edge of the zip. "See here, when the light is in a certain way, there's something written there."

Piet picked up the bag and peered at it through the sunlight. "There's something here, hard to make out, but it begins with an *s*, or maybe a *b*, hard to say, then a blank and the letter *c* another blank, and an *m*. Not much to go on but let's leave it there and see if the kid recognises it.

"What time is the flight this afternoon?"

"We're using Toby and his plane. He's a pilot the lodge uses all the time, only a short hop and an aerial game drive thrown in, plus Toby will fly us over the area where we think the girl might have travelled to get to the lodge. Sorry, we can't get there by donkey and cart. Not an impressive way to arrive at a smart game lodge."

*****

Jabu was there to meet them when they landed. He made his way to the lodge vehicle and stowed their light luggage, then handed them each a bottle of ice-cold water.

Piet lifted the bottle to his lips and downed it in one. "Phew, must be thirty-six degrees today, hey Jabu?"

"Yes, with a hot wind as well. How are you Inspector?"

Piet snorted with laughed. "No more I'm afraid. Only a private detective helping Jack with his story – showing him where he's going wrong. Just kidding, Jabu. I want to meet the kid. Jack and I between us want to follow the story and bring it to its conclusion, as we did with yours."

Jabu turned and looked at him. "Yes, you did. Something we don't talk about anymore. Too many people involved, too many people hurt. Kia and I get on with our lives now, the past is the past, it's where it belongs. Nothing can bring it back, only memories, and my sister and I have buried them all."

Jack made no comment as he climbed into the dark green tiered vehicle.

Jack could see Piet was not impressed with the wild life all around him. He knew he had been brought up on a farm in the Eastern Cape.

225

Animals to him were familiar friends, not wonders as international tourists saw them. But he watched the detective's eyes as he scanned the landscape and could see how he was trying to work out how a child could have survived in an environment such as this.

*****

Piet wasn't looking at things through a tourist's eyes, as Jack had done on his first visit to the bush. No, he was looking at it through different eyes altogether.

Through the eyes of someone who knew the bush, and its ways, well.

Chapter Fifty-Eight

Jack went on up to the cottage, Jabu showed Piet to his suite, depositing his battered overnight bag on the old leather chest at the foot of the bed, before he left to see to his guests.

Piet looked around baffled. How could it be international tourists paid thousands of dollars a night to sleep in the bush?

He showered and changed into long trousers and a pale blue shirt. Then sat gingerly on the cream cushions of one of the planter's chairs, out on the deck. The surface of the large water hole shimmered in the light, as though sprinkled with gold dust. The sounds of the bush were the sounds from his childhood.

He could have been rolled up in a sleeping bag, under the stars with no fear of wild animals, next to a warm fire, with just the same sense of peace he was feeling now.

But he understood. His childhood had been a gilded one, to be brought up in this magnificent country, his country, as a boy then a man, and accepting it all. Yes, he supposed he could see why international tourists would pay such huge sums of money for a taste of this life, however brief, something he had known all his life. He had been given a gift, and didn't know the value of it, until now. He felt humbled by it.

*****

Jabu knocked on the intricately carved door a few minutes before six that evening. "Come meet our little girl, and Grace, Piet.

"Caroline, the owner of the lodge, has arranged for an informal dinner to be served out on Grace's *stoep*."

Piet followed Jabu as he made his way to the cottages, nestled amongst the trees. He had abandoned his baseball cap, now he smoothed down his hair and straightened his shirt, he hoped he wasn't expected to wear a tie, because he didn't have one with him, or at home come to that. With the sort of social life he had in Willow Drift, which was non-existent, he didn't need one. If he was invited to a braai by one of his mates, he would have been laughed out of town for wearing one.

The first sighting of the woman called Grace was the thick blonde plait snaking down her straight back, clasped at the end with a colourful beaded clip. He was entranced before she even turned around.

She turned and smiled at him and Piet caught his breath. She wore no make-up, her hair swept back from her forehead; her smile was as warm as the morning sun. "Hello, you must be Piet. I'm Grace, and this," she said reaching behind her, "is Abby.

"Abby, say hello to Piet. He's come to help us find your family."

"Eat," she whispered.

Piet crouched and took her hand in both of his. "Hello Abby. I'm a friend of Jack and Jabu. When I was a kid, like you, I was brought up in the bush, a long way away from anywhere. I wasn't afraid of the wild animals, or the snakes, or anything."

He ran his finger down her soft cheek. "I don't think you're afraid of anything either. You know the bush, like I do. I think you're a very brave kid."

Abby stared at Piet. Grace took Abby's hand back from his, and led her through to the bedroom. "Abby has eaten, Piet," she said over her shoulder. "Caroline will be along in a moment, we thought we would eat outside. Jabu has to go back to the lodge to look after the guests, he'll pop in to say goodnight to Abby, as he does every night. He'll join us later, if the guests are not too demanding, and be here to see you back to your suite. Go sit by the fire."

Jack appeared from his room and joined Piet around the fire. "So, my friend, are you impressed?"

Piet scowled at him. "With what?"

"Well, your room, the whole place."

Piet grunted. "I haven't tried the food yet, hope it's decent. My room is alright I suppose. I want to spend some time with the girl."

Jack smiled. "Which one, Piet, the little one or the big one from Kenya? I am a great observer of people, it's what I do, I was watching you from my window. I think you like something you see here."

"You're talking *kak* Jack. I'm here to do a job, for which you are paying me. Not enough I might add. Now, when do we introduce the rucksack to Abby?"

Jack stifled a smile of innocence. "Well, I think you might need to ask Grace about this. She's the one who decides what's what with the child."

*****

Laughter permeated through the warm night air, as they gathered for dinner and drinks. The talk was about what was going on in the country, the power cuts, Caroline's travels, Jack's dog Benji, and Piet's life in the rural town of Willow Drift.

After dinner Caroline was the first one to stand up and withdraw, citing jet-lag. Jack made excuses about calling Harry and his other contacts, and left.

Chapter Fifty-Nine

Finally alone, Piet and Grace went and sat by the smouldering fire. A candle lit lamp flickered on the table in front of them. Moses re-filled their wine glasses, then melted into the shadows. Abby was tucked up in her bed asleep.

"So, tell me about your life in Kenya, Grace. How did you adapt after independence?"

Grace pulled a soft mohair blanket over her shoulders and stared out over the bush to the spiritual tree, silhouetted by the rising moon.

"I think we managed it better than you are here. Some things are out of one's control. If you can't change them, you have to go with the situation, or turn your back on it and leave the country for somewhere else. No good fighting.

"Anyway, it was a long time ago, Kenya gained its independence in 1963. South Africa's government changed in 1994, that's, what, twenty-two or three years ago?

"White Kenyans accepted the inevitable. The only way to deal with it was to take the best of all we had and keep embracing it. We still had our lovely homes, and, yes, our staff. We still lived an incredible life."

She twisted her braid through her fingers. "Holidays at the beach in Mombasa, lobster and prawns straight from the sea, dinner parties, beach parties, horse racing. Week-ends away at safari lodges. Life went on if you didn't get embroiled in politics and become bitter about how things used to be – things were as they used to be, except the government had changed.

"The Kenyan people were still friendly towards us, still smiled at us. In many ways it was a relief all round. Things had finally settled and we could all, black, brown and white, get on with our lives."

She smiled at him, the candlelight emphasising her high cheek bones. "You'll get used to it."

Piet grunted and threw another log on the small fire, then stared off into the distance, in the direction of the spiritual tree.

"We all have to deal with sadness and regret in our lives, Piet," she said softly.

Grace pointed with her glass to the blackened outline of the tree. "My son, Tim, is buried under the roots of that tree. He died in New York. Caroline brought back his ashes…it's a long story. That's how I ended up here looking after Abby."

He leaned over and covered her hand with his. "I'm sorry Grace. Tell me, what happened?"

*****

"So, that's how I ended up here at the lodge, we've turned into quite a little family, all needing each other for one reason or another, especially Abby. My son doesn't need me now but the child does. She's become quite attached to me, as I have to her, even though I know she's badly damaged, demanding and difficult sometimes, and hardly says a word. But she will. She needs to feel safe and loved."

Piet turned to her, not realising he was still touching her hand. He quickly withdrew it, throwing another log on the fire to hide his awkwardness.

"You know why I'm here Grace, why Jack is here. I'm going to help him solve this case. We're doing all we can to find Abby's family. We'll find out what happened to her and what happened to her parents, it's only a matter of time."

He paused and glanced at her. "At some point we'll come across a relative who will want to take her back into the family. You must prepare yourself for this. It will be hard for you. Abby won't be able to stay here forever, not so?"

"Yes," she whispered, "it will be hard, but I try not to think about it. Of course, her relatives must be found, she must find her family. But until then she's, my responsibility. I'll cross that bridge when we come to it.

"I know Caroline wants to keep me on here as her resident nursing sister, we've become close over the past few months. If things don't work out, I can always find a job in a hospital. They're screaming out for medical staff here, there'll always be something for me to do."

She took a sip of wine and Piet noticed her hand trembling slightly. "Now, tell me about the rucksack you've brought with you and let's work on a time and place when you need to show it to Abby.

"We'll have to pick our time, she's a moody little thing, which is understandable, and she can fly into a rage if she thinks you don't understand what she's saying.

"I suggest we invite Zuzu over tomorrow, Moses's grandson, let them play a little and then maybe introduce the rucksack, put it next to Zuzu, let him pick it up, if he wants to, and let's see how Abby reacts. She's less likely to have a meltdown, or burst into tears if little Zuzu is around. That's if she recognises it."

She stood up, smoothing down her khaki skirt. "I must go and check on her. I'll see you in the morning, I'll let you know what time Moses will be bringing his grandson. Ah, here he is now.

"Moses perhaps you'll be good enough to show Mr Joubert back to his suite?"

Piet stood and watched her walk away. Then he called out to her. "Grace, wait a minute. Tell me, have you tried to speak to her in Afrikaans?"

She turned slightly. "My Afrikaans has long been forgotten, but Caroline tried it a couple of times, she might as well have been speaking Mandarin. There was no reaction from Abby at all. Goodnight, Piet. Sorry Jabu didn't join us, we have a nearly full camp, and a few guests simply don't know when they should go to bed."

Piet smiled at her. "At the prices they charge here I'm not surprised. I'd be the last guest standing, determined to get my dollars' worth. Goodnight."

The silence of the night was broken by the buzzing of the phone attached to her belt. He waited whilst she answered it.

"I'll be right there." She held up her hand. "Wait Moses."

He watched as she disappeared into her cottage and returned carrying a medical bag.

"Someone has either had too much to drink or having nightmares about a previous life she had before she arrived here. I have to call in on her," she hesitated. "Moses, I'm afraid I have to ask you to stay here with Abby, make sure she doesn't wake and wander off anywhere."

"Yes, Miss Grace, I will wait with her until your return. Perhaps Mr Joubert, who I am thinking was a policeman at some time, will escort you to the guest's suite and wait for you. He is knowing about the bush.

You will be safe with this policeman. Then when you return, I will also escort him back to his suite."

Moses handed his torch to Piet.

Grace and Piet made their way down to the suite. He sat on the deck and waited whist Grace saw to her patient, who, she told him, had had a little too much wine then become maudlin. He led her back to her cottage where Moses was waiting.

Moses took back the torch and walked with Piet down the wooden walkway to the lodge. "How did you know I was a policeman, Moses?"

"*Eish,* it is the way you are walking. When I was a young man, we were much afraid when the police came to our villages, it was always trouble, when there was none, but they came anyway. This is how I am knowing this."

He scratched his head. "It was then the police treated us with respect, asking only questions when necessary. Today things are different, not as it was. My own people are afraid of the police now, they are more angry with us for no reason, they are looking for things which are not there. But so it must be."

Moses saw him safely to his suite and wished him good-night.

*****

Piet lay back in his superbly comfortable bed and watched as the fans above moved the billowing white mosquito net. Not a bad room after all, he smiled to himself. Rather nice actually.

It had been a long day and he was tired. The two hours at the police station had been gruelling as he signed paper after paper to gain access to the pink rucksack. Enoch had introduced him to his fellow police officers as an ex-police detective, now a private investigator looking for the family of the lost girl. They had been almost relieved someone else was being paid to follow the investigation, leaving them time to get on with all the other usual crimes and robberies going on in the town and the surrounding countryside.

Now his mind was going through all he had seen and heard, and the update from Jack. The faint letters on the pink rucksack, the dinner with Caroline, Jack and Grace, and meeting Abby.

Never having had children of his own he was surprised at the emotion Abby had evoked in him, with her big blue eyes, short pixie blonde hair and the utter desolation and sadness surrounding her.

He thought about the short flight over the bush with Toby, as he pointed out the river and the surrounding area. A thought nudged its way into his mind. He had to agree, it was highly unlikely the sister had survived the storms and the floods There was no trace of her at all.

He came back again as to how the children had arrived in the reserve. The only way anyone could move two girls around a private game reserve was by being a building contractor or someone with legitimate access to the area. Someone who would have had to check in and out with the Parks Board as they entered the Sabi Sands. There were exit and entry points. There would be a trail there. But he needed a time frame and this he did not have.

He punched the pillow and turned over. His last thought as he fell asleep was the silhouette by the fire, of the woman with the long blonde braid snaking down her back and the slight tremble of her hand as she told him about her son, Tim.

The woman called Grace.

Chapter Sixty

The next morning Piet made his way up to the cottages nestling beneath the generously leaved trees, carrying the shopping bag. He tapped on Grace's door and waited.

"Good morning, Piet, come on in. Zuzu and Abby are playing out on the patio. May I get you coffee?"

"No thank you. I'm already full of coffee and a good breakfast. They do a decent spread here, although I'm not sure smoked salmon goes with scrambled eggs. Prefer sausages myself, or a chop."

Grace laughed, warming to this gruff ex detective who didn't mince his words or try to be anything other than who he was.

He took off his cap. "I'll sit with the children, so long, then pick my moment to introduce the rucksack, Jack will be joining me. We'll try not to intrude on their games, but it's important we both see the reaction, if any."

A few moments later Jack strolled in and they both settled in the cane chairs and watched the children.

Abby and Zuzu were completely absorbed in playing with some toy cars and trucks, whispering to each other, oblivious to their audience who were watching them.

Grace came through with a tray of milk and biscuits for the children, then sat waiting for the moment they had all been anticipating..

"Out of the eleven official languages of this country, Piet, have you any idea which language she is speaking?" Jack asked quietly.

Piet didn't look up; he was watching Abby intently. "It's Ndebele," he replied softly. One of the languages of Zimbabwe, from the south of the country."

Jack looked impressed. "How do you know?"

Piet shrugged. "All our languages here are interconnected, history managed it for us. Ndebele is also one of our languages but it's a mish

235

mash of a language, part Zulu, part Matabele. That is the language the kid is speaking."

"Not a hope in hell you speak the language is there Piet?"

Piet turned his head and gave him a wintery smile. "I might be a good detective, but I don't speak all our eleven languages here, I understand a few of them because they are similar. Like a lot of European languages which have similar sounding words. Latin based.

"But, not to worry, hey. Someone will be able to translate what she's saying. It's always fascinated me how children can communicate without any particular language. We could learn a lot from them. No barriers there, only innocence. What interests me is she *can* speak, but has trouble with English."

Jack stood up. "Excuse me Piet, I'll be back, just now, as you say here. I need to let our man in Zimbabwe have our thoughts on this Ndebele angle. It might help him narrow down the search. Stefan gave me his contact details after he met him in London."

Piet turned to him. "Where does this guy in Zimbabwe live?"

"Bulawayo. South of there is not highly populated from what I can gather, only small towns, farms, a few gold mines, all the way down to the South African border."

He turned and headed for his room to retrieve Rob's contact details. Then he called him.

*****

Grace called the children to come and have their milk and biscuits. Abby reached for Zuzu's hand and led him to the table.

Seeing Jack hurrying back, Piet took the opportunity to place the rucksack with the toy cars, where they had been playing.

The children, having had their break, returned to their toys. Grace, Jack, and Piet held their breath.

Zuzu made the first move, his eyes caught by the dull glitter of the pink bag. Abby had gone back to her world of wheels and toys and didn't look up when Zuzu tapped her hand and showed her what he had found.

Abby's smile puckered, then turned to a frown as she picked up the bag and unzipped it with familiar fingers. She opened the side pocket and withdrew the empty water bottle, staring at it.

She held it close to her chest and stood up, looking out over the bush.

A howl of anguish came from somewhere deep inside her. She started to run, dropping the pink bag as she did so.

Grace knocked over her coffee and chair, as she stood up and chased after her. "Wait, Abby, wait!"

The child was quick, already making her way through the thick bush behind the cottages.

Grace paused to catch her breath, bending over at the waist. Piet was right behind her. "I'll get her, Grace, wait here."

The kid was fast, he thought, but he was faster, he knew how to negotiate his way through thick bush. With an impressive rugby tackle, one that would make any Springbok player proud, he caught her around the waist and held her tight.

"It's okay, Abby, my girl, I've got you."

She struggled in his strong arms, screaming with outrage. He held fast until she calmed down, spent from an unspeakable episode in her life which had her left her so broken.

Awkwardly he patted her back until she was still. "It's alright, my girl. Let's sit here for a moment whilst I catch my breath. *Jeez,* you can run fast, hey.*"*

He kept his arms around her, rocking her, not saying anything. Eventually her sobs subsided, she put her thumb in her mouth, her body trembling and shuddering as she leaned against him.

He lifted her chin, plucking a small leaf from her mouth. "Is this your rucksack Abby. Look at me?"

She looked up at him, her eyes red and swollen. She shook her head.

"But you have seen it before, haven't you?"

She sucked on her thumb. "Scusie," she whispered.

"Does it belong to your sister, Susie?"

Abby bowed her head, the tears dripping on to her tee shirt.

Piet struggled to his feet then picked her up. "Come on, let's go back to Grace, she's waiting for you."

*****

Grace reached out for the child, soothing her, talking softly to her, calming her as she carried her inside and lay her on the sofa, stroking her head. Moses collected his bewildered grandson and took him home.

Piet picked up the rucksack and returned it to its plastic bag. He looked grimly at Jack, who was still sitting in his chair, looking helplessly at the drama which had just played out in front of him.

"I think we may have our answer here, Jack."

Chapter Sixty-One

During the afternoon Piet was moved from his suite and made comfortable in one of the pilot's cottages, where he felt far more at home and relaxed.

He joined Jack out on Grace's s*toep* and there they sipped their cold beer and went over the entire case one more time. Grace was busy making phone calls, Abby was sleeping on the sofa. Caroline was in her office going through her paperwork, catching up on her emails and checking the onward bookings.

"So, what's our next move Piet? Jack asked. "I think we've done as much as we can here at the lodge and I know you have to get the rucksack back to the police station."

"I do, *ja*. I need to work my way through town, see what I can find out about the mysterious, disappearing hairdresser, also talk to the guy in the bookshop, see if I can persuade him to dig around in his files and find out this Elspeth's surname. He must have it, and I need it. Once I have this information, I should be able to track her family down and maybe find out where she is now. Find out why she lied to you."

Jack's phone vibrated on the table in front of him. He held up his hand to Piet and reached for it.

"Jack Taylor."

He listened intently. Piet watched him. "Thanks, Rob. I appreciate the effort you've gone to. You've worked hard on this one. I'll be in touch once I've figured out my next move. Thanks mate."

Jack pulled out his notebook and scribbled for a few minutes. Piet waited patiently.

"Rob's the guy in Zimbabwe, right?"

"Yeah. He's been doing some research for me, I offered him money, from my fast-diminishing budget, to give him a bit of an incentive. Stefan didn't have much information practically nothing, to give him to go on. Only the Christian names of the girls and where we thought they might have come from. I took over from Stefan. Made contact with Rob."

Piet could see Jack was excited by the way he jiggled his ankle over his crossed leg, as he tapped his notebook on the arm of his chair.

"Zimbabwe is a small country, the farmers there, well, the white community, what's left of them, are obviously a tight knit community, looking out for each other, according to Rob.

"Rob used his network, quickly and efficiently, as soon as he landed back home from London. He put his notes together and came up with one story which might be a fit."

Jack stilled his ankle with his hand. "There was a couple, way out in the bush, they had a small-holding. They were English. Didn't mix at any of the local watering holes or get togethers. They had two children…"

Piet leaned forward in his chair. "How long had they lived there, and where?"

"Some years apparently. It was an isolated spot, miles away from the nearest town, a place called West Nicholson. They were never seen in town buying food, or anything else. The children, according to Rob's source, were never seen by anyone.

"They had a manager out there, or a farm hand. He came into town and bought the essentials. An odd character apparently. Did the shopping, spoke to no-one and then returned to the farm. He handed a shopping list to the store keeper, didn't even speak to him."

Piet looked out towards the spiritual tree, rolling his bottle of beer in his hands. "So, who was Rob's source of information. Was he reliable do you think?"

"He was the owner of the local store, the only store, probably knew everything going on in the area. Everyone shopped there. It was the only place in the town selling everything from fresh meat, frozen fish, to bits for a broken tractor, and medicine, according to Rob. A sort of mini-Harrods, but a tad more basic. I don't think Harrods sell sacks of corn, engine bits, bolts of cloth, fertilizer, or chickens' feet."

Piet frowned. "I don't know of this Harrods place, unless it was the fancy shop in London where Princess Diana fell in love with the shop keeper's son. Yes?"

Jack smiled. Piet was one smart guy. "Well, yes, hardly a shop keeper but let's not split hairs."

Jack consulted his notes. "The store owner, Henry, also stocks a basic clothing line. Not much else to do out in the sticks but make babies. Babies grow up, they need clothes. Henry caters for everyone. He sells clothes for kids and grown-ups, nothing fancy, but all they need it would appear."

"The farm hand bought children's clothes?" Piet shook his head.

"Something not right here. A mother shops for her children, she knows what they like, what size they are." He shook his head again. "*Nah*, something not right with this. What was the name of this family, the farm manager?"

Jack looked back on his notes, unable to keep the smug smile off his face. "Keeping the best 'til last Piet.

"Henry, the store keeper, always kept a record of customers who bought things from him, his accountant insisted on it, as did the Mugabe government. They always have their beady eyes open for any tax coming their way. The name of the family who the farm hand shopped for was Beecham. He told Rob the farm hand drove an expensive looking four by four."

Piet leaned down and pulled the rucksack onto his lap, he narrowed his eyes and stared at the faded letters on the side of the zip.

"And this gives us the name in the rucksack. The only letters faintly visible here are an *s,* possibly a *b,* then a few blanks, a *c* and an *m*. It suggests Beecham to me, the *s,* is Susie. We now know the rucksack belonged to her, yes?"

Jack rubbed his hands together. "Tomorrow we leave Piet, you to work Hazyview and ask the questions. See what you can dig up on Elspeth. Me? I'm off to Zimbabwe to find out where the family lived and what happened to them."

"Rob - what else did he tell you?"

Jack pinched the bridge of his nose; he was feeling tired now.

"A couple called Richard and Maryanne Beecham were found murdered on their farm. It was the work of the so-called comrades, randomly selecting a farm and murdering all who lived there. The bodies of the couple were found in the house, in their bedroom, and it was presumed the children had also been murdered and buried somewhere on the property. Of the farm hand there was no sign."

He ran his finger along his bottom lip. "The police made a cursory investigation, concluded that's what happened, and that was how it was left. The farm hands cottage was untouched, it's possible he was murdered too, but there was no trace of his body or his vehicle.

"The main farmhouse was ransacked, not much left after a bit of a fire. The livestock were slaughtered, a few sheep and goats, left lying where they died. Two big dogs shot dead.

"That's all the information we have Piet."

Piet drained the last of his beer and wiped his mouth on his sleeve.

"That's a bad story Jack, a sad one. But look here, another way of looking at things is the farm hand took the children in the expensive looking car. He could have been elsewhere with the girls when the farm was attacked."

Jack tucked his notebook back in his pocket.

"There's more, Piet. The farm hand, if he survived, didn't report the incident to the police, or anyone else."

Piet looked puzzled. "Why not?"

Jack shrugged his shoulders. "No idea, at this point, maybe he was afraid of them, thought he would be implicated."

Piet stared at his fingers. "This, my friend, is what you have to find out. I'm presuming the Beecham's bodies were found later, if the incident wasn't reported.

"You need to check out if anyone else worked on the farm, Jack. It's highly likely they had someone to work in the house or garden. In situations like this they're likely to take off and disappear at the first sniff of trouble.

"It's possible they knew the farm was going to be attacked. In many cases the domestic staff have a hand in the events, whether they want to or not. Passing information as to the habits of a family, what time they go to bed, what the security is like. How many dogs they have? What time they have dinner, and so forth.

"Someone will have information about the family. You need to find them. You need to find out who discovered the bodies on the farm and when."

Jack clasped his hands over his head. "If you're right, then the question is, how the hell did this farm hand manage to get two girls across the border with no papers, and an expensive vehicle."

"That's the easy part, Jack. You can go through Botswana, plenty places to cross into South Africa without going through the border post, especially if you have a sturdy four by four. Same with Zimbabwe if you're prepared to take the risk."

Jack looked down at his notes. "The thing is, why would the farm worker do that. Why didn't he report it to the police and hand over the children? Someone would have stepped forward and taken them off his hands. Plenty of people in a tight knit community would want to help, the church for a start."

Pete frowned. "They couldn't have been that much of a close-knit community if no-one ever saw the family."

Jack tapped his fingers rhythmically on the side of his chair. "The other big question mark is this. Why did Richard and Maryanne Beecham never venture into town. How come no-one ever met them? They'd been living on the farm for some years, according to Rob."

Piet shook his head. "Because they didn't go into West Nicholson, doesn't necessarily mean they didn't leave the farm. There would be plenty of dirt roads, bush roads which they could have used to bypass the town. In all those years it must have been necessary to visit a dentist or doctor, maybe in Bulawayo, the nearest big town, where no-one would know them perhaps. I can't see the farm hand helping with the birth of two babies, can you?"

Jack jiggled his foot and rubbed his hands together. He could feel the story coming together.

A highly interesting one, given all the components.

Chapter Sixty-Two

Piet and Jack looked up as Grace came through the patio door of her cottage. She looked agitated.

"I've just spoken to Doctor Delamere, the doctor in charge of Abby's case. I told him about today, and her reaction to the rucksack. He thinks I should take her through to a colleague of his in Hazyview, sooner rather than later. I agree with him.

"I've made an appointment with this Doctor Meyer for tomorrow at two, he's a child specialist and has dealt with traumatised children. Doctor Delamere has highly recommended him."

She twisted her braid nervously. "I was wondering what your plans might be and whether we could hitch a ride with you if you're leaving tomorrow. If there's room?"

Piet stood up and led her to his chair. "I think it's a good idea Abby should see this doctor. I also think it would be great to take her away from the lodge. It's time she started to see more of what's out there."

He glanced at Jack. "I think you should plan on staying in Hazyview overnight, stay at the same hotel we're in. Let Abby see a more normal life, see other people, other children, shops, cars restaurants. She can't be hidden away here for months on end."

Jack nodded. "I agree, we should ease her gently back into the real world. Yes, we're leaving tomorrow. I'm off to follow the story in Zimbabwe. We may have a tenuous connection to Abby's family, we think we may possibly have her surname. But I need to check it out. Let me go and organise things with Caroline. I'll call Hugo at the hotel and book a room for you and Abby."

Grace threw her braid over her shoulder. "What do you think her surname might be Jack?"

"I'd rather not say until I know for sure, and I don't at this point. I need to make a few more calls and check in with my editor in London, bring him up to date, and let him know I'm off to Zimbabwe. I'll see you later."

Piet sat in Jack's recently vacated chair. "I'll come with you to the doctor. We can walk through town with Abby, she'll feel safe with us. I think she needs to get away from the bush for a while, away from her memories of what happened here."

He shuddered to think what her previous memories might be if Jack and his source in Zimbabwe, were right.

"You'll be with her. I'll be with you both, she won't need to be afraid."

Grace looked out towards the spiritual tree. "Yes, you're right. I do need to buy her more clothes and books. I need a break as well."

Piet leaned across and squeezed her shoulder. "Then maybe you'd consider having dinner with me tomorrow, at the hotel, with Abby, of course."

She put her hand up to her shoulder and covered his. "Sounds lovely, thank you. I'd like that."

Chapter Sixty-Three

The next day, late in the afternoon, Jack and Piet regrouped in the bar of the hotel.

"How did it go with Abby and the doctor this afternoon?" Jack asked.

Piet removed his baseball hat and placed it on the counter in front of him.

"Grace took Abby in first, they were in there for over an hour. Then she left Abby with me and went back for half an hour or so. I guess there was a lot to talk about."

He took a handful of peanuts from a bowl on the bar. "Grace was quiet when the appointment was over, hardly said a word on the way back. Maybe she'll tell me a bit more over dinner. I'll let you know.

"Now let's take a look at whichever map you have in your pocket, shall we. Tell me what your plans are for Zimbabwe."

They moved to a small table a little distance from the main bar. Jack spread his map of Zimbabwe out.

"I thought I might drive, Piet. It's a long haul but it will give me a chance to see some more of South Africa and take a look at Zimbabwe."

Piet raised his eyebrows in astonishment. "Are you mad Jack! You'll spend five or six hours getting to the border at Beit Bridge, then maybe another eight or ten, or maybe even eleven hours, sitting in a long queue of overloaded taxis, belching trucks and hundreds of people, under a sweltering sun, waiting to cross the border."

He helped himself to another handful of peanuts, brushing the shells and salt off the front of his shirt.

"It's as hot as hell up there this time of the year, the temperature can be in the high thirties. Then when you get to the Zimbabwean officials in their sweltering offices they might, or might not, let you in, depending on whether they've been paid or not."

Piet chewed thoughtfully. "They don't like journalists I can tell you, especially English ones. They chuck them into prison as spies, and your profession must be in your passport. After you've gone through seven or eight officials, with your pockets depleted of any more American dollars, it's the only currency they will accept, by the way, their money is not worth the paper it's written on. Well, that won't be the end of it I can tell you, hey."

He laughed. "You'll be stopped dozens of times, after you've crossed the mighty Limpopo River, which is only down the road from the border, you have to make sure you have a damn fire extinguisher in your car, a triangle in your boot, reflectors on your bumpers and God know what else to hinder your progress."

He stared at Jack. "No, my friend, driving is a very bad idea indeed. Especially for you as a journalist with an international newspaper. The government hates the Brits almost as much as we do."

Jack looked at him and frowned.

"*Nah*, only kidding. We kind of like you. Well, some of you," he said grinning broadly. He tipped up the empty bowl of peanuts and sighed with disappointment, dabbing at the remaining salt with his finger.

"No, the only way for you is to fly from Johannesburg to Bulawayo, hire a car and drive to this West Nicholson place. Trust me I know all about the border. Madness to even consider it. An even better idea is to get your Zimbabwean contact there, Rob, to collect you from the airport and drive you to West Nicholson."

He looked forlornly at the empty peanut bowl. "Zimbabwe used to be an easy country to navigate, but not anymore, it's on its knees. Petrol is scarce, you get stopped by the police often, road blocks all over the place, looking for bribes or food, or accusing you of things you haven't done, or even heard of, not to mention roads full of potholes.

"*Man*, you even look like a journalist. If they find this out, you're toast. Straight in the *chooky* for you. Never to be seen again, and just as I was beginning to like you," he grumbled.

He stabbed his finger at the map. "Rob knows how the country works, let him go with you, he'll appreciate the American dollars, trust me. He'll know how to handle things there. It's a difficult country Jack, you don't want to have to fight your way through all the red tape on top of following up your leads. Let Rob do the donkey work. You follow your nose, okay?"

Jack folded his map up and capitulated. "Well, you clearly know all about the border post. Okay I'll fly in then, get Rob to collect me at the airport and drive me around, if he has the time. But what about me being a journalist, I'll still be in trouble at arrivals, if you're right about this."

"Jack, Jack," he said shaking his head, "you tell me your parents, or grandparents, were South Africans, this means you're entitled to a South African passport. Leave it with me. I'll get it organised for you. Give me your British one and we'll take it from there. I'll put your profession down as a teacher, seeing as you look a bit like a mad professor with that wild hair of yours."

Jack fished it out of his pocket and handed it to him.

"I'll need a couple of passport photographs as well, make sure you comb your hair before they're taken, hey! You can pick your new passport up in Johannesburg, it'll be ready in a couple of hours as soon as you hand in the photographs. I'll give you my contacts details, no need to go through the regular channels that way. I'll email a copy of your passport through to him as well."

Piet tugged his earlobe. "Also, Jack, I'll need your car when you go. I need to hang around town for a few days, might even be here when you get back. Will you make the arrangements for me, sort the insurance out?"

"No problem. Don't go staying at another fancy game lodge, you hear? I don't want you getting used to the good life, it'll blow my budget, and you won't like the designer food, trust me."

Hugo loomed up behind the bar. "I hear you're dining with us tonight, table for three. Or should this be four?"

Piet seemed suddenly interested in the row of bottles behind the bar, and the bright patterns on Hugo' shirt.

Jack kept a straight face. "No, Hugo, keep it at three. I have a ton of work to do, loads of phone calls to make, and a column to write. I'll have room service tonight. I'd like to extend Piet's booking as well. See you tomorrow, Piet." He waved as he left the bar.

Hugo wiped down the bar. "Another beer, Piet?"

"No thanks, I have a date tonight. But something I wanted to mention to you. I walked around the grounds of the hotel this afternoon. You need to up your security, it's *kak*. Your generator has a lock on it, but easy to sabotage. What happens when Eskom strikes again as it so often does, and the generator doesn't kick in, hey?

"By the time you've found your matches and candles your guests will have been robbed blind in their bedrooms. Bad news travels fast, your hotel is well known. Not worth the risk, people won't stay here if they don't feel safe. You need someone to come and sort things out, hereabouts. I haven't seen any security around anywhere."

Hugo shook his head resignedly. "My security guy has gone to live in Australia with the thousands of other South Africans who have left the country. No better there than here, except they have more scary snakes and big grown-up, bad tempered spiders."

Hugo frowned, then his face brightened. "How about you come and fix things Piet. I know you're an ex-police detective. Jack told me you have a security business in the Eastern Cape."

"Yes, I do, it's where I live. Nice idea, Hugo, but I don't think you can afford me?"

Hugo grinned. "I think we can make a plan. Will you think about it Piet? I can offer a good package. Free accommodation, your own cottage, all meals on the house, a pension and a medical aid scheme, and a damn good salary."

Piet glanced down at his watch. "I'll give it some thought. Meanwhile I have my date with a lovely woman and her kid. Make sure we get good service, hey?"

Piet made his way back to his room, he stripped off and took a hot shower. As he dressed, he watched the lightning streak across the sky, the low rumble of thunder following seconds after. Then the slow plop of rain, gathering momentum until it came down in a thundering deluge, casting a thick grey curtain, like a shroud.

He shrugged on his jacket, looked longingly at his battered baseball cap, then smoothed down his hair and made his way to the dining room where Grace and Abby were waiting for him.

Yes, he reflected, he could easily relocate from the little *dorpie* of Willow Drift, and his cramped dusty office with the basic furniture. His camp bed with the sleeping bag out in the back, his two-plate cooker, and the lonely life he had become accustomed to over the past few years. Even the bad-tempered cat had found better, more suitable living quarters and left him. The cat, however, he would not miss.

He could close his business down. The big security companies from Johannesburg were moving in on his turf anyway, already pecking away at the tenuous business he had built up since he retired.

Hazyview had a nice feel about it. Never having had much time for English people, not really understanding them, he had found two men from that country, who he liked a lot. Not a bad bunch, the English, once you'd worked out their odd sense of humour and rather strange habit of commenting on the weather all the time.

Ja, Jack was a good guy and Hugo seemed easy enough to get along with, especially as he had lived in the country for years and had some of the Englishness rubbed off of him.

The hotel was a lively place. At least he wouldn't have to sit with his baked beans on toast, perched on a tray, staring at the television each night, or sitting in the dark with a candle when the lights went out, with a bad-tempered cat glowering and hissing at him.

If the steak and mushroom pie was anything to go by, he would get a decent dinner each night and be able to drop into the bar for a beer or two over a week-end and watch the rugby with the other *okes*. The job would be interesting. Nothing he couldn't handle.

Yes, it was well worth considering Hugo's job offer.

Of course, any decision he made would have nothing to do with the fact Grace Chambers would also be fairly close by.

Chapter Sixty-Four

Grace was wearing a long cream cotton dress patterned with sprigs of blue flowers which reflected the colour of her eyes.

Abby sat like a little ghost her eyes downcast as she fiddled with the belt on her dress.

Grace ordered the fish pie for Abby, and a salad and grilled fish for herself. Piet went for the steak and mushroom pie again.

They chatted easily to each other; Piet was careful not to get gravy on his chin. Occasionally they tried to draw Abby into the conversation but she wasn't having any of it. She stared at her dinner and remained silent.

Although Grace smiled at him often, he could see something was wrong, there was an occasional pause in their conversation and he could see her thoughts were far away, her lovely eyes troubled.

She glanced at the silent child and her untouched food. "I think I should get Abby to bed, Piet. She's had a long day. Sorry to rush dinner. I can't leave Abby alone in the room, so why don't you come back with us. I'll settle her down and then we can order coffee from room service and have it on the veranda."

Piet stood up with alacrity. "Come on Abby, show me your room and where you'll be sleeping tonight?"

Abby slid off her chair looking anxious to be away from all the other guests in the dining room. She reached for Grace's hand then tentatively put the other one in Piet's, it felt like a tiny warm mouse in his, an unusual touch in his world.

Once Abby was settled in her bed, Grace joined him out on the veranda. The rain had stopped and a watery moon had appeared along with a spattering of stars. Raindrops dripped off the veranda covering, a monotonous sound, but oddly soothing.

Pulling a light blue shawl around her shoulders she sat next to him.

"Coffee is on the way. I asked them to bring it to us out here, I don't want to wake Abby."

When the coffee was delivered, he watched as she poured them both a generous cupful, noticing the slight trembling of her hands, a sure sign she was agitated and upset.

They leaned back on the swing sofa and looked out over the garden which was lit by discreet lamps hidden amongst the dripping bushes and trees. They sat in silence, comfortable with each other. But Piet was concerned. Finally, he turned to her.

"Grace? We haven't known each other long, but I can see something is bothering you. Would you like to talk about it? Is it to do with the doctor and Abby?"

She nodded. "Yes."

He leaned over, topped up her coffee, and waited.

"Doctor Meyer had read all the reports on Abby. Doctor Delamere emailed them through to him to read before our appointment, they'd had a detailed conversation on the phone. Jack had given me the report he received from his child psychologist friend in Cape Town which I also gave to Doctor Meyer."

She took a sip of her coffee then placed the cup back on the table. Grace hunched forward, hugging her knees. "As you know I had a long chat with him whilst you took care of Abby."

She paused and turned to look at him. "She's not going to get better Piet," her voice broke. "I've tried so hard with her giving her as much love and care as I possibly can, but it's not enough. The shock of whatever happened to her is too much for her to cope with."

Piet reached for her hand. "Go on."

"Doctor Meyer thinks she may be a danger to herself at some point. He suggests she needs special care. He wants to put her in some kind of children's psychiatric hospital where they can give her the help she needs. He thinks having Abby at the lodge, being in the bush, is not helping her, perhaps bringing back too many memories which is impeding any kind of recovery she might make."

She pushed back the hair from her brow. "I don't agree with him, but he's the expert, and I'm not. It seems love and care will not be enough for her."

She turned her face away from his. "I can't bear the thought of it, Piet. Putting her in some kind of home, taking her away from our little family at the lodge. It will break her already shattered heart…"

She looked back at him, the tears now flooding her eyes. Instinctively, he pulled her into his arms and held her against his chest, feeling the wetness of her tears against his shirt.

He felt a surge of long forgotten emotion, and felt the prickle of tears in his own eyes. He stroked the long braid down her back, and knew he loved this woman. This woman who had tried so hard to put the child back together again, and seemingly failed.

Under no circumstances would he tell her what Jack's contact in Zimbabwe had discovered about her family there. If indeed it was her family. He would wait until Jack returned from his trip.

Grace composed herself and lay still in his arms. "Sorry," she whispered into his shirt, "I don't normally get this emotional over a patient, but I've come to love her you see."

He lifted her face and cupped it in his hands. "We can all see that," he murmured, "she seems to touch everyone, even though she is difficult."

He wiped away her tears with his thumb. "Look, no decisions need to be made immediately. Ask Doctor Meyer to give you some time to think things through. No-one is going to snatch Abby and take her away from you, at least not whilst I'm around, this I can promise you.

"The doctors know how hard you've worked with Abby. Delamere will support you and encourage Doctor Meyer to give you more time for the child's sake. I agree with you, to send Abby away to live with strangers in a place she has never been to before will destroy what little confidence she's gained. She seems alright at the lodge with you, Jabu, Moses, Caroline and little Zuzu. If it's all we can give her at the moment, then as far as I'm concerned, it's enough."

He closed his eyes briefly. "I want you to call Delamere in the morning and get him to speak to Meyer. Tell him Jack is following some leads in Zimbabwe which may lead to finding her family. Beg him, if you have to, but ask for more time. I'll get you some tissues."

He returned from the bathroom and placed the box next to her before sitting again. "Feeling better now we have a plan?"

She sniffed and wiped her eyes. "Yes. Much better. I'll get hold of Doctor Delamere first thing tomorrow."

"Good. Now I'm going to say goodnight and leave you to sleep, I know this is what you need.

"Tomorrow I'd like you and Abby to come into town with me. I need to talk to a few people. I'll look less threatening if I have a woman and child with me. You can buy your books; I planned on going to the bookshop anyway. Then you can go shopping and buy the things you need for Abby."

Grace gave him a watery smile. "I'm sure you can look fierce when you need to be, but it's not how I see you at all. I like you Piet. I don't feel so helpless when you're around, you give me hope, it keeps me going."

He took her face gently in his hands and kissed her lightly on the lips.

"Goodnight, Grace. I'll see you tomorrow."

Piet made his way back to his room. Although the evening had turned out to be far better than he could have hoped for there was a dark cloud hanging over his, or dare he hope - their happiness?

Little Abby.

He found the note under his door, from Jack.

Off at the crack of dawn tomorrow. Hugo fixed my flights. He has the keys to my car for you. See you when I get back. Hope I don't get chucked in the chooky at any point. If I do I expect you to come and rescue me. Thanks, for the help with my new passport, will collect it tomorrow.

Nice dinner? Did you manage to avoid the gravy on your chin – not a good look in front of a lady, if you were trying to impress her?

Jack

Chapter Sixty-Five

Grace, Piet and Abby drove through town the next morning. He parked outside the bookshop, noticing the barber's shop had the *open* sign displayed on the door.

Abby seemed to hesitate then refused to get out of the car. Piet lifted her out despite her mumbled protests. Eventually she calmed down and took Grace's hand.

"Come on Abby, let's go and choose some more books for you. I thought we might try some colouring in books for something different, and some paints, we haven't tried that have we?"

Abby looked up, a troubled smile on her small anxious face. "Peese?"

"Good girl, come on then. Are you not coming in Piet?"

"I'll be right with you, go ahead. I need to check something out."

Piet watched as they disappeared in to the shop then looked through the window of the barber's shop. The first thing he spotted was a young woman with choppy pink hair and silver studs in her ears and nose.

Elspeth the hairdresser.

She seemed to be busy. Four men, of different ages, were sitting chatting to each other as they waited their turn. Most of them were young and tanned as though they spent a lot of time under the sun, game ranger types he thought to himself. He'd noticed a couple of safari vehicles parked outside.

The door pinged as he entered and Elspeth looked up. She touched her customer on the shoulder and said something to him before making her way to the counter and her appointment book.

"Can I help you?"

Piet gave her what he hoped was his warmest smile, then immediately changed his previous plan of action. Something different was called for now.

"I can see you're busy, but I wondered if you could give my wife's hair a quick trim. No washing or drying or whatever else woman do with their hair. Shouldn't take long."

Elspeth frowned and checked her book, then looked at the four men waiting. She looked up at the clock.

"As you can see, *meneer,* this is a barber's shop, I only do men's hair."

Piet raised his eyebrows. "But you're a hairdresser, trained to cut hair, not so?"

"*Ja,* but there are plenty hairdressers in town who look after the ladies. As you can see, I have people waiting."

He glanced at her appointment book, then stabbed at the last name with his finger. "But, see here, you have no appointments after twelve. I'll bring my wife in then. Thank you."

He looked at her, his eyes hard with resolve. In her own eyes he saw a flicker of fear. He sensed she recognised a figure of authority and the only way to make it go away was to agree.

*****

Piet made his way back to the bookshop, lifting his hand in greeting at the burly bookseller, then moved around the shelves looking for Grace and the child. He found them at the back of the shop in the children's section.

Abby was absorbed in a book, sitting cross legged on the floor. Grace was making her way along the lines of shelves, her chosen books sitting on a table next to Abby.

Piet touched her arm and she jumped. "Sorry, didn't mean to startle you. I need you to do something for me. It's important."

"What is it?"

"You wouldn't by chance be planning on having a quick hair trim whilst we're in town?"

Grace laughed and touched her braid. "I haven't had my hair cut in years, Piet. Why would I want to do it now?"

"I need you to go to the barber's shop, a couple of doors away. I made an appointment for you at twelve, but I want you to go there at eleven thirty. There are a few customers there. I need you to listen to their conversation, see what you can pick up. Maybe chat to the hairdresser, her name is Elspeth, but you don't know this. Try to get her to talk about the sort of people who have their hair cut there."

Grace frowned. "This is all quite mysterious, but if it's important then I'll get a trim and see what I can find out. Is this something to do with Abby?"

"Maybe. I'm not sure yet. Take Abby with you, it might help to get Elspeth talking. I need you to take a pic of Elspeth, without her knowing. Can you do this for me?"

Grace glanced at her watch. "Alright. It gives me half an hour to choose more books. Abby can look at one whilst I have my hair done."

*****

Grace entered the barber's shop at eleven thirty, Abby clutching her hand, as always, a new book in her other which she was half looking at.

Piet escorted them in, there were only two men left waiting their turn.

As he turned to leave them Abby gave a low growl, dropped her book and sank to her knees.

Startled Grace looked at her and then at Piet, panic in her eyes.

Elspeth and her customers looked up with surprise at the noise.

"She doesn't like it here, Piet," Grace whispered. "Quick, pick her up and wait in the car for me, she's about to have a melt-down."

He picked up the book and scooped the child up, her body vibrating with an animal cry of warning, and made a hasty exit.

He felt the hair rising on his arms as he carried her back to the car. "It's alright, my girl, everything's alright. Let's sit in the car and read your new book. See here, there's a whole pile more for us to look at."

Abby twisted her head around staring at Grace's retreating back and the front of the barber's shop.

What the hell was that all about, he thought to himself. What had made Abby react like that?

*****

Grace flicked through a magazine as she eavesdropped on the conversation between the two men waiting. Elspeth finished with her customer and went with him to the till to settle his bill.

He stopped briefly to chat to the other two men, he obviously knew them. Again, she listened in, turning the pages of the magazine.

As Piet had asked her, she lifted her cell phone and took a few shots of Elspeth busy at the till.

Finally, it was her turn. Elspeth draped a black cape around her shoulders. "A trim your husband said?"

"Yes, I only need the ends tidying up," she said, as she untied her hair.

Elspeth ran her comb through Grace's thick hair and frowned. "It's so long, you'll have to sit on the stool by the window, I need you to be sitting higher up."

Grace moved and Elspeth was soon busy with her scissors. "I guess my husband didn't realise this was a barber's shop. Never mind, hair is hair whichever way you look at it. Nice looking guys your customers. They all have the same kind of look, sort of outdoors types, big and tough looking. I heard two of them chatting to each other, were they game rangers?"

Elspeth gave her a stony look, reflected in the mirror. "I have a lot of customers, some of them are, some are not. Where you from then, you're not South African?"

"No, I'm Kenyan, just passing through. We're on the way to the Kruger with our granddaughter."

Elspeth stood back, then took the cape away. "There you are, all done, you have lovely hair."

Grace quickly braided it again and stood up. "Thank you, that feels better." She followed Elspeth to the till.

Elspeth gave her the bill. "Your husband, he's South African, not Kenyan?"

Grace handed over the money. "Yes, we met here. He was with the police, now retired, but still in the same line of work. He's a private detective. We're on holiday now, he's taking some time off."

*****

Elspeth put up the *closed* sign, her heart beating uncomfortably. She had felt it the moment he had walked in and demanded an appointment for his wife.

A private detective with those cold blue eyes.

She reached for the phone and dialled the familiar number.

"They're onto us! Damn private detective! He was here in the shop. His wife was asking questions; he must have told her to do this. I didn't say much. You sort this mess, and leave me out of it."

She chewed on her nails. "Are you still there?"

"Right, well you listen to me now. The bloody detective won't see me again, and neither will you."

She started to cry. "They had a child with them…it wasn't their granddaughter. Dear God, what have I done?

"*I can't do this anymore*! Do you hear me? *I can't do this anymore!*" she screamed down the phone, the tears streaming down her face.

Once again, the phone went dead in her hand.

*****

In Johannesburg a phone purred in an opulent office in Sandton Square.

The heavy-set man reached for it, as he admired the gold signet ring on his little finger, with the long-curved nail.

Then he looked up at the pictures adorning his walls and thought of his home far away, another world in a different place, a long way from Africa, which he loathed for its heat, its politics and lack of moral standards. Something he was not used to and would never get used to here.

He listened to his caller. "We have a problem with the hairdresser. She knows too much. There was fear in her voice, the second time she's called now. She's a risk – unpredictable."

The man gave his caller instructions. Anyone listening in, which was impossible, would have no idea what language he was speaking.

The message, nevertheless, was quite clear.

"Get rid of the Zimbabwean – get rid of the hairdresser. Sort the problem out.

"They have become a liability."

Chapter Sixty-Six

Grace slid into the car, Abby reached out her arms for her, sucking her thumb she fell asleep against her chest.

Piet noticed with interest that the closed sign was once more on display, at the barber's shop and the blinds closed.

He looked at Grace. "Anything interesting happen in there?"

"Whoever she is, Piet, the hairdresser is nervous. I listened in on a couple of conversations. They were game rangers, who clearly knew each other. It seems they are the base line of her customers. I didn't pick up anything unusual from any conversation. They talked about the tourists, some of the people they had entertained on safari, how full their lodges were – nothing unusual.

"The shop might look simple enough and only deal with the short back and sides of hairdressing, but she was wearing an expensive watch. Her shoes and clothes looked expensive as well. She can't possibly make her money from hairdressing."

Piet started the car. "Maybe she has a rich boyfriend?"

"Maybe. She asked me where I came from. I told her the child was our granddaughter and we were on the way to the Kruger Park.

"She asked me about you. I told her you were an ex-police detective, now in private practice. She looked terrified. What is this all about, Piet?"

He pulled out into the traffic, indicating he was turning left. "Jack and I are following up some leads. Nothing you need to worry about. You did well, Grace. But what was with the growling noise from Abby?"

She stroked the sleeping child's short hair. "When she's frightened, she growls. There was something about the barber's shop she didn't like, something she was afraid of. I think she recognised it as a bad place for her. Don't ask me why, I just know. It's a primeval thing. The instinct for survival. It's what this child is all about."

She leaned her head against the window of the car. "The doctors are right. Abby sleeps a lot more than most children. It's how she escapes from reality. She's closing down and there's nothing I can do to help her."

Piet headed towards the hotel. "That might be so, but we're not going to give up on her. Jabu, Moses, Caroline, Jack, and yes, me, we're not going to let her go, and neither are you. You're not on your own here. Please don't think that."

He parked the car. "Come on, you two take a nap, then we can meet up for dinner. I don't want to leave you both on your own, not after today. Maybe when she's had her bath we can sit and try the colouring book together, take her mind off of everything. I'll fix things with Hugo so we can have dinner brought to your room. Would that be alright?"

Grace pulled the bag of books from the car and carried Abby on her hip. "Yes. I'm feeling washed out at the moment. A quiet evening is what I crave now. I'll see you later, shall we say about six?"

"Six is good. Oh, by the way. I saw you at the window with your hair down. You're even more stunning when your hair is let loose. You should do it more often."

*****

Grace smiled to herself and made her way to their room. Despite the fact Jack always referred to him as a grumpy ex-detective, she found Piet quite charming and not grumpy at all. He had nice eyes, deep blue, with eyelashes any woman would envy.

Maybe because they had both been born in Africa, there was some kind of empathy, or maybe they just liked each other. Grace certainly liked him, liked having him around. She felt safe with him.

Chapter Sixty-seven
Zimbabwe

Jack's flight landed at Bulawayo airport. With his new passport he cleared immigration and customs with no problem. The immigration officials were polite and welcoming.

He collected his safari bag from the flapping skirts of the carousel, and made his way through to the arrival's hall, where Rob was waiting for him, his arm held high in a gesture of greeting.

They shook hands. "Good to finally meet you, Rob."

Rob led him out of the building to his battered, mud spattered, pick-up truck, which was much cleaner inside than out, it had seen better days. At least ten years ago.

The traffic was light and twenty minutes later they were on the outskirts of the city of Bulawayo.

"I know you're keen to get down to West Nicholson, Jack, so I won't bother with a guided tour of the city. Despite the chaos you see on television, Bulawayo still has its wide streets, the jacaranda trees still blossom without fail each year and there are still some decent shops and restaurants around. But it's an African city now, so it's changed a lot over the past years since independence."

Skirting the city, he indicated he was turning right. They passed a park, a museum and a theatre, in surprisingly good shape, then a Holiday Inn with its internationally recognised gaudy green logo.

Then they were on the road heading south. They passed through a couple of small towns with dusty faded signs, the landscape dry and brown, a few hills in the distance, outcrops of rocks and the occasional goat or cow meandering across the road, dodging the potholes as they did. A railway track ran alongside the road, grasses sprouting up on either side.

In many ways, to Jack's eyes, it seemed as if time had stood still. Rob swerved between a pothole and a donkey and cart loaded with firewood.

Rob grinned at him. "Have to keep your wits about you driving here. It's not the prettiest part of Zimbabwe I have to admit, but there are many beautiful parts of the country. The game reserves, Lake Kariba, the mountains. It's a small country, landlocked, but it's a place you can lose your heart to."

He squirted some water on the windscreen to clear some of the dust, and blood-spattered remains of insects away. "Plenty of gold mines in this area, both large and small. A lot of the big producers of gold belonged to private families. They were taken over when Mugabe came into power. But there are still a few left, not great producers, so the government were not interested in them."

Jack saw the signs for Gwanda, West Nicholson and Beit Bridge, the border town, and his heart gave a jump.

Rob wiped the inside of the windscreen with his shirt sleeve.

"We're coming into what used to be cattle country. In the old days some of the finest beef and tobacco were exported from what was then Rhodesia. When the world put sanctions against us, we didn't throw up our hands in despair. No. We knuckled down to the business in hand and produced everything ourselves. Everything. It was the making of the people of this country. They were unbending in what they believed in. We believed UDI, the unilateral declaration of independence, was our absolute right, to run our country the way we wanted to." He slowed down as they came into Gwanda.

"Everything today is made in bloody China, poor quality, mass production. The rest of the world should have learned from us. They could have produced and manufactured their own products, supported their own industries. But, it's not how it works is it?

"Governments do deals, regardless of what it might mean to their own people. Ian Smith never did this. The country was the bread basket of Africa. Farmers here held world records for yields in cotton, wheat, soya and tobacco production. It worked."

He changed gear. "Greed, Jack, that's the problem with the world today. Greed and power. Who can get rich on what deal with which country, and to hell with the people who are trying to make a decent living. To hell with supporting their own people and their industries. It's all about money in the end, and who can get rich by it."

Rob sighed raggedly. "It wasn't like this here, during our war. The spirit of the people was extraordinary. We were fighting not only a war, but for survival. It brought the best out in our people Jack, all our people, both black and white. Thousands of African soldiers fought alongside us, shoulder to shoulder. Never forget that."

Jack took a sip of from his water bottle, letting Rob talk, happy to wait to ask his own questions later.

Gwanda was like any other African town Jack had seen on television, no high-rise buildings, no elegant shops or old churches to admire, only a sprawling mass of people, old beat-up cars and trucks, skinny dogs foraging for food, and traders selling fruit and vegetables from the side of the potholed road. Ragged, faded sun umbrellas shielding some from the brutal heat and searing sun. Tinny music blared out from countless shops.

Women glided past, carrying nests of firewood on their heads and babies strapped to their swaying backs. Trucks and cars belched black smoke which plumed into the sky leaving a wake of acrid fumes.

Nothing provoked his interest, except Rob's continuing story.

"Our farm had been in the family for three generations. Blood, sweat and tears went into making it a success. We bred cattle, pedigree cattle. Our two children, my boys, were brought up on the farm, being trained to take over one day. It was their heritage. It was our heritage. We honoured our forefathers who had made our life possible. We worked hard.

"Mugabe had a list you see. There was no pattern to it. It was a list described as for *resettlement* purposes. It included, tobacco farms, cattle ranches, dairy farms, flower exporters, safari parks. Thousands of farms. They took them all. The howling hordes were at the gates. One of the farms on the list was mine."

Jack remained silent, and tried to imagine what it would be like if thousands of angry people had gathered at the gates of his parent's property in the English countryside, demanding they hand it over to them and leave. He felt breathless at the thought – it was unimaginable in the world he had grown up in.

He took another sip from his bottle. "The Europeans owned over fifty percent of the land didn't they Rob. If not more?"

"Yes, they did. But you have to think about the thousands and thousands of local people these farmers employed, looked after, provided for. Under our law then, we had to provide rations, meat, vegetables, housing for anyone who worked for us. We looked after our people, Jack. We weren't all bad, they weren't servants, they were people who worked for us, and we cared for them. They were Rhodesians, like us."

Rob reached for a cigarette, blowing the smoke from the side of his mouth out of his window, his tanned arm steady as it caught the sun.

"Before the attack on our farm, an African woman had come to the kitchen door, she was well dressed, well spoken.

'I want to move into my house today,' she said. *'This is my farm now. I will be back, and you will be gone from here.'*

"I tried not to think too much about it. We locked up that night, making sure everything was secure. Called our neighbouring farmers, by radio, telling them all was quiet. Something we did each night. My wife and I went to bed, the children were already sleeping."

Jack's stomach started to curl. He had a dreadful idea of where all this was leading.

"Firelight woke me in the middle of the night. Outside the farm the war veterans had lit fires, there was singing, shouting and chanting. I checked my guns and ammunition and knew I wouldn't be able to protect my family if they attacked with their guns and machetes'. There were hundreds of them.

"I sat up all night, watching the fires burning, hearing the chanting and singing. It was like a game in many ways, I knew what the final outcome would be, the question was, how long would it take."

Rob stopped at a petrol station and refuelled. Jack didn't move. He knew the history of Rhodesia, and then Zimbabwe, heard the stories of farms being taken, but he had never heard such a raw account from one man who had been through it all.

Rob slid back into the driver's seat and started up the vehicle.

Jack put his hand on his arm. "You don't have to tell me this if it makes you uncomfortable, or if it brings back bad memories."

Rob shrugged his hand off angrily. "If you want to understand this country, Jack, then you need to listen to my story. Who knows, it may give you some insight in what you might be dealing with, with yours. Bring back bad memories? Memories are not brought back. I live with them each and every day. They will never be memories. They are my reality."

He drove as he continued his story. "After a long night the sun rose over the farm. There were hundreds of people at our gates, chanting and shouting. I went out hoping I could quell their frenzied anger.

"A woman was pushed forward; she was waving a machete in her hands. *'Out whites, out whites,'* she shouted, over and over again. I recognised her immediately. It was Nita, the nanny to our children. She had been with us for twenty years, long before the children were born. Now she was on the other side.

"I went into town to try and get the police to help me. The crowds were quiet as they let me pass. My wife and children were barricaded up inside the house.

"When I returned, without the police who didn't want to be involved, they let me back on to my farm.

"They had taken over the farm and everything in it. They had slaughtered the cattle. There was nothing left.

"I found my wife in our bedroom. She had been killed, along with my children. Nita must have watched it all happen. I thought she loved the boys…"

He wiped his tears away with the sleeve of his shirt and was quiet for a few minutes.

"They wouldn't let me take their bodies away. They tied me up and drove me away from my home. They beat me to a pulp and left me at the side of the road, not far from the farm. From there I watched my home and my family burn."

Jack could find no words to comfort the broken man next to him. No words would erase such horrific memories. He thought of Abby. She too carried memories which could never be erased. But surely nothing as shocking as what Rob had gone through.

Or perhaps she had witnessed something similar. That would explain a lot.

*****

They finished the rest of the journey in silence. Rob pulled up at the entrance of an old single storey hotel badly in need of a coat of paint. Thick curtains of crimson, purple and white bougainvillea clung as tenaciously as weeds to one side of the building. Rob turned off the engine.

"This is one of the oldest hotels in the country. Most of its trade comes from people travelling by road to the border post.

"It's nothing fancy but hopefully it's clean and the food is alright if you're hungry. Let's go and check in. I reserved two rooms for us, for two nights."

Jack looked around his room. The furniture was dark, the bed with a faded green cover hardly disguised the deep dip in the middle of the mattress.

The bathroom looked as though it had been built in the sixties with its avocado green toilet, with a chain flush, and basin. An already used bar of soap, with dark cracks, sat forlornly in a broken saucer, along with a petrified black fly. A sagging torn plastic curtain was pulled back revealing an old-fashioned rusting shower, he tried to ignore the black creeping mould in the corners, and a dead cockroach.

He had arranged to meet Rob in the bar in a hours' time.

He stripped off and reached into the shower to turn on the taps. The pipes groaned and hissed, brown water spat out of the rusting shower head, faltered then jerked and groaned once more before a thin stream of reddish-brown water dribbled onto his arm. It was ice cold.

He changed his mind about having a shower, splashed the dust off his face with the lukewarm water from the basin, wiped his face with his shirt, and left the room.

The bar had also seen better days. The bar stools, once red, were now faded, the leather split with time and use, tufts of yellow foam made their way through the surface. The lino on the floor was stained, the few chairs and tables bereft of any customers.

Rob was waiting for him nursing a beer. "What'll you have Jack?"

"A beer sounds good. The sun's still out, shall we take our drinks out into the garden?"

Rob shrugged. "Yes, I agree the gloom in here doesn't lift the spirits. I'll bring them out."

Jack looked up at the flawless blue sky. The gardens were overgrown, the iron chairs and tables pitted with rust. But it was peaceful, the silence only broken by the throaty roars of trucks on their way to the border, the faraway sound of a goat bleating forlornly and the throaty calls of starlings in the trees.

Rob brought out the beers, holding the bottles by their necks. The table wobbled as he put them down, the condensation dribbled down the sides of the glass.

Rob sat heavily. "This used to be a favourite spot for tea and cakes in the old days. Sunday lunch attracted the local crowds, always a big roast set out on tables under the trees, the place has gone downhill over the years. But there's nowhere else to stay near West Nicholson."

Jack reached for one of the bottles. He took a grateful sip then held the bottle on his left pulse, hoping the condensation might cool him down. "I've seen worse, perhaps not as old and rundown. In my career chasing cold cases in the UK, I've sat in some pretty rough places rubbing shoulders with crooks and murderers. I can handle this.

"So, Rob what's on the agenda for tomorrow. Where is this Beecham farm? How far by vehicle?"

Rob ran his finger along the dusty side of his chair. "We have a problem with that I'm afraid. No-one seems to know where the farm might have been. It's not like they have street addresses out in the bush."

Jack looked startled. "Not even Henry, the owner of the store?"

"Not even Henry. There's only one way to do this, but I needed to speak to you before I arranged anything.

"The farm hand who did the shopping for the family drove to the store, so let's say the farm must have been an hour, maybe two, within a radius from West Nicholson.

"What we have to do is hire a chopper and fly over the approximate area where we think the farm might be. I have a friend in Gwanda, George. He has a chopper and he's happy to spend as long as it takes with us to see if we can find it.

"He'll have to be paid in hard currency, into his bank account in the UK, or there's no deal. He's working on leaving the country as soon as he has accumulated enough money to survive there. He charges about three hundred and fifty quid an hour."

"I don't have a problem with that Rob. Let's book him. We can pay him wherever he wants the money to be paid, as long as it's legit."

Rob stood up and wandered around the garden, his phone pressed to his ear. Jack was way out of his depth here, but a chopper pilot, living in this area, would have flown over the bush here plenty of times. He would have an idea where to start looking in the approximate radius of the area they needed to search.

A jacaranda tree provided the only vivid colour in the otherwise tired grounds of the hotel. It's fallen blossom covering a part of the dry brown grass in a carpet of purple.

In a country so torn apart and broken, the jacaranda was a shining beacon of hope and beauty, flowering each year in spite of everything. The sun was beginning to set, the sky was a blazing palette of gold, orange and blood red.

The world would go on, he thought, but in a different way here. Bringing todays version of yesterday's places, and the poignant memories held so dear to the ones who had lost everything and moved to other countries trying to outrun them.

Having, over the years in his career, seen families and loved ones trying to cope with a member of their family who had been murdered, or disappeared, the crushing despair and heartbreak, he knew memories were something no-one could escape from. They found a way of quietly weaving their way into the most shut down of minds at the most unexpected, and inconvenient times. Rob's memories were particularly heart-breaking. His young family and his wife, wiped out.

Rob came back and sat. "Okay, all fixed. George will be here at nine tomorrow morning. He'll land behind the hotel. He's not cheap but he's good. Knows the area well. Been living here for about fifty years, but still doesn't call it home."

Jack pushed away his empty bottle of beer. "Any mileage to be had from visiting the owner of the store, Henry?"

Rob shook his head. "His store will be closed now. I've given you all the information he gave me. He'll only repeat all he told me, so a waste of time.

"I suggest we brave the dining room, such as it is, eat whatever they have on the menu and have an early night, agreed?"

"Agreed. Thankfully I'm not that hungry, but I'm feeling a bit weary. The bed doesn't look too tempting but I'm sure I'll sleep. Maybe we can split a bottle of wine, it should help."

After a meal of tough lamp chops, watery mashed potatoes and tinned carrots, Jack threw in the towel.

"I'll see you tomorrow, Rob. You've done a great job for the newspaper. It's much appreciated. Sleep well."

He turned back to Rob; his face contrite. "I'm sorry, an insensitive remark. How can you possibly sleep well after all you've been through? I certainly wouldn't be able to."

Rob looked at him, his brutal past etched deeply into his face. "Like the whites in South Africa we have always had our religion to see us through impossibly difficult situations, not all of us, of course, but most of us. It's the only thing which kept us sane in a world we thought had gone mad.

"Last year I met someone. Maria. It might work. She lost her husband and their farm. She was in Bulawayo when it happened, with her two young sons. We're both survivors, we understand the pain of losing everything.

"I'm fond of her and the boys. They're not mine, they could never take the place of mine, but they need a father figure. I'll do my best. I have some hope now, Jack. I don't want to leave my country."

Jack nodded. His throat was tight with emotion, words were impossible.

He left the silent dining room and the broken man with tentative hopes for a future where he might find happiness again.

Jack made his way back to his gloomy room. The overhead florescent light flickered annoyingly above his head, as he sat on his lumpy bed.

He thought about Rob, of all the horrific things he had seen in his life, his farm destroyed, his family wiped out, his country on its knees through shocking governance.

He wondered how he would have coped with the same situation and failed. There was only so much a human spirit could endure, he knew this from his experiences in dealing with them, and writing about them.

He thought again of Abby, and his spirits lifted a fraction. If he could find out what happened to her family it would go some way to perhaps helping her heal.

He called Piet.

Twenty minutes later he put the phone down on the stained, water marked, side table next to the bed.

The news Piet had imparted after his day in town with Grace and Abby was not good. Piet planned to re-visit Elspeth the next day and ask her a few questions.

After inspecting the threadbare sheets of the bed and checking the thin blanket for any kind of insects, Jack draped his shirt over the pillow and drifted off to sleep.

Chapter Sixty-Eight

Jack knew from experience it was nearly impossible to screw up bacon and eggs. Breakfast surely could not be as disastrous as dinner had been?

The hotel dining room dispelled that myth. The bacon was brittle with over cooking, the eggs like rubber, the coffee tasting of nothing. In the scheme of things, the toast was a triumph of *haute cuisine* from a sadly declining kitchen. Slightly burned, but slathered in butter and topped with exceptionally good marmalade, Jack filled up, anticipating the day ahead.

The thwack, thwack, thwack of helicopter blades hovered overhead, then there was silence. The dust from the blades of the helicopter added yet another layer of grime to the shabby exterior of the tired hotel.

Jack, clutching a triangle of toast and marmalade, and Rob ran towards it. Rob introduced him to the pilot George.

George was a big friendly guy, in his early seventies, with a strong Yorkshire accent and an untidy grey beard. "Good to meet you lad," he said to Jack, pumping his hand up and down. "A fellow Englishman I understand?"

Jack nodded. "Yeah, but I think I'm turning into a South African. I live there now."

"Good luck to you then, lad. Now, I have a rough idea where you want to fly over. Not much in the area. But, let's see what we can do. I heard about the murders on that there farm, but have no idea which one or where it might be. I was over in the UK visiting me daughter when it happened.

"Right, lads, let's see what we can find in this god forsaken wilderness. Meself? I long for the green and soggy dales of Yorkshire."

Rob and Jack strapped themselves in as the helicopter elevated from the ground. Jack had his map spread over his knees. They communicated through their headsets.

Jack studied the terrain below, the rains had clearly been lacking this year, the bush was dry and brown, there was the occasional outcrop of stark white rocks, straggly trees, goats, donkeys and cattle. The odd African village, with their round thatched roofs passed beneath them, the tiny figures of villagers looking up and waving. Their washing hanging out to dry on rocks near a thin river, providing a spot of colour on an otherwise flat, grey and brown, landscape.

George swept back and forth. There were tiny homesteads scattered below, some thatched, some with tin roofs, some whitewashed, other's their walls streaked black with time and neglect. None were close together. It was a vast landscape with limited pockets of habitation.

George spoke through his mouthpiece. "There's one place I always recognised. Quite big, thatched, used to have a few expensive looking vehicles parked there. Let's go a bit lower, lads, it's coming into view. This could be the place you're looking for.

"I remember seeing some signs of life down there, some washing on the line, but for the last couple of years, it's been completely deserted."

He swooped low. "None of the locals have taken up residence there, which is odd. Anything empty they move into. But not this one. No idea what it's called, or who lived there. The locals avoid it, so maybe there's something bad about it they don't like. Or maybe it was sold and there's a caretaker looking after it. Who knows? Let's take a shufti at it shall we?"

He pointed to another smaller tin roofed building set some distance away from the main house. "That could be staff quarters. Maybe there's someone living there, keeping an eye on the house."

Jack felt the familiar fizz. "Let's get down there, George."

"No problem, mate."

The helicopter swooped down, hovered for a while then set its passengers down. The dust blew up and swept around them, then the rotor blades stilled and there was only silence, except for some doves calling to each other and the ticking of the helicopter engine as it started to cool.

They climbed out and looked around.

The thatched homestead was as silent as a graveyard. All the windows were protected by heavy burglar bars, the curtains drawn. A sturdy ramp led up to what looked like the main door, which was heavily padlocked. What might have been lawn in the front garden was shrivelled, brown, dusty and dead.

Two burnt out vehicles were rusting under a tree. Rob and Jack looked at each other.

George removed his sunglasses and put his hands on his hips.

"Well, lads, if there is anyone looking after this place the chopper would have alerted them to the fact, they have visitors. Let's see what happens."

Jack wandered around on his own. At the back of the house there was the remnants of a vegetable garden, a few straggling cabbages still managing to survive. A triple strand of low-slung washing line sagged between two poles, sporting a few faded clothes pegs.

A child's bicycle, missing its wheels lay on its side next to a shrivelled bush. A wooden cart with a handle held a dozen or so colourful, but now faded, building blocks.

A small swing was suspended from a tree, its ropes fraying and the seat pitted with the trail of termites. Briefly Jack saw the ghost of a little girl called Abby, her head thrown back and laughing as her sister pushed her higher and higher, their laughter ringing through the bush.

A rusting fence surrounded what he assumed was once a paddock with a long cement drinking trough, which would have housed livestock at some point. Two large wooden kennels were backed up next to another door.

A second sturdy ramp led up to what he thought might be the kitchen. He retraced his footsteps back to the front of the house. The air was still and, for Jack, unbearably hot. He took off his sunglasses and adjusted his baseball cap, feeling the sweat seeping through his thick hair and down his spine. He wiped the half-moon crescents of dust from beneath his sunglasses, before putting them back on.

The property was completely isolated, with nothing but dry scrubland as far as the eye could see and the occasional tree dotting the landscape, with a few rocky outcrops sprouting a bit of greenery. In the far distance he could see the faint outline of some hills, distorted by the shimmering heat.

Rob was walking around the wide veranda which skirted the front and sides of the house, his hands cupped to the windows, as he tried to catch a glimpse of what the interior might look like.

Four sun bleached cane chairs, the seats sagging and rotting with constant exposure to the elements, surrounded a dusty square glass topped table. A rusting hurricane lamp at its centre.

The three men sat on the edge of the ramp and waited. Rob put his head in his hands briefly, then looked up and into the distance.

"This place is spooking me out Jack. Something bad happened here, I recognise the feel of it, sense it. I think this must be the farm where the couple and their kids lived. This is where they were murdered."

He pointed to the tree to the left of the house. "I had a look at those burnt-out vehicles. Someone made off with the number plates. Why the bastards destroyed them is a mystery. Cars, especially stolen ones, are in high demand here in Zimbabwe, always a market for them."

A sharp bark had George on his feet. "Baboons!" He put his sunglasses on and looked over the bush. "Over there where those rocks and boulders are.

"I'm going to wait by the chopper, those buggers are cheeky sods, and curious. I don't want them hopping into the seats, belting up and putting on our helmets, looking for a ride. Look here they come."

He left them there in the sun as he trotted back to the waiting helicopter. A large troop of baboons were already making their arrogant and aggressive way towards the shiny aircraft, eager to investigate.

Jack stood up, keen to find some shade from the relentless sun. He leaned against the balustrade of the veranda then suddenly straightened up. "Someone's coming, Rob," he said quietly. "I hope he's friendly, we don't have anything to protect ourselves with, if he's not."

Rob tapped his trouser clad ankle. "Don't worry, I'll watch your back, I'm armed. Be polite and friendly. I'll speak to him in his own language. Most of the local people, unless they're rabid ex-comrades, are harmless and friendly. This one heard the helicopter arrive. Let him approach us."

The African man loped towards them with surprising speed. He stopped when he reached the ramp, the sweat pouring down the sides of his glistening face.

Rob greeted him in the language of the Ndebele people and held out his bottle of water. The man took it, but didn't smile at either of them. He drank the contents in one go, then scowled at them throwing the empty bottle to the ground.

He was a strong man, powerfully built, young, around twenty-four, Jack thought, but it was difficult to tell. He was wearing baggy dark blue trousers and a stained white tee shirt, wet under the armpits with sweat. His feet were hard, dusty, cracked and bare.

"What are you wanting in this place? No-one is living here now. It is I who is in charge here. It is private property you are on without permission."

"Is this your house, my friend?" Rob asked politely, then reverted to English so Jack could follow the conversation. "Do you speak English?"

The big man nodded. "This house is being promised to me by the police, and Comrade Mugabe. Until this time is coming, I am taking care of it, then it will belong to me."

Rob nodded. "Do you know this house then, which the owners have allowed the police, and the President, to give to you in payment for taking care of it?"

The big African spat in the dust next to his feet and wiped the back of his neck with his hand. "I do not know these people who owned this house. I am knowing the garden when it was here, sometimes I was working there.

"My own father is working in this house for many years. He was paid wages for cooking and cleaning and looking after the small ones when necessary.

"What is this you are wanting when you come in the noisy machine?"

Rob inclined his head towards Jack. "This man here, comes from across the sea. From England. He is looking for his family who used to live here. This man has much money for the right information. American dollar money. He is prepared to pay for this correct information. It is his sister he is looking for."

They both saw the glint of interest in the man's hard brown eyes, as he digested this information.

Rob tried again. "The madam and the boss your father worked for here. Do you know where they are now, and the *picannins*?"

Jack saw the man's features harden. If this was one of the friendly locals, he was sadly lacking in people skills. He drew in his breath slowly, letting Rob take the lead.

"For a white man who speaks our language you know nothing. This is *our* country now, *our* land. There is no more *madam* and *boss*, the white people who are left here now have no name but their own."

He spat angrily in the dust again. "This man here," he looked at Jack with disdain, "he is British. The British are our enemies, they took our land. I will not be helping this British person who is looking for his lost sister."

Rob turned to Jack, making sure what he was going to say would be clearly heard by the hostile African in front of them.

"This man here will not be able to help you I'm afraid. I think we've come to the wrong ranch. We'll try another place where you can pay for information with your American dollars. Let's go."

Jack, picking up on the veiled message Rob had conveyed, reached for his wallet and pulled out a fistful of dollars and started to count them. He looked at the African. "Thank you for your time," he shrugged. "Someone will know what we are seeking and be happy to give my family the information."

He held up the dollars and smiled. "As you cannot help then I am not able to give you any of this American money."

He put the money back in his wallet, and made his way down the ramp. Rob followed him. The African hesitated, then stood back and let them pass.

They made their way back to the helicopter.

Rob spoke softly. "Keep walking Jack, don't look back…"

"Wait!"

"Keep walking, act as if you don't care, laugh a bit so he can hear. Keep talking to me, turn towards me and give me a friendly pat on the back."

Jack did as he was told. George threw open the doors to the chopper, ready to let them board.

"Wait!"

"Turn around Jack and look surprised. I'll keep walking."

Jack turned around. He cupped his hand to his ear, as George started up the chopper, the blades beginning to rotate slowly.

He stopped and took a few steps back; the man had been right behind him. "Are you calling me?"

The African looked at him. "Some things I am remembering, it's true," he said sullenly.

Jack beckoned to Rob who was watching him.

The African shook his head. "It is to you only I wish to speak."

Jack frowned at him. "I do not know the ways of Africa. My friend here is Zimbabwean, as you are. I will only talk with you if he is present. What is your name?"

"I am Samson."

"This, Samson," he pointed to Rob who was now standing next to him, "is Mr Thompson and my name is Mr Taylor. Now where do you wish to hold this discussion for which I will pay you dollars?"

George had switched off the engine. The silence of the bush enveloped Jack, Rob and Samson. Jack reached for his wallet and peeled of fifty dollars.

He had Samson on the back foot now. By not giving him their Christian names, he had drawn a line in the sand. Now it was all business. White, black or brown, if you were holding the dollars, you called the shots.

Samson led them back to the house and up the ramp. "Wait here."

Jack slipped the fifty dollars under the rusty hurricane lamp, making sure Samson saw what he was doing.

"I will bring more chairs for us."

He reached in his pocket and brought out a key, bending he unlocked the padlock and let the chain fall to the ground, with a slithering clatter, then he disappeared inside.

Jack turned to Rob. "Let me lead the conversation," he whispered, "let me be the bumbling British idiot, I know he loves to hate, probably as much as he hates you white folk in Zimbabwe. Try and look a bit more relaxed Rob, there's dislike written all over your face, it's not going to help. Let's get the information and get the hell out of here."

Samson brought out three dusty wooden dining room chairs, their striped green and white upholstery faded with time, and they all sat, Samson eyeing the dollars under the lamp.

"Before I give you this information for which you are paying, it is I who will ask some questions. What is the name of your sister before she is being married?"

"Maryanne Taylor, Samson, that was her name."

Samson frowned at him. "This is not good. This was not her given name. Why do you lie?"

Jack frowned, thinking quickly. Not a good start.

"Ah, well you see, Samson she is only my half-sister. Same mother, different father. But her name is Maryanne."

"How can a sister be half, if she is your sister?"

Jack tried to hide his irritation. "Look here, Samson, I don't have time to explain all these things. Let's get on with it shall we."

"This sister who is now only half of a sister. She is strong and well?"

Jack glanced at Rob. Rob raised his eyebrow and said nothing.

Jack eyed the ramp and took a chance. "When Maryanne was young, she was strong. But then there was an accident. She had to use a chair with wheels."

Samson looked satisfied with his answer. "It is my father who knew the family, as I told you. I was young when I helped in the garden, I spoke to no-one, only the little ones if they spoke with me. Then it is to school I was going, away from the farm."

Jack peeled off another fifty dollars and placed it with the other notes under the lamp.

Samson's hope for real money, Jack thought, had obviously overcome any other reservations he might have had about their unexpected visit.

"Who worked on the farm, Samson. How did this family make money to live here? To live in this big house?"

"There was my father who worked here for many years. Another man helped with the business and the animals, some sheep, goats and chickens. He lived in the house where I am now living myself. When I am given this land by the police and the President, I will also take this house, as my own, and perhaps it will be a wife I am taking."

Samson glanced at Rob. "One night, perhaps two rainy seasons ago, our President allowed for our comrades to take this farm, this ranch.

"My comrades were hungry for this land the white man had taken from us. They came in the evening and took this land back."

Jack was glad he hadn't eaten lunch. His stomach was acid with Samson's revelations, remembering Rob's harrowing story of the night his farm was taken. He glanced at Rob who was staring at Samson, no expression on his face, his body still and tense.

"The bodies of your sister and her husband were found by the police, some days later," he gestured to the two burnt out vehicles. "These fine vehicles were set on fire. This was foolish. These vehicles were much expensive. This I am not understanding.

"I am sorry, you have come from far away to seek your half-sister, but even this half is no longer here for you. Now you have no sister, not even half of one of these."

Jack rubbed his cheek with his hand. "What happened to the children, Samson? To the other people who worked here?"

Samson stared at the money. "It is not known what happened to the little ones. They say they are buried on this farm somewhere, also with the farm hand. I am thinking our comrades took them and buried them in another place."

Jack tried not to look at Rob. "My sister's husband, did you know him?"

"I did not. I am seeing him sometimes when I was a small boy. My father told me he travelled many places. This man had much money which he did not share with my father."

Jack leaned forward. "Samson, I would like to meet with your father, to know the man who looked after my sister so well, and the children."

"Then it is to the place where the ancestors go, for he is no longer here with us. It is dead you will have to be being.

"But my father is surely happy with our ancestors. He was the one who told our comrades, what it is they needed to know about the things these white people do, and at what time. It is because of my father, I will be a rich man, with some wives and this farm and the big and small house."

Jack glanced at his watch, mentally calculating the hours which had passed and George's bill, anything to keep his mind off his roiling stomach.

"One last thing Samson. Your father knew the names of the children. I need to know these names for my own family across the sea. Also, the family name."

"The two children were girl children. I am not knowing their names."

Jack kept his face calm. "The family name. Samson?"

Samson scowled. "This half of a sister she does not know her married name? She is not telling you, her brother? Hah! You British, you never tell the truth."

Jack waved another twenty dollars in front of Samson. "I think I have heard enough, and it doesn't please me. It makes me feel sick to my stomach. Give me the name of the family Samson."

Samson said nothing.

Jack gathered up the money on the table. "What you have in front of you, Samson, are two men who have seen enough of violence and killings to last a lifetime. What your father was part of defies any comprehension. Give me the goddam name or you get nothing, do you hear me!"

Rob bent down and released the pistol from its holster around his ankle. He slid it into his pocket. Samson was too interested in the money on the table, now fluttering in an unexpected breeze, to notice.

Samson reached for the money. Jack slammed his fist on the table, the glass cracked beneath his hand.

"Give me the name of the family," Jack said steadily, "before my friend here puts a bullet in your brain."

Samson sat back, looking shocked by the turn of events. He eyed the money again.

"This family name was – Beech Ham. I am not knowing the name of the other man who helped here."

Rob leaned forward. "You people," he said, his voice breaking with emotion, "destroyed my family. Destroyed my life!"

Samson smiled. "You had life, we did not. There is nothing you can take from us now. We take from you."

Rob stared at him, his eyes hard and unforgiving. "Yes, there is something we can take from you. You get no money for your treachery. I have a gun, you do not."

Jack intervened. "Come on Rob, we're leaving now. You can keep this place, Samson, with all its bloody awful memories."

*****

Samson watched the two white men head towards their expensive machine.

The white man had tricked him into telling them what happened on the farm that day.

They had not paid him, as the British man with the wild hair had promised. He looked at the wilderness around him and shrugged. What would he do with such money in a place like this?

But there was still something he had held back. The business of the farm.

The business of Richard Beecham.

He wiped the dust from his eyes watching the helicopter disappear into the distance. Once more silence descended on the bush around him, the dust settling, the doves calling to each other, the isolation of it all.

Then he sank to his knees in the dirt and wept into his hands.

Chapter Sixty-Nine

George deposited his two passengers at the back of the hotel, before taking off again and heading towards Gwanda, appearing satisfied with the outcome of the day.

Jack took Rob's arm and led him to the gloomy bar. "A rough day for you, I know. Difficult. But we've come away with a lot of information. Plus, we saved a ton of money."

"I would have shot the bastard if you hadn't stopped me, Jack."

"That would have been unhelpful, Rob. Samson wasn't the only person to hear the chopper, others saw us flying overhead. The police would have been onto us in hours."

"Only because he's an African," he said bitterly. "If it had been you or I, they wouldn't have bothered."

The barman who seemed to double up as the receptionist and dining room waiter waited for them to order. Jack hadn't seen any other members of staff. Maybe he cleaned their rooms, albeit badly, and cooked the inedible food too.

Jack smiled at him and peered at his name badge. "Two beers please, Sunday. We'll have them out in the garden. By the way, what's on the menu tonight?"

Sunday reached into the fridge for the beers and placed them on the counter, flipping off their tops with a flourish. The beers hissed as the liquid gushed out of the bottle bringing with it a light froth of foam.

"Pork chops, mashed potato and carrots."

Jack's heart sank. He picked up his bottle and slid the other one over to Rob. "Any apple sauce with the chops? Gravy perhaps?"

"Unfortunately, not." Sunday said gloomily. "I will reserve a table for you."

Jack stifled a laugh, he knew no-one else was staying in the hotel, unless there was going to be a rush on later. They made their way into the garden.

281

Jack took off his baseball cap and put it on the table. He ran his hands through his damp hair and grinned. "Is that his name, Sunday?"

"Yup. It's his name. A lot of Africans here have rather unusual names. Lemon, Surprise, Blessing, Anxious. Sixpence was popular and Lettuce. One guy I met was called Typewriter."

Jack laughed. "So, what do you think Rob. Was Samson telling us the truth?"

Rob took a sip from his bottle. "He certainly knew about the family and what happened to the couple who lived in the house. He said the farm hand and the girls were taken by his comrade friends and buried in the bush.

"However, once he had his hands on the promised ranch, he would have noticed any freshly dug graves. Those bloody comrades would not take dead bodies and bury them somewhere else. Why would they?

"In my opinion, the farm hand must have escaped with the kids. There can be no other explanation."

Jack tapped his bottle on the arm of his chair. "Perhaps the Beechams had other guests staying with them. Maybe whoever they were had taken the girls for a drive somewhere. Or even taken them back to their own ranch wherever it might have been. Could be they had children of their own and thought it would be nice for the girls to have a sleep-over at their place."

Rob looked wistful. "Children like the company of other children, especially if they live in such isolated spots. It was something all we farmers used to do. Bundle the children into the back of our *bakkies*, and head out to a neighbouring farm for a *braai*. The children would play together, have dinner, then fall asleep in the back of the vehicle, on a mattress. Then we'd all drive home.

"That's how we lived. Not now, of course."

"Maybe," Jack said, "whilst the children were staying with neighbours, they heard about the attack on the farm and made plans for them to go to a place of safety. It's also possible they may have had friends or family in South Africa and sent them there."

Rob ran his finger down the side of his bottle. "In which case, why didn't the so-called friends, if this was the case, not report the attack?"

"I don't have any answers Rob, I'm only speculating. The friends might even have been *visiting* from South Africa, taking a bush break with the Beechams. They could have taken the girls back with them for a holiday there. With the permission of the parents, they would have had all the right documents to do so."

"Yes, I suppose that's also a possibility," Rob said. "But it doesn't explain how two young girls ended up in a private game reserve in the Sabi Sands, all by themselves does it?"

Jack checked his watch. "Probably not. But I need to look at all the scenarios. What I don't have an answer to is why whoever took the children, didn't report the farm attack to the police. It was a couple of days before the bodies were discovered, right?"

Rob stared off into the distance. "Maybe," he said quietly, "the Beecham couple might not have died instantly. Perhaps one of them had time to get a message to someone, warning them not to come back to the farm because it had been attacked. Too many questions, Jack, and not enough answers for any of them."

Rob sighed, looking exhausted, he turned back to Jack. "By the way, quick of you to come up with the wheelchair angle for your long-lost sister, Maryanne. Because there were ramps up to the front and back doors didn't necessarily indicate Maryanne couldn't walk, or her husband, come to think of it."

Jack rubbed his gritty eyes. "No, it didn't necessarily mean Maryanne was wheelchair bound. But when I checked around the back garden, I saw the clothes line was lower than most. It indicated it was strung low so she could hang out the washing. The stone sink out the back was also built lower than most. There were thin tyre tracks in patches around the veranda, faint, but still there. Someone was in a wheelchair.

"The wheelchair is probably locked up inside the house, or maybe that was stolen as well."

Rob frowned. "They would probably have had a nanny to do the washing."

Jack nodded. "Yes, they might have done, but from what I know of women there are certain things they like to wash themselves, clothes that need special care. Things they don't want hurled into a washing machine. It was just a calculated guess really.

"Also, the glass table, which I unfortunately cracked, was high enough for someone in a wheelchair to be able to reach easily without having to lean down too far. Men will happily hold their glass in their hands when drinking. Women prefer to take a sip then put the glass down. The person in the wheelchair was a woman, Rob."

Jack pinched his nose, feeling a headache coming on. "Maybe it was the reason the couple never came into town to shop, or do anything else. Beecham probably didn't want to leave her on the ranch alone, helpless, with only two little girls. Perhaps it was why the farm hand was sent to do all the chores. Beecham wanted to be sure to protect his family, from the farm attacks going on. Unfortunately, they *were* attacked as we now know."

Jack stood, the sun was going down and the stifling heat was giving way to some cooler air.

"Come, let's go and eat, it's early enough the chef, such as he is, and who is probably Sunday, won't have had time to ruin the chops and make them inedible."

They were not in time. After dinner, they made their way back to their rooms.

"I'd like to make an early start tomorrow, Jack, if it's alright with you. We've done as much as we can here and I need to get back to Bulawayo. I'll drop you at the airport, of course, with plenty of time for you to catch your flight back to Johannesburg."

He paused before unlocking his room. "By the way I know to you it sounded as though I was a bit rough with Samson, and I was.

"He's not some uneducated African working the land, despite the way he talked. I know these people. He has had some education, he's intelligent and clever with his words, I picked that up when we spoke together in his own language. He's also a broken man. Broken by events in the country, or broken by something else.

"He was holding something back. I could see it in his eyes when he talked about the comrades and what happened the night the Beecham couple died.

"He was lying, Jack. I'm not sure about what, but he wasn't telling the truth."

Chapter Seventy
South Africa

Piet was there to meet Jack when he arrived back in Hazyview. Jack brought him up to date with what had happened over the past few days.

Piet was unusually quiet throughout the drive to the hotel, he pulled up, parked, and switched off the engine. Then he turned to Jack, his face hard and unsmiling.

"My old colleagues' son, from the police, Enoch, called me.

"Our hairdresser friend, Elspeth is dead. Her body was found in her car early yesterday morning. About half an hour away from here."

Jack gripped the door handle of the car. "What the hell happened to her?"

"It looks like suicide according to the police."

Piet paused to let that sink in before he continued. "There's an old land fill site out there with an abandoned corrugated hut next to it, big enough for a car. One of the local Africans was out there, going through the rubbish looking for whatever he could find. He heard the sound of the engine inside the hut and went to investigate. He called the police.

"A hosepipe from the exhaust was wedged in the front window of the car, tucked in with a thick red blanket. She wouldn't have felt a thing, if this was the case."

"What do you mean she wouldn't have felt a thing if this was the case?"

"Because, I don't think it was suicide, no matter what the police think or say. My friend Enoch, who is in charge of the investigation, well that is his verdict. Suicide. Case solved as far as he's concerned."

Jack stared at him. "But what gives you reason to think it wasn't?"

"When I went to her shop a couple of days ago, I must have spooked her out. Elspeth was involved with this whole Abby thing,

Jack, I'm convinced of it. Abby growled like a frightened dog when she saw Elspeth's shop, or maybe it was Elspeth she was growling at.

"She recognised something from her past. My visit to Elspeth's salon provoked this whole thing. Grace told her I was ex-police, now a private detective. Elspeth may have been in touch with someone involved in what happened to Abby and her sister."

Jack stared out at the cars pulling into the hotel car park, then he turned back to Piet.

"If you don't believe it was suicide, when the police clearly think this is the case, what do you think happened?"

"I think someone helped her on her way, Jack, plain and simple. Made to look as if she took her own life."

Jack ran his fingers through his hair. "What did the note say Piet?"

'I can't do this anymore! I can't do this anymore!' That was all it said."

Piet bit his bottom lip. "Elspeth had her identity book with her, it didn't take the police long to track her down through the system. There were business cards in her bag, for the barber's shop. A cash receipt for her rented apartment, with the address, and also the keys to her flat.

"They found the note on a table. The so-called suicide note. I told you what it said. Whatever she was up to, whichever way you jump with the note, she believed she couldn't go on with whatever she was embroiled in."

Jack wiped his face with his sleeve. "Well, there you have it. What makes you doubt it could possibly be anything else other than suicide?"

Piet unbuckled his seat belt. "Come on, let's find a quiet spot in the garden somewhere and have a cold beer. I've been chasing around town since I heard. Worked up a thirst. I'll tell you the rest of the story, so long."

*****

They settled away from the other guests under the shade of a generously leaved tree. After the waiter had delivered their drinks, Piet continued.

"Call it some old instinct from my police days, but something about the whole case doesn't stack up for me. In my experience when a person commits suicide, they do it in their own home, away from any prying eyes. If a person chooses to gas themselves in their car it's in their own garage. Elspeth kept her car in the garage under the block of flats.

"So, why, my friend, did she drive out into the bush and kill herself there? Why didn't she take the note and leave it propped up in the car for the police to find? Why leave it behind in the flat. It doesn't make sense to me."

He took a sip of his beer. Jack's glass sat untouched on the table. "What do you think happened then if she didn't kill herself? I see what you're saying. A note is invariably found with the body, if there's a note left at all."

"See here, Jack, for me when there's a death in the bush, I always take a different angle where I try to work out what happened. Enoch gave me a full update on where the car was found, the state of the body, found in the passenger seat, the way the suicide was committed and so forth.

"I called Caroline and asked if I could have Jabu for a few hours – on your expense account I'm afraid."

Jack lifted his shoulder in a half shrug. "Go on, expenses are the last thing on my mind at the moment."

"Jabu and I drove out to the spot. The car and body had been removed and there were signs of police activity, footprints all over the place, tyre tracks from the police vehicles and the ambulance etc.

"Jabu, in my opinion is a natural tracker, like a lot of his San ancestors he's been doing it all his life. He's exceptional, one of the best I've ever met."

Piet threw his cap on the table. "We went out there together, and I let Jabu loose. For an hour he walked around the area and the surrounding bush. He didn't miss anything, following those age-old instincts of his."

Jack sat forward. "What did he find which convinces you Elspeth didn't commit suicide?"

"Jabu found other tracks, other tyre marks and was able to differentiate them from any the police or medics had made. He told me with absolute conviction, there had been another car parked a short way from the tin hut, hidden by the thick bush, and another set of shoe prints, different from the ones the police and ambulance guys had made, which led Jabu to where Elspeth's car was found."

"Murder then, is that what you're saying?"

"Based on what he tracked, Elspeth went to meet someone there. Someone she knew. I think he overpowered her, knocked her out with something, then bundled her in the car, if she wasn't in there already, fixed the hosepipe and the blanket, closed the hut door and left her to die. Then he made his way back to his own vehicle and took off. The perfect murder, he thought. But not to me, my friend, not to me.

"The bastard once he overpowered her, drove her car into the hut and left her there. He would have wiped the car and hut door clean of any fingerprints. There are many ways of knocking someone out without leaving a bruise or any other marks."

Piet stared into the distance. "He used branches to cover his tracks from the hut, but Jabu had no problem finding them and other clues, like bent grasses, dislodged stones and other disturbances which should not have been there. We're dealing with a dangerous person, my friend.

"Enoch showed me the supposed note Elspeth left. The flat was sealed off and even I couldn't get in to take a look around.

"I don't think it was a suicide note, not for one moment. It was something she scribbled to herself after a difficult conversation with whoever this person is we're looking for. People do this, it's like a mantra they stick on their fridges. In anger, or fear, I think Elspeth was so upset she scribbled the note, then underlined it heavily as a way of dealing with her anger."

Piet lifted his glass. "This person who killed her, didn't go to her flat, or he would have found the note and brought it with him. No, she wrote the note for a different reason, as I said, maybe after a difficult conversation. She scribbled it to herself."

Jack made some notes in his book, then reached for his now warm beer. "Whoever this person was, he must have thought she knew too much about him, or something else. Where was her phone?"

Piet put his cap back on. "*Nah*, no sign of it. It would have been useful but whoever killed her took it. It wouldn't take long, with the technology we have now, to trace any outgoing or incoming calls. No, the phone will never be found, too much harmful information on it."

The waiter brought them two fresh beers and a bowl of crisp calamari, with a tartare sauce dip. They both reached forward hungrily.

"Have you shared any of what you found with your police buddy, Enoch. Your thoughts on the suicide note?"

Piet shook his head as he chewed thoughtfully on the calamari. "I'm only speculating Jack. I'm not officially on the case, Enoch is passing information to me because his father worked for me at one time."

He smiled wearily at Jack. "My thoughts are something I don't have to share, not at this stage anyway. I'll only share them with you.

"This whole story, is evolving into something a whole lot bigger than we anticipated. There are two countries involved here. Zimbabwe, we know now from what you've told me of your few days there, and, of course, South Africa.

"None of the things which have happened have been random events, they're all connected. I'm sure of it. Abby may well be the key to the whole thing."

Jack nodded his mind filtering through this new information. "Did the police come up with anything when they ran Elspeth's details through the database?"

"The police ran the number plates of her car through the system, and her identity number. We have her name now, Jack.

"Elspeth Hartman. Her parents own a farm in the Eastern Cape. They breed Merino sheep, won lots of cups and badges, or whatever they call those ribbon things they stick on sheep and cattle.

"They will have been told about the death of their daughter by now. There will be an autopsy, of course. But I can tell you now, and bet my paltry pension on the fact, that the verdict will be suicide."

Piet stared into the distance. his face troubled. "Unfortunately, we have one of the highest suicide rates in the world. Teenagers, farmers, businessmen, anyone who is overcome with life and sees no way out. This will be seen as one more, I'm afraid."

Jack finished his beer. "Doesn't matter how wealthy you are does it Piet, or how many of your fancy sheep won prizes. The death of a child stings just as much. Any siblings?"

Piet shook his head.

Jack continued. "So, her parents would have been told their daughter committed suicide, when in fact you think she was murdered?"

He watched Jack. He could almost see his mind working, making connections, dismissing some, taking a short cut here and there, filing information away to be dissected later. He gave him a few minutes, knowing he was as tired as he was, both of them troubled by their imaginings.

"It's a tough call Piet. Big difference between taking your own life, or have it taken by someone else."

Piet's blue eyes hardened as he looked at his friend. "I thought about that. The police would have told them what they found, that it was suicide. I'm not sure what would be more shocking for them. Their daughter is dead whichever way you look at it.

"We have no solid proof, not yet anyways. I think it's best to leave things as they are at the moment.

"If Elspeth was involved in any way with the disappearance of Abby and her sister, then she was up to no good. One child was never found, and presumed dead. You hear what I'm saying Jack? She could have been an accomplice in whatever happened. It's a criminal offence! She would have been in deep *kak*.

"Let them do their grieving in their own way. Their daughter is lost to them, she's not coming home again."

Jack stood and eased his aching back, driving on potholed roads and being thrown around in a helicopter for hours on end hadn't helped, nor the lack of hot water or the lumpy mattress at the hotel.

"I'm going to take a shower Piet. Then I'll call my editor and bring him up to date. I'll leave him to fill in Stefan, the guy who took my place; he did a good job tracking down Fletcher-Jones even though it didn't lead anywhere. But his contact Rob in Zimbabwe, well he turned out to be excellent.

"Then I'll tell him how much our little venture to Zimbabwe cost the newspaper. He won't be a happy man I can assure you."

Piet glanced at his watch. "I'm going back into town. Check up on the bookseller. Then I'll see if I can speak to anyone who lived across the road in those old cottages.

"Let's regroup in the bar in a couple of hours."

*****

Luxuriating in a steaming hot shower, Jack started to relax, then he heard his phone vibrating on the glass table. Quickly he turned off the mixer, threw a towel around his waist and grabbed it. The water dripped down his face as he listened to Rob.

"Sorry, Jack. You owe me another hundred dollars. When I arrived back in town, I was in touch with one of my contacts who can access births, deaths and marriages here. Not legal of course, always a price to pay here.

"Richard and Maryanne Beecham had two children, as we know. Their births were registered. Now we know for certain those two girls who lived on the farm were called Abigail and Suzanna Beecham. Suzanna was born on the seventeenth of April in 2007, she would be ten now. Abigail was born on the seventeenth of May 2009, which makes her eight. There were no death certificates for the girls or their parents, nothing he could find anyway."

Jack wiped his face. "Good work, Rob. You're doing an excellent job. This is a major step forward. Keep your ear to the ground for anything else, won't you? Cheers, mate."

He rang off, well pleased with the latest information from his man in Zimbabwe. He would call Harry again and see if he could restore his sense of humour with the latest information Rob had shared with him.

His editor had roared down the phone at him when he explained the cost of the trip to Zimbabwe, spluttering about *making bloody sure the story was going to be worth it!*

Jack would be sure not to mention that the latest bit of information from Rob had cost him another hundred dollars.

Chapter Seventy-One

The sun was beginning to set as Piet parked opposite the barber's shop.

He looked left and right then crossed the street in time to see the bookseller starting to close his shop. Gert looked up as Piet loomed up in the shadows of the doorway.

"Sorry, shops closed. Open tomorrow at eight."

"You remember me, yes?"

Gert watched warily as Piet leaned on his counter.

"Now listen here, Gert. I have bad news for you," he said bluntly. "You need to find new tenants. Elspeth was found dead in her car yesterday. Suicide."

He watched the colour leech from the booksellers' face as he steadied himself on the other side of the counter.

"Dear God. Elspeth? I can't believe it!"

"Well, it's true. I have some questions for you, as will the police when they finally get around to finding you."

Gert lowered himself onto his stool and put his head into his hands. Piet waited until he lifted his head.

"You're not in trouble with me, Gert."

He pulled his private detective card from his pocket and slid it across the counter. "Now, can you think of any reason why Elspeth would do such a terrible thing. Was she unhappy? In debt? Boyfriend trouble?"

Gert shook his head, his face white with shock. "Not anything I was aware of. I didn't ever see her with a man, she was a good decent Afrikaans girl, friendly, could talk a lot if she was given the chance.

"As I told you before, she was quiet when she arrived in town, this was over a year ago or so. After she had been here for a few months she bought a car and started to go out more. I don't know where.

Sometimes the shop was closed for a couple of days, as I told you before, but it's all I can tell you. *Ag*, man, this is a bad shock for me."

Piet left the bookshop having learned nothing new from Elspeth's landlord.

He crossed back over the street where the lights had now come on. He walked slowly past the three old cottages to see if there was anyone on their *stoep* watching the evening's passing parade, of which there was precious little.

A small dog lunged at the front gate of one of the cottages and started to yap at him. He bent and poked his fingers through the steel bars and was rewarded with the frantic wagging of its stumpy tail.

Sitting outside the house was an elderly gentleman with a cane leaning next to his chair, his back ram-rod straight, a glass of something brown, which he had noticed earlier when he passed, on the table next to him.

Piet lifted his cap. "Evening, sir, nice friendly dog you have here what's his name?"

"Japie. Useless guard dog, but noisy enough to keep strangers away. Where you from, not here or I'd recognise you."

Piet replaced his cap. "Eastern Cape. Up here on a bit of business, maybe you could help me. Not familiar with the town, but the folks are friendly here. I need to talk to some of the locals."

The elderly man chuckled. "Been living here in this cottage for forty years. Come on in and ask your questions. Could do with a bit of company. Japie doesn't have much to say for himself, don't worry he doesn't bite."

Piet unhooked the gate and let himself in, bending once more and giving the dog a pat and scratch behind the ears. He held out his hand to the owner.

"Piet Joubert. Pleased to meet you."

"Eugene Botha. Ex-South African army; saw action in South West Africa, as it was. Knew what we were fighting for then – now I wonder if it was all worth it when I watch the news. Come sit."

Piet took the faded and somewhat hard looking chair next to Eugene. Having noticed the man's glass as he passed by earlier, he withdrew a half jack of brandy, he had bought from the bottle store, from his top pocket. Eugene's eyes lit up.

"Glass in the kitchen, Piet, help yourself."

He found the kitchen, simple, clean and orderly, like the man himself. He retrieved a glass from the spotless cupboard.

Now with both glasses full, the two men talked about the army days, the police days, politics, crime and the inevitable woeful state of Eskom. As if by magic the lights went out.

Unlike the hotel there was no friendly growl of any generator. Eugene lent forward and switched on a battery driven light. He drained his glass and held it out for a top up.

Piet did the necessary, careful not to top his own glass up, he needed his wits about him.

Eugene was looking quite comfortable as the brandy coursed its way through his body.

"So, what questions did you want to ask. You told me you're retired from the police and now a private investigator. Are you here on a case, or a tourist passing through longing to go on one of those safaris? If so, you'll need to sell a kidney to afford it."

He guffawed at his own joke, and took another large mouthful of his brandy.

Piet looked at him and decided if he was going to get any information at all he would have to level with the ex-military man.

He told Eugene about the girl called Abby, and her sister who had never been found after the floods.

Eugene massaged his jaw and took another sip from his glass. "*Ja,* I heard about the girl who appeared at the game lodge. Must have had good taste to pick one of the most expensive in the country, clearly not a camping type."

Again, he laughed at his own joke.

Piet took off his cap and scratched his head before replacing it. "See here Eugene, there's a bit more to the story, which I can't share with you at the moment. I think there might be a connection with the hairdresser across the road. The one with the pink hair?"

Eugene raised his eyebrows. "Yes, I've seen her around, of course. Nothing better to do all day and night, than watch people coming and going. How do you think she's involved?"

Piet lifted his shoulders. "I think she may have been related to the girl's family, or knew the family. I'm looking for that family Eugene. The girl needs to find out who she is, where she comes from. You live right opposite the barber's shop did you ever see the hairdresser with anyone. Notice anything unusual?"

Eugene leaned his head back on the chair and Piet held his breath as he topped up his new friend's glass.

"Not really. Plenty safari types, game rangers, went to the shop to get their hair cut. Short back and sides, in and out in half an hour. Sometimes an elderly chap or two, I saw a woman go in a couple of days ago, bit unusual."

Piet hid his smile. Grace. Eugene hadn't missed much.

"The hairdresser with the pink hair has been hereabouts for some time now. I can't tell you exactly how long. Seemed like a quiet sort, but often went out in her car. Sometimes she wasn't there for a day or two, shop all shut up.

"Only unusual thing was sometimes late at night, or in the early hours of the morning, she would have a visitor, didn't see if it was a male or female, lights would be turned low, shutters down, then half an hour later, all went black. So maybe she had a lover or two, who knows."

Piet leaned forward in his creaky chair. "Ever see a strange car outside when she had visitors?"

"No, no cars. Oh, hang on, one time, when she first arrived here, I did see a *bakkie*. An expensive one. It had a Zimbabwe number plate – I remember now, parked outside her shop."

"Did you see it again, see the driver?

"No, didn't see it again, didn't see the driver. Must have been there to have his hair cut."

"You see, Eugene. Elspeth, the hairdresser with the pink hair. Well, she committed suicide."

Eugene sighed with resignation. "These young things, can't take the world anymore. We had no choice in the army, just had to get on with things even though, during the war, some thought about the hopelessness of it all. Sorry to hear this. So young. Suicide is a tough thing for a family to have to deal with. Lots of blame and no answers. I've always thought it was a selfish solution to a problem."

"Anything else you can tell me Eugene?"

He shook his head. "No, but if I remember anything I'll let you know. The body might be ageing but I still have my brain. Give me a contact telephone number. I'll see if I can remember anything else."

Piet stood, leaving the now nearly empty brandy bottle on the table.

"Thanks Eugene, once a soldier, always a soldier. I can see you haven't lost your powers of observation. Here's my card. I'm staying in town for a few days."

Using his torch, Piet made his way to the back of the barber's shop and the others. A lane ran behind the back of all the darkened shops, a service lane, littered with refuse bins. This, Piet surmised, would be where supplies for the various shops were delivered. There were no lights.

Wedged in between the back entries to the shops was a small window of light. He saw the flare of a lighter, the red smouldering end of a cigarette.

He knocked on the door. All he could hear was the faint sounds of classical music. The music stopped and a woman appeared at the window.

She was of an uncertain age, her dark hair, streaked with grey, falling around her shoulders, a colourful dressing gown wrapped around a slight and thin figure. Smoke rose from her cigarette as she squinted through the window.

Piet went up to the window and flashed his now defunct police badge, he made sure he was smiling.

"What do you want?" The voice was rasping and deep.

"Sorry to disturb, ma'am. I'm checking a few things out here, making sure everyone is safe."

"Is there a problem officer?"

"No, not at all. But I wonder if I might have a few words with you, check out your security, make sure everything is alright."

He heard the jangle of chains, the pull back of a bolt, then the door opened.

The woman stood there, her cigarette smouldering, a tentative smile on her face, her gown wrapped tightly around her body. "How can I help you officer. I've never seen the police around here before."

Piet took off his cap and, smiled warmly at her. "A couple of questions I would like to ask?"

She looked up and down the deserted lane. "I'll try to answer them if I can, officer."

"I see this is a service lane for offloading supplies for the shops hereabouts?"

She took a drag on her cigarette, pulling her dressing gown tighter around her body against the cooling night air.

"Yes, bloody awful noise they make, wakes me up."

"So, they come the same time each night, do they?"

"Yes, at night and also in the early hours of the morning. But you get used to it I suppose."

"Ma'am, over the past couple of years have you noticed any other vehicles, other than the supply vehicles?"

She took another drag then crushed the finished cigarette under her shoe. She frowned as though she was trying to remember something.

"The hairdresser woman, with the pink hair. She had a few deliveries made in the dead of the night. I mean, why do you need a small truck to deliver bloody shampoo and conditioner, I ask you?

"A guy, maybe an African, helping with whatever was being delivered. Why would anyone need a truck and help for hair products? Could easily have delivered at the front of the shop during the day. I've walked past the barber shop, no need for fancy heavy equipment in there if you ask me. But then what do I know these days?"

Piet put his cap back on. "Thanks for your help. You stay safe now ma'am, keep your door locked and chained, you hear?"

He walked back to his car and climbed in. Yes, indeed, he thought, what was Elspeth taking delivery of at odd times of the night, and apparently, she seemed to have had visitors who preferred the undercover of darkness.

Chapter Seventy-Two

Wearily Piet made his way back to the hotel. Jack was waiting at the bar, chatting to Hugo the owner, the room was relatively quiet. Most of the guests presumably enjoying dinner in the restaurant.

Hugo poured the detective a beer then enquired as to whether they would be dining at the hotel. Then he discreetly left them alone. Jack had told him about the suicide of the local hairdresser.

Over dinner Jack and Piet went over the case, speculating, arguing points, and drawing similar conclusions.

Jack finished his lamb chops, wondering how Sunday, the waiter or chef, at the Zimbabwean hotel, could have possibly massacred the ones he had cooked for him and Rob. The mashed potatoes were creamy, cooked to perfection with a sprinkling of parsley and chives, the crisp onions and prepared vegetables sublime.

Piet was once more devouring the steak and mushroom pie, oblivious to the gravy on his chin.

"I think we should make a visit to the lodge, Piet, bring Caroline and Grace up to date on what we now know. See if Abby recognises her surname and her birthday, it might help to nudge her memory.

"I think Grace might need a bit of support with our news. What do you think?"

Piet couldn't keep the smile of his face. "Great idea Jack. Let's fix it with Toby and get over there, he's bound to have a couple of seats we can hitch a ride on. Hope your expense account still has a bit of wriggle room. This Abby is starting to cost a fortune, and not just for your newspaper. Caroline is footing all the other bills, the hospital, Grace's salary, doctor's bills and the rest."

He pushed his plate to one side. "I'll leave you to make the arrangements with Caroline and Grace."

Chapter Seventy-Three

Jabu was there to meet them when they landed at the airstrip the next morning. He drove them to the lodge. Settling in the chairs on the viewing deck, he waited for them to share any new information with him.

"Caroline's away in Cape Town, at the moment. But Grace is here, of course. She's waiting for you. She seems a bit, well, all over the place, at the moment. Abby has been difficult."

Piet leaned forward in his seat. "Jabu, we have the name of the children now. Her name is Abby Beecham, her sister was called Suzanne, or Susie as she was called, and now we know their birthdays. It would be good if you could be there with us when we tell Abby this. She trusts you and she feels comfortable when you're around."

Jack then told Jabu about the trip to Zimbabwe, the death of the hairdresser and what their thoughts were.

Jabu was quiet for a few moments. "This is a lot for a child to absorb and understand. I think Grace should decide how much the little one can handle. Let's talk to her first. I will be there, of course.

"There is no doubt Elspeth, is part of this story. I followed her footsteps to her death. It is fitting that we find out what really happened to her and who was responsible."

*****

Grace was there when they got to the cottage. She led them through to where Abby was turning the pages of her book. Abby looked up when she saw Jabu, turning to him as he took her in his arms.

"Hello, little one. Jack and Piet have come to see you as well. You remember them? Come, let's go outside and see if we can find some birds for you to draw?"

Jack and Piet quickly brought Grace up to date with their news. Grace twirled her braid as she listened. Then shook her head.

"Dear God, how much more will this child be able to take?"

Grace briefly put her hand to her mouth. "The poor hairdresser. I hope I wasn't the cause of anything with mentioning you being an ex-policeman and now a private detective. Was I Piet?"

"No, of course not. But Elspeth was involved in all of this. We haven't quite figured out how, but we will."

Piet looked at Jack and nodded. "We now know Abby's surname and her birthday, she's eight years old. It's important we talk to her, see her reaction."

Grace frowned. "She's very small for an eight-year-old, I have to say. She should be a lot more active, and more advanced mentally, notwithstanding what might have happened to her."

Jabu returned with Abby and put her on the sofa. Grace put her arms around the child.

Jack hunkered down in front of her. "Hey, we found out who you are! Your name is Abby Beecham and better still, we know when your birthday is. That should make you happy, yes?"

Abby stared at him; her face completely devoid of any emotion, her eyes dull and listless.

Jack tried again, dismayed at her complete lack of response. "We went to your farm, the ranch, in Zimbabwe? We met someone called Samson. Do you remember him. His father worked on the farm, looked after your parents? They were called Maryanne and Richard, your mummy and daddy. Do you remember them, do you remember Samson or his father? Do you remember your two big dogs, what were their names?"

Abby looked out over the bush, rocking back and forth, a low growl coming from her throat. Jack and Piet looked at each other in alarm, then back at Abby.

Grace pulled the child closer as Abby put her thumb in her mouth and closed her eyes.

She looked across to Piet, and he saw the hopelessness in her eyes. Instinctively he stood up and stood behind her chair, his hands on her shoulder, trying to give her the courage she needed, when he saw what she knew was now inevitable.

"It's no good Piet," she whispered, "It's too much for her. She's gone somewhere else. We must let her to go there, where she feels safe.

It seems to me it will be kinder now. I'm not sure she even understands what anyone is saying anymore."

Jabu reached for the child. "Give me some more time with her Grace, let me take her outside again. Let me talk to her in our language, it sooths her."

Abby burrowed into Grace's arms, ignoring Jabu's outstretched arms. Grace's eyes filled with tears.

"It's no good Jabu."

Having had no response from Abby, Piet and Jack decided to return to their hotel.

Toby was waiting for them on the airstrip, ready to take them back to Hazyview.

*****

Piet didn't say much as he gazed out of the small window of the aircraft, watching the bush speeding beneath them.

When they arrived back at the hotel, Piet seemed to be in a hurry.

"You go ahead, Jack. I have something to do here. I'll meet you back at the bar around six."

Jack raised his eyebrow. "What are you up to Piet? You seem to be somewhat preoccupied, looking a bit shifty in fact. Is it something to do with Grace by any chance?

Piet looked uncomfortable, and rubbed his cheek. "Maybe. See you later."

*****

Jack called Daisy in Franschhoek. She was unusually subdued, not her normal noisy self.

"Something wrong Daisy?"

"It's the scruffy dog, Mr Yak. I was taking him for a walk in town. This man stopped me and said the dog was his, he's been looking everywhere for him. He wanted to take him."

Jack frowned into the phone. "You didn't let him take Benji did you Daisy?"

"*Neh*, of course not Mr Yak. But Benji seemed to recognise him, wagging his tail and so forth. He knew him. Now what must Daisy do? The dog is looking sad now."

"Okay, Daisy, this is what we will do. If Benji does belong to this man then he must be given back.

"You'll find the number of his vet on the fridge door. Call him and make an appointment. Did you get the number of the man who says Benji is his?"

Daisy sniffed. "Yes, Mr Yak, this I did. He said the dog was called Atty. He was right, this dog is knowing his real name, it's true Mr Yak."

"Okay. Now listen. Once you have made the appointment with the vet, I want you to call him, arrange to meet him at the surgery. Doctor Steyn will be able to work out if Benji does belong to this man. If he does then we must give him back, you hear me?"

"Yes, Mr Yak, I hear you. But now Daisy will be sad with no scruffy dog to look after."

Jack squeezed the top of his nose. "We'll both miss him, Daisy. But it's the right thing to do. If the vet says this man is the owner, then you *must* hand Benji over, okay?"

"Yes, Mr Yak," she whispered down the phone. "But what will happen to Daisy now, with no dog to look after? I'm liking your house Mr Yak. I don't want to go home to my noisy family, with all their arguments and shouting."

"Then you shall stay in my house. It will still need looking after, don't worry about it. Let me know what happens with Benji. I'd be interested to know what language he speaks?"

The familiar roar of Daisy's laughter echoed down the phone. "This dog, Mr Yak, is speaking only Afrikaans. This is why he would not do as you told him. It is Daisy he understands. It is you he is not understanding."

Jack put his phone on the table. He would miss the little fellow, but it sounded as if his real owner had been searching high and low for him.

Benji would go back to the home he knew, back to his family. He hoped Abby would be given the same chance. To find someone in perhaps her wider family, although from what he now knew, this would seem unlikely.

He tried not to think about how empty his cottage would be when he finally got home. Daisy would still come in every day, but the nights would be long.

Jack had had such high hopes when he decided to move to South Africa. But, he reasoned with himself, might as well be lonely in a beautiful place if one is going to lonely at all.

However, it was hardly what he had had in mind when he made his decision to leave England and make a new life for himself.

Chapter Seventy-Four

As arranged, Jack was at the bar at six, waiting for Piet. He jerked his head back when he saw him walk in. Piet was grinning, looking pleased with himself.

He wore a dark green uniform, with the hotel logo embroidered on the pocket of his shirt and a discreet bronze badge, announced he was now *Chief Security Officer* for the hotel, it glinted in the light from the bar counter. His battered baseball cap was perched on his head.

He sat down. "I've done it, Jack. Made the decision. There's nothing for me in Willow Drift anymore, this is where I'm going to live now."

Jack signalled for the barman. "What about all your things in Willow Drift. Your cottage and the security business?"

"I don't have much Jack. My ex-wife cleaned me out after the divorce, the bloody cat also left, went to somewhere where the food was more to her liking, probably took what was left at my place as well.

"I have nothing to tie me to Willow Drift anymore. An old buddy from the police wants to take over my lease of the office and cottage, also he's keen to take over the business. Any personal bits and pieces he'll send on here.

"I have a decent cottage provided for me, with a proper bed and bathroom, food is on the house, good salary, medical aid, a hotel vehicle." He smoothed down his shirt. "Feels good to be back in uniform," he said cheerfully.

Jack shook his hand with gusto. "Great news! Congratulations. I can think of someone else who's also going to be happy to hear you're moving here."

Jack took a handful of peanuts from the bowl on the counter and tossed them into his mouth. "I hope you'll still be able to help me with the case, Piet?"

"Sure, I will. I've already spent some time walking around the property, made a list of what needs to be done, where the security can be improved and so on. Working for Hugo will be okay, I like him, even though he's an Englishman..."

He stole a look at Jack through his thick dark lashes, waiting for some kind of reaction – there wasn't one.

"What kind of vehicle have they given you."

"One of those safari long wheel base vehicles, dark green with the hotel logo on the side. Hey Jack, I'll be able to drive around the bush anytime I want, with a vehicle like this and my uniform," he looked at his shirt and shorts. "I'll look like a game ranger."

Jack stared at him; his glass steady as he slowly put it back on the counter. "That's it, Piet," he said softly. "That's how all this worked," his voice tailed off as his mind raced.

Piet looked surprised. "Are you going to share with your buddy what you're thinking here?"

"What I'm thinking Piet, is that the man we are looking for is a game ranger, someone who can move around the bush without worrying about the authorities. He wears a ranger's uniform and he drives a safari vehicle with a lodge logo."

Piet nodded slowly, thinking this theory through. "It's possible, yes, very possible."

Jack reached for his phone. "I need to call Jabu. He's the only one who will be able to give me the information we need."

Piet stood up. "Let's go find a place out in the garden. Something tells me you'll be spreading your big map out. We need somewhere with a bit more space."

Jack reached for the map in his pocket. "Are you not on duty, Piet? Don't need to prowl around the perimeter fences and make sure we're safe and not going to be murdered in our beds anytime soon?"

"I start next week. Just wore the uniform to impress you. Come let's go into the garden, or perhaps you might like to come to my place, I've already moved in."

Piet's cottage was well appointed, equipped with all he needed including a basic kitchen if he became fed up with eating steak and mushroom pie every night, something Jack doubted.

They spread the map out on the low wooden table and anchored the corners with whatever came to hand.

Jack pulled out his note book then picked up his phone and called Jabu. He knew it was a busy time of the day for a lodge manager. He would be checking all was in order and awaiting the return of his guests, back from their game drive. He would have to be quick.

"Jabu? Jack here. Sorry to call you at a busy time, I have a couple of questions for you. Have you a few minutes? Good, I'll try and keep my questions short.

"I know there are many lodges in the Sabi Sands, most of them at the high end of the market. I also know some owners have their private homes there. But my question is this?

"Are there any run-down lodges, perhaps with the owner not being able to afford to refurbish and keep up with the big boys. Any sort of back packer places? Any small basic lodges in your area, say in a forty-kilometre radius?"

He listened intently as Jabu replied. His eyes, and finger, traversing the map in front of him.

"Do you know the name of it?"

He stared at the map, thanked Jabu, closed his phone off and looked at Piet, who was examining his new safari boots, although he had obviously been listening to the one-sided conversation.

Jack studied the map; all the lodges were marked on it.

"What are we looking for here, Jack. A run-down lodge I heard you say. What did Jabu come up with? You have this look on your face, and you're jiggling your foot. Makes me nervous."

"Jabu told me there's a lodge called Trackers. It's small with only four guest rooms, quite basic apparently. It used to cater for the lower end of the market, so it only attracted the local tourists. Over the years it slowly ran down and eventually closed."

Piet leaned over the map and looked to where Jack was pointing.

Jack circled an area with his finger. "Here it is. Trackers. It looks really isolated. The perfect place to hide two children, away from prying eyes. No guests, no staff."

Piet scanned the area. "Yes, it's possible. But quite far from Infinity. I can't see two kids making this journey."

Jack's foot beat a rapid tattoo on the floor. "But supposing the girls didn't walk all the way. Maybe a vehicle was involved. Something happened and the girls were abandoned?"

Piet shook his head. "A vehicle would have been found. As would the driver. Someone would have discovered it sooner or later. Whoever it was would never have dumped two kids in the middle of the bush Jack, surely no-one could have been that cruel."

Jack tried to contain his excitement. His instincts told him he was on the right track. "We need to go find this lodge and take a look around."

"You'll need a search warrant for it, my friend. Can't go busting onto private property, it may be empty but it doesn't mean the owner isn't going to be around, maybe brandishing a shotgun."

Jack stood and paced around Piet's sitting room. "What about your friend Enoch. He could get a search warrant for us?"

Piet sat back in his chair. "We'll have to give Enoch a good reason to do us this kind of favour. It means bringing him into the whole thing, telling him everything.

"However, if I can persuade him with the promise of solving the case of the lost girls, well, I think he would do it. He's an ambitious man, anxious to get a promotion or two. It means you'll have to give him the facts Jack, about how you came to these conclusions, not that they're conclusive at this stage. The media will be hungry for a story like this. If we have a story that is."

Jack sat abruptly. "I have the exclusive on this Piet, my paper gets it first. No argument. That's the deal. Harry has dished out a lot of money to get this story. That's the first thing Enoch will have to understand and accept. No media involved."

He stared at the map again. "But here's what I'm prepared to do. Once we have the full story of what happened, and we're not there yet, I'm happy to let Enoch take all the glory for cracking the case. What do you say? Do you agree. Do you think he'll agree?"

"*Ja*, it seems fair. Let me see how he's fixed for the next few days. I'll give him a call now."

"Maybe call Grace," Jack said innocently, as he left. "Give her the news about your job. She looked as though she needed something to cheer her up. That last session with Abby was disturbing to say the least, and very concerning for all of us, especially Grace."

Chapter Seventy-Five

Back in his room Jack called Caroline at the lodge.
"We're making some progress, Caroline, but I'm afraid I have to ask you another favour."

He felt the silence at the end of the phone. "What is it, Jack?" she said edgily.

"I need to borrow Jabu for a few hours possibly tomorrow or the day after. Toby says he'll probably have room for Piet and I to cadge a lift. From there we'll pick up Jabu, if we may, and be on our way to one of the lodges we want to look at. Jabu identified it for us, he knows where it is, we need him to guide us there. We also need your permission for a police vehicle to enter your property to collect us. Would you arrange it?"

He heard her sigh heavily. "Look Jack, I'm as eager as you are to solve the mystery of Abby, to help in any way I can, but I have to say it's beginning to cause a few problems.

"I'll arrange for the police vehicle to enter the property, of course I will, they'll have to come through the back entrance, I obviously don't want my guests to see it. This is now sounding quite serious, but I don't have time to ask you about what's going on at the moment, but I trust you if you think it necessary. We have a full lodge and we're all flat out, it's high season.

"I need Jabu here, to look after my lodge. I can't keep letting him go to sort things out for you. I know it sounds uncaring, but it's not. I have a business to run here.

"A few guests, over the past couple of weeks have complained about hearing a child shouting and howling. They were more concerned than accusing, but even so it's becoming a problem. Guests pay a huge amount of money to stay here. I can't have the guests' safaris interrupted with concerns of a crying and howling child.

"As you probably know most game lodges won't take children under the age of twelve, and there's a good reason for this. Sounds carry over the bush. Look I'm really sorry Jack."

Her voice softened. "Grace has told me what the doctors recommend, and I have to say I think it's for the best. Abby may have to leave. I've done as much as I can. I think Grace knows none of us can help the child anymore. She needs care with professional specialists, we need to accept that, hard though it may be. You *do* understand don't you Jack? I have to put the business and my guests, before anything else. I've invested a great deal of time and money in Infinity, and the lodge is my top priority.

"Moses helps Grace out when she needs him, but it's not what he was hired for. I need him to carry out the duties he's trained and paid to do, especially at the moment when we're so busy. I appreciate that Abby can't be left alone at any given time, but I need to have Moses back to do his job as a personal butler."

Jack thought quickly before he replied. "Yes, I do understand, of course I do. If I could borrow Jabu one more time, then it will be the last time, I promise."

He closed his phone. They had one more shot with Jabu and then he would have to respect Caroline's wishes. He could understand her concerns with the guests and the use of her staff to look after Abby, the time Jabu had given them and her generous hospitality when he and Piet needed to stay overnight.

He wondered how Grace would feel about Abby having to leave, her life at the lodge would be empty without the little girl. He doubted the odd occasion when her nursing skills were needed would be enough to fill her days and nights.

He knew Grace had been the answer to a daunting problem when medical supervision was necessary to get permission for Abby to stay at the lodge, and he knew the two women were close. The relationship had worked well for everyone. But now it looked as though it would all be coming to its predictable, and inevitable, end.

With that in mind he knew he and Piet would have to work fast and try to solve the mystery of Abby before she had to leave the lodge. Once she left, they would have no more access to the girl, she would be swallowed up by an institution who would certainly care for her, but not love her as Grace did. Difficult though Abby was they had all become attached to her, and he included Caroline in this. It was true she had spent a lot of time, and her own money, making sure Abby was safe and cared for.

It didn't bear thinking about. But he tried to console himself with the thought of Piet now resident in Hazyview, that there might be a glimmer of hope for Grace and her future.

Losing Abby would break her heart, but perhaps Piet might be able to fill the empty space Abby would leave. Grace would easily find work in town, if she wanted to, and be able to rent a flat, or house, of her own and, hopefully, a more permanent relationship with his grumpy detective might evolve.

Jabu, had appointed himself as guardian of Abby. He would be another matter altogether. Jack knew he was fiercely protective of the girl whose life he had saved, and his deep connection to her because of this.

His phone rang, it was Piet.

"Hey, Enoch is available tomorrow, he'll have the search warrant needed for Trackers. He's keen to get involved. What arrangements have you made with Jabu – we're going to need him."

Jack told him about the conversation with Caroline. The decision she had made about Abby's future at the lodge.

"*Jeez*, it's going to be tough for Grace and Jabu. But let's not worry about it now. We need to get out to Trackers tomorrow and see what we can find, not so, Jack?"

"Yeah, I'll call Caroline back. We need to ramp up the case now. There's pressure on with the decisions which have been made about Abby. We have to find out exactly what happened. I'm not sure the outcome will make much difference. But if we can find out anything more, we may be able to buy a bit more time for the child and my story."

Chapter Seventy-Six

Inspector Enoch Coetzee and his police sergeant collected Jabu, Jack and Piet from the delivery entrance at the back of Infinity.

Enoch followed Jabu's instructions as they made their way through rough bush tracks which would lead them to Trackers.

An hour later, having passed no other safari vehicles, road workers clearing bush trails, or supply trucks delivering to other lodges, they pulled up in front of the run-down lodge called Trackers.

The gate to the property was heavily chained with a large rusted padlock, and a faded sign warning anyone to *keep out*.

Enoch edged out of the vehicle and indicated to his police sergeant he should cut the padlock and chains to let them in, his search warrant tucked safely into his uniform pocket.

Slowly the vehicle made its way through the thick grass which was battling to eliminate the dirt road to the lodge. The air was still, the heat intense, there was not a sound of any bird life, or any life at all.

Enoch gave a brief beep on the horn and waited to see if anyone might come out of the sagging main entrance. Only silence permeated the air.

The men climbed out. Jabu held them back with a gesture of his hand, as he made his way through the entrance and on to the ragged path which led to three collapsed *rondavels,* their thatched roofs already ravaged by birds and small animals who had helped themselves to whatever was available to build their own homes somewhere else. His eyes and instincts missing nothing.

Only one *rondavel* was in a reasonable state, and Jabu headed for this one. He gestured for the others to follow.

He pushed open the matting door, ducked his head, and looked around.

It was basic but had signs of recent habitation. A simple kitchen, a table and four chairs, and two rooms leading off to sleeping quarters.

In one of the bedrooms, Jabu found what he was looking for – evidence that at some point a child, or children had lived, or stayed, there.

On both of the two single beds, tee-shirts and shorts had been thrown in place of any drawers or a wardrobe. Some children's books piled up on a crate in the corner, childlike drawings tacked to the wall.

Jack and Piet followed him around, making their own observations, coming to their own conclusions.

They checked the second bedroom out. It was sparsely furnished. A single bed with a side table, and a small cupboard. Inside the cupboard they found a man's clothing including shirts with the Trackers logo on the pocket.

Jabu turned to the other men. "I'm going to check the rest of the property. See what else I can find."

Enoch and his sergeant cast a cursory glance around, happy to let the three men follow up on whatever information they had gathered and were now pursuing. Enoch was satisfied with this, and the facts they had shared with him. He could see his promotion looming in the future and was content to let the retired detective, his father's old friend, follow the leads.

Seeing how small the place was and not wishing to get in their way, the two police officers retreated outside and waited under the shade of a mopani tree, quietly talking together and enjoying a smoke.

Jack and Piet examined everything, convinced this was where the girls had been hidden away. Jack noted the now familiar map of the Sabi Sands area tacked to the wall in the small sitting room.

Elspeth had had the same map, as did he.

On a wooden table beneath the map was a pair of heavy binoculars, a two-way radio and a battery powered lamp. Nothing unusual as far as he could tell, the sort of things any manager of a lodge might have in his office.

The shadow of Jabu filled the small door to the *rondavel*.

"I think you need to come and see what I have found."

He led them to the back of the property. A sheet of corrugated tin once held up by four wooden poles had collapsed on its side.

"This," Jabu said, "would have been where the lodge vehicles were parked."

Jabu hunkered down and pointed. "See here. Tyre tracks. The front right-hand tyre has an uneven tread. This comes from the vehicle tracks I found close to where Elspeth's body was discovered." He stood up. "Come, I'll show you what I found."

Deeply camouflaged by thick bush behind the thick girth of a towering tree was an old Toyota land cruiser, with a faded Trackers logo on the side. The other an expensive looking 4x4 with Zimbabwe number plates.

Piet was taking shots of the licence plates and the tyres of the dust covered Toyota. Jack tried the handles on the driver's doors, both were locked.

The Zimbabwean vehicle was immaculate inside, no sign of empty bottles or shopping bags.

The old Toyota was as battered inside as it was outside. He rubbed the window with his sleeve and peered in. Empty bottles on their sides lolled in the well of the passenger seat, an empty packet of cigarettes on the seat alongside a book of maps and a pair of heavy binoculars.

Jack went around to the back of the land cruiser and wiped the dust from the high rear window. An old double mattress filled the space, two pillows and a faded blanket were pushed to one side.

He recalled Rob's conversation.

"It was something all we farmers used to do. Bundle the children into the back of our bakkies, and head out to a neighbouring farm for a braai. The children would play together, have dinner, then fall asleep in the back of the vehicle, on a mattress. Then we'd all drive home."

Jack looked around for Piet and found him looking at the tyre tracks with Jabu. "Hey, guys, come and check the inside of the Toyota, found something interesting in the back."

Piet took more shots of the interiors of both vehicles. Then slipped his phone into his pocket. He turned to Jabu. "I think you need to show Enoch and the sergeant what you found. He'll need to make some notes and take his own shots of the vehicles and the tyres on the Toyota. At some point he'll want to tow these vehicles back to the station to be dusted for prints. I have no doubt they'll find prints from the children in the back."

Jabu nodded, and went off to find Enoch and his sergeant. Piet and Jack headed back to the dilapidated lodge and the one surviving *rondavel*.

Jack stood in front of the map, saying nothing. Piet rummaged in the cupboards of the kitchen until he found a glass. Turning on the tap he started to fill it, then looking at the colour of the water he changed his mind, emptied it down the sink and put it back.

"This is a pitiful place to hide two children, not so, my friend?"

Jack shrugged. "Yes. But someone must have been looking after them. There was tinned food and boxes of cereal in the kitchen cupboard."

Piet nodded in agreement. "The oldest child was ten, Jack, she would have been able to open a can or two. These two girls had to look after themselves, but, yes, there must have been an adult here as well, the manager or the ranger. But I'm not sure he was here all of the time."

Jack stared at him. "You think the girls were left on their own here now and again?"

"Yes. Whoever was looking after them, if you can call it that, must have had other things he, or she, was involved in, otherwise why just sit here out in the bush with two small kids and do nothing? What would be the point of that?

"My thinking is that Elspeth might have made a few visits, and stocked the place with food for the kids and whoever the person was who was responsible for bringing them here. The two are connected, of this I have no doubt. In fact, I would say they were close friends, if not lovers.

"Whoever he was he obviously didn't go into town to do any shopping; he hid out here with the girls. But not all the time."

His forehead creased into a frown. "You see, Jack, it's the mattress in the back of the land cruiser. Who slept on it? The ranger? Or the two little girls, and why when they could sleep here?"

Jack ran his finger along his bottom lip. "I think you're right. Elspeth and this ranger were probably lovers, certainly very close. But how did she get in and out of the reserve on what looks like now, a fairly regular basis, with all the strict rules laid down by the Parks Board?"

Piet narrowed his eyes as he looked at him. "Not difficult. This man could have met her at one of the entry points, perhaps told the officials he was collecting his groceries from a girlfriend who was parked outside the park gates.

"Africans, on the whole, are friendly people, these guys have a boring job, checking people in and out of the reserve, they were probably grateful for anyone who took the time to chat to them.

"Our man could have walked over to Elspeth, picked up the shopping and walked back into the reserve. Perhaps over time the officials got used to seeing Elspeth, perhaps she brought them a few gifts now and again, a six pack of beer for when they came off duty, food, cigarettes. She could have become friendly with them. They would have seen her as nothing more than a girl visiting her boyfriend. Seeing her as harmless they probably broke a couple of rules and let her drive in and out to Trackers."

Jack nodded thoughtfully. "Shouldn't be too difficult to check the entry points with the guards and ask them if they remember a young girl with pink hair and studs in her nose. But if your theory is correct, they wouldn't have a record of her entering and exiting the reserve."

Jack rubbed the back of his neck. "So, whoever this ranger was, and based on what Jabu found with the identical tyre tracks, he arranged to meet Elspeth out in the bush near Hazyview, and killed her. She obviously trusted him, had a relationship of some kind with him. Young girls don't have clandestine meetings with strangers after dark in the bush.

"Whatever those two were up to I think she became a threat, Piet, and he had to get rid of her, or someone did, using the Tracker's vehicle, one she would recognise. That would have put him in a difficult position. Who was going to run his errands for him and look after the girls when he was out and about doing whatever it was he was doing?"

Piet shrugged and took a final look around the lonely tired room. "Come on, let's get Jabu back to Infinity. The police guys will need to be on their way. We can get a lift back to town with them and discuss these latest developments."

Chapter Seventy-Seven

Jack was busy in his room at the hotel, writing up his notes by the dim light the generator was producing, and finishing his weekly column for Harry in London.

The visit to Trackers lodge had produced some tantalising information. He and Piet had spent the best part of the rest of the day analysing all they had, arguing the points, agreeing and disagreeing on possible motives.

They were making good progress, but apart from the Zimbabwe connection with the girls, there still wasn't the thread they were looking for to pull it all together.

Piet, he knew, had planned to phone Grace and tell her about the empty lodge and the evidence they had found that this was possibly where Abby and her sister had been living, or had been kept. He would leave that to him. He had another plan.

Jack had phoned Grace and briefly explained what they had found. "I'll leave Piet to fill you in on all the details, he's going to call you shortly. We would like to take Abby out to Trackers, with Jabu, and watch her reaction, there would definitely be one. But Caroline won't allow it. I promised I wouldn't ask her any more favours. I would need Jabu again to find the place. He must have time off during the day, or at week-ends. Maybe he could use that time to help us. Caroline surely could not object to that. He'd being doing it in his own time?"

Grace had interrupted him. "No, Jack, I can't put Abby through any more trauma. She's just not strong enough. I'm sorry." Her voice had broken and then she had ended the call.

There was a tap on Jack's door, he turned to find Piet standing there his face crestfallen.

"Hey, what's up Piet. Come on in, take a seat. I'm just finishing up my report. I'll be with you in ten minutes. You might want to check out the generator, it hardly generating enough power to see the end of my nose, hope you have it on your to do list?"

Jack completed his task, saved the document, closed the lap top down, and turned to face Piet.

"So, have you come up with anything from all your shady, and might I add expensive, contacts Piet? By the way, I phoned Grace to see if there was any way we could take Abby out to Trackers, with or without Jabu, but she was adamant and said it wouldn't be possible."

"Did you call Grace?"

He still looked gloomy. "*Ja*, I called her. The doctor wants to see Abby again, he's putting pressure on her to do the right thing and let him take over responsibility for her. Caroline, as you know, is encouraging her to do the same thing."

He took off his baseball cap and rubbed his hair anxiously, an unusual gesture for him. "Grace is bringing Abby into town tomorrow. I'll go meet her and give her some support. She can't do this by herself."

Jack stood up and stretched his back. "The doc won't take Abby tomorrow surely. I mean is Grace going to be prepared for this? What will Abby think if she sees all her books and toys being packed up. This is a bad idea, Piet, she's not ready for another upheaval."

Piet rubbed his eyes with the back of his hand. "Grace is going to ask for more time, maybe a week or so, but if the doc doesn't agree he can use legal channels to force her to hand over Abby, in what he considers, her best interests. After all the police had to give their permission for her to stay at the lodge. It's still an open case, even though we have Enoch on our side now.

"Grace isn't the mother or even the legal guardian, she has no rights whatsoever. We didn't move fast enough Jack. We still have no family for Abby."

His phone vibrated in his pocket and he held up his hand to Jack. He frowned into his phone then a look of disbelief passed across his face as he looked at Jack, who had all his attention now, as he listened to the one-sided conversation.

"Are you one hundred percent sure about this. No chance the information can be wrong?"

Slowly he returned his phone to his pocket and stared at Jack.

"What Piet?"

"My contact ran the Zimbabwe plates through the system. Gave me the name of the person the vehicle is registered to. Looks like a dead man drove the vehicle here.

"The owner of the vehicle is Richard Beecham. He drove the vehicle across the border."

Chapter Seventy-Eight

Piet met Grace and Abby at the airport, pleased to see she didn't have a suitcase with the child's meagre belongings. He held out his arms to take her, but Abby put her arms around Grace's neck and buried her face in her neck.

Grace held her left hand out to him, holding it tight.

"Thank you, Piet. I can do this if you're with me. But I'm *not* handing over this child to anyone, they'll have to rip her from my arms if they try. I'm not sure how much she understands anymore, but she's definitely sensing something and she doesn't like it, she's frightened."

She kissed the child's cheek. "Hush, Abby. It's alright. No-one is going to take you away from me, I promise. No-one!"

Piet took her arm and led her to the car. "You said the appointment is at noon?"

Grace nodded. "I've brought a change of clothes for both of us," she lifted the light holdall she was carrying, "in case we have to stay overnight for any reason."

Piet took it from her and stowed it in the boot of his car. "Then it gives us time to have a coffee and maybe an ice-cream for Abby. Would you like that, my girl?"

It was high season in the town and the rest of the country. Everyone was on the move heading for their Christmas holiday destination, the town was packed with people, vehicles and long crowded tour buses.

They found a restaurant with chairs and tables set out on the pavement. Once settled Piet ordered their coffee and a pink ice cream for Abby.

They both watched her as they sipped their drinks. Abby stared at her ice-cream, watching it melt into a puddle on the plate. Grace looked at him her eyes full of despair.

Piet picked up a spoon and scooped up what was left. "Come on, my girl, everything will be alright. We won't let anything bad happen to you, I promise. Have a taste of this, it's the best ice-cream in town, I know because I've tried it."

With the speed of a streak of lightning, Abby stood up and bolted. Grace and Piet rose as one and ran after her. "Abby! Abby! Wait," Grace shouted.

The driver of the vehicle would recall later, that the child seemed to have appeared from nowhere – he didn't have time to even touch his brakes.

The dull thud brought other patrons in the restaurant to their feet as they looked in horror at the child lying in the road, their hands to their mouths, their eyes wide with shock.

Cars swerved, their brakes screeching as they tried to avoid another collision in the chaotic traffic.

A bright pool of blood surrounded the back of her head like a halo. Grace sank to her knees a cry of despair erupting from deep inside her as she tried to gather the child to her.

Piet knelt next to her. "Don't lift her Grace, someone will have called for an ambulance. It'll be here in minutes."

She shook off his hand on her shoulder and lifted Abby into her arms. "Oh, Abby, Abby. Don't leave me now…"

The child's eyes fluttered open at the sound of Grace's voice, a voice Piet knew she had come to love and trust. "Ace? Mommy?"

"I'm here my darling, as I've always been. Ace or Mommy, I can be whatever you want me to be just hold on, help is coming. You'll be alright."

Abby's eyes closed, her mouth moving slightly. Grace bent her head. "What is it, Abby?"

"Scusie? Mommy? Peese?"

"They're right here with you, Abby," she said softly to the child, "waiting for you…"

Her head dropped back in Grace's arms, the breath leaving her body in a whispered sigh. Grace doubled over as she held the child, a low keening sound coming from somewhere deep inside her, the child's blood seeping into her shirt as she wept.

The ambulance had arrived, the sirens now quiet, the light flashing on the roof of the vehicle turning silently. The medics stood helplessly. It wasn't an emergency anymore.

The crowd, which had gathered around, were silent, gazing at the woman who held the dead child so tightly in her arms, a few crossed themselves.

The young waiter who had served them in the restaurant was clutching Grace's handbag which she had left on the table in her haste to follow Abby. He tapped Piet's arm and handed it to him, looking as shocked as everyone else.

For the first time in his life Piet felt powerless as he watched the woman he had come to love, collapse with untold grief in front of him. He felt his own tears welling up as he looked at the broken body of the child, he too had become so fond of.

The medics moved forward to take the child. But Grace refused to give her up. "She needs me to hold her. Don't take her away from me. Please don't do that," she whispered.

Piet put his arms around her, holding them both. "It's alright Gracie, I'm here. I'll come with you and Abby, but we have to let them take us to the hospital. We'll go together. Come, no-one will take Abby from you, I promise."

Like a sleep walker Grace allowed Piet to lead her to the back of the ambulance, amidst the chaos of the hysterical driver of the car which had killed Abby, and the swelling crowds.

Grace wouldn't let go of Abby, and the medics looked on uneasily. The child could come to no more harm.

*****

Grace, knowing she had left them, finally allowed the doctor at the hospital to take Abby from her reluctant arms.

The stretcher took her away, covered in a sheet. She knew they would clean Abby up, wash away the blood, and the tears. Grace waited until the stretcher disappeared around the corridor then made her way unsteadily back to the waiting room.

Piet was waiting for her there.

"Come, Gracie," he said huskily. "Let me take you home. The doctors here will make all the necessary arrangements. I've taken care of everything."

He took her back to his cottage, driving with one hand, the other holding her as she wept.

He fetched one of his shirts and helped her out of her blood-stained clothes. Making her comfortable in his bed, he covered her with a warm blanket and left her to her grief. Something he knew, with his years of dealing with distraught relatives, he couldn't help her with.

Grief was the longest and loneliest road to travel, and it was done alone. A pain that could not be shared, or understood, by anyone.

He bundled up her blood-stained clothes and took them through to his kitchen, then phoned Jack asking him to call the lodge and let Jabu and Caroline know what had happened. He knew it would be a difficult call to make, especially for Caroline. She would be devastated knowing the decision she had made had led to this, although it was not her fault in any way.

The death of Abby.

*****

Jack arrived at Piet's cottage, his face creased with worry and concern.

"How is Grace? What a terrible thing for her to witness, she must be beside herself. Is there anything I can do?"

Piet shook his head. "She's sleeping at the moment. I feel as if we've let her down. Not finding Abby's parents or any relatives, well, until yesterday, with the possibility that her father brought her here. Now this."

Jack squeezed his shoulder. "We're not giving up, and you haven't let her down, neither of us have. We've been doing all we can. We still don't know where her father is, but we'll find him eventually. Until we do there's no way of letting him know Abby is dead, and his other daughter is missing."

Piet wiped his weary face with his hands. "The fact he hasn't come forward to report his girls missing gives me reason to believe he might not be around either. Dead or alive."

Jack patted his friend's shoulder, trying to comfort him. "Jabu wants to come and see Abby. He needs to say goodbye to her in his own way, the way of his people. He's arriving tomorrow afternoon, with Toby. I'll collect him from the airport."

There was a movement from the doorway, Grace was standing there, a blanket held tightly around her shoulders although it was hot both inside and out. Her eyes were red and swollen, her face white and pinched, grief had briefly sucked the beauty and serenity from her stricken face.

Both men looked up. "Jabu's coming tomorrow, you said? I'd like to be with Abby when he arrives at the hospital."

Piet gestured to the sofa he was sitting on. "Come and sit, Gracie. He moved over as she lowered herself down next to him.

Jack hunkered in front of her, taking both her clenched hands in his own. "I'm so sorry Grace, so very sorry. What a terrible thing to have happened. I don't know what else to say, how to make things better, but I know I can't."

She squeezed Jack's hand. "Abby was leaving us anyway, withdrawing from everything, shutting down. I've watched her closely these past few weeks. She missed her sister, she knew because she hadn't been found that Susie wasn't coming back.

"I'm not sure what she saw on the farm in Zimbabwe....whatever it was and what happened afterwards destroyed her. She wasn't strong enough to take any more bad news, too small, too fragile, and deeply unhappy despite all we tried to do. But she's with them now, with her sister Susie…and her mother. I have to believe that."

She dabbed at her swollen eyes. Her shoulders began to shake as she put her face in her hands.

The two men looked on helplessly.

Grace seemed to pull herself together, then looked at them both. "I can only hope the love and care I gave her, we all gave her, especially Jabu, went some way towards making her last few months a little happier. I came to love her very much, fractured, difficult, and broken though she may have been.

"To have her locked away in some institution would have been more than she would have been able to handle. No, it's better this way. There will be no more nightmares for my Abby. I can only pray she didn't understand what was going to happen to her, I have to hold on to that thought. That she didn't understand that we were going to have to let her go. That's not why she ran into the traffic is it? I can't think about it at the moment."

She pulled her blanket tighter around her shoulders and straightened her back. Piet reached for her hand and held it in both of his own.

"I'm not sure what religion she was brought up with, but I would like her to have a Christian burial. I'd like her to be buried with the family bible, Melody, gave to her.

"Perhaps we could ask Jabu to bring it when he comes. It's next to her bed in the cottage at the lodge."

"Of course," murmured Jack, "I'll be sure to ask him."

"Also, if it's alright with the authorities, we might be able to arrange for a priest to come out to the lodge. I'd like Abby to be buried next to Tim, under the spiritual tree, especially as there appears to be no other family to make any alternative arrangements. I don't think Caroline will have any objections, but I will have to ask her, of course, the tree is on her property."

Tears spilled down her cheeks. Piet silently handed her a box of tissues from the side table next to him.

She took a handful. "Tim will watch over her, she won't be alone. She'll never be on her own again, he'll be beside her."

Grace stared sightlessly out of the window. "We could put up a headstone with her name," she murmured. "Abigail Beecham, and her date of birth and death. It will give her the dignity she never had when she was alive, when she didn't know who she was, when no-one knew who she was. It broke her heart when no-one came looking for her."

Jack stood. "I'll see what arrangements can be made, Grace. I'll call Caroline and ask for her permission to bury Abby next to Tim. I'm sure she won't have any objections whatsoever. I'll see what I can arrange with the local priest here in town."

"Thank you," she whispered, then turned and went back through to the bedroom.

Piet went through to the kitchen, retrieving the blood-soaked clothes he bundled them into a plastic bag then handed them to Jack.

"Best get rid of these for me Jack. She has a change of clothes in her bag, I don't want her to see these again. I left Abby's overnight bag at the hospital, there's a change of clothes for her in there.

*****

Later during the evening, having been unable to tempt Grace to eat anything, Piet kept her company until he saw she was beginning to wilt from the events of the day.

"Stay here with me Gracie, I want to be near you, look after you. I'll sleep on the sofa in case you need me."

Sometime during the night, he awoke to the sound of her anguished crying. He lay down next to her, gathering her in his arms holding her as she wept, waiting for her to fall asleep again.

"You called me Gracie," she whispered to him. "Only my mother called me that, it brings me comfort hearing you say it, Piet. I feel so tired now."

He stayed there until morning. His mind running through the events of the past few weeks, turning the facts over in his mind trying to make some sense of them.

Then, exhausted, he too fell asleep.

Chapter Seventy-Nine

Jack drove Jabu to the hospital, the journey made in silence. Knowing Jabu, Jack knew he would not want to speak. It had always been Jabu's way of dealing with the unexpected.

He led him to the room where Abby lay, then closed the door behind him, and went to join Piet in the waiting room.

*****

The room was lit with candles. Grace was sitting next to Abby stroking her arm. When she saw Jabu she stood up shakily.

He came to her swiftly and put his arms around her saying nothing, her tears soaking into his shirt.

After a few moments, she looked up at him. "Would you like to be alone with her Jabu?" She said softly. "Would you like me to leave you both together?"

He shook his head as he approached the little girl whose life, he had fought so hard to save. Her guardian.

He bent over her, cupping her cold cheeks in his hands as he murmured to her.

"I heard your voice on the wind today, little one. I've come to say goodbye and wish you well in the world you have gone to. The world of stars and brightness where you can play and have joy in your life again. There you will find the family you have lost. Susie is waiting for you," his voice broke, "she will be happy to see you again."

Softly he sang to her, sending her on her way, setting her spirit free with words only he understood. Letting her know she was no longer alone and he, Jabu, would hold her in his heart, guiding her spirit to the next world.

He removed the turquoise bracelet from his wrist and placed it gently between her cold hands, holding them together before he whispered to her again. He wiped his tears from her still face.

"Go well, little one…your time was before, I should have let you go then, not tried to keep you when your spirit wanted to leave. But I will remember you, for I knew you had only been lent to me for a short time.

"In this time, I learned much from you and you gave me the gift of your love and trust. I will see you again, my child. You will be waiting for Jabu and I will find you, as I found you before."

He turned to Grace, the tears running silently down his cheeks. He touched her shoulder and let himself out of the room. The candles flickered as he opened the door.

He looked back briefly at Abby, and then he was gone.

Chapter Eighty

The priest waited patiently beneath the spiritual tree.

His pure white robes, the skirts lifting slightly in the warm breeze, contrasted sharply with the blackness of the dead tree's branches.

With his bible open and ready, he watched the funeral procession approach, the gold and red bookmark the only visible colour on the landscape.

Abby's white coffin was lifted from the back of the lodge vehicle carried by Jabu and Jack. Grace, Caroline, Piet and Moses followed slowly behind. Piet with his arm around Grace's shaking shoulders.

Once the priest had concluded the short service, he indicated to the gardeners, who had prepared her grave that they should prepare for the burial. Then suddenly the priest held up his hand, a slight frown on his face as he turned to look up.

In the distance came the sound of clear pure, harmonious voices. The African staff had congregated on the lawns outside the lodge where the spiritual tree was clearly visible, and the small group of mourners who congregated beneath it.

The staff at the lodge had not met Abby, but they knew about her and here they were sharing this sadness, singing the child on her way to another world, giving comfort to the ones who had been left behind with their brutal grief.

Their voices carried across the still bush as they sang to the child's spirit saying their own goodbye to her, with no need of music or song books, religious or otherwise.

Jack felt the hairs on his arm prickle. He had never heard another song as beautiful, or as moving, as the one the staff were singing. The innocence and harmony of their untrained voices brought tears to his eyes.

Africa was the most magical place he had ever been to. A place where despite great sadness, such as the funeral of a lost little girl, there was still beauty, song, and the greatest spirit of all – the spirit of humanity.

Chapter Eighty-One

Christmas came and went. Piet had started his new job. The hotel was booked solidly until the end of January. The game lodges were full as were all the hotels and guest houses in the area. This was the time of the year all businesses worked towards, making good money to see them through the quiet winter months ahead.

Jack went back to Franschhoek which was also heaving with tourists from all over the world. He avoided going through to Cape Town where the traffic was almost impossible, the hotels also full and the restaurants packed. Parking was at a premium all over the city.

Jack retreated to his cottage and spent his time writing up his article, and his weekly column, for Harry in London, although it had no ending at this point.

On the wall he had pinned a large sheet of paper noting all the links so far with Abby's case. He spent a long time working on it, then standing back running his finger over his lips to see if any kind of pattern was forming, any angle he might have missed which would unlock the bigger picture.

Daisy was a cheerful presence, delighted she had Mr Yak back to fuss over and cook for.

The scruffy dog, Benji, had indeed been returned to his rightful owner. Daisy begged him to adopt another dog but Jack had said no. His job took him away too often and to leave a dog, albeit in Daisy's capable hands, didn't seem fair to him.

He was itching for the season to be over, when Piet wouldn't be as busy as he was now, and they could settle back to putting the final pieces together in the case of Abby and Susie Beecham.

*****

Grace's grief over the death of Abby, according to Piet, never seemed to leave her, but Jack knew, with time, the pain and absence of her would lessen. But he knew she would never forget the little girl called Abby.

With Infinity booked to capacity until the end of February, she was busier than normal. But not enough to keep her occupied each and every day.

As evening fell, Grace would sit out on her patio and gaze across the bush, watching the sun set behind the spiritual tree, where Abby and Tim lay together, and the tears would come and fall into her empty arms.

*****

Gert, the second-hand book seller, was too busy in his shop to look for new tenants for the barber's shop and Elspeth's flat. He was waiting for her parents, or a relative, to come and claim her few belongings before he could start to look for a new tenant to take her place.

Like everyone else in the country, if they weren't heading for the coast for the Christmas holidays, her parents would be staying put, avoiding the heavy traffic on the motorways and the busy towns and cities.

Piet was a few steps ahead of Gert. He had called him two weeks ago and told him he would like to show a friend of his around the place. Someone who was looking to move into town and would, if she liked it, probably want to move in.

Piet wanted to spend time in Elspeth's flat to see what he might find. He wanted to get in there before the family, or a relative, took all Elspeth's things away.

He knew Gert would not let him wander around on his own, knowing Piet was a private detective. However, he would surely be quite happy to let Grace take a look. Gert wouldn't be following her around, he had his hands full with the shop, cashing in on the tourists like everyone else.

He called Grace at the lodge and asked if she could get away for a few hours and come into town. He cleared a few hours for himself with his boss Hugo.

Grace called him back and said she could catch a flight with some departing guests, spend a couple of hours in town, then fly back in the early evening with the new guests.

Satisfied he would see her in a few days' time he called Gert, told him Grace would pick up the keys to the flat on Saturday afternoon and decide if she wanted to rent it.

Gert apologised in advance saying Elspeth's things were still waiting for collection.

Piet was delighted with this news.

*****

Some of the guests at the hotel were more difficult over the season. Now they were paying high seasonal rates they were more demanding.

Over and above the overall security of the hotel he was often called upon to find missing objects guests had misplaced, either through over indulgence of alcohol when they couldn't remember what they had done with their valuables, or because they perhaps planned on claiming on insurance once they returned home, for a so-called stolen piece of jewellery.

Piet was seeing another side of life here. Couples had loud arguments, other guests complained and he was called in to calm the situation down. There were rowdy parties on the lawns of the hotel which he had to break up. Police work, of the past, seemed a quieter way of life, far more disciplined when things went by the book.

He too was longing for the end of the season and all the silliness it brought with it.

Saturday was only three days away. Three days before he could be with Grace again, after what felt like months but had only been a few weeks.

*****

He waited impatiently for Grace to appear in the arrival's hall, and when she did, he instinctively held out his arms to her.

After a few minutes he held her at arm's length in front of him and frowned. "You've not been eating all the fancy food at the lodge, have you? You've lost weight. Come, we'll have a quick lunch, then I need to ask you a favour.

"Hey, don't look so alarmed, it's nothing much I need you to do, but it might help with finding some more out about Abby. Jack and I are going to solve this if it's the last thing we do. We want to do it for Abby, and for you."

They chatted easily over lunch, swapping tales of difficult guests, the crowds, the heat, the traffic, the frantic days over Christmas, anything but Abby.

He watched her pick at her food. "Come on, Gracie, the food's good here. You know better than anyone the body needs food to function well.

"What I need you to do might not be easy for you, but I'll be right there next to you. Finish up and let's get going."

Grace pushed her plate aside and it was deftly swept away by a waiter, anxious to clear the table so he could seat the queue of guests waiting outside.

Piet paid the bill and they made their way back to the car. "What is it you want me to do Piet. If it's to help with Abby, well, you know I'll do anything at all. Tell me."

"I need you to collect some keys from the book shop we went to with Abby. They belong to the flat where Elspeth lived, on top of the barber's shop. I want to take a good look around to see what I can find. Elspeth's things are still there. The book seller won't let me in, he's highly suspicious about my motives.

"I need you to pretend you're interested in viewing the place with a possibility of renting it. Will you do it for Abby?"

She nodded and quickly wiped her rapidly filling eyes.

Grace collected the keys as she was asked. Gert gave her the easy directions to the flat and the number, apologising he couldn't take her himself and show her around, he was too busy with all the tourists still in town.

Piet was waiting for her at the entrance to the flat, anxious to get inside.

The flat smelt musty from lack of habitation. The curtains were drawn keeping out the heat and light.

Piet moved across the room and opened them letting in the sunlight, motes of dust floated in the stifling air. Grace looked around, shivering slightly at the memory of the hairdresser, and what had happened to her.

Piet went through to the bedroom and rummaged through the drawers and cupboard finding nothing of interest. He wandered back through to the sitting room where Grace was standing looking at the large map tacked to the wall, one corner now slightly curling, like a puppy's ear, as it peeled away from the wall.

She turned as Piet came back into the room.

"What an odd thing to hang on your wall. I mean, why not frame it or something. Why would a hairdresser use such a thing to decorate a room?"

Piet joined her and they both studied it together. Then he leaned forward to get a closer look.

"And why," he said softly, "are these small crosses here, leading into the Kruger Park? Here, here, and here."

Grace took a step back and lowered herself into one of the chairs, her brow puckered.

"To me, Piet, it looks like some sort of a project map. The sort of thing tacked up on a wall on a building site, you know, a temporary working map. Not something which would be a permanent fixture.

"Or maybe, because of all the game rangers she had as clients, this is where they worked or perhaps the area they worked in, and she liked to keep track of who worked where.

"Rangers move around quite a bit, from lodge to lodge, maybe it was some kind of project for her, keeping track of her clients. Sounds a bit crazy, an odd thing to do, but it's what comes to my mind anyway."

Piet turned to her, a big smile spreading across his face. "You, my girl, are a genius. That is exactly what it is. A map showing where her game ranger clients worked, the area they worked in.

"Our young Elspeth must have been up to her decorated ears in this whole thing."

He whipped out his phone and took some close-up shots of the map where Elspeth had left her crosses.

He checked his watch. "Better get the keys back to the book seller," he said urgently. "I need you to buy a map from him, identical to this one. I know he sells them. Tell him you need one showing all the game lodges, the entrances and exits to the parks, and the dirt roads leading to the lodges, you'll recognise it when he shows it to you. Then I must get you back to the airport.

"You can tell him the flat's too cramped for you and you won't be taking it. Well done, my girl, you've done a great job."

Bemused and not quite understanding what she had helped him with, she hooked her bag over her shoulder, picked up the keys and left the flat with him.

When they returned to the airport he hugged her again, telling her when the tourists started to leave town, they would spend more time together. Something he was looking forward to.

Grace turned to go then stopped, looking back at him. "Seeing the flat made me think, Piet. Perhaps I should think of moving into town. I'll find a job easily enough. If Caroline needed me for anything, apart from a guest with a hangover, I could always fly out, it only takes twenty minutes to get there as you know.

"With Abby gone I have too much time on my hands. I want more work, to take my mind off things. I need to do something useful. I know where Abby and Tim are, I can always go back and visit. At the moment watching them from my cottage is almost too much to bear. I think I need a change. What do you think?"

The wide smile on his face was enough, no words were needed.

With a brief wave she was gone.

*****

Piet returned to the hotel and went straight to his cottage to change into his uniform, ready for work.

Then he opened up the map Grace had bought and tacked it to the wall in the sitting room. He scrolled to the shots he had taken of Elspeth's map and copied across where she had made her small crosses. He enlarged the crosses on his phone and peered at some pencilled numbers next to them.

He placed the numbers next to the crosses he had made on his own map. Satisfied he stood back.

The map had been the key to the whole thing. Now he thought he knew what the connection was with the hairdresser, the game rangers, and the vehicle registered in Zimbabwe.

There were still unanswered questions.

How were the two girls involved?

How had Richard Beecham been involved? Had he driven the girls across the border, or was it the farm hand?

And who was the man who was found dead in his wife's bed, if it wasn't him?

Chapter Eighty-Two

At the end of January Jack was back to Hazyview. Now he and Piet could pursue their case without being impeded with thousands of tourists who had now all left town and gone home.

Piet was waiting for him. They shook hands, delighted to see each other again. They drove to the hotel and arranged to meet in the gardens once Jack had unpacked and settled himself back into his old room.

It was the week-end and Piet was off duty, on call, but off duty.

"So, my friend," he said to Jack when he joined him. "Warm enough for you?"

Jack kicked off his safari boots and wriggled his toes. "I had no idea how hot Franschhoek could be, forty-three degrees one day. That's a geometry angle not a friggin' temperature. Suffice to say I'm not used to that kind of heat." He squinted into the fading sun. "It's still hot even now." He put his sun glasses back on.

Piet grinned at him. "It's why we live here, my friend, we like the heat. It is the height of summer after all."

Piet wiped the back of his neck. "*Ja*, it's a bit warm. Hotter up here than most places and will be until April. Now, finish your beer, I have something to show you."

"How is Grace doing, Piet? He asked as they walked towards his cottage.

"I saw her recently. We went to Elspeth's flat together. She was the one who came up with the map maybe being some kind of working document.

"She's thinking of moving from the lodge and finding work here in town. Maybe renting a place. She needs more work, Jack. She's far from over Abby, none of us are. But it's particularly raw for her. There's a rural clinic here, she wants to get involved in that as well."

They went inside Piet's cottage and he showed Jack the map, where he had made all his crosses and numbers.

"Now, let's take a careful look at this, my friend. Things are now beginning to form a pattern."

He put his glasses on. "The crosses mark certain places, off the beaten track, deep in the bush. The numbers possibly reflect times, see here, all similar numbers, just before dawn. I think what we're looking at here is a highly sophisticated network of poaching. It's the connection we were looking for. This is what it's all about, my friend – poaching. What do you know about it in my country?"

Jack lowered himself into a chair, not taking his eyes off the map on the wall.

"Well, what I know is the Kruger National Park has the world's largest white rhino population, and there's a huge demand for rhino horn in the Far East. They seem to think it can cure everything. Per ounce it has more value than gold."

Piet smiled at him. "In fact, chewing your own finger nails is about as effective, and cheaper, than paying for a bit of ground-down rhino horn, but go on."

Jack continued. "I know there's an insatiable appetite for rhino horn and the ivory from elephants. Ivory, in parts of the world, is used to make jewellery, chess pieces and ornaments. Used to be used for making piano keys, but not sure if Steinway would get away with that these days. I wonder what they use instead?

"Rhino horn is, they think, as I mentioned, the cure all for every ailment, an aphrodisiac, and anything else you need to sort out in your life over there in the Far East."

Jack stood up and examined the map closely. Then he turned, sat back down again, and continued.

"I also know the anti-poaching units spread across South Africa, have had high levels of success with catching poachers and retrieving the ivory and rhino horns. But they're not winning the war. Apparently, a rhino horn can be removed from the animal and be out of the country in twenty-four hours, that's what I heard."

Piet interrupted him. "There's not enough funding available to finance all the sophisticated equipment the anti-poaching units need, despite the generous private funds from all over the world, from people and companies who have a real concern for what is happening to the wild life here in Africa. People who come on safari here want to protect what they have seen.

"Private reserves pay a huge amount of money to security companies to protect their land, and the wild life, but they're not winning.

"Zimbabwe has a much bigger poaching problem. The people are starving. It's understandable. But wrong. Sometimes there is no other recourse than to get involved with the business of poaching. They certainly don't have the resources there, privately or otherwise, to stem the flow of killing and export of ivory and rhino horns, you hear what I'm saying, Jack?"

Piet turned on the light, illuminating the map in front of them.

"See Jack, what we have is a highly sophisticated crime syndicate raping our land of its endangered species.

"We're not dealing with the odd rhino horn or a couple of elephant tusks. This is on an unimaginable scale.

"The masters from the Far East have a network of people who they manipulate in order to harvest what they want, and now we must include the pangolin on their shopping list. Much sought after for their scales which are again used in traditional Chinese medicine. It's the most valued trophy on the planet."

Jack looked puzzled. "Pangolin?"

Piet nodded. "Yes, pangolin, much in demand. They look like an artichoke with a long snout and a bendy tail. They're rarely seen, but much sought after as another prized trophy. They are nocturnal so difficult to find, but when faced with danger they roll up into a ball – easy for poachers to pick them up and pop them in a shopping bag.

"You see, Jack, they have runners here on the ground, people desperate for money. These are the guys who locate where the rhinos and elephants are at any given time, pangolins are trickier to find. The runners move in, normally before daylight. To use lights at night would alert the anti-poaching units.

"They use guns, yes, but also poisoned arrows. They bring the animal down. Silent and deadly. They chop off the horn, or the tusks, and leave the animal to die a slow and agonising death, sometimes with a female rhino or elephant, the calf stands by and watches. No value of course as they have no grown horns, or tusks, worth anything. But they make a note of them – long term investment if you like.

"The runners either bury the horns or ivory, for collection later, by organised pick-ups. Poachers have a sophisticated way of disposing of their trophies.

"Their Far Eastern masters own shipping companies in Africa, road haulage companies, courier companies, railroads."

Piet obviously knew what he was talking about. He spoke with passion and determination clearly incensed by these criminals raping the land of its iconic species.

Piet continued. "They have our own people at customs all over the country, who turn a blind eye to certain shipments coming in and going out of South Africa. It's all about money, my friend, greed, yes, survival also.

"From the lowly road builders to diplomats at various Embassies. It's massive leaving no trace.

"They have a network, Jack. It's what we're looking at now. A network, so sophisticated, so powerful, it took a little girl called Abby's arrival at the water hole, to attract our attention to it."

Jack looked puzzled. "So, you think this Richard Beecham was involved in something like this. So where is he now then?"

Piet brushed a moth off the table in front of him. "Like I said, I think he's dead. I think he holed up at Trackers with the girls. I think he was part of this poaching syndicate. I checked with the guy who ran his vehicle through the system, we went a bit further than before.

"He used a contact at Immigration. It seems Beecham made visits back to Zimbabwe on a few occasions, only for a day or two."

He rubbed his hands together. "Now, my thinking is he was moving things he shouldn't have been moving – like rhino horn and tusks.

"When he made these visits, he left the girls behind. I think Elspeth went to Trackers and looked after them. It would explain why she disappeared, now and again, for a day or two. Remember Gert the bookseller noticed she wasn't around and also the ex-soldier across the way from the shop?

"If you recall, I told you about the activity in the service lane behind the barber's shop at odd times of the night. Elspeth could have been hiding some of the trophies until Beecham made his next trip to Zimbabwe. He wouldn't want to keep them at Trackers because the girls were there."

Jack took out his note book and scribbled a few notes to himself.

"So, Piet, where do you think Beecham and the hairdresser met then?"

"This I don't have the answer to I'm afraid, but I'm working on it, so long. Elspeth could have met him at her shop. Maybe Beecham had a haircut there and noticed her clients were mostly game rangers, it might have been what he was looking for. A golden opportunity.

"Game rangers chat amongst themselves. Poaching is always a topic of conversation with these guys. It's highly likely they mentioned more remote areas they knew the rhino, or elephant, moved around in. Pangolins were more difficult, of course, being nocturnal. But they would have been spotted, not often, but maybe in a certain area. That's all the *bleddy* poachers need. Innocent talk with deadly consequences."

Jack was catching up fast. "So, what you're saying is Elspeth listened to these conversations then made notes on her map where the potential trophies might be located, with crosses, then passed this information to Beecham, who in turn passed it onto a contact, or whoever was running this international poaching syndicate?"

Piet was now pacing around the room, clearly agitated and angry. "It's exactly what I'm saying, my friend! She would have been paid a great deal of money for her information. The times scribbled on her map were maybe the pick-up times for the meet up with the poachers.

"Then the runners move in around the area, kill the animal and bury the trophy. Perhaps Beecham was waiting with his Trackers truck and met them wherever they were, simple enough to plan with two-way radios. He could easily have taken away the trophy, kept it in the back of his truck until Elspeth pitched up to take it away."

Jack drummed his fingers on the side of the chair. "You think he would have left the girls on their own at Trackers whilst he made the pick up?"

"It's possible, but he might sometimes have taken them with him, if Elspeth wasn't available, asleep in the back of his truck, on the mattress. Poachers normally kill the animals before light, harder for the anti-poaching units to spot them if it's not pitch dark. The kids would have been fast asleep if they had been with him.

"It would only take minutes to load the trophies and make his way back to his camp. It's not as if he was busy every night of the week collecting trophies. Maybe once every couple of months. It would all have had to be carefully planned.

"If anyone in the anti-poaching unit had spotted him, he would have raised no suspicion at all. The unit would have a list of all vehicles allowed to travel around the reserve. He had every right to be there in his safari vehicle, driving around as the sun came up, having a bit of a private game drive himself."

Jack was making notes. "Right, so let's say we now have Richard Beecham with his trophies hidden in his truck. What happens after this, how does he get them through customs on both the South African and Zimbabwean side?"

Piet shrugged. "The syndicate would alert some tame customs official that there were some sensitive goods coming through. They would be waiting, making sure Beecham passed through the border, with no problem.

"Once through the border he could have met up with his crooked pals, handed over the goods ready for transportation to wherever, probably making its way to Mozambique where the syndicate would have one of their shipping companies based, and there you have it. It's how they get the trophies out and send them on their way to the Far East. They also use private aircraft to move stuff around. I think you get the picture Jack."

Jack flipped back through his notes. "It's also possible Richard Beecham, over the years, used his ranch in Zimbabwe to hide trophies coming through from South Africa. Maybe it's why no-one ever saw the family. They didn't want to take any chances someone might find out what the family business there was. To my mind he was in the poaching business there as well.

"Maybe when the farm was attacked, he had to make another plan. He took the girls, came to South Africa to the abandoned game lodge, then set up business from there. For all we know the syndicate might even have owned Trackers, hiding ownership behind another name, a shell company. Perhaps the original private owner was a bit short of cash, needed the money and allowed it to happen. They'd probably been poaching for many years."

Piet nodded in agreement. "We're not dealing with amateurs here, Jack, this is a highly sophisticated international crime operation."

Jack stared at the darkening sky outside, the clouds heavy with the promise of rain.

"Thieves fall out, Jack. My thinking is Beecham went out one night, took the girls with him. Maybe it was an unexpected pick-up he had to make.

"Something happened, an argument, and he was killed by the poachers, or maybe he was taken out, a contract. Perhaps he was getting too clever, knew too much and became a threat to the entire operation.

"Whatever. I think he's dead. They would have buried his body somewhere. Now, they have to get the vehicle and trophies back to

Trackers, hide them and the vehicle, and make another plan to have them retrieved by someone else.

"I think the girls could have been asleep in the back of the truck, maybe whatever happened out there in the bush, woke them up, and they started to make a fuss. The poachers pulled them from the vehicle and left them in the bush."

He saw the shock and disbelief on Jack's face.

Piet continued. "Yes, I know it's a shocking thing to think about, but it makes sense, not so? These poachers are bush hardened, unfeeling criminals, all they care about is making money. They wouldn't think twice about dumping two kids to cover their tracks.

"When we took Grace to have her hair done, Abby reacted to something. She growled like an animal as we entered the barber's shop. It wasn't anything to do with the place itself. The kid recognised Elspeth and associated her with something bad in the past."

Jack looked at him with some admiration. "Well, I can see you didn't only have Grace on your mind these past few weeks, Piet. What you're saying makes a lot of sense. However, there are still some questions we need answers for aren't there?"

"Yes, Jack and you're the only one who can find the answers. I'm thinking another trip back to Zimbabwe is called for."

Chapter Eighty-Three
Zimbabwe

Having cleared it, with some muttering from Harry, Jack called Rob and arranged for him to collect him from the airport in Bulawayo, the following afternoon.

"I'd like you to drive me to the rather forgettable hotel we stayed in," he told him, "and please book George and his chopper, for the following morning.

"I think it might be a better idea if I went back to the ranch on my own, Rob. There was definitely no fuzzy and cosy feeling between you and the soon to be new owner of the Beecham place, the hostile and unfriendly Samson.

"I think if I flash enough dollars around, he might give me the information I need about the Beecham family, and what happened there. Despite what he told us before. I think you were right. I don't think he was telling us the truth."

*****

The following day George picked him up in the chopper, behind the hotel, and they flew back to the Beecham ranch.

George landed in front of the house. Jack sat and waited for the re-appearance of Samson.

Within twenty minutes, Sampson appeared, sweating profusely, as before, after his run through the bush from the farm hands cottage where he had apparently taken up residence.

He stared at Jack, hostile and unsmiling. "So, you return. What is it you are seeking now?"

Jack proffered his hand which was pointedly ignored. "Hello, Samson. I need your help again. I've had no success in finding out what happened to my sister Maryanne and her husband."

"Why is it I should help you now? When before you did not pay me the American dollars for the information, I gave you then?"

Jack wiped the sweat from behind his neck. "I think the information you gave me then was wrong. I think it was information you were given by the government before they allowed you ownership of this ranch and the farm hand's cottage."

He reached for his wallet and extracted fifty American dollars. "In good faith I hope you will help me with my search for the truth, I will give you this money now."

Samson's dark eyes wavered as he took the money. "I am thinking we can talk Mr Taylor, *Nkosi*," he said softly. "Now I have this money in my hands. Come, let us sit here and speak of things you wish to know."

Jack took off his sunglasses. "I would like to see the place where the farm hand was living. It will help me understand what happened here."

Samson inclined his head. "It is not far, but we will have to walk."

Jack's heart sank, the heat was brutal but he wasn't going to give up. "Show me the way Samson."

Thirty hot minutes later they arrived at the farm hand's cottage. Chickens pecked away at the dry dirt in front of the place, two sturdy brown goats watched the men approach, their yellow eyes unwavering and showing no interest. A washing line was strung between two spindly trees bereft of any washing.

Samson indicated Jack should sit out on the patio. He sank into a cane chair grateful for the shade of the thatched roof surrounding it. His heart was pounding in his chest and he was desperate for something to drink.

Samson went inside and returned with two chipped mugs full of brackish water. Jack was so desperate he took the mug and downed the liquid in one go, knowing the water was probably not boiled and he would suffer later.

He wiped his handkerchief over his face and neck, then leaned forward, his hands loosely linked together.

"Samson, I want to apologise for how I treated you when last I was here. I would like to tell you the truth of what I am looking for, and in return, I would like the truth from you. It's true I'm not the brother of Maryanne Beecham. I'm looking for information about what happened to the girls. I'm a journalist working for a London newspaper."

Samson threw the dregs of his water onto the ground. "I can tell you nothing more, *Nkosi*. This is the only information I have which I have given to you."

Jack thought for a moment. "You see Sampson, the two girls who lived here on the ranch went to South Africa. But it is with great sadness I must tell you both the girls died there, one only recently. I need to know what happened. They didn't die on the farm here. We now know this. I have the proof.

"We think the father of these girls, Richard Beecham, took them across the border to South Africa. The man who died in the big house was not him. So, who was he?

"I think, Samson, you knew the father took the children, right?"

Samson's brow puckered with concern. "I am sorry to hear this *Nkosi*, I did not know the girls well, but I knew them. We Africans have a great love for children, they are the future of our families, we wish for no harm to come to them."

Without warning Samson bent forward in his chair and covered his face with his hands. Deep keening sounds coming through his now wet fingers.

Jack stared at him nonplussed at this strange turn of events. The arrogant hostile African was now weeping uncontrollably.

Jack let him. Waiting for him to compose himself, unsure of where he should pick up the conversation.

With a deep shuddering sigh Samson pulled a grubby handkerchief from his pocket and wiped his face. He sat back in his chair, his forehead creased into a frown, his once hostile eyes now filled with sadness.

"Look, Samson. We didn't get off to a good start before, did we?"

Jack held out his hand, Samson responded and shook it this time.

"But I want you to know I mean you no harm. I haven't come to take the farm from you, it's not mine to take. All I'm looking for is the truth, and I think you know what the truth is, don't you?"

He paused. "My friend who came with me last time, said you were a man with an education, he also thought you had many problems, and you didn't tell us the truth."

Samson rested both his large hands on the sides of the chair as he stared out over the dry and dusty bush, his face still damp with tears.

"It's true I have had an education. I wished to become a teacher. But when my father died there was no money to complete my training.

"With no money I had to come back here to the farm after the funeral of my father. I tried to find work but there was none. I took the house of the farm hand and made it my own. There was no-one living there, and I needed somewhere to stay."

Jack frowned. "So, the government didn't give you the main house, the farm or this house then. So why did you tell us they did?"

Samson shook his head. "This government is a hard, unforgiving, government. If the people of the country did not vote for them, or agree with their angry talk, then they would be killed. They would send their thugs to the ones who wanted to see change here, and then murder them.

"There are many of us who wanted to see change, who did not agree with the ways of the government, and how they treated our people. There was no money here, *Nkosi,* no food to eat, no petrol – no future. But to stay alive we went along with what the government wanted to hear. It is true a man wants only to survive. In such times a man starts to believe what the government is telling them.

"I have lived in fear for many years, it is easier to lie sometimes than tell the truth. Then a man starts to believe the lies and they become the truth."

Jack nodded. "Yes, I understand what you're saying. So, the story of the comrades coming and shooting the Beecham's – this was not the truth then?"

Jack leaned forward again. "I need to have the truth Samson," he said urgently. "Two girls are dead because the truth was not told. I came to know the girl called Abby. She was deeply troubled by what happened to her here on the farm. Her mind had gone to another place, I'm not sure what this child saw."

He reached into his pocket and took out his phone, scrolling through until he found the enhanced photo of Abby. "This is Abby, Sampson, isn't it?"

Sampson stared numbly at the photograph, then nodded. "Yes, this is Abby. She was a happy child, always smiling and laughing."

Jack told Samson how Abby had been found at the water hole, how her sister must have perished in the floods that followed.

"We tried to help her, tried to give her hope, but it was not enough. There was an accident, she ran into the traffic and was hit by a car. She died. Will you tell me the truth Samson, for the sake of this little girl?"

Silent tears ran down the big man's face. "I am sorry to hear of her death and also the death of her sister Susie. Too many innocent people have lost their lives to the war in this country.

"I have lived with the burden of lies for too long. What is it you wish to ask of me? I will tell you the truth as I know it, *Nkosi*. This I will do for myself. I do not wish to be paid American dollars for this truth."

Jack sat back and took a deep breath. "I need to know what happened on this farm. I need to know the name of the farm hand who worked here."

Samson kicked at the dirt beneath his feet then pulled a sharp thorn from his heel.

"His name was Beecham."

Jack frowned. "No, Samson, the name of the farm hand, not the owner."

"The name of the farm hand was Beecham."

Chapter Eighty-Four

Jack stared at Samson as he digested this information. His eyes were no longer hostile, only filled with a heavy sadness.

"Beecham?" Jack said incredulously. "His name was Beecham?"

"Yes, he was the brother of the owner. This is where he lived, in this place where we are now. You thought this farm hand was an African?"

"Yes, we had no reason to think otherwise. What happened then Samson. The body of the man found in the house was then the brother of the owner, would I be right?"

"Yes, this is the truth. Many times, when Richard Beecham was away his brother, Mark, this was his given name, would stay at the house to watch over the wife and the children. But it was not in the other bedroom he was sleeping. He was sleeping in the bed of his brother's wife.

"Then one afternoon, it was when the sun was going down, the husband returned when he was not expected. The children were here where we are sitting now. This brother did not want them to see what he was doing with their mother.

"They were safe here. Many times, there was a nanny here to look after them, when he went to the big house, but at night the children stayed at their mother's house.

"When the father returned to his house, this is where he is finding his wife and brother in bed together. It was at this time I had returned from my father's funeral and I was looking for work, any kind of work.

"I was thinking it possible there was something I could do to earn some money, maybe some work on the farm somewhere. The husband did not know I was waiting at the back door, waiting for Mrs Beecham. It was a long time I waited.

"I heard the shouting from the two brothers and the screams from the woman. Then, many shots were fired. I was much afraid of what was happening and hid in the shed near the kitchen, where the firewood was kept. Then all was quiet and so I came softly out to see what was happening. Mr Beecham was putting petrol over the two vehicles parked there, and the chair with wheels, then he made the fire.

"The two dogs were also frightened by the noise so he used his gun again, then he killed the sheep and the goats. Already he was making the big house look like the comrades had come and killed his wife, his children, and his brother.

"Then he took the big car, the BMW, and drove away. From what you tell me now, he came here, to his brother's house, and picked up his children. From there he left the farm. I saw the dust from this vehicle when he drove away, the evening was still, the air heavy, the dust left the mark of his leaving. I was very much afraid and ran away to hide in the bush.

"There was no nanny there this time, she was away in her village, she was my cousin. Two days later she returned. It was she who discovered the bodies and contacted the police.

"When the police arrived, she was gone. Much afraid she would be in trouble for whatever reason."

Jack shook his head in disbelief as the story unfolded. "The gun he used, Samson, was it a shotgun or a rifle?"

Samson frowned. "I am not knowing which is which. This gun he used was the one he used when he went hunting."

"Did he do a lot of hunting. What did he hunt Samson?"

"My father told me he would shoot small game for the cooking pot. There is nothing else to shoot here. My father also told me, from the kitchen window, he saw many times small sacks being loaded into the vehicle. These sacks only appeared when a vehicle was heard in the night.

Samson rubbed his chin. "When my father told me this, I am thinking Mr Beecham is involved in the business of poaching. This is bad business which makes much money. There was no other way to make money on this farm. No farming, not many livestock."

Jack frowned. "Tell me, Samson. Do you think the girls saw what happened to their home, to their mother and, um, their uncle?"

Samson shrugged. "No. I am thinking they did not see any of this, they were here, where we are now. They did not see what their father had done. It would have been the anger and crazy behaviour of their father they would have known, as he drove them away. These children would not have understood what had happened, only the anger of the father who had been responsible for everything. They would have cried for their mother, their home and their dogs. All this their father had taken from them."

The big African's eyes filled with tears again. "Sometimes the not knowing is harder than the knowing. The children would not have understood anything, only they were being taken away from all they had known and loved. This is a cruel thing to do to young children, they were happy children."

As the pieces fell into place Jack took a furtive look at his watch, then stood up. Samson also stood. "I will show you the way back to the helicopter, *Nkosi*."

They walked in silence for a while. Then Jack spoke. "Thank you for telling me the truth Samson. It is a good thing you have done. What will you do now? Will you stay here?"

He shook his head resignedly. "What choice do I have, *Nkosi*? There is no work anywhere. Here I have a place to live. There is nothing else I can hope for."

The helicopter was waiting for him. George started up the engine when he saw them. Jack held out his hand in farewell. "My newspaper will pay for your story; it will help you plan a future for yourself."

"What will I do with money, Mr Taylor," he said bitterly. "What will it buy for me here?"

Jack frowned. "You might need it someday, Sampson. I've been thinking whilst we were walking. The man Rob Thompson who came with me when we first met you. He's a good man, Samson. Like you, he has suffered for many years under this government, and lost his own family and his home. When he hears the truth of the story you told me I think he might help you?

"In the end you are all Zimbabweans. I know from the history of the country there was a time when all who lived and worked here got on well together, they seemed to live happily as one people. The people I work for in London will pay well for your story. Your name will not be mentioned, to protect you. I will see this money gets to you. I will ask Mr Thompson to deliver it himself.

"The money should be enough for you to finish your degree as a teacher, Sampson. Mr Thompson, I think will help you, because you have done nothing wrong. There will be no need for the police to know who you are and what you saw.

"I will ask Mr Thompson to take you to Bulawayo so you can continue your studies. He would do that for a fellow Zimbabwean who had the courage to tell the truth. A fellow Zimbabwean who also wants change in this country. It is better to fight this change as friends, and not as enemies."

Sampson's face lit up, the smile spreading across his face, words seeming to fail him as he pumped Jack's hand, then clasped them both in his own.

"Thank you, *Nkosi,* this I should like to do. Your friend Mr Thompson, he will know where to find me. I shall be here at this place and welcome him back in friendship which is the way of our people here, the way it always was before the war."

As the helicopter lifted away, Jack looked down at the fast-diminishing figure of Samson.

He was well satisfied with the way things had turned out and grateful the compelling truth about Abby had brought one man a future and another perhaps, the first tenuous hand of friendship with the man called Samson.

He also thought he knew now why Abby's hair had gone from blonde to brown, as Susie's would have done.

A killer on the run would need to hide with two children, dying their hair would have given them a different look as he tried to cover his tracks, in case he was being pursued by the authorities.

Elspeth the hairdresser would have done that, touching the roots up on her visits to Trackers.

Chapter Eighty-Five

Once more Piet, alone in his cottage, off duty but on call, stared at the map on his wall. He knew it had more to tell them, but he couldn't figure it out. He picked up his phone where he had taken shots of Elspeth's map in her flat, then called Jack in his room.

"Get over here, my friend, I think I may have found something. I need your eyes for this one."

Jack arrived, the rain thundering on the hotel umbrella. He shut it down, propped it against the door, and shook the rain from his hair.

"What have you found now, Piet, something you need the eyes of an Englishman to sort out?"

"Maybe. *Kak* weather hey, Jack, but we need it. I've tried to work out the numbers here on the map. It looks like some sort of code, but there is something which gives it away. The first numbers are zero one, one. Perched up here in the right-hand corner of the map. Then further down a few more. Muddled in with the other crosses and numbers on the map."

Jack frowned as he peered closer. "What is all this?"

Piet tried not to look too pleased with himself. "Zero, one, one is the country code for Johannesburg, or whatever they call it now. I've linked up the other numbers hidden in between all the other crosses, numbers, dates and times, and so forth.

He stabbed his finger at the map. "Here, we have a telephone number."

Jack looked down at the number Piet had written on the right-hand corner of the map.

"So, have you called it?"

"No, my friend, this is a long road we have travelled. I thought it best we made this call together, not so?"

Jack smiled at him. "No doubt you have traced the number with all your shifty, and not so shifty, friends."

"*Ja*, of course! I don't think you'll be surprised, given what we think we know now. It's the final link in the chain, Jack."

He pointed to his phone. "Give the number a ring, my friend. Let's see what's on the menu tonight?"

****

The other commercial phone in the plush office in Sandton purred. The heavy-set man with the intricate gold ring on his finger, glanced at the pictures of Chinese landscapes and temples, on his wall, then he put it on speaker phone and sat back in his chair, as he looked over the city of Johannesburg and all it contained, and promised. He often listened in on calls made to his various restaurants around the country.

The phone picked up on the second ring. A sing-song voice gushed over the line. "Take out Africa! How may I take your order this evening?"

The man smiled to himself. The perfect name for his chain of Chinese restaurants all over the country.

Take out – that's what he did.

****

Jack had a different smile on his face. "This is the link then, Piet. It's possible whoever owns this restaurant, or chain of restaurants, is the contact, even the mastermind of what you think could be a poaching operation."

Piet grinned at him. "*Ja*, the last link in the chain. We have him now."

"It's time to meet with the anti-poaching unit and give them all the information we've put together."

Jack rubbed his hands together. "And, it's all because of Abby, right. A little girl, so innocent, so damaged, who might have broken this whole thing open."

"Yes. She was worth so much more, but didn't know it. Didn't even know who she was. A deeply disturbed child, who might, just might, have busted an international crime cartel of poaching in southern Africa."

Chapter Eighty-Six

The anti-poaching unit descended on the abandoned game lodge called Trackers. Their forensic team crawled all over the place, finding traces of rhino horn and ivory. The map on the wall told them everything they needed to know; they took it down to use as evidence.

The two impounded vehicles were combed for any traces of having carried any kind of trophies. The anti-poaching units found what they were looking for.

Whilst the team were gathering their evidence, they came across the fact that two young girls had indeed lived at Trackers. Hairs from their clothes and brushes had been taken away, for analysis. The police forensics team had found finger and hand prints from two small children in the back of the Toyota land cruiser.

Using the information in the anti-poaching network they had managed to trace back the information to the farm in Zimbabwe. With the help of Sampson, they matched the prints from the Toyota with prints inside the deserted family home, which proved without any doubt, the girls were from the farm, and had ended up in the camp called Trackers.

The police moved in, closing down all thirty Chinese take-away businesses, called *Take Out Africa*, spread around Cape Town, Johannesburg and Durban. Now they were hunting for the mastermind, the man, behind the whole operation of poaching and smuggling trophies out of the country.

The Chinese businessman, with the heavy gold ring and the long fingernail, was arrested in his opulent offices in Johannesburg and charged with rhino and ivory poaching, and other crimes including the involvement in the murder of Elspeth Hartman and Richard Beecham, and being complicit in the deaths of Abigail and Suzanna Beecham.

As promised by Piet and Jack, Inspector Enoch Coetzee, took the credit for cracking the biggest case he was ever likely to see in his career.

He became something of a legend, the hero who had exposed the international crime organisation dealing in poaching and exporting illegal trophies from Southern Africa. Enoch's promotion was swift, and Piet knew he had a friend for life should he be needing any favours in the future.

To his credit it had been Inspector Enoch Coetzee who had been swift to act on the information he had been given by Piet and Jack. Doggedly using all the facilities made available to him by the police department, he used their huge network across the country to hunt down the mastermind behind it all, then arrested him, and everyone else who worked for him.

It had been Enoch who had processed the paperwork necessary to give anonymity to a senior employee of the Chinese syndicate in exchange for information.

Shortly afterwards that man was deported back to China where he went into hiding, in fear of his life. His body was found some months later floating face down in the harbour in Hong Kong.

The anti-poaching unit were also swift to move on the information they had. Using Piet's map, Beecham's two-way radio, and the confiscated Trackers vehicle, they set a trap to snare the poachers. A trap within a trap.

This resulted in eight of them being arrested and two more being shot as they tried to escape through the thick bush.

The information extracted from the arrested poachers led to other poachers being caught, although what had happened to Richard Beecham remained unknown.

The international crime syndicate who had time and again raped the country of two of their greatest treasures, the rhino and gentle pangolin, collapsed.

Inspector Enoch Coetzee and his team, the anti-poaching unit, and Jack and Piet knew that although the destruction of the syndicate had been highly satisfying, it would only be a matter of time before another syndicate moved in and resurrected the despicable world of poaching.

Chapter Eighty-Seven

Caroline, Grace, Jabu, Piet and Jack gathered down on the viewing deck, overlooking the water hole where the story had begun, when a little girl, ravaged by fever and tormented by her past, had wandered into their lives, desperately seeking help.

As the sun set, the sky changed from blue to cream and gold and finally blood red. Down at the water hole the animals came to drink, lifting their heads cautiously, alert to any predators, their hooves leaving rutted imprints in the soft mud around the water. The air was warm and still, as birds called to each other and headed back to roost in the safety of the trees.

The silence of the evening was broken by the splashing, grunting and growling of a pod of hippos in the water. Their loud calls sounding like deep uncontrollable laughter.

Jack and Piet brought everyone up to date on the events leading up to the collapse of the poaching syndicate and all who had been involved in it, answering the many questions they all had.

****

Jabu and Grace were unusually quiet and Jack knew their thoughts were far away with Abby, how she had come into their lives for a brief period of time, and how they had come to love the strange unpredictable child.

Piet sat next to Grace. He too was thoughtful. If it hadn't been for Abby, he would still be living in Willow Drift, his lonely life stretching out night after endless night with only a bad-tempered cat for company. He wouldn't now be living in Hazyview, with a good job, and, of course, he would not have met the woman from Kenya called Grace, who he was now hopelessly in love with.

Piet's thoughts went back to the past week-end and the soft knock on the door of his cottage, he had been expecting it.

Grace had been sitting on the sofa, leafing through a magazine. She was staying with him whilst she looked for a place to rent in town. He had generously offered her his bedroom; he took the couch to sleep on.

Piet had opened the door and taken delivery of the small wicker basket, then placed it on the table in front of her.

Grace had looked up in surprise. "Picnic supper Piet?"

"It's for you Gracie. Open it."

She leaned forward curiously as the basket moved slightly. Lifting the lid, she looked down at a furrowed golden face with big brown eyes, its tail whipping back and forth, soft sounds coming from its throat.

She lifted the puppy out and held it close to her neck. The puppy wriggled in her hands, licking her face with excitement.

"Oh, Piet, it's adorable." She did a quick check. "She's adorable!"

A smile spread across his face. "I know you're looking for somewhere else to live, but should you change your mind, I've cleared having the puppy here, with Hugo," he looked down at his slightly trembling hands, "and for you to stay, if you'd like to."

Grace gave a tentative smile. "You want me to come and live here with you Piet?"

He looked at her nervously. "Yes. I'd like that very much."

Grace buried her face in the puppy's soft fur. "I'll certainly give it some thought, it's a nice idea, I quite like it. No, I like it very much Piet."

He felt his heart somersault in his chest. "She'll officially be our security dog at the hotel. So no making a big baby out of her, you hear me? She's going to be a working dog," he said gruffly, trying to hide his emotions.

He scooped the puppy from her arms and looked around the living room, frowning. "She can sleep in her hamper, in the kitchen, until we get her a dog basket in the morning."

Grace stood, a shy smile on her face, and reached for the puppy. "Let me cuddle her, Piet?"

She took the still wriggling and excited puppy from his hands. Holding it close to her shoulder she headed for the bedroom, holding her hand out behind her.

"Come Piet. She'll be lonely out here all by herself on her first night. Let's settle her in your bed, shall we?

"There should be enough room for the three of us. Oh, by the way you might want to take your clothes off, the puppy has weed on you.

****

Caroline, although disappointed Grace had decided to leave the lodge and move to town, was pleased she now had someone to fill the empty place in her heart which Abby had filled so briefly, then left empty again. In fact, she now had two conduits for her love. Piet, now the not so grumpy ex detective, and a golden Labrador puppy who they had named – Hope.

****

Caroline was tormented by the thought that she had somehow been responsible for the death of little Abby. It would be something she would have to live with, although no-one was blaming her for what happened.

Jack, Piet and Jabu had assured her she was not to blame. Her decision for Abby had been based on her medical condition and also a business decision. The rule in most of the lodges of not allowing guests under the age of twelve was made for a very good reason. It was dangerous to mix small children with wild animals. An excited child could not be expected to obey the rules of other guests, out on a game drive, to stay still and quiet when they were up close to a herd off elephants or other big game.

But still…

Caroline made an anonymous donation of two anti-poaching vehicles equipped with the best equipment her money could buy.

She told no-one about her generous gift.

She did it for Abby.

Chapter Eighty-Eight

Jack's story was a huge success. Harry, was delighted. He ran it over four weeks in the Sunday supplement of the newspaper.

His readers devoured every word, many of them had lived in Africa at some point in their lives. The story brought back memories and nostalgia during the cold bitter month of February, in the UK. A tear or two was shed by many as they remembered the sounds, the smell of the much-anticipated rains when they came, and the vast blueness of the endless skies there, in a country they had left - and the little girl called Abby.

The story was big in South Africa and Zimbabwe, making headlines in every newspaper. Hazyview was awash with speculation and gossip about Abby. Everyone had an opinion, people came forward with their own stories, things they had remembered which was of no use to anyone any more.

With Jack's story making headlines globally, celebrities, politicians, wealthy individuals and corporations from all over the world donated generously to the Abigail Anti-Poaching Foundation, or AAPF Foundation as it became, which had been set up in her memory, by Caroline.

The funds allowed the foundation to purchase more sophisticated equipment to deal with the scourge of poaching in the game reserves, which never seemed to abate, leaving the rhino and pangolin in a perilous position as the iconic animals neared extinction.

****

Jack sipped his beer as he too looked out over the bush, remembering Piet's map and the numbers and crosses. He knew that soon the predators would be out in the darkness, eager to fill their empty stomachs. He also knew other predators were no doubt out there, stealing through the night with their weapons.

He thought about Zimbabwe. The donations their anti-poaching team would receive would be shared with Zimbabwe, and go a long way to helping save the rhino, elephant and shy pangolin. But what pleased him more was that Rob Thompson had reached out to the African called Samson, and taken him under his wing.

It was a tentative beginning to forging a relationship between the two Zimbabweans who both so desperately wanted to see change in their country.

It was a start.

Samson was now enrolled at a college in Bulawayo working towards attaining his diploma in teaching.

****

A well-known artist in Nairobi who specialised in working with bronze wanted to donate a statue of Abby to be erected in a place of Grace's choosing. He had recognised her name from the newspaper story and was touched by how hard she had worked to help the child, and he wanted to help a fellow Kenyan.

Caroline, Jabu and Grace had discussed where the statue should be erected and all agreed it should be placed under the spiritual tree. Grace had sent the artist in Nairobi a photograph of Abby.

The finished work when it arrived at the lodge was small, but beautiful. Abby kneeling on the ground her arm resting on the back of a baby rhino, a taller version of herself stood behind her, both hands resting on her little sister's shoulders, as they looked into the distance, towards the water hole.

****

The group down on the viewing deck were unusually quiet as each one sat with their memories and all that had happened over the past few months.

The waiter moved silently around them refilling their glasses before gliding away and leaving them to their thoughts.

Caroline raised her glass towards the distant bush to the left of the deck. "Here's to the little girl who blessed us with an unexpected visit and changed all our lives."

They raised their glasses towards the spiritual tree, standing sentry over the little girl's grave as the sky darkened. The discreet light Jabu had placed there earlier that morning, sprang to life behind the statue, silhouetting the kneeling child, her sister Susie, and the little rhino calf.

Piet reached for Grace's hand as she stared in surprise. "Oh, that's beautiful, they look so perfect there, and Tim is with them. They're safe now." The tears slid down her face and Piet squeezed her hand, a lump in his own throat, as he passed her his handkerchief.

"Caroline?"

"Yes, Grace?"

Caroline took a deep breath. "I want to thank you for everything. For bringing Tim and I back to Africa, for trusting me with Abby and giving me the new life, I so desperately needed. Without you none of this would have been possible."

Grace stole a look at Piet. "You not only reached out to a troubled child but you generously made sure she wanted for nothing. Your kindness and love gave Abby a few months in a place where she knew she was finally safe, where she could once again trust the people around her. That's something to be very proud of, and the Foundation will be a living memorial to her."

Caroline looked at the lovely tableau beneath her magical tree unable to hold back her own tears at Grace's words. "Thank you." She dabbed at her eyes. "I must remember to send some shots of Abby's grave and statue to Doctor Olivia and the American woman Melody. I want them to see where she is now, here with me at Infinity."

She stood up unsteadily. "I'm going to do that right now…"

****

Jabu stood as well, wanting to be alone. He looked up at the stars now appearing, then back at Abby kneeling there.

Tears ran unashamedly down his dark face as he whispered to her in his language, the gentle language she seemed to have understood and took comfort from.

"Your spirit will come to this place, where you were lost, then found. Jabu will be here waiting for you," he whispered to her.

"Go well, little one. I will find you again, for you are part of me now."

He lifted his arm towards her, as if in farewell, then melted into the dark shadows of the night.

****

Jack leaned forward in his chair, and held his breath. The outline of a massive elephant had come silently into view next to Abby's grave.

The old bull stood there, then ran his trunk over the statue, laying it over the baby rhino as if he somehow knew how special this child had been. Then as quietly as he had approached her, the elephant melted back into the black shadows of the night, the rustling and crack of a branch was the only sound carried back on the still air.

Hardened though Jack was, having seen more than enough of the violence and tragedy in the world during his career, he felt his own eyes prickle with emotion.

Africa, he knew could be unpredictable, frustrating and violent, but it had a gentle enduring side to it. It was a place like no other.

A place he had made his home.

*****

If you enjoyed reading this book and would like to share that enjoyment with others, then please take the time to visit the place where you made your purchase and write a review.

Reviews are a great way to spread the word about worthy authors and will help them be rewarded for their hard work.

You can also visit Samantha's Author Page on Amazon to find out more about her life and passions.

Also by Samantha Ford:

The Zanzibar Affair

A letter found in an old chest on the island of Zanzibar finally reveals the secret of Kate Hope's glamorous, but anguished past, and the reason for her sudden and unexplained disappearance.

Ten year's previously Kate's lover and business partner, Adam Hamilton, tormented by a terrifying secret he is willing to risk everything for, brutally ends his relationship with Kate.

A woman is found murdered in a remote part of Kenya bringing Tom Fletcher back to East Africa to unravel the web of mystery and intrigue surrounding Kate, the woman he loves but has not seen for over twenty years.

In Zanzibar, Tom meets Kate's daughter Molly. With her help he pieces together the last years of her mother's life and his extraordinary connection to it.

A page turning novel of love, passion, betrayal and death, with an unforgettable cast of characters, set against the spectacular backdrop of East and Southern Africa, New York and France.

Amazon Reviews

"This book will keep you guessing; that's a good thing. I could barely put it down and one night dreamed about it so much I woke up and read more. It's unbearably sad in some places and wonderfully happy in others. Fantastic!"

"This book takes you on a safari round Africa. It is a compelling story with so many twists. It is beautifully and hauntingly told. The details and descriptions made me feel the heat, smell the ocean and slap the mosquitoes. Thank you."

"I loved The Zanzibar affair. I felt I was there sensing the smells, the sea and the warmth of Africa. The way she weaves the characters into the story is quite fascinating, leaving the reader spellbound and wondering where it's going to end. Always with an unexpected twist. A fabulous storyline and book which I could hardly put down. Highly recommended."

The House Called Mbabati

The Mother Superior crossed herself quickly. "May God have mercy on you, and forgive you both," she murmured as she locked the diary and faded letters in the drawer.

Deep in the heart of the East African bush stands a deserted mansion. Boarded up, on the top floor, is a magnificent Steinway Concert Grand, shrouded in decades of dust.

In an antique shop in London, an elderly nun recognises an old photograph of the mansion; she knows it well.

Seven thousand miles away, in Cape Town, a woman lies dying; she whispers one word to journalist Alex Patterson – Mbabati.

Sensing a good story, and intrigued with what he has discovered, Alex heads for East Africa in search of the old abandoned house. He is unprepared for what he discovers there; the hidden home of a once famous classical pianist whose career came to a shattering end; a grave with a blank headstone and an old retainer called Luke - the only one left alive who knows the true story about two sisters who disappeared without trace over twenty years ago.

Alex unravels a story which has fascinated the media and the police for decades. A twisting tale of love, passion, betrayal and murder; and the unbreakable bond between two extraordinary sisters who were prepared to sacrifice everything to hide the truth.

Mbabati is set against the magnificent and enduring landscape of the African bush - where nothing is ever quite as it seems.

Amazon Reviews

"It is a long time since I have been so absorbed by a novel about Africa. Reading it, I vacillated between willing it to last longer as I was enjoying it so much, and wanting to get through it to reveal the outcome. There can be no greater praise for this novel than its endorsement by the late John Gordon Davis, to whom the novel is dedicated. Anyone who has read any of JGD's novels, in particular his classic 'Hold My

Hand I'm Dying' will understand that Samantha Ford's novel is in the same league."

"What a wonderful story where you have a stormy love affair set in the heart of Africa. It twists and turns as the plot unfolds and you will surely shed a tear or two along the way. For those who have been on an African safari you will not put this book down. Such intelligent and beautiful writing."

"The book is captivating from beginning to end. It takes you on a riveting journey where the story develops and keeps you guessing. Loved it! Didn't want it to end!"

A Gathering of Dust

Through the mists of a remote and dangerous part of the South African coastline, a fisherman stumbles upon an abandoned car and an overturned wheelchair.

Thousands of miles away in London, an unidentified woman lies in a coma. When she recovers she has no memory of her past or where she comes from. As fragments of her memory begin to return, the woman has to confront the facts about herself as they begin to unfold. A disastrous love affair in the African bush: a missing husband: and a sinister shadowy figure who knows exactly who she is and where she comes from.

Tension builds as images and secrets begin to resurface from her lost past – rekindled memories that plunge her back into a world she finds she would rather not remember.

Set against the magnificent backdrop of East and Southern Africa. A Gathering of Dust is a fast-paced story of love, betrayal and murder scattered along a trail of deception and lies, with a single impossible truth, and an unthinkable ending.

Amazon Reviews

"What a writer this author is! So cleverly written and with twists and turns you never see coming. I am an avid reader and this authors books are the best I have read in a long time. Her books have everything, mystery, murder, romance, intrigue, suspense etc etc. Well worth a read."

"My husband knows when I am reading this author's books that there is little that will get my nose out of them. Her descriptives of even the simplest things create such a vivid picture. She has made me fall in love with Africa and her story lines are captivating and intelligently

thought out. I never want to finish one of her books only because I don't want them to end."

"Superb. Absolutely brilliant. I simply couldn't stop reading, turned TV off and just read and read, even ignoring my hubby. Can't wait to read the next book!!!"

"A gripping read, with many gut-wrenching twists and turns. I had trouble putting the book down to eat, sleep or work! Fabulous."

The Ambassador's Daughter

During a violent storm deep in the African bush, a child disappears.

Sara, the ex-British ambassador's daughter, and mother of the child, is arrested.

Twenty years later, journalist Jack Taylor, travels from London to the magnificent landscape of the Eastern Cape, in South Africa, where the unforgiving bush hides long-forgotten secrets of loss, hate, betrayal and revenge.

A staggering story awaits. A deadly secret threatens to destroy the lives of people who thought themselves now safe - a story which has fascinated the media for decades.

Only one person knows exactly what happened on that day - a nomadic shepherd called Eza - but can Jack find him?

Amazon Reviews

"This is simply the best book I've read in a very long time. This talented lady brings Africa alive. Wilbur Smith you have some competition..."

"A cracking good story with a totally unexpected twist at the end!"
John Gordon Davis – author of Hold My Hand I'm Dying

"Having read all Wilbur Smith's books, this author ranks up with the best of them. Best read I've had for years!" Peter C. Morgan